THE WINTER PLACE

THE WINTER PLACE

ALEXANDER YATES

SIMON & SCHUSTER

First published in Great Britain by Simon & Schuster UK Ltd, 2015
A CBS COMPANY

Published in the USA in 2015 by Atheneum Books for Young Readers,
an imprint of Simon & Schuster Children's Division, New York.

1 3 5 7 9 10 8 6 4 2

Simon & Schuster UK Ltd
1st Floor, 222 Gray's Inn Road
London WC1X 8HB

www.simonandschuster.co.uk

Simon & Schuster Australia, Sydney
Simon & Schuster India, New Delhi

A CIP catalogue record for this book
is available from the British Library

PB ISBN 978-1-4711-2383-2
EBook ISBN 978-1-4711-2384-9

Printed and bound by CPI Group (UK) Ltd, Croydon, CR0 4YY

MIX
Paper from
responsible sources
FSC® C020471

Simon & Schuster UK Ltd are committed to sourcing paper that
is made from wood grown in sustainable forests and supports the Forest
Stewardship Council, the leading international forest certification organisation.
Our books displaying the FSC logo are printed on FSC certified paper.

for my parents,
Barbara and Michael
and for her parents,
Tuija and Pertti

Acknowledgments

I would like to express my deep gratitude to Ellen Levine and Caitlyn Dlouhy. Ellen is the best advocate any writer could hope for, and this novel is so much stronger for Caitlyn's generous, rigorous editorial eye. I would also like to thank good friends and early readers Brett Finlayson and Calvin Hennick, who gave valuable advice and support though various drafts of this project. I'm also particularly grateful to Mary Clare Cole for her enthusiasm and her art—I'm not sure I completely saw Tess or Axel until I saw them through her eyes. And years later, I remain flabbergasted at the good fortune I had to attend the creative writing program at Syracuse University and I am deeply grateful for my time there.

But above all, I thank my incredible wife, Terhi Majanen. Words fail me. Thank you. Thank you.

PART ONE
Bear in the Backyard

Then the mother sought the strayed one,
Dreading what mischance had happened,
Like a wolf she tracked the marshes,
Like a bear the wastes she traversed

—*KALEVALA*, RUNE XV

1

The Battle at Mud Lake

Tess was out in front of her house, sitting next to a boy, when the knight rode up. The boy had been trying his best to kiss her, but Tess wasn't having it. Still, she wasn't happy to be interrupted. The knight brought his horse across the road at a canter and charged right into the front yard. His armor flashed in the afternoon light, jangling like a set of expensive pots. The boy turned from Tess as soon as he heard it, sliding away on the wooden step. The knight was named Sam, and he was Tess's father. The boy had a name, too, but it hardly matters. Tess would remember him only as the boy who tried and failed to kiss her on the day that her life changed forever.

"Tess!" the knight said, his mail-draped horse stamping the ragged grass that passed for their front lawn. "Tess? Is that you, sweetie?" Her father had trouble seeing through the visor of his helmet.

"Nope," Tess said.

"Honey," Sam huffed, gathering his patience. He dropped the festooned orange reins and snapped his visor up. "You know I don't have time to fool around."

"I told you that thing was dangerous," Tess said. "You're going to break your neck."

"I don't need to see faces for the battle," Sam said.

That's why he was done up like a gleaming tin idiot. Tess's father was a member of the local Medieval Society, and in just over an hour he would take part in the opening ceremonies of their Annual Battle Re-enactment. It was, far and away, Sam's favorite time of year, leaving Thanksgiving and Christmas and all birthdays well in the dust. It used to be Tess's favorite time of year too. Not that she was telling.

"Listen," Sam continued, waving his hand in the air as though to shoo flies. "Did Axel leave yet?"

Axel was Tess's ten-year-old brother. "He's still inside," she said, "sewing up his tunic and putting dirt on his face." The boy beside her stifled a sort of hiccup-laugh.

Her father's horse shifted and threw her head back. Sam hardly moved in his saddle. He wasn't a bad rider, even in that heavy armor. "Good," he said. "The road is getting busy, and these out-of-towners drive like lunatics. I want you to walk him to the battle tonight. I'll bring you both home when it's over."

"It's not even half a mile," Tess said. "Axel isn't—"

"Hey." Sam cut her off, jabbing an armored finger into his chest. "Parent." Then he pointed at Tess. "Kid. It isn't a lot to ask." He zapped her his most guilty-making look, a tactic that usually worked whenever it had anything to do with her brother.

"Fine," she said. "We'll take him in a minute."

Sam's bushy eyebrows perked up, disappearing into his helmet. It was as though he hadn't been able to see the boy until Tess said "we."

"Who's your friend?" Sam said.

"Rod," she said.

That was not the boy's name.

"Pleased to meet you, Rod." With the lightest press of his heel, Sam urged his horse closer to the front stoop. He leaned down to shake hands.

"And you, sir. Your Highness."

"No, no," Sam said, apparently oblivious to the boy's mocking tone. "I'm no royal. Just a knight of the realm."

"Understood." The boy was trying so hard not to smile that he actually frowned.

Sam straightened up in his saddle and turned back to his daughter. "Remember that I'm teaching tonight, so I'll need to bring you and Axel home immediately after the battle." As if being a knight weren't nerdy enough, Tess's father was also a professor specializing in forest ecology and lichens. *Lichens*.

"Come on, girl," Sam said. "Come on, sweetheart." These last words were directed not at Tess, but at the horse. Technically, she belonged to the Medieval Society, but Sam had been performing with her for the past five years straight, and they had sort of a thing. The mare gingerly turned herself around while Sam petted her neck and cooed. Tess slipped her phone out of her pocket. She dialed her father, and seconds later the sound of Gregorian chanting began to emanate from his groin area. Whether he was in front of a lecture hall full of dozing students or fighting for the king, Sam always forgot to switch his phone to silent.

"Hell," Sam muttered, patting himself down. Then, noticing the phone in Tess's hand, he said: "You know, the smart-ass thing is not so adorable."

"Who says I'm going for adorable?"

Sam smiled, maybe in spite of himself. Tess knew that her dad didn't simply love her; he also *liked* her, most of the time. He dug the person that she was, even now that she'd begun to do her teenage best to communicate that this was in no way mutual. "You know what," Sam said. "It's actually kind of fitting." Then, with a ridiculous "Ya!" he pressed his mare into a gallop, crossed the paved road with a heavy clopping, and vanished into the trees on the other side.

The boy couldn't hold it in anymore. He laughed so hard that he fell off the stoop, getting mulch on his nice new jeans. "How the hell did you save yourself from that?" He gestured down at the trees into which Tess's father had disappeared. "With a dad like that, you should *so* be a loser."

Truth be told, this boy was kind of a bully and a jerk. Tess had no illusions about that.

"I'm not sure," she said. "Must have been a miracle."

The town Tess lived in was called Baldwin, and it sat smack-dab in the middle of New York State. She and her brother had been born there and—excepting the occasional trip to Florida to visit their grandfather—they'd never left. Baldwin was made up of a handful of shops, a drugstore, and a diner, all strung along the sluggish glitter of the Seneca River. Everything beyond that was hilly farmland, save the little county park where the Baldwin Medieval Society held their re-enactment every fall. The park was called Mud Lake, and it consisted of a few miles of blazed trails running from forest to meadow to marsh, lassoed around a lake that took its name for the algae and goose poo that thickened the shallows to pudding every summer. The park was generally as quiet as the town it was stapled to, save these two weeks in October when it was positively bursting with costumed fools.

Tess opened the front door after Sam left and found her little brother racing through the living room. "Train leaves in five minutes!" she called after him.

"Go on without me," Axel hollered. He ran into Sam's bedroom, and Tess heard the sound of closet doors opening and slamming.

"Don't think I don't want to," she shouted. The boy joined her in the living room, casting his gaze over the grotty furniture. There was a chest to one side of the room, the lid yawning wide, filled with replica daggers, maces, and war hammers. The boy snorted. This was the first time he'd ever been inside Tess's place, and it seemed to be living down to his expectations.

"I can't find Dad's shield," Axel said, charging back into the living room. Tess's brother was dressed in a burlap cowl and tunic falling over sheer Peter Pan leggings. This was ostensibly for a reason—for the first time Axel would be taking part in the battle, playing their father's squire. But honestly, Axel would have dressed up whether he was being paid to or not. His cloth shoes curled up festively at the tips, and he'd buffed them over with cooking oil and fireplace ash. He'd also dabbed his tunic, arms, and face in the stuff. The kid didn't so much resemble a squire as he did a forlorn Christmas elf afflicted with mange, or rabies.

"Wow," the boy said.

"I know," Tess said. "He puts my dad to shame." Then, to Axel: "Do you really need it?"

"Of course I *need* it," Axel said, totally ignoring the older boy. "The squire is supposed to present the knight with his shield. I can't go without it."

The boy stepped over to the big open chest of weapons, and he began to root around. "Screw the shield. How about this bad boy?" He plucked out a short, one-sided ax with a mean spike at the pommel. Like all the other replicas, and like Sam's full set of period-accurate armor, this was little more than an overpriced toy. Still, it would have ruined your day to get clobbered with it. The boy made as though to toss the ax at Axel, who flinched.

"That's not even the right era," Axel said, sort of sheepishly.

"'Course it isn't." The boy let the hand ax fall to the floor, where it scuffed the hardwood as it landed. He shut the heavy chest and then paused for a moment before reaching around behind it. From the space between the chest and the wall, he produced a diamond-shaped shield with polished copper edging—it must have fallen back there when Sam opened the lid to get his weapons.

"Thanks!" Axel said, rushing over to take the shield. But the boy held fast.

"What do you say?" the boy asked.

"I said it already. Thank you?"

"No." The boy might have been a bully, but he was a practiced and patient one. "The word I'm looking for is 'please.'"

"Oh," Axel said. He shot his sister the briefest look. "Please," he said.

The boy smiled and let go of the shield. "That's right," he said.

"Come on," Tess said, unable to meet her brother's eyes. "You're going to be late."

¤ ¤ ¤

They locked up the A-frame and cut across the yard, heading for the Mud Lake gates down the road. Soon Tess began to hear the first strains of music drifting through the park. Flags and banners whipped in the breeze, flashing through the canopy. Axel hurried ahead, Sam's heavy shield bouncing across his narrow spine.

"He doesn't look that sick to me," the boy said. "At least not, you know, not *physically*."

This brought Tess up short. Rumors regarding Axel's condition were rife in Baldwin, but no one had ever confronted her so directly.

"He's not sick at all," she said. It sounded like the lie it was, but the boy had sense enough to leave it at that.

They reached the park gates, where a cloth billboard was draped over the Mud Lake sign, brightly announcing the start of the battle. Sam's picture was on the billboard—the good white knight. For the next two weeks he'd fight the evil black knight twice daily. Sam would win and lose on a predetermined, rotating schedule, as committed to his own defeats as to his victories.

Axel showed his performer's badge to the leather-capped steward at the ticketing kiosk—shaped, unsurprisingly, like a castle battlement—and nodded his head in the direction of Tess and the boy. "They're with me," he said.

"Pass, then, young sirs," the steward responded in a strangely piratical English accent. "All is well. You may pass. But mind you make haste. Their majesties convene the contest on the hour!"

Translated from high-nerd, this meant: "You're late." Axel didn't have to be told twice. He gave Tess a parting glance and then disappeared among the interpretive displays and vendors' tents that had spilled out of the parking lot and into the meadows. Tess made to turn and go, but the boy took her lightly by the arm.

"If you think I'm missing this, you're crazy," he said.

Oh well. Watching the battle with him was probably as good a way to spend their afternoon as any, even if it was just so that they could laugh at Sam and Axel. Tess certainly wasn't above this. Never mind that last year she'd been right there with them. She'd grown out of all that. Maybe "grown" isn't the right word. It was more an act of will than an act of nature. Tess had *decided* to grow out of it. High school had come for her. It was every kid for themself.

"It's not going to be as fun as you think," she said, pulling her arm from his hand and stepping past the kiosk.

"I don't think it's going to be fun at all," the boy said, his smile sharp and hungry.

The battlefield was set up in a meadow at the far end of the fairgrounds, just beyond the ax-throw and court-of-foods. On almost any other day of the year you could see whitetail deer grazing here, or maybe a skunk nosing through the wilted growth. But today every sensible animal had found its way to the deeper woods and marshes. A ten-foot riser had been erected at one end of the field, flanked by miniature cardboard towers, and bleachers lined both sides of the green. Tess and the boy found seats on the lowest level, where a sign warned: YOU WILL GET MUDDY! in cheerfully ornate script.

A sudden commotion rippled through the crowd, and some people started clapping. It took Tess a moment to realize that this was for her brother. Axel stepped out from behind the riser, joined by an older boy who must have been playing the squire for the evil black knight. They certainly looked the parts of grim, downtrodden urchins. The knights themselves appeared moments later, galloping out of a large opening at the center of the riser, down to the end of the green and back. The crowd erupted, shooting to their feet, hollering and wolf whistling. Sam gave them a wave, then unsheathed his sword and twirled it in the air, the sun bright upon the blade. He accepted his shield from Axel with a curt nod and turned to give the king and queen, seated on thrones atop the riser, a deep bow. Tess was struck, all at once, by how strange it was to be watching her father from the audience like this. Every inch of Sam was concealed. Tess couldn't see his face, or his fingers, or even a thread of his long graying hair. But he wasn't *hidden*—that was Sam up there. That was her father's truest self. He may as well have been naked as covered in plates of tempered steel.

For as much time as they'd all spent practicing, the battle didn't last very long. The knights retrieved their lances and charged leisurely at each other, while their squires led the crowd in coordinated cheers. The boy not only participated in this but, much to Axel's chagrin, he way overdid it. Whenever Sam scored a point, the boy would jump to his feet, fist pumping the air like he meant to bruise it, hooting with luxuriously insincere delight. Whenever Sam lost a point, the boy would boo and hiss, spitting on the ground. Tess tried her best to ignore it, staring blankly across the field. Axel did no such thing. He couldn't exactly interrupt his performance, but he made a point of passing by their bleachers between the runs and staring daggers at the boy. Tess wished Axel wouldn't—nothing good would come of it.

Nothing good did. After the battle was over, Tess and the boy went to the makeshift stables, where Axel had just finished putting the horse their father had been riding into her stall. Tess could tell that her brother was still fuming. The boy slapped Axel's back a little too hard. "Not bad," he said. "You were by far the least stupid part of that."

"This one's a bigger jerk than usual," Axel said. It would have been a brave and rather foolish thing to say, had it been in English.

"Hell is that?" the boy said, his hand still on Axel's shoulder. "Elvish?"

"*Suomea*," Axel answered. It was Finnish, for Finnish. Only Tess understood what he'd said, on account of she spoke it too.

"Snow-ma?" The boy glanced back at Tess, a hint of irritated confusion behind his pasted-on grin. It was clear that Axel had gotten under his skin.

"Don't be like that," the boy said, more a threat than a plea. "Come on—what's that you're speaking?"

"What do you care?" Axel said, switching to English.

"Be nice," Tess said.

Axel turned to look at her, and at once Tess realized that this had nothing to do with the fact that the boy had been nasty to him. This was happening because the boy had made fun of their father. Then he looked back at the boy. "You know that she's going to be bored of you in a week or two," Axel said. "So I wouldn't bother trying to learn it." His eyes went wide, blazing with certain awareness of his own foolishness. "Not that you could, anyway."

The boy snatched the collar of Axel's tunic, backing him up into a broad patch of horse-trod mud. He seemed almost sad as he did this—the boy must have realized that he'd been checkmated. Nowhere to go from here but down, so he gave Axel a hard push that sent him sprawling feet over face into the mud. Axel landed flat on his back, the wind knocked out of him so hard that Tess could actually hear his lungs empty. She knew that this was restraint on the boy's part. He could have done a lot worse.

"Stop it," she said, pushing past the boy and stepping into the mud to help Axel sit up. He was gulping air, trying very hard not to cry. "I think you should go," she said, not even turning to look at the boy.

That was restraint, too. It wouldn't have been impossible—or even all that difficult—for Tess to have put that bully back on his ass. She had the advantage of staggered puberty, to say nothing of the element of surprise. Because who expects to be leveled by a willowy girl with thin arms and post-goth hair? Certainly not this boy. But Tess could have done it.

She should have.

She knew that.

They found their father waiting in the employee lot, the engine of his rattletrap pickup running, his armor and weapons trembling in the bed. Sam knew that something had happened the moment he saw Axel's muddied costume and bloodshot eyes—the look of bruised pride was not uncommon in their house. He reached across to open the passenger door.

"Get in," he said.

"I'll get the seat dirty," Axel said.

Sam smiled lamely. "The seat's already dirty." His expression darkened as he turned to Tess. "You too."

They pulled out of the lot without uttering another word. The drive home didn't take two minutes, but it was a long two minutes. Their house lay just ahead, all alone between the park and the surrounding farmland. It was a boxy little single-level, above which their father had erected a sort of high-peaked, timbered bivouac, designed to keep the winter snows from flattening them. From the road the house appeared to be a traditional A-frame, but from up close it looked more like a shanty under a wooden tent. Sam turned down the driveway and put the truck into park, leaving the engine idling. "There are potpies in the freezer," he said. "Tess will make you one." There was a long silence. Nobody got out of the truck or said anything. "Give us a second, little man." Sam had been calling Axel that for years, but only recently had the phrase taken on an air of unintentional mockery. Because Axel was little—too little.

"She didn't do anything," Axel said, loyal to a fault.

"Obviously, she did." Sam waited, but Axel didn't move. *"Out,"* he said, his voice loose and gravelly; about as close to yelling as he ever got.

Axel slid across Tess's lap to dismount the truck. He whispered over her, light as Pinocchio, hardly bending the grass when he landed woodenly in the yard. He accepted the key without a word, leaving them to it.

"So I take it that's the kid's idea of flirting with you?" Sam said. "Who is he?"

"Nobody," Tess said.

"Not nobody. Somebody. Somebody who'd hurt your little brother."

"Yeah. Because I knew he'd do that."

Sam gave her a look. "And now that you know?"

"I'm not going to talk to him anymore." The

answer was automatic, but it was also true. The boy, who'd meant little to her before, now meant nothing at all.

"And if he does it again?"

Tess squirmed, eager to be out of the vibrating pickup and free of this conversation. "I don't know, Dad. I'll kick him in the balls. I'll give him a nosebleed. I'll break his arm in three places."

"Gosh, that'd be smart. Get yourself good and suspended. And who'd look after your brother then?"

Sam was always saying stuff like that. It hardly surprised her anymore. "Yeah, it sure would be a shame for Axel, me getting suspended," Tess said.

Her father opened his mouth, ready to chop that sarcasm off at the neck. But he caught himself. "Sorry," he said. "I know you were kidding. But the point is that . . . You know the point."

Tess was quiet. Given the circumstances, her poor ground in this fight, an apology from her dad should be pretty close to victory.

"Want me to put a pie in the oven for you?" she said.

"I'm doing a session at the writing clinic after class," her father said. "I'll pick something up in between."

"All right," Tess said, stepping out of the truck. "See you."

Sam reached across the passenger bench and pulled the door closed behind her. The window was still open, and he called to her through it. "I love you, honey." Nothing but a throwaway had it been any other day. For years to come, Tess would play this moment over and over again in her mind. It was only a fluke, a temporary and benevolent glitch in the universe, that she answered the right way.

"Love you, too, Dad," Tess said.

Sam nodded, glanced at the dash clock, and drove away.

2

Inexplicably
Brown Bear

Axel immediately sensed that there was something strange going on back at their house. A smell hung in the air—animal, but unfamiliar. It struck him faintly as he got out of the pickup, and by the time he'd reached the front door it became undeniable. Some raccoons had been after their trash cans last spring, but this smell was different. There was something aggressive about it, something musty and rotten. Odd. But when Axel shouldered open the front door, the scent faded. The A-frame smelled exactly the way it was supposed to—like hearth ash and canned chili. Like holly and old paper. Like home.

Axel shut the door behind him and peeled off his muddy tunic and tights, draping them over the back of a wooden chair to dry. Then, wearing nothing but his underwear, he plucked a book from what he and Tess called the "school shelf" and planted himself on the couch to wait for his sister. Axel knew that he was at least partly to blame for what had happened that afternoon, and if Tess was getting chewed-out on his account, loyalty demanded he wait for her. The book he'd chosen was one of Tove Jansson's Moomin stories. It was in Finnish. Most of the books squeezed into their little living room were a mix of English and Latin—work stuff for their father's job. These included botanical field guides, graduate-level textbooks, and crisply bound student theses on the minutia of lichens and soil nitrogen. But everything on the school shelf was in their mother's native language. An old leather-bound edition of the Finnish epic *The Kalevala* held the place of honor at the top, followed closely by their full set of Moomin books. There was an abundance of filled-in grammar readers, a collection of Astrid Lindgren novels—translated into Finnish from the original Swedish—as well as enormous Finnish editions of Tolkien, Grahame, Adams, and Holdstock. The reason they called this the school shelf was that every evening their father would take one of the books down for an hour and a half of Finnish lessons. Sam always said that knowing the language was a way of knowing their mom—a way, even, of knowing themselves. Axel wasn't so sure about that, but he kept up with the practice all the same. It made his father happy, and besides, he liked the stories.

Tess came in before he even finished a page, shutting and bolting the door behind her. Axel closed his book and stood.

"I just want to say—"

"Please don't. Turkey or veg?" She meant the pies.

"Turkey," he said after a pause.

She nodded, crossed through the living room and entered the kitchen at the back of the house. Axel watched her pull two potpies from the freezer and thumb the frost off one of the boxes to read the cook temperature. She knelt to set the oven and slid the unwrapped pies inside.

"Call me if I don't hear the beep," she said, fast-walking to Sam's office and closing the door behind her. The computer was in there, and she'd no doubt be locked up with it well into the evening. Axel remained on the couch for a moment, contemplating his sister. It wasn't just that Tess was a different person these days; she seemed to be many different people. He hoped that whatever personality she settled on in the end was one that he liked. Because he really used to like her.

Axel put the Moomin book back on the shelf and went into the kitchen to pick up some lettuce for Bigwig, a hare they kept as a pet. But when he opened the door to his bedroom, he got two more indications that something was vaguely wrong. For one, the wheelchair was there, glowering at him from beside the bed. It had never come inside their house before. It was the old-fashioned kind—lightweight and collapsible, with folding footrests and a sagging leather seat in hospice-navy-blue. It wasn't a real wheelchair. Nobody but Axel could see it, and even *he* couldn't see it most of the time. But on bad days he could hear its oiled wheels swishing behind him, and sometimes he'd turn to catch it rounding a bush or a stump. One morning it rolled insanely after his school bus, bouncing over potholes and stones, as though fastened to the hitch with a twenty-foot length of invisible bungee. Axel had no idea why it had started to follow him. He'd come across it in Mud Lake Park that summer—worn from use but totally clean—and wheeled it to the nature center so he could drop it off with Lost and Found. The poor lady at reception just stared at him, her pained smile shellacked into place. When Axel looked down at his hands, he found them empty, clutching tubes of air where the handles had been. "Do you want me to call your daddy?" she asked, soft and cooing.

Needless to say, he'd never told Sam or Tess about the wheelchair.

The other clue that something was off was Bigwig herself. She was a snowshoe hare, and just about as tame as those animals ever get. She'd darted in front of Sam's truck a few years ago, when he was returning from a lecture at the Ranger School on Cranberry Lake. Their father brought her home all bound up in splints. Bigwig healed quickly and had grown more or less accustomed to their touch and to the unpredictable sounds of a human house. So it was exceedingly strange to see her now, tight as a basketball in the far corner of her hutch, ears flat against her back, whiskers pert, shivering like it was the end of the world.

Axel opened the top of the hutch and made to pick her up. Then he thought better of it— Bigwig looked like she'd take a chunk out of whatever came near. And she stank—her whole inner den was in tatters, littered with pellets. Sam had cut a passageway into the wall, which led to another enclosure out in the yard. Bigwig normally passed droppings out there, but now the floor was covered with them. The wire and wood framing the hutch was bent and splintered. It looked like she had spent the whole afternoon inside, flipping out.

There must have been something in the woods.

No raccoons could have put Bigwig into such a frenzy of fear. Could be a coyote was skulking about, or a fisher, but more likely than not it was just a stray dog.

Carefully, Axel reached into Bigwig's hutch and dropped the lettuce. She'd upended her water dish into the wood chips, so he retrieved it and went into the kitchen to refill it. Their old oven was protesting, sounding like a workshop of busy elves, clinking and tinkering. Tess sounded much the same, through the thin door to their father's study—a mania of typing.

"Something's the matter with Bigwig," Axel called.

Tess stopped typing briefly. "Is she sick?"

"She's scared. Really scared."

There was a pause. "She'll be fine," Tess said.

Back in his room, Axel set the fresh water at the far end of Bigwig's hutch and dug a dry pair of pants out of the hamper. There was a faint creaking sound, and he looked back to see that the wheelchair had rounded the bed and was approaching him, like some kind of screwed-up doom-pet. He gave the chair a kick, sending it backward into the wall, where it shattered into loose gears and smoke and disappeared. Axel had only just finished getting dressed when he heard more creaking. The chair—the mirage, the hallucination . . . whatever it was—was rarely this persistent. "Leave me *alone*," Axel said, wheeling back around.

But it wasn't the wheelchair this time. It was Bigwig, gnawing and pawing at the edge of her hutch. She was suddenly insane with fear, a froth of spit and blood around her mouth from chewing at the wood. Whatever had been terrorizing her must still be out there. And if she didn't stop soon, Bigwig could really hurt herself. Quick as he could, Axel rushed out the door, yelling "Ya! Ya! Ya!" which didn't sound all that menacing, even to him. He grabbed up a broom that was leaning against the stoop and started slamming it on the ground in front of him. He ran around the A-frame, still yelling: "Ya! *Ya!*" so that whatever it was would get good and gone. When he got to the backyard, he stopped.

There was a brown bear sitting in the garden patch, staring at him. For a strange moment it was like Axel was just looking through it. Like it couldn't be any more real than the imagined wheelchair. But no. It was a bear—a huge one. Axel's broom made a thwacking noise, and he realized that he was still hitting it against the ground. He stopped. The bear looked him over. Axel thought a bunch of things all at once. He flew through all the sometimes helpful, sometimes contradictory bear-encounter advice that he'd gleaned from park rangers and his father and the Internet. Was he supposed to make noises so the bear knew what he was? Was he supposed to keep quiet so the bear wouldn't be startled? The literature was sometimes vague, and species dependent. Basically, what it all boiled down to was: Don't run. Lie down and protect your organs. If you have to fight, do it like your life depends on it, because it does. Axel didn't run. He put his free hand over his belly, snorted at how ineffective that'd be, silently scolded himself for snorting. The brown bear just stared. That was another thing he thought—and this much more intensely than the survival tips—that the bear was *brown*. Totally, inexplicably the wrong color. There were no brown bears in Baldwin. Black bears. New York State had black bears. So where the hell had this thing come from?

As if in answer, the bear huffed. It got up off its haunches and took a step closer. Axel suddenly began thinking nothing at all. The bear took another step. The palms of its forepaws were so short, almost human, the back ones elongated and beastly. The bear's head was larger around than Axel's torso, and it swung from left to right, rhythmically. Axel had been avoiding eye contact with the animal, but he stole a glance and saw that it wasn't looking at him anymore. The bear was staring over his shoulder, at the little house from which he'd just emerged. Maybe it smelled the pies in there? Or Bigwig? Or Tess? Maybe it just wondered if Axel were alone. Would it be allowed to eat him in peace, right here? Again Axel wondered: Where did you come from?

What happened next did not happen quickly, but for how fast Axel reacted it could have passed in just a second. The bear began to approach. Axel couldn't seem to get his body to do anything, other than shake, as the bear closed in. But the thing didn't swipe at him, or bite. It walked right past Axel, knocking him with a shoulder big and looming as a hooked side of frozen beef, sending him toppling backward for the second time that day. The bear then made for the kitchen window. Its front paws seemed to clap at the ground lightly before lifting off, standing on its hind legs to peer into the kitchen. Tess was there—Axel could see that now. The animal blocked glare from the setting sun, leaving a bear-shaped patch of darkness on the window glass. In that patch he could see Tess, staring out.

Axel actually felt the ground *thwump* as the bear fell back down onto its forepaws. The animal rocked its head again and gave a sort of low groan—it sounded distinctly dissatisfied. Then the bear turned and made its way around Axel, back through the vegetable garden, departing with a slow, discouraged gait. It seemed no more than a second later that Tess's arms closed around his chest. She lifted him right up into the air. And then he was in the kitchen, on his hands and knees. Tess was bolting the back door and cussing not a little. "What the hell, Axel? What's wrong with you?" He meant to answer, but he couldn't just yet. He realized he hadn't been breathing for a while. He started again.

"Are you, like, broken?" Tess said.

"Did you see it? It was brown," he was gasping, giddy. "Why was it brown?"

Tess glared at him, but her disdain seemed almost forced. She was giddy too. "Next time you go outside and you see a damn *bear*, come back *inside*. Even if it's purple. Too complicated?" Still pressing her weight against the door, she shifted slightly to peek out the window.

"Where did it come from?" Axel said. He got up and pressed his nose against the glass. The bear was trundling through the dying light in the garden.

"Don't know," Tess said. "Zoo? Or was there, like, a dancing-bear thing at the event?"

"I didn't"—he was still catching his breath— "see one." The bear was disappearing. What was wrong with him? Why was he just standing there? Another minute and it'd be gone! "Keep an eye on it," Axel said, darting back through the living room.

"I swear to God if you go outside I'm just going to watch!" Tess hollered from the kitchen. But Axel was only looking for Sam's camera. He found it on his father's desk, stacks of paper swishing away as he grabbed it. By the time he was back in the kitchen, the bear had already reached the edge of the yard, skirting slowly into the deepening shadows beneath a knot of birch trees.

"You don't have enough light," Tess said.

"No one will believe us otherwise," Axel said. He rested the lens on the windowsill and pressed his eye to the viewfinder. The image of the brown bear was just about as clear as your middling Bigfoot picture, a ball of dark against lesser dark. But the road beyond the papery birches was open and lit by a huge bar of setting sunlight. Sure enough, the bear surfaced from the birches edging their yard and stepped onto the road, at once brilliant and distinct. Axel pressed the shutter, but nothing happened. He pressed it again. The camera was off. He turned it on, but it was too late. The bear had submerged into the murky parkland, its shape blending to nothing.

"Stupid," Axel said to himself. *"Stupid."*

Tess didn't seem to notice that he'd failed to capture the necessary proof. "Dad is gonna flip," she said.

Axel was quiet for a while. He was, as a rule, hard on himself. He had to be. "You won't tell him what happened, will you?"

Tess smashed her lips together. "I'm not an idiot. Don't think for a second it's not me he'd blame." With the bear gone, she unbolted the kitchen door, laughing to herself a little, maybe at how utterly useless the flimsy thing would have been to protect them. "We're supposed to get rain tonight," she said. "Why don't you take some pictures of the prints? They might not be there tomorrow."

So she had noticed that he didn't get a shot.

Axel followed his sister outside and started snapping pictures of the torn-up old garden and the big, claw-bristling prints. Their preposterous size was proof enough that the animal was not resident. Plenty of black bears lived up in the Adirondacks, and some occasionally strayed as far as Baldwin. But Tess and Axel had seen their tracks, and they weren't half this big. Together they did a circuit around the house. Evidence of the bear was everywhere. As though it had done nothing but walk rings around their house all afternoon. The deepest scuffs were below the windows. Axel imagined the bear standing to peer inside, investigating each and every room.

"Maybe it was looking for somebody," he said.

"Dude," Tess said, "sometimes it's like you're not even trying to be normal."

They'd returned to the kitchen door, where the final set of needle-pointed prints led off through the garden and between the bone-white birches. Axel judged they still had a half hour before it was totally dark. There was really no question in his mind that they were going to follow this bear. You don't grow up the way Axel had grown up and then *not follow an unexplained bear*. Tess, for her part, seemed to recognize as much.

"So really," she said. "I mean . . . it has to belong to the Medieval Society, right?"

"Maybe." Axel nodded. "It's totally possible. I think I saw something in the catalog about it." A lie, but if Tess was going to let them talk themselves into this, Axel was sure as hell going to aid and abet.

"There's probably some trainer in a coxcomb going crazy with worry," she said.

"It's tame," Axel said. "It's gotta be tame."

"If you tell Dad—"

"Not even . . . I wouldn't—no." Quickly, before she could think better of it, Axel turned and picked up the broom. It was so light in his

hands, making him feel strong. Not just strong—
mighty. He braced the shaft across his shoulders
like the thing was a spear and slung the camera
over his neck. Then he set off for the road, cutting
right through the vegetable garden the way the
bear had.

"You're bringing the broom why, exactly?"
Tess caught up to him in a few long strides.

"No reason," he said. They passed through the
garden, approaching the birch grove at the end of
the property. "I just like to carry it."

"Okay." She stared at him for a moment. "You
know it's just a broom, right?"

Axel sort of laugh coughed. "Come on, Tess,"
he said. "I know what's real and what isn't."

And with that, the two of them headed up the
road. Or rather, the three of them, if you counted
the wheelchair, which had reappeared among the
birches. It followed creakingly, at a distance.

3

The Keeper

Tess knew, of course, that this might not be the smartest thing to do. Even if the bear were a tamed, dancing fugitive from the Battle Re-enactment—which really, it had to be, because where else could it have come from?—that was hardly a good reason to put themselves into the woods with it. And Axel's promise to keep mum about this little adventure would last exactly as long as their father's classes that evening. Her little brother's enthusiasm would boil over, and when Sam found out, he'd come down on Tess like a hailstorm. So why do it, then? Tess wasn't sure, but it had something to do with that moment when the bear stood up, staring right at her through the kitchen window. She couldn't explain it, but there was something in the animal's expression that she'd almost recognized. Worse yet, the big, horrible thing seemed to recognize her right back.

They passed into the birches edging the yard, thick with the smell of the bear, where Axel paused to take a few more pictures. Their mother had planted these trees, and they were still only saplings when she died. The birch orchard was supposed to give them some privacy from the road, but for that any old trees would've done—plenty, indeed, would've done better. When Tess asked her father about it, his answer had been typically roundabout. "These are *Betula papyrifera*," Sam had explained. "American white—you see the oval leaf, the fine toothing? Doesn't look totally dissimilar, at a distance, from *Betula pendula*. Silver birch. A European variety." He'd left it there, using the Latin, and the lesson, as a hiding place. Sam could just as well have said: "Your mother planted these trees because they reminded her of home. But they're not exactly the right kind."

When Axel was done, they crossed to the far side of the road. To the south the park entrance was still crowded—knights and jesters heading home for the day—but up here it was quiet. Axel searched the gravel embankment. "There you are," he mumbled to himself, having rediscovered the trail. The bear tracks didn't veer off into the welcoming shelter of the park, but rather stuck to the road, traveling due north along the embankment. The tracks disappeared once, in a wallow on the shoulder, but emerged again on the far side, the course just as straight as ever. There was something distinctly un-wild about it, like the bear was paying a neighborly call. Like it knew exactly where it was going.

The sun had been swallowed up behind the park, but there was so little cover on the far side of the road that twilight was still bright enough. Beyond the low hedges and blackberry were farm plots, ripe pumpkins scattered across them like orange marbles. Day laborers were still in the field, drifting toward a repurposed school bus that sat at the far end of one of the plots. None of them looked like they'd seen a bear. A jay screeched and whistled from somewhere above and was answered by the cries of other jays, deeper in the park. A warning passed from bird to bird. Back in the field the little school bus began to rumble and whine. The driver flipped the high beams on and started working it carefully out of the plot. One of the tires pinched a pumpkin, and it burst. Tess couldn't explain why, but the world suddenly felt tight as a drum.

Up ahead was Mrs. Ridgeland's place—an

enormous house sulking inside a rough ring of trees, brassy outdoor lanterns casting light out into the countryside. Mrs. Ridgeland was their only real neighbor, which was a shame, because the woman was a grade-A creep. She owned all the farmland opposite the park, including the puny house that Tess shared with her brother and father. Every month their dad would walk up the road to slip a rent check into her mailbox, but Mrs. Ridgeland never came out to say hello. Never asked after their family or if there were any problems with the house she was renting them. But that's not to say they never saw her. Nine times out of ten you could spot Mrs. Ridgeland in one of her many windows, gazing back at you through an old-fashioned telescope. That's how she spent her days, going from window to window to spy on the workers in her fields or on unfamiliar cars passing on the road. Exactly what she was on the lookout for, nobody could say.

"It's cold," Axel said. Tess glanced back at her brother, ready to scold him for not bringing a jacket. But it was the trail he was talking about. The paw prints had veered into the center of the road, where they disappeared like a track crossing a river. Axel got down on his knees and peered expertly at the asphalt. He picked up a handful of fallen leaves and sniffed them. He consulted the air. "There," he said, pointing to a muddy half-moon on the far side of the road. Sure enough, the tracks reappeared on the opposite embankment, cutting down the slope toward the big, bright house.

"She must have seen it," he said.

Tess had spoken to Mrs. Ridgeland only a handful of times, and she had no particular urge to add to her tally. But if anybody was liable to notice something out of the ordinary, it would be their landlady. "We can ask," Tess said. "But that's it. After that we're going right home."

Axel grinned and nodded. Together they followed the tracks down through the ring of hardwoods that circled Mrs. Ridgeland's house. The branches above hung a net of tracery over the property, their trunks marking out airy chapels in the yard. This churchy impression was helped along quite a bit by Mrs. Ridgeland's particular obsession with angels. Stucco and fiberglass statues were strewn among the trees—women with trumpets, men with swords, winged all. The statues were clearly supposed to look like old stone carvings, but mostly they just looked cheap. Tess and Axel lost the trail again just shy of the front stoop. The bear seemed to have stopped between a pair of sinister cherubs, strutting their potbellies and gross baby thighs.

They continued up to the front door and knocked. Eventually two shadows appeared beneath the door, but it was a while longer before it opened. "What are you two doing?" Mrs. Ridgeland said. Their landlady had thrown a robe on over her pajamas. She held the door open wide, but didn't invite either of them in.

"Good evening, madam," Axel said, coaxing a tiny smile from her—adults rarely saw his word choice for the liability that it was. "We apologize for disturbing you, but we bring urgent news."

"Does your father know you came all the way over here?"

"Sam's at work," Tess said.

"So much more reason for you two not to be out wandering," Mrs. Ridgeland said, already making to close the door. Then, a little reluctantly: "Do you need me to help you find your way back?"

It was a ten-minute walk without a single turn, but Axel answered with total sincerity. "No, ma'am, thank you. We just came to ask, did you see the bear?" For the briefest moment it seemed to Tess that a look of unguarded surprise passed across Mrs. Ridgeland's face. But the expression vanished before it had a chance to settle. "A brown bear," Axel continued. "A grizzly."

"A bear?"

"Indeed. Yes."

"I can't say I have." Mrs. Ridgeland glanced at the broom Axel was carrying and shot an annoyed look at Tess. "Are you two playing hunters?"

"We really saw one," Tess said, staring hard into the woman's face, looking for a trace of whatever had just passed. "A brown bear came into our garden."

"No bears in Baldwin," Mrs. Ridgeland said, meeting Tess's gaze. The black/brown distinction seemed totally lost on her, one bear as impossible as the next.

"Actually, that's not entirely accurate," Axel said. "Up in the Adirondacks there's a population of—"

"The Adirondacks are a long ways off." Mrs. Ridgeland looked over their heads at the darkening trees. "I think it's time the two of you got along."

"The footprints are right there," Tess said, pointing to where they'd lost the track. "If you want to put some shoes on, we can show them to you." She wasn't being insistent out of any desire to be believed. She simply didn't like Mrs. Ridgeland and wanted to impress the woman's own wrongness upon her. Their landlady's expression hardened, and it was now no longer a question of whether or not a bear could happen—it was a contest. The grizzly would have to pop out from behind a tree and start tipping over angel statues for her to admit it to evidence.

"We tracked it from our garden," Axel said. "But the track ends here." If seeing the bear wasn't enough for him, his week was likely made by getting to say the word "tracked." "We've got some pictures of the footprints, if you don't want to come outside." Helpfully, Tess's little brother offered up the camera for Mrs. Ridgeland's inspection. She made like she didn't notice.

"Well, now . . . if I had to guess, I'd say that bear probably went *back* the way it came," Mrs. Ridgeland said. "Why don't you two go home and check again, before it gets completely dark." Then, to Tess: "Step inside with me for a minute. I want to give you a flashlight for the way back."

Instead of allowing her to follow, Mrs. Ridgeland actually took Tess by the arm and pulled her inside. She shut the heavy door behind them, sealing them both up in a dark hallway overflowing with stacks of faded, glossy paper. Her skin seemed somehow whiter in the darkness, her complexion matching the stucco angels out front. The woman gave the impression of being just as dry and hollow on the inside.

"Playing with your brother is fine and good," she said, "but this is too much. It's odd." Mrs. Ridgeland whispered the word "odd" like it was a malignant, disfiguring disease. Like she meant to quarantine the afflicted.

Tess stared at her for a moment. She was getting bolder as she got older. Ruder, too. "You saw it, didn't you?" she said. "You gave us a look when Axel—"

The older woman scrunched up her brow, cutting Tess off with a dismissive huff. "It's solid oak my dear." She reached over Tess's shoulders and rapped on the door behind her. "He can't hear you through it, so there's no need to keep up the act. Now listen. A little pretend from time to time is harmless enough, but your brother doesn't understand . . ." She trailed off. "It seems to me like you might be taking advantage of him."

Tess opened her mouth to speak, but then she thought better of it. Her father could forgive a lot, but cussing out their landlady would be too much, even for him.

"You've got him convinced he's tracking a real live bear," Mrs. Ridgeland went on. "It can't be good for his condition, traipsing all over the place, and at this time of year. You're going to wear him out."

"His *condition* is fine," Tess said.

Mrs. Ridgeland sighed, her eyes suddenly glistening. "Oh, honey," she said.

Tess felt either a scold coming or a forced hug. She didn't care to get either, so she said a loud "thank you!" and used that ink cloud to slip back out the door, closing it firmly behind her. Axel had gone down the front steps to wait in the yard. He usually had a good sense of when people were talking about him and would make himself scarce for their benefit.

"The flashlight?" he said.

"No batteries." Tess set down the steps. "Come on." Axel picked up his broom, and together they passed through the angel-crowded yard and left Mrs. Ridgeland's house behind them. Everything had grown closer and larger in the dark.

They walked back home in silence. The A-frame burned through the birches up ahead, alongside the taillights of the last cars still trickling away from Mud Lake Park. Tess was still mulling that look of surprise that had flashed over Mrs. Ridgeland's face, wondering if maybe she'd imagined it, when she caught sight of a tall, slim silhouette standing against the glow of their house. At first it looked like their father, but he wasn't supposed to be back from teaching for another few hours. It was a stranger. Tess shushed Axel—he'd been yammering about irregular weather patterns as a potential catalyst for a confused, migratory grizzly—and they approached quietly.

For his part, the stranger didn't seem to notice

them coming. As the man came into fuller view, Tess saw that he wasn't tall—he was *towering*. He skimmed the underside of seven feet, if you counted his boots and hat, but he was just about as skinny as Axel, which made him look like some gaudy marionette from a stop-motion movie. He wore a long duster, patched here and there with patterned swatches. No question this joker must have been a member of the Medieval Society, done up for the battle. He even had an elaborate wizardish walking stick, which he used for support as he lowered himself into an odd squat: free hand on his knee, his narrow butt waggling out like a mockingbird's. Tess realized that he was talking to somebody in the woods—a second stranger, among the trees. That was enough for her. Medieval Society or no, oddly dressed strangers in the night were to be avoided. She took Axel's wrist and made to lead him silently across the road.

"Maybe he knows where the bear is?" Axel whispered.

"Who cares where the bear is," she said, tugging on his wrist. He wouldn't budge.

"Come on, now!" the stranger was yowling. He had an accent, but from where Tess couldn't be sure. "You're being an infant. If it's too early, then it's too early. You'll just have to wait and come back later."

Whoever was in the woods made no reply.

"Having a sulk?" the stranger said. "I bring you all the way to this armpit and you're having a *sulk*?"

Again Tess pulled on Axel's wrist, but he set his heels. The kid weighed almost nothing, but when he wanted to, he could make himself leaden.

"I'm going to go ask," Axel said, twisting out of her grip and continuing down the road. Slowly, the stranger began to grow more distinct. His patchy duster was neatly tailored, with suede elbow pads, and on his feet was a pair of mud-spattered knee-high gum boots. His head was roughly the shape of a sideways egg—so oblong that Tess wondered for a moment if it might be some kind of fancy prosthetic makeup or a well-fitted mask. He wore a beat-up old fedora with a sprig of lily of the valley sprouting from the band. He'd apparently decided to attend the battle dressed as either a depression-era wizard or a vaudeville hobo.

"You think I won't go back without you?" The stranger stood up to his full height, his body unfolding. "I can do that. See how well your sorry self makes it home without me." He gave his head a sad, violent shake. And as his face whipped about, he caught sight of Tess and Axel approaching. "Oh!" he said, startled. He looked back into the woods and then at them again. "No pictures," he said.

"What?"

The stranger pointed at the camera slung over Axel's shoulder. It took Tess a moment to realize that the finger he was pointing with was one of only three on that hand. The stranger had been badly mangled, and the ring and pinky fingers of his left hand were missing entirely. Hard to fake that with makeup.

"It'll cost you," the man said. "We have a booth for that. You need to get tokens." He flashed them a smile, and wow, was it ugly. His mouth was thin and stretchy, and his teeth . . . It's hard to describe them. They were clean and even. But they seemed to vibrate slightly. They looked like they wanted *out*.

Axel, for his part, was totally unfazed. "What makes you think we want your picture?"

The stranger smiled again, and Tess wished he wouldn't. "Not mine," he said. "Hers." He nodded at the dark patch of woods, and there it was—not it, *she*. The brown bear. She was lying down in the shadows, her big head resting on her front paws. She did look sulky.

"Oh," Axel croaked.

"That is, more or less, the desired effect," the stranger said, with a pixie-dust wriggle of his three fingers.

"Are you her trainer?" Axel said.

"I can't say that, no. I haven't the temperament for hoops or balls, and I'm afraid that she doesn't, either. I'm just a lowly *Keeper*." The stranger said this word like it was some kind of official title. He even gave a little bow and doffed his cap, revealing a single lick of red hair on his otherwise bald head.

"But you're *her* keeper, right?" Tess said. "You know that she escaped?"

"Escaped?" The Keeper jabbed his walking stick into the crook of his elbow and clapped his hands once. "*Escaped* would imply that I get a vote in where she goes or what she does when she gets there."

From inside the woods the bear got up onto her haunches and seemed to moan, or growl. Axel took a step back, cupping the camera in his free hand. Tess saw that he was trying to be discreet about adjusting the settings, flipping open the flash.

"Well, she came right into our yard," Tess went on. "She could have hurt somebody."

"You're telling me," the Keeper said. "Old girl is a monster." Then, to the still grumbling grizzly: "Quit it, you drama queen." He removed his fedora, took a mantislike step into the woods, and batted the bear across the muzzle with it. Amazingly, she didn't eat his face. She behaved neither the way a wild bear would nor the way a tame one should.

Axel's broom fell away as he lifted the camera and snapped a picture. But no sooner had he taken it than the Keeper reached over and snatched the camera away.

"Hey!" Axel sounded more surprised than anything else.

"I said no pictures." The Keeper was calm but plainly annoyed.

"That's our dad's camera," Tess said.

"Trust me, he won't miss it." The Keeper brought the camera up to his face, seeming to puzzle over it.

"He's a knight of the realm," Tess said, her cheeks warming. "He'll get you kicked out of the re-enactment."

"Some realm," the Keeper said. Then, without any warning whatsoever, he lifted the camera high above his head and let it drop. It landed on the embankment with a heavy, glassy crunch. For a moment, Tess and Axel just gawked at him.

"You're going to break it!" Axel shouted. He scooped up his broom and swung it at the Keeper. To Tess's horror, the ragged head caught the strange man directly across the face. Everything went quiet. The Keeper stared down at them, and Tess made ready to grab Axel and sprint for the house.

"Good reach," the Keeper said. For a moment it looked like his face had turned red. But it wasn't just him—the whole roadside was bright and blinking. Tess glanced back at the road and saw a police car driving up, very slowly, cherry top whirling. It turned down the dirt driveway to the A-frame, where it stopped. Someone must have called to complain about the bear.

"I'm going to tell them what you did," Axel said.

"Be my guest," the Keeper said, unfurling his mangled left hand in the direction of the police cruiser. A pair of officers had gotten out, walking slowly toward the front door of the A-frame. They took such tiny steps.

"You think I won't?"

"I'm sure you will," the Keeper said. "Have at it."

Axel hesitated, maybe reluctant to leave his sister alone with this crazy person. Behind the Keeper, in the shadowed park, the bear let out another groan. She stood, quite suddenly, on her hind legs. "Hey, now," the Keeper said, sounding nervous for the first time. The bear groaned again and then rolled her haunches so that her front paws landed to one side. She spun around and charged deeper into the woods, away from her keeper, lost in the firefly-dotted depths of the park.

"Stupid thing," the Keeper said. "She's going

to get lost." Then he turned back and gave them one last look. He reaffixed his hat to his broad, ugly head, then picked the camera up off the embankment and tossed it to Tess. The view screen blinked and sizzled—the thing was definitely broken. "It was nice to meet you both," the Keeper said. "And I'm sorry."

"Don't be sorry," Axel virtually hissed. "You can't just wreck our dad's camera and then say *sorry*."

"That you had coming," the Keeper said. "What I'm sorry for is everything else. Everything that's about to happen to you."

And with that cryptic bit of garbage, he took his walking stick in hand and bounded jauntily into the woods after the bear.

4

The Fortune House

The two policemen had reached the front door and were tapping on it gingerly. Axel cut through the birches and then around the A-frame, coming right up behind them—a young officer and an older one, both in strange, dark blue uniforms. These were city cops, Axel realized, not the troopers who normally patrolled town. The bear must have covered a lot of ground.

"Hey, you just missed them!"

The men spun around. The younger one had his hand on his belt, not six inches from his holster. *Stupid,* Axel thought. Not them—him. He knew better than to sneak up on city people.

"Whoa, kid. You shouldn't . . ." The older officer looked flustered. He glanced at his partner, and it seemed like they were having a silent argument over who would speak next. The older one finally gave in. "Do you live here?"

Axel nodded impatiently. "Listen, they're just in the park, but they're getting away." He pointed across the road, into the murk of the woods, still flickering with siren light.

"Who is?" The younger officer glanced into the evening. It was plain to see that he was still half spooked.

"The bear," Axel said. "She's with her keeper, but I don't think he knows what he's doing. Also, he broke my dad's camera!"

The officers looked at each other and had another long stretch of talking with their eyebrows. "I don't know about any bear," the older one finally said. "But I do need to talk to your mom—I mean, Mrs. Fortune. Is she home? Is this the Fortune house?"

Axel stared at them both. Police coming up from the city, asking for his mother, not knowing enough not to. Axel's own knowing started that very moment, but for the next few minutes he'd resist it.

"Our mom is dead," Tess said. She'd appeared in the middle of the driveway, her arms hanging slack at her sides, the camera dangling so low that it grazed the gravel under her feet. "But this is the Fortune house."

"That's your sister?" The younger officer said, his voice creaky. He seemed to have had enough of kids appearing out of the darkness.

"My name's Tess." Axel's sister sounded weirdly hesitant—like her name was somehow up for debate.

"He's getting away," Axel said. "The bear is, too."

"Okay, now," the older officer said, nodding like he was listening. But he wasn't—his attention was on Axel's sister. "Are there any adults in the house, young lady? You have any other brothers or sisters?" Then, as a little aside to Axel: "Mind that's not a question you should normally answer to a stranger, all right? We'll just make an exception this time." As though Axel were growing younger under this nice old dude's gaze. The officer had started out talking to a ten-year-old, and now Axel was maybe six or seven to him, tops. All the proof he needed that something was wrong. Wrong in a new kind of way, as big a kind of wrong as had entered his life since he was a baby. Still, he kept himself blind to it.

"We have a neighbor," Tess said, her eyes a little cloudy, the muscles of her face loosening. "Mrs. Ridgeland. She lives just . . ." Instead of saying where, Tess simply pointed up the road. Her finger was shaking. Her whole arm was shaking.

"That's fine," the older man said. "All right.

Rick is going to go and get her. How about that, Rick?" He looked at the younger officer, who nodded.

"Why do you need Mrs. Ridgeland?" Axel said.

"I'm James," the older officer said, stepping down off the front stoop and holding out his hand for Tess to shake. She didn't. "Do you mind if I come inside for a minute?"

"It's open," she said.

"Well, all right." James smiled, the effort behind it plain enough to see. He stood there for an awkward moment, and when it became clear that Tess wasn't going to give him more of an invitation, he returned to the front door and swung it wide. Rick, the jumpy young officer, was already back inside his cruiser. The siren light spun silently as he pulled off the shoulder, back onto the county road.

"I said, why do you need Mrs. Ridgeland?" Axel was getting annoyed now.

"Why don't you come on inside?" James said. "We can talk in here."

Tess was the first through the door, pausing for a moment to grip the frame. James and Axel followed. Inside, the house smelled of butter and of burning. A greasy film of smoke hung about the light fixtures on the ceiling. "Oh dear," James said.

"There are pies in the oven," Tess said, her voice flat. "We forgot them."

"Shouldn't leave the house with the oven on," James said, sort of to himself. He went from window to window to air out the A-frame. When he opened the oven, a hefty belch of smoke slurped out. Waving a pot holder in front of his face, he retrieved the two pies and dropped them in the sink with the water running. They sizzled like doused campfires. Tess lowered herself onto the couch. Axel wanted to shake her. He wanted to be big enough to shake this old police officer, too.

"Doesn't anybody give a crap about the bear?" Axel all but shouted it.

Tess just looked at him. She was crying, now—God, why was she crying? It was more a sound than anything else, like awful hiccups caught between her belly and her throat. Like she was choking on the air. It made Axel so angry. The bear was getting away, and Tess was just sitting there and the cop was condescending to him the exact way every stupid adult always condescended to him. His sister reached for him, but Axel pulled away.

"Honestly, son, we haven't heard boo about any bears." James coughed a little as he exited the kitchen. He saw what was happening with Tess and sat down next to her. It was only now that

Axel noticed how sad the man looked. His eyes were red and wet, too, but also hard. "I can ask around, though. You say you saw a bear, and I believe you. Sounds like something that should be looked into."

Nobody said anything more, and a clean night chill slowly filled the house. Before long they could hear the crunch of tires on the dirt drive outside. Mrs. Ridgeland pushed her way into the A-frame before the younger officer had even unbuckled his seat belt. She was still in her pajamas and robe— she hadn't even bothered to put shoes on. James stood to greet her, but she went right past him, setting on Axel. She took the boy into her arms and virtually carried him over to Tess and glommed her into the embrace as well. Axel could feel the shudder of Tess's crying, thrumming through the trunks of Mrs. Ridgeland's arms. But all he could think was: How could they? How could they tell her before they told us? He's our dad. He's *ours*, and they told her first.

An accident. A crash on 690, eastbound into Syracuse. The barest of bare bones, and it's all they got. The police persuaded Mrs. Ridgeland to unlatch from the children and then spoke to her for a good long while. As though Tess and Axel had been rendered deaf—as though they'd slipped out the open doors and windows with the rest of the smoke. Though, to be fair, they'd all but done so. Axel had never seen his sister like this. He'd seen Tess cry, sure, but only once or twice. And even then it was just a few neatly controlled tears, a perfect distillation of a particular moment of anger and frustration. But this was something else, horribly alive and unselfconscious. Axel, on the other hand, felt anything but alive. It was almost as though he'd been ejected from his life and was watching this whole maudlin scene unfold on high-definition television. It was strangely comforting. As though, if things got too bad, Axel could simply change the channel.

Over at the kitchen table Mrs. Ridgeland was telling the police about how Saara, Axel and Tess's mother, had died a decade ago. The children had no aunts or uncles that Mrs. Ridgeland knew of, and no grandparents, either. At least none who ever visited. She thought it was a safe enough guess that any family they had were either dead or else not on speaking terms.

"We have a grandfather," Tess said, her bleary eyes turning to the bookshelves. There was a picture of Grandpa Paul right there in the middle, just as rangy as their dad but older and more used up. He was sort of smiling, sort of squinting, seated in a canvas camp chair on the edge of a clear pond, the skin on his shoulders pink and peeling. He wasn't smoking in the picture, but you could tell from it that he was a smoker. "He lives in Florida," she said. "He's afraid to fly. We visit him."

"That right, honey?" Officer James said. "You know where in Florida?"

Tess didn't answer right away. She and Axel had been to their grandpa's actual house—if you could give such a name to a single-wide trailer with only occasional electric and plumbing—only a few times. It was on the outskirts of a little town called the Boils, named for the warm freshwater springs that burbled up deep in the juniper prairie of the Ocala reserve. The trailer didn't exactly have a street address, and what's more, their grandpa liked to move it from time to time. He said it was to change up his view, but even Axel knew that it was more to change up his neighbors. Grandpa Paul could be a hard man to get along with, as evidenced by the fact that their dad got along with basically everybody on the planet except for him.

"Not exactly," Tess said. "I know his number." She took out her phone and read it aloud. Rick, the younger of the two officers, stepped into Sam's study to call. He emerged less than a minute later, mouthing "out of service" to James and Mrs. Ridgeland.

"He doesn't have a lot of money," Axel said. He hadn't quite articulated this before, to himself or anybody else, but wow was it ever true. He thought of his granddad, groomed and quaffed whenever they met, reeking of aftershave and effort, wearing clothes that sometimes still had outlet-store tags on them. Axel supposed they'd live with him now, and that was as weird a thought as any. It rivaled the backyard bear in oddness.

"Nothing to worry about," James said. "We'll find a way to get in touch with him. Until then, is there anyone else? Somebody closer by?" He waited, looking at Tess.

How could it be possible that the answer was no?

It was decided in very short order that the kids would go home with Mrs. Ridgeland. She and the two officers waited by the front door while Tess and Axel emptied their backpacks of schoolbooks and stuffed in their pajamas and their toothbrushes. Axel felt strange as he wandered the house, as though he had just minutes to save a few possessions before evacuating the area, the A-frame a loss, doomed to be consumed by a forest fire racing down on them from the hot heart of the leafless park. He made one last stop to drop some more food and water into Bigwig's hutch before closing the door to his bedroom for what would be exactly the second-to-last time.

"Do you two have any questions?" Officer James asked once they were all packed.

"Not about . . . just . . ." Axel sensed it was wrong, but he couldn't help himself. It wouldn't leave his head. "About the bear. I want to know if somebody is going to go look for the bear."

The adults just stared at him.

The angels in Mrs. Ridgeland's yard blazed white one by one as they caught the high beams and fell back into nothing when the cruiser passed them by. Tess was still crying when she stepped out of the car, but it had cooled now to a sort of teary daze. Mrs. Ridgeland and Axel got out as well, and the sound of their doors shutting seemed loud enough to knock the trees over. Officer James lowered his window and explained that some-one from Social Services would be around in the morning, to work out a better arrangement until next of kin could be located. Mrs. Ridgeland said that the children could stay with her as long as they needed to.

The cruiser backed cautiously down the drive, and Mrs. Ridgeland fumbled with a big ring of keys. She led them through that cramped hallway and into a sitting room swollen with yarn and con-struction paper, old photographs spilling out of open boxes on the floor. "You two probably aren't hungry," Mrs. Ridgeland said, "but you should try to eat something all the same."

Axel nodded. He was actually starving. The pies had immolated, and he hadn't eaten a thing since the sweet barrel pickle he'd bought at the court-of-foods that afternoon.

Mrs. Ridgeland waited for another moment and, getting no indication either way from Tess, she said: "I'll see what I can find. After that, we'll sort out a place for you to sleep." She was talking mostly to herself now, fading in the direction of the kitchen.

The children sat silently on opposite ends of a little love seat facing an enormous picture window. Mrs. Ridgeland's giant, copper-plated telescope was set before the window. It made about as much sense as the angels cavorting out in her yard. Axel thought, once again, of the bear. It was out there too. "Dad is gonna flip when we tell him about it." It was only when Tess turned to stare at him that Axel realized he'd said this aloud.

"We're going to have to make do," Mrs. Ridgeland said, returning to the sitting room. She held a tray with three mugs on it, a box of crackers, and an assortment of store-brand dips in plastic tubs. "I'm used to shopping for one." She squeezed in between Tess and Axel, orange construction paper crumpling beneath her, and made space for the tray by whisking her forearm across the coffee table.

"I'm afraid the bedrooms are a bit . . . messy." She opened each of the tubs and gave the contents a good sniff. The onion dip and the southwest dip were promptly recapped and set off to one side. "But there's a couch in the basement," she went on. "It doesn't fold out, but it's a sectional. I think you two should fit all right."

"Thank you," Tess said.

"None of that." Mrs. Ridgeland put a hand on Tess's cheek, not even trying to brush away the heavy gloss of tears. "Listen," she said, turning to Axel and putting her free hand on his. "This is awful. This is a terrible thing that's happened to both of you. But it *happened*. It's real, and it's permanent. You can feel whatever you need to feel, whenever you need to feel it. You can be as tough as you want to be right now. Denial, I've found, is underrated. As long as it's only to delay pain, have at it. But understand—the facts are forever. Your father was . . ." She trailed off, her eyes drifting to her telescope. Axel followed her gaze and noticed something moving in the yard. It was a dark thing, slithering serpentine between the statues. Not the bear—the wheelchair. It entered the rectangle of orange light cast out the window and seemed to stare up at him patiently. It seemed, for a weird moment, like Mrs. Ridgeland could see it too.

"To be honest," she continued, "I never knew your father that well. But he seemed like a sweet man. He's gone now, and he isn't coming back." This last bit seemed directed at Axel in particular. She stared down at him as she said it, and her voice had a strange, pleading ring to it.

Tess pulled away from Mrs. Ridgeland, whose hand stayed exactly where it was, clutching the air where her cheek had been. "You're *terrible* at this," Tess said.

"That's fine," Mrs. Ridgeland said. "As tough as you need to be." Whatever the point of her bizarre little speech was, she seemed satisfied that she'd made it. She clapped her hands on her knees, hoisting herself up off the love seat. "Let's go see about those beds." They followed Mrs. Ridgeland into the basement and helped her tuck sheets between the cushions of a big L-shaped sectional, the short end of which was just long enough for Axel. It was a lot less cluttered down there, but the air felt close. A black workout bench sat opposite the sectional, flanked by two hulking sets of free weights. Axel couldn't explain why, but it was among the most depressing things he'd ever seen.

Mrs. Ridgeland left, and they both changed into their pajamas in the dark. Axel lay still, looking at the shadows of the workout gear, listening to the wet rattle of his sister's breathing. Listening to the night and the creak of the wheelchair as it rounded Mrs. Ridgeland's big house. There was a little window near the top of the wall, which was just at ground level. Through it Axel could see the curve of black rubber, the greased spokes of the wheel. It was bumping gently into the brickwork. If the wheelchair could have stooped down and crawled in through the window, it no doubt would have. Axel wondered if he would ever sleep again. It certainly wasn't going to happen now. He sat up. His brain was buzzing, but not with thoughts about his father. He was thinking about the bear.

Tess must have heard him slip out of bed, but she didn't say anything. Silently Axel crept back upstairs. With all the junk in the house, there must be a computer somewhere. He'd see if the *Post-Standard* had anything about a loose grizzly on its website. He could even double-check this year's catalog for the Battle Re-enactment, on the slim chance that there was an exhibit he'd missed. Mrs. Ridgeland was on the telephone in the kitchen; Axel could hear her dialing as he snuck through the sitting room. She wasn't having much luck— she dialed and hung up, dialed again and hung up again. If she were trying to reach their grandpa Paul, she'd need her patience.

The stairs were so cluttered that it was hard to get up to the second floor without making too much noise, but Axel found that if he stepped mostly on the piles of clothes, he was all right. He checked the master bedroom first and got lucky. Not just a computer, but several of them. Mrs. Ridgeland even had decent Internet.

The word "bear" appeared nowhere on the front pages or associated blogs for the *Standard*, or YNN, or any of the network affiliates. Axel even checked the papers out of Albany, Rochester, and Binghamton, but found zilch there as well. There was a story that did repeat on a number of the pages, usually above the fold of the scroll bar, but it had nothing to do with animals. One website bore a photograph of what looked like a sword sticking out of a beaver mound, paired with the seemingly unrelated headline: SLEEPY TRUCKER CAUSES HAVOC. Axel clicked on it, thus stumbling backward into the story of his father's death.

It had been a long-haul driver, just starting his trip from the Canadian border down to Austin. In an attempt to bypass interstate construction and the choke point of downtown Syracuse, this trucker had put himself and his rig on the same road Sam used to travel from Baldwin to his evening class. The trucker had, apparently, missed three signs advising drivers of the low clearance of a pedestrian overpass, which spanned the highway and allowed residents of a new subdivision to access the jogging trail around Onondaga Lake. The top of the rig tore into the overpass, scattering suitcase-size chunks of concrete across the road. A pickup traveling behind the rig was struck directly and rolled into the embankment. The driver of this private vehicle—who later died en route to hospital, the only fatality of the accident—was a performer at the Annual Battle Re-enactment. As he had failed to secure his costume materials in the bed of his truck, they, too, were scattered. Banded armor and mail, a helmet half crushed under a slab of the ruined bridge, and the sword flung well clear of the road, stabbed deep into the dome of a beaver mound, Excaliburesque. It would have been news either way, but this twist made the story irresistible. The whole road had to be closed down, and a member of the cleaning crew had cut himself on a battle-ax and would require stitches. Axel kept reading past the end of the article—there had to be more than just: "a performer at the Annual Battle Re-enactment"—and into the comments section. The trolls had beat him there. *Should have used a warding spell!* sat right at the top. Below several people wasting their typing breath admonishing the idiot, another charmer had written, simply: *No more HP?*

Axel turned the monitor off. He unplugged the A-cord from the tower, unplugged the keyboard and mouse as well. He wanted to put his foot through something, but he couldn't find anything soft enough.

Axel went back downstairs, now making no attempt at all to be quiet. But Mrs. Ridgeland still didn't hear him. She must have gotten through to somebody, because she was shouting into the receiver like a woman calling against a stiff wind. "England . . . what? Say again?" There was a long pause. "No, I don't. I see. Well, how am I supposed to call there, then?"

She still didn't hear Axel when he reached the landing and trudged heavy-footed into the sitting room. He went right up to the window and pressed his face against it. He knew it was out there. "Come back," he said. He put his hands on the glass, and they left smudges. Why did he want to see it so badly? "Come back, please," he said again, louder this time. He was crying a little now, which was good, he guessed. It had been weird that he couldn't do it before. Though it was only slightly less weird that he was now standing outside of his own crying self, appraising it for normalcy.

"Bear," he said. "Please."

Suddenly Tess was standing right behind him. He didn't know how long she'd been there, but she turned him around and hugged him and said: "It's going to be all right." They were the first words his sister had spoken to him since they'd left the Keeper. The first words they'd shared since they found out that Sam had died. He didn't believe them for a second.

5

Oakwood

Sam's funeral was set for Monday, though later postponed to the middle of the week. Nobody would tell Tess why, but it wasn't hard to guess. It was because of Grandpa Paul. He'd probably need at least a few days to shake off the smell of bourbon and pawn his way to an airline ticket. The fact that her grandfather was a total, irreparable screw-up was the worst-kept secret in the Fortune family. And Tess thought that was saying something.

He called her on the night Sam died, a few hours after she'd brought Axel back to bed. Tess hadn't been able to tell who it was at first, because her grandfather was using a pay phone and because he was a good deal drunker than usual. Of course, she wasn't supposed to know about her granddad's troubles, but honestly. Two years ago when they'd visited him at home, Grandpa Paul had greeted the family in a yard littered with shattered empties, cigarette butts, and the forest-green shells of discharged buckshot. His closet-size shower and dinky, waterless sink had been filled with uncapped bottles, saved for the dregs in their bottoms. Sam had put on a wooden smile, depositing the children up on the bank of the steaming pond out back and telling them that the first one to spot the endemic Florida scrub jay would win a milk shake. Then he disappeared back into the trailer, where Grandpa Paul was singing a song about horses. Tess had never heard a fistfight happen so quietly, and for the rest of the day neither her father nor her grandfather would acknowledge the black eyes they'd given each other. It was the last time she or Axel had set foot in the trailer; every visit since was anchored to the safety of a strip mall, fast-casual food, and hugs good-bye in skillet-hot parking lots. Still, Tess knew that Sam loved the old man. She did, too.

"Oh, baby girl, my darling." Grandpa Paul was lilting on the phone, trailing off. He must have had a bottle to his lips since hearing the news.

"Hi, Grandpa," Tess said. She whispered it, so as not to wake Axel up.

"If this isn't a bucket of awful, I don't . . ." He

paused. A sob escaped him like a belch, high and tinny. "Listen. Listen." He was steeling himself against crying, or trying to, at least. "We're coming, baby girl. Don't you worry about a thing."

Tess sat up on the sectional. She turned her back to her brother and then hunched over to make her body a catcher's mitt for her voice. "Who's *we*, Grandpa?"

If Grandpa Paul heard what she'd said, it certainly didn't register. "You. Your brother. Both of you, now. You are going to be taken care of. Hear me? Plenty to be sad about right now. Plenty." He paused again to master his breathing. "But nothing to *worry* about. I want you to know that, Tess."

"Grandpa, are you bringing somebody with you?" She spoke a little louder now.

"Of course I am, sweetheart. I'm coming, and I'm bringing your grandma."

"Please, whoever she is, don't call her that," Tess said. Grandpa Paul had a girlfriend more often than he didn't, though never for more than a few months straight. By her count, Tess had met at least three would-be stepgrannies at various Olive Gardens scattered throughout central Florida. "Please," she repeated, "could you just come alone?"

"Nonsense. I just spoke to her. When you meet her, you—"

"I don't want to meet anybody, Grandpa."

"Can't help you with that, honey." Grandpa Paul didn't say anything more for a while. Tess could faintly hear music on the other end, the buzzing whoosh of a truck driving on a wet road. There was a single tavern in the Boils. She knew because it was set right up against the drop point for one of the Ocala canoe runs, and they used to stop by for early waffles before putting in. Tess imagined her granddad standing outside now, broom-skinny in an old phone booth, ferns and palmetto reaching darkly from the bank. Did he have any idea that it was one of his son's favorite places in the world? Whatever woman he was seeing must have been in the tavern, waiting on another round, maybe planning her upcoming trip to New York. Tess wondered if he'd even told her it was for his son's funeral.

"How's your brother doing?" Grandpa Paul said, sort of suddenly.

Tess turned to peek at Axel on the short end of the sectional. He was either asleep or faking it well. "I don't know," she whispered.

"Come on, now," Grandpa Paul said. "Yes, you do."

Tess and Axel went back to the A-frame every day to feed Bigwig, but on the morning of the funeral they were surprised to see that somebody had boxed up nearly all of their possessions. The library shelves stood bare, and the furniture was shoved against the walls. There were open crates everywhere, many already labeled in thick blue marker. BOOKS—ENGLISH and BOOKS—NOT ENGLISH, as well as KITCHEN and, oddly: WEAPONS. Tess and Axel stood speechless on the threshold.

"Most of your clothes got packed yesterday afternoon," Mrs. Ridgeland said, "but I left a few options out on your beds. Nothing is quite right for today, I'm afraid, but there's no helping it. We don't have time to shop."

Neither Tess nor Axel said a word. Axel made for his bedroom, pausing on the way to grip the rim of an overflowing box. Tess followed him, picking a few spilled books up off the floor. One of them was an old Finnish grammar reader, the recycled pages gray and soft as newspaper. It lay open to a worksheet on families—*äiti, isä, sisko, veli*. Mother, father, sister, and brother. Beside the words was a space where you could practice writing them, dark with shaky pencil marks. Tess recognized her brother's handwriting. He'd written only one of the words, over and over, stretching out beyond the dotted lines. *Äiti-Äiti-Äiti-Äiti*. Mom-Mom-Mom-Mom. All his life,

Tess's little brother had longed for a missing parent. Now it was two for the price of one.

"Get angry," Tess thought. Actually, she did more than think it. She whispered it aloud. Because anger was the only alternative she could see to sinking to the floor right then and there and crying for a month or so. She slapped the workbook shut, focusing on the revolting thought of Mrs. Ridgeland's plump, plaster-white fingers on it. It's not that Tess had any illusions. She didn't think that she and Axel would keep living in the A-frame by themselves, taking the bus to school in Baldwin, ordering groceries online, and drilling each other on Finnish verbs every evening. And she knew that Grandpa Paul would never leave his juniper woods to live up here with them. But still, the speed with which they were being booted out was ridiculous. "You should have told us," she said.

Mrs. Ridgeland paused to consider this. "Maybe," she said, breezing through the maze of boxes like she owned the place. Which, to be fair, she did. "But it had to be done, and you couldn't have changed it. If you want, you can come by tomorrow morning to help finish up. In the meantime, you've got to change."

The service was scheduled for midday, in the Oakwood Cemetery down in Syracuse. It was a big, old cemetery that abutted the south end of the SUNY College of Environmental Science and Forestry, where their father had taught undergraduates about lichens and hardwoods. The Oakwood was also where their mother was buried, and Sam's plot would be right beside hers. Grandpa Paul was supposed to land in the late morning, presumably with his new lady friend in tow, and would meet Tess and Axel at the cemetery. Tess hoped that her granddad would be able to hold it together and make it through the day. She hoped that she'd be able to, as well, because whenever she lost her immediate focus on the boxes, or her clothes, or spying on Axel to judge his energy levels, the world went flimsy. Tess felt a sadness so deep and desperate that it was like the sun—she was sure that if she looked right at it, she'd go blind.

"I know that was a shock," Mrs. Ridgeland said as they left the A-frame and got back into her car. "I'm sorry about that. I don't mean to make you feel like you're being pushed out. But we have to be realistic." She backed them down the dirt drive. A minute later they were on 690, heading southeast. It was the exact same route their dad had taken, not even a week ago, on the night of the brown bear.

"Everything's been worked out with a moving company," Mrs. Ridgeland went on. "Your stuff should arrive at your grandparents' place in no time at all."

"What about Bigwig?" Axel said, tugging at his shiny sleeves—the only thing he had that approached funeral attire was a costume tux from the previous Halloween. "I think we'll need special papers," he went on. "It's not the same for a hare."

"What's that?" Mrs. Ridgeland eyed him in the rearview.

"As a rabbit," Axel said. "I mean, I think it's easier for a rabbit." They stared at each other via reflections.

"I'm not following."

Axel sighed. He kept his voice reasonable. "Bigwig is a *hare*. She's technically a wild animal. We need a permit to take her out of the state."

"I see. We'll have to look into that." Mrs. Ridgeland nodded up in the driver's seat, and Tess knew that there wasn't a chance in hell that the hare would be coming with them. A tiny loss, in comparison, but Axel would take it hard. He loved that little animal.

They passed the exit for Camillus and came abreast of Onondaga Lake, on the final stretch to Syracuse. The lake was lined with a low, marshy forest. Red-winged blackbirds tilted among the reeds, trilling. Up ahead were the remains of the concrete pedestrian bridge. It looked like a diving board now, terminating in a crisscross of caution tape, a full stop, a drop into the passing lane. They glided under it without a word.

"Grandfather," Tess said.

"What's that?"

"You said grand*parents*. It's grandfather, singular. No matter what he told you."

"None of my business," Mrs. Ridgeland said, sounding relieved that it wasn't.

The funeral was a lot bigger than Tess had expected. A good portion of the faculty and student body of the College of Environmental Science and Forestry turned out, along with the Mud Lake Birding Club and the Medieval Society. As they approached the site, Tess was horrified to see that Sam's fellow knights of the realm were attending in full-on costumes—swords snug in scabbards, colored plumes sprouting out of their helmets like gouts of flame. Kilted bards played a running dirge on lute, bagpipe, and fiddle. The bizarre crowd parted as Tess and Axel approached, and people shushed one another, all of them apparently nervous about making eye contact with the newly minted orphans. Tess heard someone say her name, and only then did she recognize her grandfather among these strangers. He'd shaved, and his hair was pulled back into a clean, puffy ponytail. He wore a pressed but ill-fitting suit, and when he hugged her he smelled of toothpaste and nothing else. And he was alone, thank God.

Grandpa Paul led them to the core of the gathering, where Sam's casket sat bedecked with wreaths of nettle and blackberry. As they arrived, a Lancelot-looking dude stepped out of the milling mourners. He dropped to one knee before Tess's little brother, presenting Axel with what appeared to be Sam's replica sword, leathered hilt first. After a moment Tess recognized him as the black knight—rather, she corrected herself, the acned grad student who played the black knight every year in exchange for a handful of meal vouchers and ax-throw tokens. Her brother accepted the blade with the same solemnity with which it was offered. Then the knight turned to Tess and fell to his knee once again. Her father's shield was strapped to his back, and he unslung it and made to hand it over. Tess gave him a look that could have pierced any shield, replica or not. The black knight got up and backed away. The music stopped, and somebody started speaking into a wireless microphone, which she guessed meant that the funeral had begun.

"Be nice," Grandpa Paul whispered to her. He was right—these people weren't trying to be anything but comforting. And besides, Tess knew that this was probably how her father would have wanted it, if he'd been around to cast a vote. So she did her best to quarantine the cornered, angry part of herself. It wasn't easy.

Slowly the microphone moved through the crowd. Grandpa Paul said a few words when it was his turn, but he had to stop when his voice fell to pieces. Sam's students took over, sharing their memories of a professor generous with his time, a professor as pleased with their successes as they were. The pretend king talked about an excellent rider. A member of the birding club used the word "grace." Tess scanned faces as these strangers spoke, but found that she kept coming back to one in particular—an older woman with silvery, boy-cut hair. She'd elbowed her way right up to the casket, but now that she'd arrived, she seemed not the least bit interested in the service. Instead the woman stared intently down at the plot immediately adjacent to Sam's— Tess's mother's grave. The marker was simple, but the Finnish name on it—Saara Kivi—made it conspicuous in this cemetery. The woman had an odd, cold look on her face. It seemed almost like she was angry. She must have noticed Tess watching, because her gaze snapped up like a sprung trap. She was the first person at this whole thing who wasn't the least bit shy about looking Tess right in the face. They stared at each other until a commotion erupted among some of the birders, and Tess, distracted, glanced away.

"Indigo bunting!" It was a spontaneous shout, and the plump gentleman who'd loosed it slapped a hand over his mouth, mortified. The gathered mourners gawked, first at him and then up at the peak of an old oak, where a little blue bird was chittering about. It was late in the season for a bunting to be seen, and the birder must have been so excited that he couldn't help himself. There was a long moment of awkward silence. It was Axel who eventually broke it.

"Mockingbird," he said. He used the hilt of Sam's sword to point up at the arched roof of a family mausoleum, where a little bird was showing off with a song. Now the silence deepened. Some people smiled, and some who'd been crying cried harder. Tess had never imagined that in the midst of all that fakery and costume, she'd feel her dad so strongly. She should have guessed it would be Axel who'd bring him to her.

"House finch!" somebody at the edge of the crowd called.

"Woodpecker!" yelled Grandpa Paul, nodding up at a catbird. Nobody bothered to correct him, because it didn't matter.

Even their landlady got in on it, going for an easy one with: "Robin!"

It went on like that for a while, as the crowd searched the trees above for birds. There was a siskin and a junco and a white-breasted nuthatch. Finally, after they'd named everything they could see, they went silent again and listened.

As surprised as Tess had been by the turnout at the service, she was even more shocked when, after it was done, the old woman with short, silvery hair came to stand beside Grandpa Paul. She seemed not in the least bit his type—too quiet, too orderly, too altogether icy. Tess's grandfather suggested that they go someplace where they could talk, and not a half hour later, the four of them—Mrs. Ridgeland had made herself scarce the moment she handed the kids over—were seated around a table in a nearly vacant Chinese restaurant. Grandpa Paul took off his tie, ordered a second beer before finishing his first, and slowly melted into his rumpled old self. He cleared his throat a few times. It took him all of two minutes to explain why Tess and Axel couldn't live with him. His reasoning was sound—he was a disaster. He even used that word. "I'm a disaster. You both deserve and need more than I can give you. You're going to live with your grandma. You're going to live with your mom's mother."

"And my husband," the short-haired woman said. It was the first time she'd spoken, and her accent was movie-bad-guy thick. Tess had listened to plenty of recordings, but she realized that she'd never before heard a real live Finn speaking English. "Your *other* grandfather. He's waiting for us, in Helsinki."

Tess and Axel gaped at this strange woman. She gathered her sweater coat around her, as though cold. The waiter arrived with the food they'd ordered some minutes ago, in an entirely different lifetime. He set the plates down, sensed the nuke-level weirdness, and fled. "Don't look at me that way," the old woman finally said. "I'm not happy about it, either."

PART TWO
The Summer Place

But thy home thou now art leaving,

To another home thou goest,

To another mother's orders,

To the household of a stranger,

Different there from here thou'lt find it

In another house 'tis different:

Other tunes the horns are blowing,

Other doors thou hearest jarring,

Other gates thou hearest creaking

Other voices at the hinges.

—*KALEVALA*, RUNE XXII

6

An American
Mutant in Helsinki

Axel took it better than Tess did. Like, by a mile. After a long stretch of silence, his sister tumbled into what could be fairly described as a shit fit. She made it clear to everyone at the table, and indeed everyone else in the restaurant, that she did not want to go to Finland. She had friends here. A life here. Florida would have been bad enough, but *Finland*? You don't do that to a person. You don't just tell them they're moving to another country. You don't take them out for Chinese food after their dad dies and announce: By the way— you'll be living in the Arctic, like it or not.

"Most of it isn't in the Arctic," Jaana said, her calm voice razor sharp in the wake of Tess's yelling. Jaana Kivi—that was the name of their new grandmother. Or, not new, but new to them. Jaana, similar to their mother's name, Saara. They had *a*'s in all the same places, which Axel found strangely appealing. Nobody had touched their food, but Jaana was fiddling with her break-apart chopsticks, trying to separate them evenly. "It's just a little bit colder there than it is here," she said, keeping her eyes on the sticks. They finally snapped, clean and splinterless.

Tess was, for a moment, rendered speechless. "I don't care if it's *tropical*," she said. Her voice had gone dangerously casual. "That's not the point. The point is that Finland isn't our home. And you aren't our family."

"Whoa, there." Grandpa Paul lifted his coffee-colored palms from the tabletop and held them flat in the air. "I know you're upset, but that's an ugly thing to say."

Tess slid her chair back and stood. She turned on her grandfather. "Don't you think that if Dad wanted us to live with her, we might have met her before? Or at least known she existed?"

"I'm sure your father *wouldn't* have wanted you to live with me," Jaana said. She set a chopstick down on either side of her plate, aligning them flush with the place mat. "It won't surprise you to hear that the two of us didn't get along. And I understand that this isn't an ideal solution.

It certainly isn't ideal for me. Otso and I hardly have room for one of you." Otso—that was their grandfather. Axel had two of those now. "So if you want to be angry with someone, be angry with him." She nodded in Grandpa Paul's direction. "He's the disaster."

Tess looked the old woman over, and Jaana returned her stare impassively. Axel imagined his sister with a rapier, probing her opponent's guard for holes, or blind spots, silently infuriated by how difficult it was proving to land a cut. Whenever warriors fought to a draw in one of his books, they always ended up becoming fast friends and questing buddies. Axel was often criticized for how his imagination bled over at the edges, but even he couldn't picture that happening with Tess and Jaana. "Today was the first time you saw our mother's grave, wasn't it?" his sister finally said. "I guess you didn't get along with her, either."

"Jesus," Grandpa Paul said.

Jaana didn't blink, but something happened in her face. She was still in control, but it no longer seemed quite so effortless. "I don't go where I'm not welcome," she said.

"Neither do I," Tess said. She must have figured she wouldn't get a better exit line than that, because she jolted suddenly toward the door, leaving nothing behind her but the jangling of a bell affixed to the frame. The table was silent, though everybody else in the restaurant was chatting noisily, making like they hadn't been eavesdropping. After a moment Grandpa Paul got up and followed Tess out the door, looking lost and foggy. Axel and Jaana were left alone at opposite ends of the big, round table.

"You're angry, too, I suppose," Jaana said.

Axel didn't say anything. The uncomfortable truth was that even with everything that had just happened to them, Axel found the idea of moving to Finland a little bit exciting. The country had always loomed large on his bookshelf, and in his brain, as a fairy-tale wilderness of fir trees and silent lakes. It was where the monstrous Groke sulked, leaving behind her a wake of hoarfrost. It was the land of the red swan, home of the first real wizard, a graveyard for wandering Vikings. They could just as well have told him he was moving to Mirkwood. But this feeling seemed way inappropriate, given the circumstances. And besides, Tess was his sister. Loyalty demanded a unified front.

Jaana waited a long time for him to answer. Then, when it became clear he wouldn't, she said: "Not that I blame you." She reached across the table, and for a second Axel thought she was going to try to hold his hand. But instead his new Finnish grandmother wrapped her fingers around his wrist, just below the itchy fabric of his funeral clothes. She seemed to be appraising him, gauging his girth.

"Eat," she said. "It's getting cold."

That nearly empty Chinese restaurant might just as well have been the business end of a catapult, for how quickly Axel and Tess were to be launched across the Atlantic. Sam's funeral was on Wednesday, and before the end of the week, movers had come to cart away the boxes that Mrs. Ridgeland had packed. They were scheduled to fly out the following Monday. Tess confidently told Axel that applying for passports would slow them down, but as it turned out, they already had them. One each for Sam, Tess, and Axel, all issued on the exact same day the previous summer. Tess and Axel's passports contained old yearbook photos on the info page, and their father had illegibly forged their signatures before locking up the documents in his desk, where Mrs. Ridgeland eventually discovered them. Why he'd hidden the passports, or even applied for them in the first place, was a minor mystery, overshadowed by a slightly larger one—a fourth passport. Jaana paged through it and gave it to Tess, who glanced at the thing only briefly before throwing it into the garbage so hard that it nearly bounced back out again. Axel waited for Jaana to empty the trash into the aluminum can out back before fishing the fourth passport out. It was for Tess, though the fat-cheeked toddler on the info page could just as well have been him. The passport was expired, and it contained just two stamps. Entry to Finland, reentry to the United States. Tess had, apparently, already been to this place she said she'd never go to. But when Axel checked the dates on the stamps and did the math, he found that she'd been tiny at the time. No way she remembered. His sister hadn't kept anything from him—their father had kept it from them both.

The day of their departure came quickly, and it was rough. In retrospect, Axel really should have seen the Bigwig thing coming. Bringing a hare to Finland was a nonstarter—forget about the airline regulations; they'd never get a wild invasive through customs. But Grandpa Paul promised them, moist-eyed, that he'd take care of her. He'd cancel his return flight to Florida, rent a car, and road-trip back down the East Coast with their grizzled, adorable pet. He had plenty of chicken wire at his trailer in the Boils and could set up an enclosure for her, no problem, wouldn't take but an afternoon. "Besides," Grandpa Paul said, "she'll be thankful for a permanent vacation from cold weather." Axel should have seen the scope of this promise as a warning sign, but he chose to believe his granddad. Grandpa Paul said he'd pick Bigwig up on Monday morning, when he came by the A-frame to say good-bye. But the coward never showed.

Jaana waited with them in the front yard longer than she had to. Then she plucked Bigwig from her hutch, the hare made limp by her utter lack of hesitation. The children followed Jaana across the county road, to the edge of the park. This was almost exactly the spot where they'd last seen the brown bear, where the Keeper had smashed Sam's camera. Axel realized that he hadn't thought of either of them all week. They must be long gone by now, all their scent rubbed out by the wind and autumn rain. Jaana set Bigwig down atop a splay of browned ferns.

"She's going to get eaten for sure," Tess said.

"Don't be morbid," Jaana said. "The way you've fed her, nothing could choke her down." She was right on that count—Bigwig would have been a middleweight among dogs. And most of it wasn't even fat.

"But what if she doesn't know how to survive in the wild?" Axel said.

"What's to know?" his grandmother responded. "Eat. Sleep. Sometimes hide. Besides, this isn't exactly wild." She gestured into the woods, through which they could see one of the mulch walking paths and a series of little plaques announcing the Latin names of the trees they were affixed to. Axel supposed it was true. As long as Bigwig stayed in Mud Lake, she'd be playing with a net.

"Go on," Tess said. She was speaking to Bigwig, who stared up at them, confused. Jaana brought her hands together for a single, surprisingly loud clap. The sound carried through the trees, and Bigwig bolted. They watched her go, the last shred of their old life, a mottled puff of tail bounding deep into shadow, under and over the steadily falling leaves.

They had a direct flight from New York City to Helsinki. Axel got the window seat, watching baggage handlers in jumpsuits loading suitcases onto a tilted conveyor. He half expected to see the wheelchair there, stowing away with the luggage, pretending to be benign and real. Or else rolling furtively around the tail fin, looking for a way to sneak aboard. He was glad to be leaving the thing here in the States. Though the longer he looked, the more afraid he was that it might jinx things. What if simply searching for the chair was enough to conjure it? Axel turned his gaze into the cabin and shut the shade on his porthole.

As soon as the airplane took off, Tess buried her face in a book. Jaana, seated by the aisle, placed her hands neatly on her knees and stared straight ahead. It looked like she was watching the little TV embedded in the seat back in front of her, but the only thing on the screen was a mosaic of old fingerprints. Axel passed the time by watching his fellow passengers—his new neighbors, his *countrymen*. They were, by and large, ridiculously good-looking and stupidly dressed. Tights and goofy-large sunglasses, checkered coco-brown suits, harem pants, and mullets were *in*, apparently. Axel could detect only the slightest hum of chatter floating above these people, hardly audible over the sounds of flight. It took him some moments to recognize that it was indeed Finnish, a language he used to think he spoke fluently. An hour of eavesdropping in the Finnair economy cabin cured him of that silly idea. Axel's was little-kid Finnish. Picture-book Finnish—Moomintroll Finnish. His go-to vocab was cutesy, largely onomatopoeic, and maybe worst of all, inflected with a thick Yankee—or, *Jenkki*—accent. And now he'd been dunked into a soup of advanced varieties. Business Finnish. Backpacking-trip-before-university Finnish. Distressingly-beautiful-teenager-with-a-pixie-haircut Finnish. All of it more capable and authentic than his own.

Somewhere between Iceland and Ireland,

Tess jammed her book into the seat-back pocket, shut her eyes, and went to sleep. Jaana seemed to be waiting for this, and she suddenly became as chatty as she'd been the entire flight, which is to say: She used actual words. She leaned over Axel's sleeping sister and whispered: "You know, I assume that your mother had this thing as well."

By "this thing" Axel could only guess that his grandmother meant his particular variety of muscular dystrophy—a condition that seemed to define *himness* to the outside world, his friends and loved ones included. And of course he knew it. "Yes," he answered simply.

"But do you also know how she died?" Jaana's face was totally relaxed as she said this, her voice flat. A stranger listening in could hardly have guessed that she was talking about someone so intimate to them both. Axel took a moment to respond, because the question had knocked him back a bit and because the answer itself was complicated. He'd never actually been told how Saara died—or, more precisely, he'd been told only lies. The going story was that his mother had passed when he was just under a year old. She'd had an emergency appendectomy and succumbed swiftly to a complication from the anesthesia. Axel never doubted his father's intentions for inventing this story, but that Sam thought his flimsy lie had staying power hurt Axel's pride a little. There wasn't a single picture of him as a baby, cradled in the arms of a living, breathing Saara. And in a town as small as Baldwin, most people get obituaries, and those obituaries are easily findable when librarians think you're darling. To say nothing of the research Axel had done into the disease itself. He and his mother shared a rare form of dystrophy, owing to a mutation in their genes. One of the sequences repeated, like God fell asleep on the job, his fingers heavy on the keyboard. Of course, there could be worse things for a nerd to be than that—a *mutant*. But genes are complicated things, and most changes to them are, in fact, for the worse. Their variant of the disease wasn't nearly as debilitating as some others, but it did present big problems for pregnancy and labor. Axel's mother had known this—had decided to have him and Tess in spite of it. She'd gotten lucky on her first try, less so on her second. Axel *was* the complication.

"Yes," he said again.

Jaana raised her eyebrows, the first thing to happen on her face that could fairly be deemed an expression. "Your father told you?" She sounded incredulous, and given that she hadn't liked Sam, that was reason enough for Axel to lie.

"He did."

"Well. Good." She didn't say anything more for a time. "So you understand then, that . . . Forgive me. My English." Jaana turned away, facing the dark screen once again. She rubbed her face with her hands. Axel was about to tell her that they could try talking in Finnish when she spoke again. "You understand that very little is known, yes? You understand that your mother was a special case, because she was pregnant. You could be my age before you have any real problems from this."

What Jaana was trying to tell him was that he wouldn't necessarily die young. She didn't have to. Axel had given death plenty of thought, especially in the last few days, and he had no intention of doing it, ever.

Otso—their grandfather, apparently—met them at the roundabout outside of the small, glassy Helsinki airport. He was seated in the back of a stretched minivan-taxi, with some kind of mechanical lift bolted beneath the sliding door. Jaana climbed aboard while the driver loaded their luggage, sitting in the very back beside her husband. Axel and Tess took the next row up. Otso exchanged cheek pecks with Jaana and loosed a pitifully lame smile up at Tess and Axel. The old man had a full-speed-ahead beard, totally wild and food-speckled. The driver joined them, his reddish muttonchops curling up into a wickedly bushy mustache that curtained over his top lip. Medieval facial hair all around.

"Moi," the driver said, addressing his dashboard but speaking loud enough so that they could hear him in the back.

"Moi," Jaana said. In Finnish, it could just as well have meant good-bye as hello.

"I'm very sorry," Otso said, still gazing up at them. "I'm so sorry." His pronunciation was deliberate and practiced. Axel wasn't sure if the old man didn't know what else to say, or if that was all he knew *how* to say.

The words caught the driver's attention. He glanced at them in the rearview. "English?" he said, without turning.

"Amerikkalaisia," Jaana answered for them.

"Welcome to Finland." The driver smiled gamely into the mirror.

"We won't be staying," Tess said, earning a glare from Jaana.

"This is good." The driver coughed mirthfully. "Winter is approaching." He waited a moment, shy eyes in the oblong frame of the mirror. When no one chuckled at his joke, he put the taxi in drive and pulled onto the road. The weather here was more or less identical to what they'd left behind, and a light drizzle streaked across the windows, partially obscuring Axel's view of his new home. His mother's country looked mostly familiar, like a middling replica of Upstate New York. The taxi turned onto a smallish highway lined with fir trees and some leafless deciduous, maybe ash or elm. Beyond the trees Axel saw a series of modest suburban developments, mostly single-level houses painted in barnish white and red, their yards and exteriors immaculate. The sidewalk was broad and lightly trafficked, pedestrians with eyes on their feet and umbrellas held against the wet breeze. They passed a gas station that looked exactly like the gas stations back home, except that the placards read in liters and euros. It had an attached café with some forlorn tables scattered out front, where, despite the weather—and the hour; it was only morning here—a man in an old suit sat drinking a froth-capped chalice of beer. Birds wheeled madly against a low ceiling of clouds. Axel didn't recognize a single one of them.

"The boy doesn't look so bad." Otso spoke under his breath, in Finnish. "I thought it was more advanced than this."

"I'm not sure," Jaana said, also in Finnish. "Paul was useless, of course. He didn't know anything." Like her husband, Jaana was half whispering. Did she not realize that Tess and Axel could hear her?

Was Otso maybe going a little bit deaf? "I made an appointment for him with Dr. Virtanen," she continued. "Heavens knows what kind of care he's been getting. He doesn't look right at all."

Even considering what Axel learned about Jaana over the last few days, he was still knocked windless by this sudden burbling of unedited honesty. She was totally nonchalant about it, gazing lazily out the window as she spoke. Tess must have been just as surprised, because she said nothing.

"Does he have any symptoms?"

"All I can tell is that he gets tired sometimes."

Otso caught Axel looking back at him, and he forced another weak smile. Then he turned to Tess. "She's so beautiful," he said.

"And a brat."

"You're surprised?"

Jaana sort of snorted. "I shouldn't be."

"She looks exactly like her."

"I'm not so sure," Jaana said. "Her eyes aren't quite right."

Axel felt like an idiot for not realizing until that moment that Jaana and Otso weren't whispering on his account, but rather so that the taxi driver three rows up wouldn't overhear. Because that man spoke Finnish, and it apparently went without saying that Tess and Axel *didn't*. Their new grandparents hadn't even bothered to ask! Of course their father, when he was alive, couldn't be bothered. He hadn't cared nearly enough to teach them. Jaana and Otso sure would feel lousy when Axel piped up to join the conversation. And rightly so.

"Are we almost there?" Tess said loudly, and in English. She'd put a hand on Axel's arm and clamped down hard. Making like she was scratching her nose, she pressed a finger hard against her lips in a very unambiguous shushing motion.

"Getting closer," Otso said. "We live nearby to the city center, now days."

"Now days?" Slowly Tess released Axel's arm.

"We just moved," Jaana said. "We used to live out here." She gestured vaguely at the houses beyond the trees. "But the garden was so much work. We wanted something smaller. Bad timing."

"Never mind," Otso said. "We can manage."

They rolled on. The closer they got to downtown Helsinki, the more unfamiliar the scenery outside became. The buildings grew taller, pressing in against one another beneath copper-green roofs. The facades were simple, adorned only with a series of identical windows and a coat of cheerless pastel paint. The roads became narrow, and stone and brick overtook plaster. Trams passed them by, rumbling under a neat web of cabling. Jaana and Otso continued to talk in hushed Finnish for the rest of the ride. They covered the funeral and how awful it was. The A-frame and how awful it was. Grandpa Paul and how awful he was. By the time they stopped at the foot of the Kivis' condominium, Axel was in as foul a mood as he'd been since that first night at Mrs. Ridgeland's place.

The driver got out and went around back to unload their luggage. Jaana fumbled through her wallet, sorting the euros from the dollars. Otso unbuckled his seat belt but stayed exactly where he was. Axel opened the sliding door and jumped out, fuming. And how perfect it was that the wheelchair should appear at that moment. He saw it, all saggy and creaking and forlorn, standing right at the back of the minivan. Like it had been waiting for him here all along. How stupid to have thought he could fool the thing and leave it behind. You can't strand a hallucination. You just have to figure out how to unhallucinate it. Either that or learn to live with it.

"Go *away*," he hissed, giving himself a running start before kicking the wheelchair across the road, into the path of a slow-moving bus. He'd never been able to destroy the thing for good, but it was still gratifying to watch it shatter into fragments and smoke.

But then something awful happened. The bus reacted as though the driver could actually *see* the wheelchair. Slow as the bus was, the brakes still screamed as it came to a sudden stop. Not sudden enough—the bus hit the wheelchair lightly, knocking it onto its side in the middle of the road, the upturned wheel spinning dizzily. Cars behind the bus slammed on their brakes and tapped noncommittally on their horns. The bus driver opened his door and stepped out into the street. Axel felt utterly stupid. God, he should have figured that one out. He only had this condition because Saara had passed it on. There were two people in the world who could have given it to her, and it obviously hadn't been Jaana. That's what the lift on the minivan was for. That's why the old man hadn't gotten out to greet them. How freaky it was that Otso's real wheelchair looked exactly like Axel's imaginary one.

His grandmother was already out of the van, approaching the bus driver, speaking calmly in Finnish. "I'm so sorry. Is everyone all right?"

The bus driver answered her back, but Axel recognized none of the words. This, too, was a vocabulary lesson. Because what could they possibly be other than the most awesome and elaborate curses?

7

At the Harbor

Talk about an awkward elevator ride. The four of them were silent in the brightly lit, mirrored box as it carried them up to the Kivis' condominium. Otso rolled his creaking chair a quarter turn forward, a half turn back, trying to be sly about checking it for damage. Other than a slight asphalt burn on the left armrest, it seemed fine. Axel, on the other hand, not so much. He was dangling over the rim of a good shame-and-fury weep. Tess was embarrassed for him, too. His normal flavor of weird was strong enough, but they were entering uncharted territory here. What could he have been thinking?

"Well," Jaana said as the elevator stuttered open. "An excellent start."

She took Otso by the horned handles of his chair and rolled him down a paneled hallway, to the door of their flat. The sound of her key in the lock was crisp and lonely, and when she turned the knob, a soft muddle of outdoorsy light poured into the corridor. Jaana took a single step into the flat and removed her shoes, setting them beside the door, heels to the trim. Otso did the same, though Tess wasn't sure what the point was—with his feet in their stirrups, his shoes wouldn't have touched the floor anyhow. "I will give you a tour," Otso said, turning himself around by anchoring one wheel with his hand and pushing lightly on the other, sort of like ruddering a canoe. "You should visit the toilet first, however." His beard opened up to reveal a smile. "It will take a long time."

Hilarious. The tour took forty seconds—just about ten for each Ikea-neat room. The front door opened onto a sort of den/hallway, the spine of the flat. It was bright and sparsely decorated, rigid with cheer. A white leather sofa sat against the far wall, presiding over its own reflection on the shining hardwood, with some kind of woolly animal pelt—maybe a reindeer?—thrown over the back of it. Over by the window was a low wooden breakfast table dotted by a shifting constellation of shadows from the rain-specked window. There was only one chair pulled up to the table. Otso's traveled with him, and guests were apparently infrequent.

The rest of the flat was just as showroomy, looking almost like it'd been explicitly designed to be the opposite of their old A-frame. The kitchen was stocked with shiny copper pots hanging from hooks embedded in the faux-earthen tiling, two big wall calendars sporting pictures of the beckoningly melancholy Finnish countryside, and a chromed espresso machine. The bathroom had no tub, just a retractable showerhead affixed at about waist height, with an attached mini sauna no bigger than a phone booth. Jaana and Otso's bedroom was small as well, but it had an expansive view of the city, a fogged-in hint of the Baltic beyond. Hothouse daisies drooped in a Moomintroll-print vase on the end table. The ruthless way that Jaana had taken a hatchet to even the slightest hint of clutter seemed right in keeping with Tess's first impression of her, though what remained hardly matched her temperament. As though the old woman were trying to give the impression that she was cheery, warm; and really she was the precise opposite of that.

The last room was a study, and that at least looked lived-in. Otso had been a poetry professor at the University of Helsinki, and a great deal of his work seemed to have followed him home over the years. Reproductions of famous Finnish paintings hung lopsided on the walls—Tess recognized several from the illustrated *Kalevala* that Sam had given them—alongside tacked-up photocopies of the relevant passages from the Finnish myth. It was all harpies and glowing forges, big-ass beards and undead swans, with Otso's tiny annotations scrawled everywhere.

"You two should get some rest," Jaana said, indicating the two twin beds drifting at odd angles in the middle of the study—clearly an afterthought. "It's still very early, and we have a busy day."

"There is cheese in the freezer," Otso said.

"Refrigerator," Jaana corrected.

Their grandfather winced a little. "Refrigerator." Then, to Jaana, in Finnish: "Tell them they should help themselves whenever they want. Can they eat? Have they been eating? I should have asked what they like. Tell them they're welcome."

"They're not babies, *ukko*." *Ukko* was a vaguely rude word for "old man," certainly an accurate descriptor in this case, but Jaana seemed to be using it as a term of endearment. "They know they're welcome." Then, switching back to English: "Do try to rest. Don't worry if you fall asleep. I'll wake you when you're needed."

"Sleep tightly," Otso said as Jaana wheeled him backward out of their surrendered study. "And without insects."

"You should probably leave the talking to me," Jaana said, closing the door softly behind them. The wood was pulp thin, and their voices came through almost as loudly with the door shut.

"I was so nervous that I forgot to tell them about the salami," Otso said. "And I bought pickles!"

"It can wait, *ukko*."

The sound of feet and wheels faded to the other end of the little flat. Axel approached one of the beds and prodded it, like he wasn't quite sure what it was made of. Then he hopped aboard, hardly wrinkling the tightly tucked sheets. Tess got on the other one, and the two of them stared wordlessly at the ceiling. They could still hear their grandparents talking in the kitchen. Jaana in particular made no attempt to quiet her voice, imagining Finnish to be all the hush she needed. She told Otso about Saara's grave and the Oakwood Cemetery—how big and showy it was, how totally unlike their daughter. Saara would have hated it, they agreed. Oh, Sam knew it. How could he not have known it? Saara would have wanted to be brought home. She would have wanted to be buried alongside her grandparents, up at Talvijärvi.

"She still can be," Jaana said.

"It's too soon for that," Otso said. "No. It wouldn't be appropriate."

There was a silence, through which Tess could

hear the exertions of their obnoxious coffeemaker. At that moment she felt so adrift, and she missed her father so intensely, that Tess thought she might actually throw up.

"Shall I tell Dr. Virtanen about what happened this morning?"

"You mean downstairs? I hardly think that's worth mentioning."

"I see. That's normal behavior for American children as you understand it?"

"Don't be snippy, *rakas*. Imagine the week he's had."

Tess turned in bed to face her brother and saw that he looked just as lost. Axel rolled his shoulders so that she wouldn't see him crying and turned his face to one of the epic paintings on the wall. It was a picture of Väinämöinen, who was basically a pre-Christian Finnish wizard. Väinämöinen and his men were on a small boat, defending the magical Sampo from the flying hag queen of the north. The wizard held a sword in his left hand, the tiller in his right. A thicket of spears sprouted up at his knees. This painting had appeared on the cover of their illustrated *Kalevala*. When Sam used to read from it, during their Finnish lessons, he would do all the voices. His Väinämöinen was the best.

"I don't think so," Jaana was saying from the

far end of the flat. "If anyone were to act out, it'd be the girl. The boy has hardly made a peep since it happened. And did you see how he looked afterward? Like he was surprised?"

"So what are you saying?"

"Just that it's foolish, *ukko*, to rule anything out."

"Sam's letters never mentioned anything neurological."

"And you think he'd have told us?"

"Hey," Tess whispered, trying to get Axel to turn back around. But his gaze was anchored to the painting. The hag's name was Louhi. Her green-black wings darkened the upper third of the frame, and upon them sat her army, their bearded faces leering over her feathers.

"Well, all right. You can ask. But I don't want you to make him feel . . ." Their grandfather trailed off in the kitchen.

"I wouldn't. Of course I wouldn't."

"Hey," Tess whispered again. Finally Axel turned back to face her. His cheeks were pink, and his shoulders jolted up toward his ears like he had the hiccups. "Don't be afraid," Tess said. "I promise that I'm going to get us back home."

Neither of them slept, but they were both still in bed when Jaana returned to collect Axel some hours later. She planned to bring him by bus to

Dr. Virtanen's office, which was all the way out in someplace called Vantaa—trust and recalcitrance kept them going to the same physician they'd always used, even after moving into the city center. "After that we'll meet at Kauppatori," Jaana said. She was informing, not consulting. "It's the harbor market. We can eat, and we need to shop." She took Axel by the hand and led him out of the improvised bedroom. "Your grandfather's in the sauna," she said to Tess. "He can get in and out just fine by himself. There's no need for you to do anything."

Excellent. As though Tess really would have helped a naked old stranger in and out of that upright wooden steam coffin. She followed them through the den, up to the front door. "Do you want me to come?" she asked Axel.

"No," Jaana said. "It's not for you to worry about."

Tess looked at her grandmother. She didn't want to be that girl, but if Jaana didn't back off at least a little bit, then things would get very ugly, very quickly. "If he wants me to come, I'm coming," she said.

Axel must have heard the danger in her voice. "It's fine," he said. "I'll see you at Kauppatori."

His pronunciation was so good that it almost let the Finnish cat out of the bag right then and there. Janna eyed him for a moment, surprised. Then she called out: *"Ukko! Rakas!"* Geezer, my love. "We're going!"

"Hyvä!" came the muffled cry from the sauna.

Jaana shut the door, leaving Tess alone in the den. She waited until she heard the elevator chime and then hurried back into the study. Tess hadn't seen a telephone during the tour, but she still had her old cell phone from Baldwin. She meant to find it, call Grandpa Paul—he'd promised to sort things out with the phone company—and talk some sense into him. Because they couldn't stay here—it was *ludicrous*. They'd only even come this far because Jaana had Tess at a temporary disadvantage. Her father's death and the sudden appearance of surprise Finnish grandparents had tilted her off balance. But Tess's resolve had returned on the flight over, as she watched the incomprehensible Finns over the rim of her open book. Even more so during the taxi ride, as she listened to Jaana and Otso dismiss everything that made her life *hers*. She and Axel should be living with their grandpa—their real one; Otso didn't count—down in the Boils. It might not be home, but it was a hell of a lot closer than this. Paul had some serious problems; Tess wasn't denying that. It was pretty lousy the way he'd bailed on them without even saying good-bye. But really, what was worse: not showing up for a single—admittedly important—afternoon, or not showing up for well over a freaking decade?

Tess fished her phone out of her bag and switched it on. The little screen said *Searching* for a good minute before giving up and settling for *No Service*. The cell phone contract that Sam had signed apparently didn't include coverage in Finland—hardly a surprise, now that Tess actually stopped to think about it. Plan B, then: She'd send her grandfather an e-mail. Paul didn't have his own computer, but Tess knew that he checked his messages at least once a week, down at the little public library in the Boils. It might take a few days, but he'd write back.

An old laptop sat on the desk in the converted study, emerging from a moraine of crumpled loose-leaf notes. It took a while to boot up, the icons landing one by one, speckling the wallpaper. The desktop background was a scanned photograph—a shot of a much younger Jaana, her hair waist long and nearly platinum. She was squatting in a flower bed before a single-story wooden house, holding a trowel in one hand, using the other to shade the sun from her face. There was a skinny girl with Jaana in the garden, about Axel's age, her hair sprouting sideways in stubby braids. Dirt smudged her bare feet and ran up past her knees. She was just standing there, staring into her own cupped hands. It was impossible to tell what she was holding—maybe an earthworm or a quartz-veined rock—but whatever it was, it seized the little girl's attention completely. It took Tess a few moments to realize that this child was her mother. As soon as she did, her fingers jolted up and away from the keys.

Tess had seen pictures of Saara before, of course. Sam's old bedroom back in the A-frame had been all but a shrine to the lost wife and mother of the Fortune family, where framed photographs of her crowded the walls. There was a shot of Saara on skis and another of her in a flower-print dress, a shot of her sleeping on a picnic blanket and another of her treading water in a deep blue lake. But Tess's mother had looked the same age in all of those pictures—the only evidence that any time passed between them was that in some she was pregnant. This desktop background was the first picture that Tess had ever seen of Saara as a child. It must have been taken in front of the home that the Kivis had so recently sold. Otso wasn't in the shot, but the long shadow thrown up against the house was probably his. The shadow looked tall, like Otso was standing up, but that could have been a trick of the sun.

As the computer sputtered to life, it buried the young Kivi family under a slow drift of icons. Tess realized, with a chill, that these, too, were pictures. They were *all* pictures—all labeled with Saara's name, followed by a date. Jaana and Otso must have gone through their old albums and scanned every last shot of their daughter. It was strange—they didn't hang it out in the open the way Sam had, but the Kivis had a shrine too. Tess moused over to one of the photos, but she couldn't bring herself to open it. Because Tess didn't know that little girl any better than she knew Jaana, or Otso. She didn't *want* to know them. Tess wasn't looking for a connection—she was looking for a way out. So instead she opened the browser so that she could write to Grandpa Paul and convince him to let them come home.

"It does not work."

The sound of Otso's voice nearly startled her out of her seat. She hadn't heard him roll into the study, but there he was, right behind her. His thinning hair and beard were still damp, his cheeks a bright young pink—an envelope of heat had followed him out of the sauna. He wore a long white robe, and Tess wondered how he'd gotten in and out of the sauna, the robe, the chair, without any help.

"Not the . . ." Otso chewed his fuzzy lower lip and glanced up at the ceiling, as though there were an English cheat sheet scrawled up there. Then, finding the word, he smiled. "Not the *computer*—the Internet. We do not have it yet. A man comes, next week."

"I need to write to my grandfather," Tess said. No point trying to keep it hidden. Otso squinted a little, but she couldn't tell if it was because he didn't approve or simply didn't understand. She considered, briefly, switching to Finnish. "I need to write to Paul."

"Paul," Otso said. That he understood. "A man is coming next week. We will have Internet, and you can do it." With surprising ease, he spun his chair around and started to leave the room. "You take a sauna?"

"No."

"I will turn off." Then, just as he was leaving the room, he turned back to ask: "We go to market now. There is *munkki*—you know *munkki*?" Tess didn't know if *munkki* was a person or an item or a beverage. Otso grinned at her silence. "It will be a nice surprise. Are you hungry?"

No amount of reticence could make her answer with a lie. "Very," she said.

The Kivis' building let out onto a narrow street, scaled with neat, rectangular cobbles that glowed dully under remembered rain. Otso glided down the sidewalk with his polished loafers pointing the way in their little metal stirrups. He didn't look back, assuming Tess would follow. She did.

At the corner it got brighter, and the cityscape

opened up to make room for a sand-colored train station, big as a sporting arena. Legless stone giants stood out front, cupping lanterns of frosted glass and looking distinctly cool, withdrawn and Nordic. A copper-plated clock tower sprouted up at the front end of the station, beside an arched pedestrian entrance.

"We go there tomorrow," Otso said, nodding his sharp-tipped beard in the direction of the station. "We must take a train."

"Why?" Tess said.

"The summer place. It is not nearby."

Tess missed a step. They'd been in Helsinki for all of five hours, and already the Kivis were planning another relocation? "What's the summer place?" she said.

"It is our place," Otso said after a pause. His wince let Tess know that he was aware of what a crap answer this was. Apparently, it was the best he could do with the words he had. "Better wait for Jaana," he said.

Leaving the train station behind, they turned onto a larger street, with trams rumbling through dedicated center lanes. Otso's chair didn't have a motor, but despite those stork-skinny arms, he was able to move at quite a clip. His fingerless gloves hardly seemed to touch the wheels as he brushed his hands cleanly over the curved rubber, and Tess found that she had to rush to keep up. After a few blocks she caught herself staring at him—gauging Otso the way she sometimes gauged Axel. The kind of dystrophy her brother had was highly variable. One patient could get off easier than the next, so the fact that Otso had made it to this old age with so few problems was predictive of nothing. But still, it was kind of cool to see him zooming down that sidewalk. Otso was, in a way, the best possible outcome. He was also the root cause for all this trouble. His genes had killed Tess's mother and made her brother sick. But then again, they'd also allowed those people—and her—to exist in the first place.

The two of them turned down an esplanade lined with bare trees and cafés. Finns sat at French-style outdoor tables, not to be cowed by the October chill, downing espressos and beers—some seemed to be drinking both. In the distance ahead Tess could see the copper dome of an orthodox church sprouting out of the low Helsinki skyline. Some of the surrounding buildings looked like factories, with pale plumes of smoke discharging out of their upturned snouts. For a moment it appeared that the buildings were moving—swapping places ever so slowly. But then Tess realized that she was looking at the upper decks and smokestacks of cruise ships. They'd arrived at the harbor.

Kauppatori was a densely packed market

square, set right up against the water. From a distance Tess could see nothing but a quilt of identical orange tarps under a wheeling haze of gulls, but as they approached, the shop stalls began to distinguish themselves. Despite the late season, there was still produce for sale—carrots and peapods, gooseberries and blueberries and plastic troughs of gooey cloudberry. There was also plenty of fish: cooked and raw, whole and cleaned, smoked, pickled, and dried. Otso unfurled a canvas bag from one of his pockets and rolled into the grid of stalls, his chair bumping and hopping on the irregular paving stones. "We need provisions!" he said. A word taken right out of Axel's mouth—the adventuring equivalent of groceries.

"So, how long will we be gone?" Tess said, trying again.

"One week. Or more, if not too cold." Otso had reached one of the tented tables, where he greeted the vendor with a subdued nod. "There is time. For school, you wait for November. We must find a teacher for your Finnish." He passed over the greens without a glance, going right for a bin of cleaned mushrooms, all twisty and golden. "These are *kanttarelli*," he said, holding up one of the mushrooms for Tess to see. "At Talvijärvi—that's where we have the summer place—the woods have many. Autumn is excellent for hunting." Otso stuck his face into the bin itself to give it a deep, almost passionate sniff. He asked the vendor how long she'd had the mushrooms and where they came from. Her answers must have been exemplary, because he bought the entire lot.

"Why are we going to the summer place?" Tess said.

Otso turned to look at her, confused. "It is beautiful." He made an attempt at a game smile. "Your grandmother, Jaana . . . We think it will be good. It is so quiet. It is somehow peaceful, and we think—"

"Peaceful isn't going to fix anything," Tess said. "And Jaana never asked us if we wanted to go. Since my father died, she hasn't *asked* me anything."

Otso squirmed in his chair and made a brief escape by turning to pay for the mushrooms. Tess felt a little ruthless, pressing her advantage on the old man by forcing him into lame, partial English answers. Especially when it would have been so easy to let him explain himself more fully in Finnish. But she couldn't quit pretending now— the ammunition she'd been collecting was just too good.

"You are right," Otso said, placing the plastic bags of mushrooms into his larger canvas sack. "But please, don't be cruel to Jaana." If he had a bigger vocabulary, he probably wouldn't have used that word, "cruel." He probably would have been less honest.

"She cares very much," he continued, "and she is also very, very sad. We have been for a long time. But we are trying hard. We want only what is best."

"Jaana doesn't even want us here." Tess's face flushed with her own wickedness. But it was true, wasn't it? She'd said as much back in Baldwin.

Otso shook his head patiently, like an instructor offering gentle correction. "You are wrong," he said. "You don't understand anything." Again the old man's partial grasp of English made him unsettlingly direct. "Jaana loves you."

"I don't believe that," Tess said.

"You don't have to." Otso made no more answer than this. He balanced the plump sack of mushrooms on his lap, pushed away from the stall, and rolled deeper into the market. They did the rest of their shopping in silence.

8

Real Elephants

At the doctor's office, Axel knew the drill. Height and weight and make-happy chitchat. Measuring tape wrapped around his upper thighs and arms, where his imaginary quads and biceps bristled with veins. An electrocardiogram to chart his dependably spiky heartbeat, followed by an echocardiogram, the ultrasound jelly cold on his chest and upper back. Dr. Virtanen asked about his energy and his breathing and made him move his neck in circles and read letters of various sizes from across the room. Basically, the same routine here in Finland as it was back home—a festival of prodding and discordant cheer. The only difference was that now, instead of Sam and the doctor retreating to another room to have their private conversation, it played out right in front of him. Jaana either thought that Axel had received nothing better than Medieval-caliber medical attention back in the States—barbers bearing castor oil and leeches—or that he harbored secret intentions of dying, soonish. She gave Dr. Virtanen a grilling like Axel had never seen.

"Did you look for the murmur? His father spoke in letters about a murmur."

"A slight murmur, yes," Dr. Virtanen said, his eyes still on his notes. "But the boy's heart is healthy. To be honest, if I hadn't seen his paperwork, I'd be hard-pressed to say he was even positive."

"How can you be serious?" Jaana crossed her arms tightly over her chest and pressed herself into the wall. "Just look at him."

"He's scrawny, absolutely. But scrawny isn't a diagnosis. Nor is it necessarily a symptom. There aren't any signs of dystrophy in his proximal muscles." The doctor turned back to Axel, still up on the examining table in his skivvies. "For all you know, he could have a growth spurt coming."

"So that's it, then. Not a thing in the world to worry about." This prospect seemed to distress Axel's grandmother even more than the alternative.

"There never is. Until there is."

Jaana sucked her teeth viciously at this, but Dr. Virtanen seemed totally at ease. She must have been abusing him over Otso's care for decades. "I know that it's frustrating," he said, "but this is the best I can offer. The boy appears to be asymptomatic now, which is excellent news. But also not at all uncommon in a patient so young. Will he be asymptomatic next month? Next year? All I could offer would be a guess, no more valuable than anybody else's."

Jaana uncrossed her arms and smoothed her trouser legs. She glanced briefly at Axel, and when she spoke again, her voice was hushed. "What about cognitive symptoms?" Axel didn't recognize most of the words that followed, but the familiar medical terms came through. The Finnish word for "hypersomnia" was, apparently, "hypersomnia." Jaana said: "persistent confusion." She said: "hallucinations." It was no surprise that she was up on her research—Axel was, after all, the third member of her family to be subject to the whims of this illness. But what did surprise him was the extent to which his loved ones had sold him out. His father had apparently called it "more than just an overactive imagination" in one of his letters. Shortly after the funeral, Paul had admitted to Jaana that Axel would spend hours in the woods looking for things that simply couldn't be there. Mrs. Ridgeland had even claimed that he hallucinated bears and accused Tess of playing this mental deficiency for laughs. Axel wanted to correct them on this point—the wheelchair was one thing, but that bear was real and his sister would never do such a thing—but all that came out when he opened his mouth was a gout of dragonish flame. The shock wave blew Jaana and the old doctor off their feet, and lucky for them, because otherwise they'd have been char-becued with the rest of the office. The fire burned an ash-ringed hole in the wall, and Axel, still in his underwear, jumped through it and into the wet morning. It was cold out there, so he breathed more fire. Did Finnish cops even carry guns? He would destroy them, either way.

"You get tired sometimes?" Dr. Virtanen asked, switching to flawless English.

"What?" Knocked out of his daydream, Axel looked back at the doctor. Jaana eyeballed him, as though Axel's momentary distraction were all the proof she needed of a profound medical calamity heading his way, fast.

"Sometimes you feel very tired. Sometimes you feel a bit weak. Is that true?"

"Yes," Axel said.

The doctor smiled. "Me, as well. Naps. They are the ticket."

Jaana was not amused.

¤ ¤ ¤

Axel left Dr. Virtanen's office that morning thinking that his sister was right—really, they couldn't get out of this stupid place soon enough. But he amended this thought a little later, when he got his first bite of something called *lihapiirakka*, at the harbor market. It took about an hour to travel there from Vantaa, and by the time they arrived, Tess and Otso had just finished their shopping. A canvas tote brimming with vegetables sat on his grandfather's legs like an overhanging beer gut. Jaana pecked Otso on the lips, relieved him of the tote, and peered inside to inspect his purchases. Whatever was in there earned a curt grunt of approval.

Otso led them to a tented café near the center of the market, about which some picnic benches and tables had been set. A sign affixed to the tent proclaimed that they sold the best *lihapiirakka* in the market, though the word "market" had been crossed out and replaced with "Helsinki," which had itself been dashed in favor of "Finland." It was basically a soft, hot doughnut filled with spiced meat and exactly as delicious as that sounds. Axel ate two of them, followed by something called a *munkkipossu*—the same deal but with jam, dusted with sugar, and in a slightly more whimsical shape—while his new grandparents sipped coffee and looked gratified. The caterers who ran the court-of-foods for the Battle Re-enactment could have learned a thing or two from this market café. The food here was simple, vaguely rustic—it could totally have been served in a mead hall, atop a big pewter platter set beneath a boar's head center-piece—and it was a hell of a lot more delicious than funnel cakes or corn dogs.

"Otso told me that we're going someplace," Tess said. She'd been quiet as she ate, straining to repress all signs of pleasure. There was still a little bit of jam in the corner of her lip.

Their new grandparents looked at each other. "What?" Otso said in Finnish. "It's some kind of secret?"

"We're going to Talvijärvi, up north," Jaana said. Translated literally, it meant: "winter lake." "We have a house there. Not a house—a cabin. It's our summer place." A summer place on winter lake. Axel hadn't yet been in this country for a full day, and already it struck him that there could be nothing more Finnish than this.

"Why are we going?"

Jaana and Otso looked at each other, like this question exposed a weakness either in their grand-daughter's education or her character. "To *be* there," Jaana said.

"It's beautiful," Otso said, inching his chair closer to their table. "It's very beautiful."

"But why? What's up there, other than the cabin?"

"Nothing," Jaana said. "That's the point." She waited for Tess to return the volley. When she didn't, Jaana went on: "It used to be your mother's favorite place."

Did she mean for that to sound as provocative as it did?

"Can I have a little bit of money?" Tess said suddenly and with an oddly insincere brightness. It wasn't the response anybody expected of her, especially on the brink of what could become another light show of an argument.

"What for?" Jaana said, duly skeptical.

"I saw something over at one of the white tents. A souvenir. I'd like to get it for Mrs. Ridgeland. Just, you know, to thank her for everything."

Axel knew, of course, that this was utter crap. Jaana seemed plenty suspicious as well, but even she wasn't quite cold enough to call Tess on it. Otso hooted "Of course!" and handed over a small wad of euros. Tess slipped out of her chair and said she'd be right back. She even did an excellent job of hiding her annoyance when Axel announced that he was coming too.

"Don't be long," Jaana called after them. "We have packing to do this afternoon!"

Tess fast-walked away from the tented café, with

Axel right on her heels. "Where are you going?" he said under his breath.

"Not a word." She turned to glance back at Otso, shrugging off his wave. "He's not so bad, but she's awful."

Axel didn't think that Jaana was awful, exactly, but he didn't waste any breath sticking up for her. His grandma had yet to prove that she deserved even a small portion of the loyalty that Axel had invested in his sister. Tess moved quickly through the market. The tarp awnings up ahead changed from orange to white, where Kauppatori turned from a fish and vegetable market into a souvenir bazaar packed with tourists. There was plenty that Axel would have liked to take a closer look at—reindeer pelts, rune-scrawled knives and wooden drinking cups, candelabra made of antlers. One guy was even selling dulled battle-axes and Viking armor. Children's sizes were available.

"Nope," Tess said, reading his expression. "They can still see us from here." She turned a sharp right, heading for a low seawall that ran along the rear edge of Kauppatori. The water was thick with frothy wavelets, harbor taxis and ferries shuttling hither and yon, gulls bobbing atop their perpendicular wakes.

"What are you doing?" Axel said.

Tess answered him by fishing an unfamiliar

and painfully old-fashioned cell phone out of her pocket. Axel could only guess that it belonged to Otso, or Jaana, and that Tess had swiped it as they ate. He didn't have to ask whom she meant to call.

Tess dialed, and there was a long pause. Finally, she said: "Grandpa?" The connection must have been bad, or maybe she'd woken Grandpa Paul up, because she had to repeat it a few times. "Stay put," she mouthed to Axel before backing away from the stalls, crossing to the very edge of the water, where the sound of small waves churning against the seawall offered some privacy. Still, Axel had no trouble hearing her end of the conversation. Tess was trying to convince Paul to let them come back to America, to live with him. Axel found this sort of odd. It's not that he didn't want it to happen, but Tess must have known how terribly unlikely it was. Axel had only a tenuous grip on real-world probabilities, and even he knew it. If keeping them had been too high a hurdle, how would Grandpa Paul ever manage to bring them back?

He scanned the market as his sister talked, inching back toward the stall that was selling the Viking gear. Tourists clustered here and there, bundled up against the gentle autumn chill in ski pants and draped frock coats, puffy down jackets and layered scarves. One guy wore a long Western-style duster, patched here and there with floral-print fabric. He was perusing the iced catch spread out over the fishmonger's table, and even though Axel couldn't see his face, there was something familiar about him. The guy was a monster—the tallest person in a crowd of tall people. His body language indicated haggling, or giggling, or some other kind of jumpy vibrato commiseration with the fishmonger. Finally the slim giant settled on a fish, a lock-jawed salmon ugly as sin, and dropped the whole thing into his knapsack without so much as wrapping it in butcher paper. Then he adjusted his hat with his mangled left hand and turned to leave. There was no question that Axel had seen this man before. Just once—an ocean away, a lifetime ago, last week.

It was the Keeper.

Axel stood there for a moment, utterly dumbfounded. The old man was already at the far end of the market, headed in the direction of the esplanade and disappearing fast. Axel turned to call his sister, but she was still by the water, pleading with Grandpa Paul, and she paid him no mind. The Keeper was disappearing fast, and Axel made a decision. He rushed along the line of stalls, darting around shoppers with their plastic totes of peas and berries, careful to stay clear of the tented café where Jaana and Otso were waiting. The Keeper had reached the edge of Kauppatori, where a bicycle lane and a set of tram tracks hemmed the market in from the rest of the city. He paused there briefly, while a column of spandex-clad riders whizzed past. The Keeper had slung his still-open knapsack over his right shoulder, and the salmon's bulldog skull peeked out, jellied eyes staring back in Axel's direction. In his mangled hand the Keeper held the same gnarly, driftwood-looking walking stick that he'd used on the night of Sam's death. His gum boots had been washed, and the lily of the valley in the band of his fedora had been replaced with a few sprigs of starflower.

Axel had mostly closed the distance when the last bike ticked past, but the Keeper turned a sharp left, heading quickly up the water's edge. There were a few boats here, tied off in wet little paddocks demarcated by scum-lined concrete breakers. Teenagers sat with their legs dangling over the water, sharing headphones and plastic bottles of fizzy cider, puffing conspicuously on blunt cigarettes. Up ahead was a low building, made of multicolored bricks, set against the water—it looked like an old customs house. The Keeper disappeared inside, and Axel followed. The building had been redone as a covered arcade filled with amber-lit food stalls, but the Keeper strode past without even a glance, banging through a set of saloon-style doors at the far end. Axel lost sight of him as the doors swung closed, so he picked up the pace. A second later he was through the doors as well, standing outside again in a big parking lot, completely alone.

Axel ventured a few steps into the lot. There were some parked cars, though none of them big enough to conceal somebody so tall and spider-gangly. He turned to peer around both sides of the narrow customs house, in case the Keeper had realized he was being followed and doubled back. But he wasn't there. Beyond the lot was a small city park, but it was too distant for the Keeper to have reached, even if he'd gone at a flat sprint the moment those saloon-style doors swung shut behind him. It was as though the man had simply disappeared.

Here is where things started to get weird. More weird than was usual, even for Axel. A haze of exhaustion came over him, sick and sudden. There was a bench set up against the wall of the customs house, and it was all Axel could do to take the six or seven steps required to get himself to it. He sat there, feeling faint as he gazed out into the park. It seemed unusually lush for this time of year and this far north. Way too lush—bizarrely tropical, in fact. The trees were heavy with broad leaves, draped in webs of woody vines, gem set with orchids. There were animals in there, moving among the trees. Not waddling geese, or dogs on leashes, or sad little ponies hauling kids around a track. *Elephants*. Live ones, wandering beneath the forested canopy, pulling down branches with their trunks to browse on new growth. This seemed not at all strange to people—joggers bounced along the park perimeter without so much as a glance at the preposterous goings-on inside. Then, right before Axel's eyes, the trees began to shiver and shrink. Suddenly the park was grassy, dotted with buffalo. A moment later the trees were back—or no, not trees. Cacti. It was a high desert, snow dusting the spiny, rounded heads of the cacti, terrified owls peeking out from holes in their desiccated trunks. Then it was nothing but a city park again, leafless and bare, as was appropriate for Finland in the fall.

"Moi," someone said. "Hello again." The Keeper was seated beside Axel on the bench, as though he'd been there all along. His knapsack rested between his knees, the salmon bearing its scraggly underbite up at them with dead pride. "Tell me, do you prefer English or Finnish?"

Axel just gaped at him. He was thinking two things: the first was that he really hoped he wasn't imagining this, because if that were the case, then it'd be as big a red flag as had ever flown atop his sanity. The second was that he sort of hoped he *was* imagining it. Because if this were actually happening, then it represented a much graver red flag.

This was a massive point against a world that was supposed to make at least a little sense.

"All right, then," the Keeper said. "I prefer Finnish, so Finnish it is. But remember that you didn't vote, so you don't get to complain." He reached into the open knapsack and pulled out a long, elfin pipe, slick with rubbed-off salmon scales. He tapped the pipe bowl against the underside of the bench, producing a musical clonk and discharging a knot of ashes onto the cobbles below. Then, plucking some tobacco from inside his duster, he began the work of stuffing the bowl. "So," he said, glancing diagonally across the water, back at Kauppatori. "Looks like you made it a whole four minutes before giving up. Bravo." With the pipe stuffed, he produced a box of wooden matches. His lips puckered awfully as he puffed. "I don't mean that," he said. "I'm being sarcastic. You did terribly."

"You're the man we saw at my house." The obviousness of this statement was enough to make Axel wince, but it was all he could think to say. The Keeper made no answer, sucking busily on his pipe, like he was still waiting for their conversation to begin. Axel could feel the exhaustion ebbing out of him and other things ebbing in. "How did you know that I was following you?" he said. The shape of Finnish words felt oddly natural in Axel's mouth.

The Keeper uncorked the pipe from his face and pointed the delicate stem back at the market. "I was following you before you were following me. A waste of time, I'm afraid. Because clearly"—he scowled at the distance between Kauppatori and their bench—"you're not nearly up to the task."

Axel was savvy enough to know when he was being baited—it happened plenty at school. He was supposed to ask: *Up to what task?* And boy did he ever want to. But hallucination or no, it was probably a bad idea to play into this creeper's hands. "Where was I supposed to go?" he said. "You disappeared."

"Further proof." The Keeper blew a smoke ring so thick it looked like a doughnut. "You think you get to *see* what you're looking for? You think anybody does?" He gestured dismissively at the harbor market with his busted hand. "Best run off to Grammy and Grampy."

Axel reached down and touched the zipper tag of the Keeper's knapsack. It sure felt real. The man smiled ever so slightly, like a fisherman who's sensed the first tug on his line.

"How did you get here?"

"Straight to the point." The Keeper let his smile blossom. "We hoofed it, I'm afraid." He began scratching at his temple with the spent end of his match, leaving an ashy rune on his pink skin.

"I mean here, as in Finland," Axel said.

"Do you not know what 'hoofed it' means?" The old man seemed patently delighted by how impossible an answer he was giving. "We *walked*. Flights are so expensive these days, and of course, a brown bear does present certain complications."

"The bear is here, too?" Axel asked.

"Not exactly," the Keeper said. "But close enough. The old girl is resting up."

"So . . . were you working at the Battle Re-enactment, then? Are you two on tour?"

The Keeper's thin lips collapsed, his smile imploding. "Of course we weren't working at the re-enactment," he said. "But if you insist on being dim about it, then sure, I suppose you could say we're on a tour. Or, no—call it a hunt. 'Hunt' is a far more appropriate word."

"Okay, then," Axel said, figuring he might as well take the bait. "What are you hunting?"

"The same thing you are," the Keeper said. "Sam Fortune."

The sound of his father's name would have been enough to knock the wind out of Axel, if he hadn't already been holding his breath. "How do you know that name?" he said.

"I had hoped this would be obvious," the Keeper said, grinning once again because he knew it so wasn't obvious. "I learned it from the bear."

There wasn't much Axel could think to say to this, and they both fell silent. The tobacco ember crackled in the Keeper's pipe, and out in the harbor one of the cruise ships sounded its tremendous horn. Axel wondered how much time had passed since he'd slipped away from Tess. She'd probably finished talking to Grandpa Paul by now and noticed that he was missing.

"She doesn't want to stay here," the Keeper said, as though he'd read Axel's mind. "She's still trying to charm your old drunk of a grandfather. Trying to shame him into letting you both go back to America to live with him. It's never going to happen. Paul Fortune is a building on fire." Whatever that meant, the Keeper fell silent for a moment to drive it home. "The Kivis want to take you up north, to a place called Talvijärvi. This *must* happen."

How the old man knew about Jaana and Otso's planned trip to the summer place, or Grandpa Paul's problems, it was impossible to say. It was no more bizarre, certainly, than him muttering the name of Axel's dead father. Or the fact that, just some minutes ago, Axel had been watching wild elephants foraging in the jungles of downtown Helsinki.

"She's up in Talvijärvi right now," the Keeper went on, "in the woods, by the lake. She's waiting for you." Axel opened his mouth to ask whom he meant, but he felt like he had a pretty good guess. The bear was waiting for him in Talvijärvi.

The Keeper flicked his match into the harbor, braced his mangled hand on the head of his walking stick, and stood. He scooped up the knapsack and slung it over his shoulder again. For a moment he seemed about to walk away. But then he turned back to Axel, all his playfulness suddenly drained. "Your sister isn't the only one who is trying to stop you," the Keeper said. "*It's* still out there—you can't think that you've lost it. Only a matter of time before it follows you here."

"The wheelchair . . . ," Axel said. The words escaped him almost on their own, but he had little doubt that's what the Keeper was talking about.

The old man raised an eyebrow. "It looks like a wheelchair to you?"

"It's real." Axel didn't mean this as a question, but that's how the Keeper took it.

"As real as I am," he said. "As real as the elephants. It's the Hiisi."

Axel recognized the word. It could mean slightly different things in different contexts, though most of them weren't particularly nice. A *hiisi* was a wood spirit. A *hiisi* was a troll, or demon. A *hiisi* was, apparently, following him. Axel knew he shouldn't be delighted by any of this.

"When it finds you," the Keeper continued,

"and it *will*, you need to keep your distance. None of that silly shit you like to do—pushing it, kicking it. Don't even *touch* the thing."

"Why not?" Axel said.

"You'll know soon enough," the Keeper said, "next time you see it. The Hiisi likes to put on disguises. It dresses up as something it knows you fear. But underneath the disguise—that's so very much worse." The Keeper went quiet for a moment, his gaze again drifting out across the water, to the tented market. "You should get back to them," he said. "If you get Granny too worried, she might cancel your trip." Then, without another word, he turned, taking high swamp-walker steps across the parking lot. He was heading in the direction of the little park, which for the moment looked utterly normal.

"Where are you going?" Axel called, not a little worried that it might seem crazy if he was yelling at an empty parking lot.

"Home," the Keeper said, without turning back. "See you up there!"

9

Talvijärvi

Axel behaved strangely for the rest of the day. He didn't say a word during the short trip back to Jaana and Otso's flat, and once they arrived he marched straight into the study. Tess followed, watching as he ransacked his suitcase. Clothes unfolded and books butterflied as he tossed them over his shoulders. When he found what he was looking for—their father's camera, the most expensive thing he'd ever bought, counting the truck he died in—Axel scooped it up and switched it on.

"I thought that was busted?" Tess said.

"The screen still works." Axel planted himself on the edge of his bed and began to flick through the pictures. When he came to the one he was looking for, his eyes widened. Axel stayed quiet for a long moment, and when he finally spoke again, his voice was thin and shaky. "I think you should sit down," he said.

Quickly, Tess joined him on the bed. She took her brother's chin in her hands and turned his face toward her. He didn't have bad days often, but when he did, they started out like this. "Are you all right?" she said.

Axel made no answer, other than to pass her the camera. Tess looked down at the cracked display, threaded with blue, and saw the very last picture her brother had taken. It was the brown bear, sulking among the sugar maples edging Mud Lake Park. The bear looked smaller in the picture, though no less terrifying. How strange—she'd hardly given the animal or her keeper a second thought since Sam had died. But had the encounter happened on any other day, it probably would have been a highlight of her year.

"I think she's here," Axel said, his voice sort of faraway and breathy. "She's waiting for us."

Tess flicked the camera off and looked at him. "The bear?"

"No," Axel huffed, impatient. He seemed about to say something more but caught himself at the last moment. "Wait. . . . You see a bear?" His tone was so flat that she almost didn't realize that this was a question.

"Um, yes?" Tess handed the camera back to her bug-eyed brother. Again, she inspected his face. "What's going on with you?"

Axel didn't answer for a long while, and the "nothing" he finally uttered was totally unconvincing. Then he lay back on his bed, clutching the busted camera to his chest. He didn't say anything more, but behind that grim, jet-lagged stupor, there was a kind of lightness seeping in. It almost looked like her brother was happy.

The rest of the afternoon went by quickly, but that was largely because the sun set at half past four, dousing Helsinki in darkness. Jaana and Otso kept busy in the kitchen, cooking for the trip. The cabin at Talvijärvi had no stove or running water—Otso announced this cheerily, as though it were an excellent feature, something they'd be sure to put in the listing if they ever sold the place—so anything that couldn't be cooked over an open fire had to be prepared in advance. That meant that dinner was a smorgasbord of samples: sausages, thick hoops of raw onion, a bizarrely viscous gooseberry pudding, and a funky mushroom casserole that looked a good deal worse than it tasted. Tess was starving, but Axel hardly ate. He stayed silent throughout the meal, fiddling with the camera, earning suspicious and worried glances from Jaana and Otso. When it was time for bed, he took the camera with him, the display casting a flickering glow over his face. It wasn't until Tess was about to fall asleep that her brother spoke again.

"What did Grandpa Paul say?" he asked.

Tess took her time. "He said to give it a week. He said we should see how the first week goes and then call him back." She turned onto her side. "If we still want to go home after that, he'll see what he can do." Paul had, of course, said no such thing. Tess hadn't had high hopes for their conversation, but it actually went even worse than she'd expected. Paul's voice came through clogged and woolen, eking its way from word to word, like just making the sounds required more effort than he was capable of. Tess's first assumption had been that he was drunk—where Paul was concerned, that was generally a safe bet to make. But as the conversation meandered and doubled back, she began to realize that he was sober. This was, in a weird way, even more troubling.

"I'm just so sorry," Paul had said in a leaden voice. "You both deserve better."

In a moment of anger, Tess has allowed herself to answer, "Yes, we do."

Axel lay quietly for a moment on his bed, pulsing with the glow of the camera. "Good," he eventually said. "I think we should *try*, you know? I think we should give them a chance." Axel seemed to realize that this wasn't the answer Tess was expecting. He looked up from the camera to stare at her, forcing eye contact, almost like he was selling something.

"Don't you miss home?" she said, a little lamely.

"I miss everything." Axel switched off the camera and set it on the floor beneath his bed. "I miss Dad."

"Me too."

A moment passed. A long one. It seemed like the accident had happened a year ago. Or a minute ago. It seemed, for a moment, like it had never happened at all.

"He'd want us to stay here, I think." Despite everything, chances were that Axel was right. Considering the alternatives. Still, Sam wouldn't have been happy about it. He'd put in zero prep work for their relationship with Jaana and Otso. Tess had never thought that her father was the kind of man to hold a grudge, but the fact that he'd kept this one going so long meant that something truly terrible must have happened between him and the Kivis.

"What do you think they did to him?" Tess said.

"I don't know," Axel said. Then, after a moment: "Are you sure it was them?"

"What?"

"How do you know they started the fight?"

She stared at him, incredulous. All the available evidence pointed to Jaana as the maker and sustainer of the decade-long, arctic-silent grudge.

"Maybe it was Mom," Axel said, already woozy and drifting. Tess could hear Otso's spokes echoing through the wooden flat. The street below hummed with the complaint of tramcars and a brief eruption of boisterous singing.

"What do *you* know about Mom?"

"Nothing," Axel said. "Neither of us does."

Their train was scheduled to leave at dawn the next morning. Tess kept an eye on her little brother, but he seemed more or less restored to his normal self. Axel grinned down at his paper ticket, at the looming sandstone giants, at the train waiting to convey them all to Talvijärvi. The thing was sleek and podlike, modern as a cell phone, but her brother couldn't have been more pleased if it were a steam engine, quaintly greased and smoky, worthy of platform nine and three-quarters.

The trip took only a few hours, but that accounted for most of their meager allotment of daylight. Otso unfolded a map over his knees, tracing their route as they went—north out of Helsinki and east toward the Russian border. Tess watched as the flat, lake-pocked terrain blurred past her window. The farther they went, the greener things got. The autumn-brown ashes and elms fell away, replaced by spruce and stands of orange-barked pine. In some places there were no trees at all but a heathland of yarrow and hops and yellowish cloudberry bogs so wet that they reflected the sky. Tess imagined that her father had probably taken this same train journey years ago. She pictured Sam seated exactly where she was now, gazing out at the green and unfamiliar world beyond the windows.

Wow, Tess thought. He would have *loved* it. And just a moment after these words flitted across her brain, she had to turn away from Jaana and Otso, so that they wouldn't notice her wiping her eyes. God, it kept getting the jump on her. The depth of Tess's sadness was somehow a never-ending surprise. Her grief would jump out from behind some unexpected corner, yell "boo," and freaking ruin her.

They transferred to a bus at the Talvijärvi train station, disembarking at the mouth of the Kivis' long driveway. And no sooner had the summer cottage come into view through the trees ahead than Jaana began divvying out chores. Otso was to bring all the dry goods into the kitchen and deliver the perishables to the hillside cellar. Firewood was stacked beneath the eaves of a freestanding sauna adjacent to the cottage, and Jaana put herself in charge of making kindling and stocking the fireplace and the woodstove. Axel's job was to go inside the cabin, open up all the linen closets, and air out bedding—no heavy lifting there. It was Tess, unsurprisingly, who got the shit shift. Literally. No running water meant they used a composting outhouse, and her job was to uncork the toilet and add some wood chips. After that she should go down to the lakeshore and get the boat off its blocks and into the water. Oh—and could she bring all the heavy suitcases inside? Again Jaana seemed ready for Tess to fight her on this—she seemed, almost, to *want* it. Tess didn't know why her grandmother had decided to poke the dragon, and she didn't much care. She gave the old woman a blank smile and did as she was asked.

Tess started with the job least likely to involve poop or spiders, following her brother to the front door of the cottage and hauling each suitcase inside. If the Kivis' new condo in Helsinki was the exact opposite of her old A-frame back home, then their summer place was a sort of medium between the two. It had the same grotty odor of wood and books—Otso must have left a great deal of his work here over the years—the same worn floorboards covered in a concealing patchwork of rugs. The cabin was just about the same size as the A-frame, but it felt a good deal bigger because there was simply so much less *in* it. With people this old, you'd expect a knickknack or two, but Jaana had been just as merciless with the clutter in here as she had been in their city flat. Where couches and chairs were needed, there were couches and chairs. The table was perfect for a couple and could accommodate up to four, but not a person more. There were exactly two beds. It wasn't lost on Tess that the smaller one had been her mother's.

Axel stalked the cottage for closets, opening each door with a kind of cinematic swish, as though he half expected to discover a fawn-trod snowscape on the other side. The fact that all he found were sheets and comforters, thick with the stink of mothballs, seemed to do nothing to dim his enthusiasm. Tess stashed a suitcase in each of the bedrooms—there had better be a cot some-where, because no way was she sleeping with her brother—before helping Axel unfurl the musty linens. Then she left him in the cottage and made for the outhouse, which was set up against a low hill opposite the lakeshore, looking out from a copse of winter-tortured birch.

There was a covered plastic tub of peat and wood chips sitting just outside the outhouse door, with a big scooper perched atop the lid. The toilet seat looked like a regular one, but when Tess lifted it, there was nothing beneath but a gaping black hole—the kind you definitely don't want to hang your naked butt over. She dropped in a few scoops of woody mulch and got the seat closed as quickly as she could. Then it was down to the water. On her way, Tess passed the freestanding sauna, which looked rather like a jumbo replica of a Lincoln Logs play set, made of raw timber, jointed at the corners, with a capped tin chimney jutting from the roof. Jaana was already out behind the sauna, using a hand ax to split birch logs into kindling. She worked the ax into the wood with a few gentle taps. Then, once the blade was lodged, a quick thump splintered the log neatly down the middle. Jaana called out as Tess passed.

"Your brother, he swims?"

"He knows how to swim," Tess said.

"Well?" Jaana kept her eyes on her work as she spoke. She might as well have been addressing the ax, or the wood.

"Well enough," Tess said.

"The oars are in the front room of the sauna. Better grab a life jacket, too. We have a small one." Jaana looked up briefly, to stare out at the lake.

The water was ice-flat, broken in the middle by a small, rocky island, just big enough to support a pair of stunted pines. There was something swimming around the island—a swan, lit pinkish by the autumn sun. "We've got some time. If you're quick, we can go out before dark."

Jaana had said that the rowboat would be behind the sauna, up on blocks, but when Tess rounded the outbuilding she couldn't see it. The blocks were there—three rough hunks of wood jutting from the untended lawn—and beside them a balled-up tarp, but no boat. The grass had all been trampled, and a smooth trail indicated which direction the boat had been hauled. But if it was the work of thieves, they were at least lazy ones. The drag path led down to the Kivis' dock, where a small rowboat was already tied off.

Tess headed down to the dock, which was glimmering strangely in the late sunlight. As she got closer she realized that the shine was due to broken glass—whoever had borrowed the boat had enjoyed a drink or two at the water's edge. Actually, it was more than a few drinks—they'd put on a lakeside party. The bottom of the rowboat was littered with chicken bones, cigarette butts, and empty plastic bottles of hard cider. The borrowers had also failed to bail the boat, so that everything floated in a gross, inch-deep slurry.

There was a box in the stern, and Tess knelt down to open it, hoping to find a dipper in there. Otherwise she'd have to drag the rowboat onshore and tip it empty.

"Hey, you!" She was startled by the shouted Finnish, which came from a little farther down the water's edge. "Back off!"

Tess looked up and saw a guy about her age, approaching fast. He held a fishing rod in his hands, the bobber bouncing on the grass behind him. The guy was heavy, with bangs falling over his freckles, but he knew how to square himself to look more solid than fat.

Tess didn't answer or back off.

"That's the Kivis' boat," he said, reaching the edge of the dock. His hook got stuck on a root, compelling him to stop and set the rod down, which dissipated his would-be bulldog energy just a tad.

"I know," Tess said.

"So don't touch it!" Despite the chill, this kid was in shorts and barefoot. His shirt was a fitted, button-down plaid, and his shorts had creases. His fishing rod bore all the bright, boastful hallmarks of being overpriced.

"I'm sorry, but who the hell are you?" Her first full sentence gave her away as a foreigner, and that knocked the guy back a bit.

"That's my house," he said, pointing a ways down the water, to the only other home visible on this side of the lake. It was a multilevel with big windows and a stilted deck stretching out over a boathouse. Tess and Axel had definitely lost the summer cottage lottery—that place no doubt had flush toilets and heated bathroom tiles. There was a gas grill out on the deck and pretty college-age kids sprawling on loungers.

"Okay." Tess thumbed over her shoulder at Jaana and Otso's comparatively dinky summer place and said: "Well, I'm staying there. The Kivis are my grandparents."

"Oh," the guy said. He looked down at his feet, at the glass around his feet—it was a wonder he hadn't cut himself—and the stagnant filth inside the rowboat. "Crap," he said. "I'm sorry."

"You did that?"

Instead of answering, he stepped into the water, getting his nicely pressed shorts all wet. He steadied the boat with one hand, peered inside, and made a disgusted grunt. He reached in and started plucking out leg bones and cigarette filters, laying them out neatly on the edge of the dock like caught fish, washing his fingers in the lake between each pluck. "We have a boat, but it's not big enough to fit all of my brother's friends. Your grandparents never come here in the fall, so . . ." He glanced at her, either shy or grossed out. "They promised they'd be careful with it."

She watched him for a moment before squatting down on the dock to collect the larger shards of glass, adding them to the pile he was making. The guy leaned against the stern so that the standing water flowed down toward him, bringing with it the last of the mess. He grabbed at it daintily, revolted but determined.

"I'm Kari," he said. "I didn't know the Kivis had grandkids."

"I'm Tess," she said. "And until last week, I didn't know who the Kivis were."

Kari stared at her, maybe wondering if inflection was different where she came from. Was he misunderstanding a joke? He laughed, too late and too loud.

"My parents will be happy to hear they came up. Give me a hand?"

He'd untied the boat from the dock and started to pull it up out of the water. Tess came around to meet him, and together they heaved it onto the grass. There was indeed a dipper in the stern box, and Kari used it to add some clean water to the inside. They rocked the boat back and forth to rinse it out. It took both of them to tip and drain it.

"They're in Barcelona," Kari said.

"Who is?"

"My mom and dad."

Tess just blinked at him for a moment. "What are they doing in Barcelona?" she asked.

Kari looked at her like this was a dumb question. "Seeing Barcelona," he said. "Dad hates the fall. And the winter. And besides . . . the architecture! We're having some work done on the house, so Kalle and I came up for the week to keep an eye on things." Kari shoved his hands into his pockets and assumed a look of knowing, weary responsibility. "You know how it can be with contractors. Anyway, Kalle, that's my brother." He pointed back at the deck over the boathouse, at a blond guy manning the grill. Like Kari, Kalle was dressed in stubborn disagreement with the season. But in Kalle's case, it was by no means a bad thing. Even from a distance Tess could tell that Kari's older brother cultivated the kind of glossy, tanned shirtlessness that you usually saw only on your computer screen. But the evidence at the bottom of the rowboat suggested that among his friends there was at least one jackass, and that made the prospects pretty dim for him as well.

"Where do you live, then?" Kari had switched languages, and Tess could tell right away that his English was better than her Finnish. Not that that was super hard.

"New York."

Kari went a little bug-eyed. "I *love* New York." No need to tell him that Tess lived farther away from the city than this sleepy little lake was from Helsinki. "So your parents," he went on, "did they come too?"

"No. They're in Zanzibar." The lie came out so unexpectedly, so very easily. This is everything that Tess knew about Zanzibar: It was a place.

"Awesome," Kari said. "Do you want it on the blocks or back in the water?"

Jaana interrupted them before Tess had a chance to answer. "Mr. Hannula," she called out in Finnish, "do you mean to steal my boat?" Tess's grandmother had rounded the sauna and approached with a pair of oars slung over her shoulders, making her look irritatingly intrepid. Axel was with her, already fastened tightly into one of the bulky life jackets, which jutted up around his collar like a dog's veterinary cone, making him look the precise opposite of intrepid. Jaana's sudden appearance seemed to scare Kari not in the least. In fact, he smiled wide.

"I wasn't stealing it," he answered. Then, in English, he told Jaana that he'd only borrowed it. Tess couldn't tell if Kari had switched languages as a courtesy to her, or rather to keep showing off how good his English was. Either way, it saved her little lie from falling apart then and there.

"Well, I don't see any problem with that," Jaana said, also in English. "As long as you took good care—" She caught herself when she saw the empty bottles and soggy cigarette butts. Jaana peered across the lakeshore at the stilted deck. Seeing Kalle and his friends, she sighed. "So young and so determined to hurt themselves. Tell me you didn't smoke any of these."

"Of course not," Kari said. "No, ma'am."

"And look at you, no shoes in this weather. And with glass! Tarzan feet will get you only so far! You think there were broken bottles in the jungle?" *Tarzan feet* was clearly an inside joke between them, years past its expiration date by now. It made Kari blush. Tess blushed too.

"I suppose . . ." Jaana looked up at the deepening sky and back down at the messy dock. "We have all day tomorrow," she said. "No need to be greedy. We'll finish tidying up and go rowing in the morning." She leaned her oars against the sauna wall and popped back inside to get a bucket and a broom. It took only a few minutes for the four of them to sweep the dock clean, set the rowboat back in the water, and tie it off again.

"We cooked too much, if you'd like to join us for supper," Jaana said.

"No thanks," Kari said. "Kalle's grilling."

Tess's grandmother nodded thoughtfully at this. "Well. Regards to your parents. And ask your brother to pay me a visit when he's got the time."

Kari's expression darkened almost imperceptibly. "Yes, ma'am."

Jaana turned back to the little cottage, leaving them. Axel hesitated for a moment, glancing furtively between Kari and Tess. Then, in his patented face-palm style, he said: "Am I interrupting anything? Do you two require privacy?"

Tess told her brother not to be stupid, and he grinned because that meant he could stay. The three of them sat at the end of the dock. Axel took his time unlacing his shoes and folding up his socks before letting his feet trail in the water. But it was way too cold, and seconds later he had them tucked under his thighs. He seemed to be in no hurry to take off that dumb orange vest.

"So, you know our grandmother," Axel said.

"I do," Kari said.

"What do you think of her?"

Sometimes Axel was great to have around—you never had to be the one to ask awkward questions. Kari glanced at Tess, as though for help, and when none came he said: "Your grandmother is one of the nicest people I know."

"Fascinating. That doesn't match our own

experience, thus far." Axel thrust a palm at Kari. "Axel Fortune," he said.

Kari took a moment to see if he was for real before accepting the handshake. "Kari Hannula," he said, his formality matching Axel's without mocking it. "Welcome to Talvijärvi."

"Thank you kindly," Axel said. "So, I'd like to pose a question to you. It's going to be weird. Is that okay? Can I ask you a weird question?"

"God, Axel," Tess said. She'd only just met Kari, and already her kid brother was laying it on thick.

"It's all right," Kari said. "Ask me whatever you want."

"You've been coming here for a long time, yes?"

"I have. Every summer, since I was five."

"Excellent," Axel said. Then, looking suddenly worried, "But that's not the question. The question is: Have you noticed anything out of the ordinary lately? Has anything strange been happening in Talvijärvi?"

"What do you mean strange?"

"Supernatural."

Kari didn't even blink; nor did he give Tess a chance to make her usual excuses. "That's so funny that you should ask," he said, pointing out at the middle of the lake, where the twin pines loomed atop their tiny island. The swan was still there, swimming a slow circuit around the rocks. The sun was almost down, and the swan was the color of blood. "You see that island?"

Axel nodded, obviously holding his breath.

"Totally haunted."

"Shut up," Axel said. His laugh hit bottom, bounced a bit, and skidded into what could only be called a squeal of delight. Tess hadn't heard anything like that escape him since the night of the brown bear. He turned to her. "Can we go?"

"Of course we can," she said.

10

A Ghost Story

Just yesterday in Helsinki Axel had been right on the edge of a full-scale flip out. He'd felt dizzy enough to puke, giddy enough to shout as he tore through the suitcase, searching for his father's busted camera. He'd needed to see the picture he'd taken of the bear. Though, of course, she was more than just a bear; Axel was sure of that much already. He knew it in his legs and lungs, in his stomach and heart just as sure as he knew when a bad spell was coming over him. According to the Keeper, he and the bear had come to Baldwin in search of Sam Fortune. And now the bear was waiting for Axel up at Talvijärvi. A single word ran through his head on a loop—*Äiti. Äiti-Äiti-Äiti-Äiti.* It couldn't be her, and it couldn't be anyone else.

Axel switched on the camera, and the last shot he'd taken on that awful night flickered across the cracked display. And there she was—a youngish lady looming in the middle of the photograph, dressed like some kind of hippie art teacher. The image went fuzzy as Axel's eyes filled up with fat, frantic tears. He rubbed them away and scrolled back through the other shots, just to be sure that nobody was playing a trick on him. But everything else was exactly as it should have been. Axel saw the torn-up garden and overturned trash can; he saw the shadowed wells of bear tracks that had skirted his home. But the *bear*—the bear had disappeared from the photograph, and this young woman had taken her place.

The woman stood pale in the light of the flashbulb, jagged rows of black maples sinking into the velour nothing of the night around her. She wore denim overalls, paint-spattered and rolled up to the knees. There was a burst of color running up one of her legs that at first Axel mistook for a bright sock. But on closer inspection he saw that it was a tattoo, the ink curling above her calf, disappearing below the denim of her overalls. This was a photograph of Saara Kivi—Axel's mother. The fact that this was impossible made it no less true. Never mind that he'd seen the bear with his own eyes—smelled it, touched its matted fur when the thing knocked him over with a careless haunch. The bear had reeked of earth and musk and reality. Never mind, also, that so many things about this woman were strange—not just unfamiliar, but *wrong*. Her tattoo, her ironical horn-rim glasses, the way she'd twisted her lips into a pissed-off grimace. But despite all of that, there was no question in Axel's mind. The bear was his mother. Or, rather, his mother's ghost.

Freaking awesome.

Of course, Axel never intended to keep any of this from his sister. His first instinct was always to be honest with her. Tess might not have believed that he'd seen the Keeper at the market if she had nothing more to go on than Axel's word—it was, after all, a pretty preposterous thing to have happened—but the photograph of their long-dead mother was proof that something paranormal was going down. Except that it *wasn't*. When Axel gave her the camera, Tess couldn't see anything but a picture of a brown bear. And while a bear in Baldwin was odd, it was hardly evidence of magic. Again Axel had to consider the possibility that this was all in his head—a much more pleasant hallucination than the wheelchair, but maybe more troubling, sanity-wise. He decided to stay quiet, doing his best not to seem too excited on the train ride up north, keeping his cool as they walked from the station, taking his time rooting around the little lakeside cottage. There'd be plenty of opportunities over the coming week to explore the woods out back. Hours upon hours to search for signs of his mother.

But Axel's calm and steady course got scrapped the moment that Kari kid uttered the words: "totally haunted." He damn near fell into the lake when he heard it.

"Don't mess with me," he said. "Do not make fun of me, because it's cruel."

"What?" Kari glanced between Tess and Axel, worried he was missing something. "You're the one who asked."

"But what do you mean haunted? Like, haunted how?" Axel said.

"There's a ghost on the island. People see her at night sometimes."

Her. Promising. Axel pressed for more information. "What people? Have you seen her? What does she—"

"Okay," Tess cut in. "How about we cool it a little bit?"

"I have," Kari said, totally deadpan.

"You shouldn't encourage him," Tess said.

"I'm not encouraging anybody," Kari said. "I've seen the ghost, and my parents have seen the ghost, and my brother, Kalle, has seen the ghost. Last year, just after midsummer." Here he trailed off for a moment. The sun sank behind the fir trees, and the swan went ashore on the rocky little island, apparently untroubled by the resident spirit. "It was one of those evenings when you don't get any real night, just a few hours of twilight," Kari went on. "No darker than this. My father had some people from his work staying with us, and we all went out on the boat so he could show off the midnight sun. They were Greeks, these people. When we were coming back home, we noticed a lady on the island. She was all alone. We asked if she needed a ride back to her cottage, but she didn't say anything. My mom thought that maybe she was a foreigner, so we tried Swedish and English. The Greeks tried Greek. But she wouldn't answer. So we just left her there. And by the time we got home, we couldn't see her anymore. My mom made us go right back out. All around the island. She was so upset. She thought that the lady had drowned."

"Did you notice tattoos?" Axel said. "Was she wearing glasses?"

Tess had been pretty patient with him so far, but that was apparently the limit. "Damn, Axel. Weird much?"

"I didn't notice," Kari said, as though this were a perfectly reasonable question. "In the morning my mom went around to all the cottages on the lake, to see if anybody had guests staying with them. To see if anybody was missing. But nobody was missing. Everybody was accounted for."

Kari lifted his feet out of the water and let them drip dry for a moment before standing up. In the brief time it took him to tell his story, the twilight had ripened to full dark. Stars blasted holes in the sky one by one, and cottage windows ignited along the distant shore. "Are you two really rowing out to the island tomorrow?" He glanced at Tess, not quite making eye contact. As lost as Axel was in his own thoughts, he'd have to be blind not to see that this chubby rich kid was into his sister. Poor guy.

"Probably," she said. "He'll drive me crazy until I take him there."

"That is correct," Axel said. "That is absolutely true."

"Well, I'd better come with you," Kari said. "The lake gets shallow around the island—a lot of rocks just under the surface. There's only one place where you can row ashore, and it's hard to find if you don't already know where it is." This all came out a bit too quickly, but it worked. Tess told Kari to meet them at the dock the next morning. As a compatriot in awkwardness, Axel found himself happy for the older kid. The problem was that he sometimes didn't think before speaking.

"Well played, sir," he said.

Kari burst into a flame blush and retreated to his bright house for dinner. Tess and Axel stayed outside for a while longer, saying nothing, watching the two pines disappear against the lake.

The next day couldn't begin soon enough, and it made no effort to—these late sunrises were really getting to be a drag. Axel rushed through a breakfast of cold cuts and buttered rye, then fidgeted as Jaana outfitted him with layered sweaters, knit socks, and a scarf as thick as a folded bath towel. Over the entire woolen riot, she buckled his puffy life jacket. Jaana didn't make the same effort with Tess, but did insist she bring a jacket as well, slung over her shoulder if not fully fastened. The two of them seemed to have argued each other to a stalemate.

Outside the weather was windy and cold, as though they'd tipped from autumn's summer edge to its winter one overnight. The breeze kicked up wavelets on the lake. Frost had left the grass brittle as spun sugar under their feet. A single dainty icicle hung from where the drainpipe met the gutter. As they rounded the freestanding sauna they saw that Kari was already at the dock, hugging himself on the rear bench of a beautiful power rowboat—it must have belonged to his parents. Axel wondered how long he'd been out there, bobbing and shivering.

Jaana followed them outside, and she called out to Kari as soon as she saw him. "Mr. Hannula, that boat had better be a joke!"

"Morning, Mrs. Kivi!" He waved from inside the boat, his unbuttoned shirt cuff flapping in the breeze. "I promise we'll be careful."

"There isn't a chance," Jaana said. "Not in that thing."

As Kari's house was to the Kivis' summer cottage, so was his rowboat to the Kivis' rickety skiff. It wasn't that it was bigger—though it certainly was—so much that it was slicker. The bow tapered sharply into an elegant elfin stem, and there was a shining black outboard motor at the transom. The oarlocks were of polished brass, and the entire thing had the white, woody look you associate with yachting and New England.

"There's no such thing as careful. Not in that," Jaana said.

"But we won't use the motor," Kari said. "We *can't*, even. There isn't any fuel. Kalle used it all up."

"I see." Jaana squatted down on the dock and rested a hand on the gunwale. As short as her hair was, the breeze was still stiff enough to ruffle it. "Do I need to check the gauge, or can I trust you, Mr. Hannula?"

Kari's expression looked so sincere that it almost couldn't have been. "You can trust me," he said. "You can also check the gauge."

Jaana stood. "To the island and back." She helped Axel get aboard and settled on the stern bench, where he propped his feet atop a foam cooler. "Look after him."

"*I'll* look after him," Tess said, climbing aboard as well. The boat rocked under her, then steadied. She dropped her life jacket on the bench beside Axel.

"You're who I was talking to," Jaana said, untying them and tossing the line for Kari to catch. "I'd better not hear a motor."

Their grandmother stayed on the dock, watching as Kari set the oars into the oarlocks and took his spot on the bench, his back to the little island. This struck Axel as strange—he was used to canoes, and in a canoe everybody faced forward. Grandpa Paul had a whole fleet of them out behind his trailer, some salvaged or stolen, but most bought bargain basement from a summer camp gone bust. No matter how poorly their trips down to the Boils went, Sam and Paul always quit fighting for long enough to take the kids out onto the steaming creeks and springs. Everybody had a paddle, and everybody was expected to use it. A rowboat was different—you couldn't exactly share the work. But Kari didn't seem to mind.

"We'll have to go around it . . . and let the breeze carry us to the north side . . . where we'll put ashore," he said between pulls on the oars. They'd gone all of ten nautical yards and already there was sweat speckling Kari's forehead. "It'll take a little longer, but we don't have a choice."

"Your brother's not going to miss his boat?" Tess asked.

Kari sort of snorted. "Kalle won't be awake for hours." In order to compensate for the wind, he struck a diagonal course roughly between the pine island and his own summer house. Though perhaps that name wasn't fitting—the Hannula house seemed to be battened against anything Finland could possibly throw at it, summer *or* winter. It was a fortress of warmth, four chimneys stabbing out of the roof like the jeweled peaks of a crown. A sauna was attached to the house via a glass walkway, and the skeleton of a new wing bulged from the east wall. The deck above the boathouse bore all the evidence of revelry; empty cider bottles along the railings and paper plates smeared with mustard, scattered by the weather.

"It's Tuesday," Tess said. She left it at that for a moment, allowing the words to be carried away on the breeze. "Don't you all have school?"

"My brother's taking a semester off," Kari said. "Mom and Dad are paying him to supervise the work on our house."

"But you?" Tess asked.

"Kalle told my school I have mononucleosis." Kari smiled hugely and toothily, as though trying to convince all three of them that this was a good thing.

"So. About the island . . ." Axel had held off as long as he could. "Do you know if anyone else has ever seen the ghost?"

"Of course they have. Plenty of people," Kari said. "She's sort of a local legend. The newspaper down in Savonlinna even did a story about her."

"Oh." Axel wasn't sure why, but the fact that sightings were relatively common struck him as not necessarily a plus. People saw Bigfoot all the damn time. "Does she always look like a lady?" he asked.

Kari took a brief break from rowing, and the wind pushed them sideways. They were nearly abreast of the island now, and Axel could see that the discussion about underwater rocks from the previous evening hadn't just been an excuse for Kari to tag along. Gray-green shadows drifted just beneath them like a herd of petrified manatees.

"What do you mean?" Kari said.

"I mean does she ever appear in a different

form? Does she ever look like something else?" Axel chewed his lips, debating. He didn't want to give himself away to his sister, but he couldn't resist. "A bear, maybe?"

Tess had been staring back at Jaana and Otso's summer place, but now her attention snapped toward Axel.

"I don't know about that," Kari said, pulling on the oars again to get them out of the path of a granite boulder kissing the surface. "I mean . . . we *do* have bears here. But they stay deep in the forest. As long as you aren't dumb with your garbage, you'll never see them."

They pulled past the island and doubled around, making for a pebbly beach no broader across than a bathtub. Kari slid over to the backseat, where he stood and used one of his oars to push off against the underwater rocks, punting them the final distance.

"Anything you want to tell me?" Tess whispered, leaning in to her brother.

"Nope," Axel said, unable to look her in the face.

The gravel rattled under the hull as they struck bottom, and Kari jumped into the shallows, crossed to one of the pines, and tied off. Then he turned to help them ashore, offering his hand first to Axel, then to Tess.

Smart boy.

The island was just about as large from coast to coast as a volleyball court, with the two pines sticking out at either end. The swan they'd been watching the night before was nowhere to be seen, but there were signs of her everywhere. Feathers and down coated the rocks like puffy white lichen, cemented into place by a dried film of swan crap. The island had looked pristine from a distance, but in the moments when the breeze died down, the stench was considerable. There was also some evidence of human activity—a few discarded fishing weights and the mangled skeleton of a demon-jawed pike. It even looked like there had been some kind of structure here, once upon a time. In the middle of the island, exactly between the pines, were the remains of a brick foundation. Some pots and coiled piping were heaped into a corner, rusted and crumbling, just one rough winter away from being turned to dust.

Kari lugged the cooler to the little ruin, dropping it into the foundation and then jumping down after it, taking a seat against the old brickwork. Axel and Tess joined him. The shallow dip of the foundation kept them mostly out of the wind, but still afforded them a view of the distant lakeshore, bleak and magnificent. The Kivis' humble cottage and Kari's lake villa were the only houses visible against a wall of evergreen. Axel saw smoke rising from the tin chimney atop the freestanding sauna and could faintly make out Otso's wheelchair sitting empty beside the open door. Over at the Hannula house, some gulls had collected on the deck, screaming insanely atop the leavings from last night's party. Axel eyed the birds and the forest. There was something else there, farther away, faintly visible above the tree-tops. Something made of stone.

"That's Erikinlinna," Kari said when he'd asked. It meant, roughly, "Erik's fort." Or, more promisingly: "Erik's castle." The way Kari said it was so cool, like a castle was no big deal. Oh, it's just the castle—hundreds of years old, filled with knights' spirits, whatever. Axel couldn't help but grin like a fool. It seemed like everything at Talvijärvi was eminently hauntable. If his life was ever going to get magical, this was the place for it to happen.

"Snacks?" Kari asked, plainly tickled that his little outing seemed to be going well. He opened the cooler to reveal a stash of cold sodas and salmi-akki—a kind of Finnish licorice that Sam used to get mailed in from a specialty store in Michigan. It was an acquired taste. Axel and Tess loved it because they'd grown up with it, but their father said it was like chewing on boiled-down sweat.

He ordered it only because he missed Saara and got a kick out of the fact that his kids liked it as much as she used to. Just like he got a kick out of hearing them speak Finnish. What would Sam have thought if he could see the two of them now? Axel suddenly felt something deep inside, lurching for the surface. Tess must have felt it, too, because when she spoke her voice cracked.

"Sure." Tess coughed. She quickly took a cold cola and handed another to Axel, who held it through his scarf. The three of them sat silently, sipping and snacking. The sun, for all its sluggish rising, shown brightly and clearly now. Down on the far shore, Jaana stepped out of the sauna, ran down the dock, and dove into the frigid water. They were too far away, thank goodness, to tell if she was wearing a skin-tone swimsuit or if, in true Finnish tradition, she was stark naked.

"This place doesn't exactly seem haunted," Tess said.

"Well, it *is*." Kari had all the showy enthusiasm of a scoutmaster. He was shivering like mad but seemed gleefully determined to ignore it. "You don't even know. We're at the epicenter." He pointed meaningfully at the foundation walls.

"What do you mean?" Axel shifted position to get more comfortable and realized that his legs had gone stiff. They must have just fallen asleep.

"You know what this used to be?" Kari said. "A *still*. There used to be a little hut here, and the woodsmen who lived on the lake would row out to the island to escape their wives and children and get drunk on homemade vodka. That was right after the war, when a lot of people came from the east, because their old homes were now in Russia." By "the war," Kari could only have meant the Continuation War, which was what the Finns called their part in World War II—they hadn't been in one since. That made the ruins at least sixty years old. Axel started to get the very beginnings of a bad feeling. The more of this story Kari told, the less promising it sounded.

"You can still see what they used to make the vodka." Kari nodded at the rusted pots and coiled piping at the corner of the foundation. "The way the story goes is that there was this woodsman named Väinö. He had a beautiful wife named Aino, and he loved her very much. But he also loved to drink. All the money he had, the woodsman put into the still and drank. One summer he even went so far as to sell the family boat. The island wasn't that far away, and he could always paddle out to it on a raft. But it made Aino furious. So she decided to sneak out one night and wreck the still."

Here Kari paused again, rubbing his fingers against the foundation. The blackened bricks were weather-pocked, cracked from years of winter and thaw. "She waited for the lake to freeze. Then, after Väinö fell asleep, Aino lit a lantern and walked out across the ice. She'd stolen her husband's wood ax, and she used it to break open all the jars of vodka and to cut the roof and walls to pieces. Nobody knows if she dropped the lantern by accident, or if she was really trying to set the whole building on fire. But either way, the thing went up. Like—*boom*." Kari cupped his hands in the air and flung them apart.

"So the lady died in the fire?" Tess said.

"Almost," Kari said, trying his best to look severe. "The explosion woke her husband up, and he saw Aino running away from the burning still, her night coat all in flames. Maybe if it had been later in the season, she'd have had time to get the coat off or jump into the snow. But the ice was still so thin. Aino was going to burn to death. But instead she fell through the ice and drowned. She's been haunting this little island ever since."

Under normal circumstances Axel totally would have appreciated the breathy, painfully rehearsed flourish with which Kari had ended his story. But as it was he couldn't even muster a smile. Because it was the wrong ghost! Even if Saara were hiding behind a false story, the timeline didn't fit. Her ghost should be as old as

Axel was, *to the day*. This Aino lady, real or not, was a stranger to him. He had no time for her. Axel stood, which took more effort than it should have.

"You could have told us that story back on the dock," he said, suddenly testy.

Tess looked at her brother, surprised. Kari seemed a little lost. "But I thought . . . Didn't you want to come here?"

Axel said nothing. He bent over and rubbed his hands up and down his legs, trying to rid them of pins and needles.

"And what about the woodsman?" Tess said—a peace offering for poor Kari. "What happened to him?"

"Actually, that's part of the story," Kari said, glancing at Axel, trying to reel him back in. "Väinö had been a pretty bad drunk before, but after his wife died, he went a little crazy. He started telling people that he'd met a strange man living in the castle. Now, you understand, this was impossible. The castle had no roof or heat, and there was no chance anybody could survive there in the winter. But Väinö insisted. He said that this man had promised to bring him into the underworld and reunite him with his dead wife."

At these words Axel's head snapped back up, the growing numbness in his legs forgotten.

"You mean *that* castle?" He pointed out across the water, at the emergent little chunk of Erikinlinna.

"That's the one," Kari said, looking relieved to have Axel aboard once more. "And you know, that's not even the weirdest thing. During this time, Väinö also became obsessed with trolls and goblins. He was convinced that one of them was following him—a *hiisi*, you know? He said that it was guarding the underworld, keeping him from his wife. He even tried to get the villagers to go into the woods and help him kill it. But, of course, nobody took him seriously. So one day he packed his rifle and some clothes and extra food and marched off into the forest all by himself." Kari paused, but they all knew what was coming next.

"It was the last time anybody ever saw him."

That certainly seemed consistent with the Keeper's vague warnings about the Hiisi. But it also wasn't reason enough to slow down. "Do you know how to get to Erikinlinna?" Axel asked. "Is it far?"

"It's not," Kari said. "The shoreline cuts around that way. We could take the boat, but maybe we'd better save that for—"

"Let's go." Axel straightened up and hoisted himself over the shallow lip of the foundation, trying hard not to show how difficult this had suddenly become. He reached the pine and began to untie the rowboat. It was only when Axel climbed inside and began to work the oars back into the oarlocks that they realized he meant *now*.

Kari rowed them around a little spit of birch land, bringing the boat ashore onto a bank of yellow grass. The sun had melted away most of the frost from that morning, but it persisted in the retreating shadows of the trees—the outlines of an ice forest drawn across the ground. Kari walked well ahead of them, either because he was getting ready to be done with this little outing or because he had sense enough to give Tess and Axel some space. They lagged out of earshot.

"What's up with you?" his sister said.

"Nothing's up with me," Axel said, trying his best to keep the effort of walking out of his face. There was no more denying what was happening to him. A bad day was coming, and it was coming fast.

"You're lying," she said. "And you shouldn't be taking advantage of him like this." She nodded up at Kari, who was blazing a careful path for them around a big patch of stinging nettles.

"You're the one leading him on, not me," Axel said. He regretted this even before his mouth closed. His sister missed a step, and in the brief moment before anger flooded her face, he could tell that he'd hurt her. Of course she wasn't leading Kari on. She only wanted a friend. "You guys don't have to bring me," Axel added quickly. "I can probably find it by myself from here."

Tess eyeballed him for a minute and then went to join Kari up ahead. Axel had to push to keep up with them, his legs going rubbery beneath him. There was no question in his mind that the man in the story, the man who lived in the castle, was the Keeper. And he had to find him before the numbness and exhaustion took over. Whenever it came on this quickly, it tended to take its sweet time letting him go again. For all Axel knew, he was looking at two or three useless days, stuck in his little bed in the Kivis' cottage.

It wasn't long before the ruins became visible through the trees ahead. Minas Tirith it sure as hell wasn't—all that remained of Erikinlinna were a pair of low towers flanking a stone archway and beyond that a courtyard filled with stunted trees and rock confetti. It was obvious, even from a distance, that the puny castle had been done up for tourists. There was a covered picnic area out front and shiny new garbage bins with swinging lids. Plaques and posters had been tacked up within the picnic area—a sort of mini-exhibit on the history of the castle. Kari led them here first, pausing by a glass-capped display table that housed a tiny model of Erikinlinna as it was thought to have looked some eight hundred years ago, bedecked with banners and primed for siege. Stenciled lettering beside the model told of how the castle had been built by the Swedish count Erik Kagg—a boss name, which Axel would have appreciated more if he weren't so focused—and went on to detail how the castle had served as one of the easternmost outposts of the Swedish kingdom. In its long history, Erikinlinna had been seized by the tsar's army, bartered back to Sweden, only to be seized once more. It had served as a rallying point for the White Guard in the Finnish Civil War and a munitions cache during with Winter War with the Soviets. Axel glanced from the model to the crumbling ruin beyond it, wondering how long the Keeper had lived there. After all, if Kari's ghost story was true, the Keeper had already been an old man sixty years ago. But was he as ancient as those towers? How much of this history had he seen?

"Back here," Kari said, continuing on to the rear of the picnic area. There was another plaque there, bearing a single laminated photograph. Text at the top of the plaque read: THE FAMOUS GHOST OF TALVIJÄRVI, AND HER MAD HUSBAND. "What did I tell you?" Kari said, tapping his finger on the picture—a family photo. "Here they are."

Old, black-and-white portraits have a tendency to be supercreepy, and this one didn't disappoint. Aino stared out at them over sunken cheeks and a long, squared chin. Her hair was covered by a white shawl, which was tucked neatly behind her ears and flowed loosely down her neck. She wasn't beautiful—not even in that hard-bitten way that people in difficult circumstances can look beautiful. But her husband, Väinö, looked even worse. He stood slightly apart in a patchy suit, both hands shoved deep into his pockets. His face was nothing but a blur—a fleshy gray cloud with diagonal lines for eyes and a dark mess of indistinct hair. Väinö must have turned his head to look at something just as the camera went off, and the unfocused effect made him look just as mad as the little plaque claimed him to be. Between Aino and Väinö was a kid, about Axel's own age. He already seemed braced for what was to come.

"You didn't mention they had a son," Tess said.

"Oh." Kari shrugged. "The son isn't really part of the story."

"He should be," Tess said. "It makes what his father did even worse. Running off like that."

"Do you think he ever found her?" Axel asked. Both Kari and Tess turned from the plaque to look at him. "What? You said that he was looking for his wife. Do you think he found her?"

"He was just a crazy drunk, Axel," Tess said.

"That's right," Kari said. "And anyway, he died."

"But I thought you said nobody ever saw him again."

"Not alive," Kari said. "They found his body the following spring—he'd frozen to death, in the castle. His family was so angry that they refused to go to his funeral. According to the story, they didn't even want to take his body back."

Axel wasn't going to lie—that last bit was troubling. He made a note to ask the Keeper about Väinö's fate as soon as he found him and then followed Tess and Kari out of the covered picnic area. They stepped through the arched entrance of Erikinlinna, into a courtyard thickly carpeted with feathers and weeds. A few spruce trees had managed to push their way through the stone-laid floor, and they stretched skyward, their trunks like columns in the big open space. A flock of strange birds seemed to have taken up residence inside the courtyard. Some perched in the lower branches of the spruce trees, stretching their wings. Others peered down at Axel from atop the scant remains of a bombed-out keep. They looked like crows—similar to crows back home but done up in gray jackets and executioner's hoods.

One of the birds leaped from its perch and flitted heavily down to the courtyard floor. It landed a few paces from Axel, its wrinkly black feet gripping an upturned corner of stone, and stared up at him. "Go away," it said very clearly in Finnish. It didn't sound the way a supernatural, possibly undead crow should sound—not shrill or deep or echoing. It was a perfectly normal voice, but for the fact that it had just come out of a crow.

"I'm looking for the Keeper," Axel said. Tess and Kari turned to him, startled.

"He isn't here," the crow said. "You shouldn't be, either. You need to leave."

"I won't," Axel said. Though, *I can't,* would have been just as accurate. Axel's exhaustion had been slowly mounting on him all morning, but the moment he crossed beneath the archway of Erikinlinna, it seemed to boil over. His legs turned to soft wax beneath him. And where had his knees gone? He used to have knees.

"You won't what?" Tess said, crossing to Axel and taking him by the arm.

"It's following you," the crow said. "You're going to lead it here."

"I'm not going anywhere until you tell me where the Keeper is," Axel said, trying his best to sound hard. The numbness had come up past his waist now, making his tummy feel sick and loose. It was horrible and painless.

"Hey. What's going on with you?" Tess put a hand around Axel's chest as he began to slump forward toward the crow. The bird didn't flinch.

"You don't belong here," the crow said. "This place isn't for you."

"Kari," Tess called out. "Help!" The older boy came around and grabbed Axel's other arm—it felt as though they were attached to his shoulders by nothing more than glue and staples. Slowly, they lowered Axel onto his back, making it look to him as though the trees were shooting up all around, a forest in fast-forward. There was a bird in every tree, two eyes in every bird.

"Now you've done it," the crow said, flapping back up onto a low branch so that it could peer down at Axel. "You've drawn it out, you selfish little rat."

"What's wrong with him?" Kari said.

"I don't know," Tess said. Then she said some more stuff, questioney stuff, all directed at Axel. But he wasn't listening—not to her, anyway. He listened instead to the familiar ticking sound that had just filled the courtyard. The Keeper had warned him that this would happen. It had been bound to find him, sooner or later. The wheelchair rolled smoothly through the castle entrance, wheels bouncing over the cracked stone.

"Send it away!" the crow screeched, its feathers standing on end.

"I can't," Axel said.

"What can't you do?" Tess shouted.

But Axel hardly heard her over the riot of squawking. The birds scattered, shattered, poured their wings and screams into the lake-blue sky. They fled the trees and the cracked battlements, the tower walls and balustrades. "Hiisi!" they shouted. "Hiisi! Hiisi!" The word rose up all around Axel—doubling, tripling, flocking.

11

No Halloween

It had been so long since Axel's last bad day that Tess had allowed herself to hope that they might finally be over and done with. No such luck. Her brother looked like he was about to fall asleep right there, in the middle of the crumbling courtyard. She and Kari were finally able to get him back onto his feet, but he couldn't take even a step unassisted. More worrying than that was the sleep-talk-caliber nonsense that Axel was uttering. The Hiisi was coming. The Hiisi had arrived.

Kari was clearly trying his best not to panic. He didn't have Jaana's or Otso's number programmed into his phone, and when he called Kalle it went straight to voice mail. "Okay," he said. "Okay." He looked as though he might throw up.

"It's all right," Tess said. "It's happened before."

"Okay," Kari said, nodding as though to calm himself down. It seemed to be the only word he had access to, for the moment.

"Where does that path go?" Still steadying her brother with one hand, Tess pointed to a well-kept mulch track that led away from the covered picnic area and disappeared into the spruce wood, white blazes marking the trunks.

"Out to a parking lot, on the main road," Kari said.

"Can we get back to the cottage that way?" Axel was in no shape for a walk, but they couldn't take him back out onto the water in this condition, life jacket or no. Kari's rowboat was out.

"That's not the right direction," he said. Then, turning to the spruces, "We'd have to cut through the woods. It isn't too far, but . . ."

"We've got time. This isn't an emergency." Tess didn't actually believe this until she said it. But somehow hearing the words, even in her own voice, made them true. It wasn't an emergency. This had happened before, she said again, this time to herself. Axel was going to be all right. They each took one of his arms over their shoulders and left the castle ruins behind at a measured pace. Her little brother's sneakers barely grazed the grass underfoot, and his head dipped and lolled.

"Sorry," Axel mumbled. "I'm sorry." He was staring down at his legs, as though trying to will some life back into them. Their doctor back home had described this as "daytime sleepiness" and "fatigue." Their doctor back home had a crap vocabulary.

"Don't be dumb," Tess said.

"Yes. You have no . . ." Kari paused, maybe a little shy about intruding. But this was already so intimate, walking three abreast, arm over arm. He couldn't be in any deeper than this. "Nobody chooses when to get sick."

"Not talking . . . ," Axel said, his voice thick and groggy, "to you."

Tess and Kari exchanged a look. They continued on without saying anything more, under the whorled branches of the spruce forest. Soon enough they caught a glimpse of the Hannula house through the trees ahead and the Kivis' summer cottage well beyond it. Kalle and his friends were all awake by now, framed by a double-paned window, playing one of those video games where you have to actually get up and dance. They were wearing bathing suits and neon wigs, because the world was inexplicable.

Jaana was out on the dock when they reached the cottage, using an old pair of binoculars to scan the pine island, probably wondering why she couldn't see Kari's rowboat. But whatever scolding she'd been cooking up was shelved the moment she noticed the three of them emerging from the trees. Jaana helped them bring Axel inside and interrogated him only very gently about how he felt. Otso, resolute in his belief in the restorative effects of a good steam, rolled himself down the back ramp and went to go add logs to the still-warm woodstove in the sauna. Jaana had baked little blueberry tarts, which they ate silently as they waited for the fire to get going. Tess kept expecting her grandmother to flip, and Jaana kept not-flipping. Perhaps there was an upside to that fine-tuned Finnish pessimism. Expecting the worst all the time made a thing like this seem inconsequential—a reprieve from more awful possibilities.

Axel stayed inside for the rest of the day, tethered by his own exhaustion to the couches and chairs. Tess spent most of the afternoon with him, watching as her brother walked a slow circuit from window to window, wading through the air. But whatever Axel was looking for outside, he wasn't keen to tell her what it was. Moreover, he flat-out refused to talk to her about what had happened at the castle. Tess recognized the word he'd been mumbling—Hiisi—from the folklore that had been a mainstay of their old Finnish lessons.

A *hiisi* was a sort of forest-dwelling demon from pagan times—God, Axel could just as well have been repeating the word "unicorn" or "goblin." But when confronted, her brother pretended not to remember having said it. It wasn't like him at all. Tess could usually count on Axel to be maddeningly chatty—far more likely to overshare than to withhold. Why he would start lying to her now, she had no idea. It made Tess a little angry, actually. They were all each other had left, and *now* Axel was going to start keeping things from her? Well, fine, she thought. If he wants his secrets, then he can keep them.

It took a few days for Axel to get his full strength back, but the time passed quickly for Tess. A lot needed to be done to get the summer place ready for its winter hibernation, and the work fell squarely on her and Jaana. The fireplace had to be scooped of ashes and scrubbed down with a wire brush, the woodstove in the sauna cleaned, the Nordic spruce benches sanded pale. Shoddy shingles on the cottage roof had to be replaced, and the chimney seam needed caulk, to say nothing of the filth-choked gutters. Not that Tess minded any of this. The tasks helped keep her mind off everything that had happened in the last few weeks. Off everything that was *still* happening, because that's what it felt like—a slow, continuous dissolve. Tess's life was falling away piece by piece, the loss somehow bigger every minute she spent with it. Sometimes she'd look up from her work, see her father standing just beyond a scrim of unfamiliar trees, and have to hold fast to the cottage wall, lest she fly away on the breeze. How terrifying it is to know how much you love your parents.

Kari came by every afternoon, dressed in his own overshot approximation of working clothes, eager to do whatever Jaana told him to. Tess found it sort of cute and sad the way Kari followed her grandmother around like a puppy, and she wondered briefly if the Barcelona that his folks were visiting was as imaginary as the Zanzibar where her mom and dad were supposedly sipping umbrella drinks. But Jaana confirmed Kari's story and offered her own typically merciless assessment.

"They'll be in Spain until the day after Christmas," she said. "Lousy people, worse parents."

Like Tess, Jaana seemed happy to be busy. With each job finished—the hillside cellar door replaced, for example—she'd brew a cup of coffee and bask for a moment, sipping and surveying her handiwork. When the cup was drained, it was time to check on the progress Kari and Tess were making and to begin her next task. Otso, on the other hand, was not so pleased. The normally cheerful, bashfully quiet man didn't like their Talvijärvi itinerary one bit. The wheels of his chair cut deep troughs into the lawn as he rolled to and fro, trying and failing to make himself useful. He met every new project that Jaana embarked upon—or set Tess and Kari against—with similar reservations. "This really has to happen now? These outhouse hinges—they're an emergency?"

One morning, during their predawn breakfast, Jaana and Otso had an out-and-out argument about it—the first that Tess had ever witnessed between them. Otso had called the bank in town, trying to arrange for an appraiser to come out and take a look at the property. He held his hand over the receiver to check the suggested times with Jaana, who kept saying: "Nope. Won't work. Inconvenient." Finally, Otso surrendered and hung up the phone.

"Why break your back if you won't even let them look at it?" he said, frustrated.

Jaana stared down at her poached egg. She nicked the yolk, and it bled out slowly over the blue ceramic. "I'm not breaking my back," she said.

Without drawing much attention to himself, Axel slipped away from the breakfast table and hobbled woodenly back to his bedroom. Tess knew that he'd become uncomfortable with their eavesdropping. The truth was that she had, too. But her lie of omission had calcified over the course of the week. And the longer Tess put off admitting that they both understood Finnish, the more impossible it felt.

"That's childish." Otso brought his coffee to his lips, mustache curtaining over the rim. When he spoke again, his voice was soft—too soft. "You know we can't keep it forever."

"I never said forever. But now isn't the time. Not with the kids."

"Now is exactly the time," Otso said. "*Because* of the boy and the girl." It would have been easy enough to use their names, but he clearly didn't want to drop any obvious clues to Tess that she was being discussed. "This is all right for now. I mean, it's wonderful. But in a few weeks the lake will be frozen and the cottage will be colder than an icebox. And we'll be four of us in Helsinki, in a flat with one bedroom. One bathroom. We need the money."

Jaana stood and began to clear the table. She hadn't finished her egg. "You're so rosy, *ukko*. How much do you think we could get for this place? It's not in fashion." Tess guessed from her dismissive tone that this was a reference to the Hannulas' upmarket vacation palace. "Besides, winter isn't the selling season."

"So we'll list it in the spring. We can do one last trip before midsummer, and—"

"I am not trading our summer place for an extra bedroom in Helsinki. We'll get on fine without the office."

"But the office isn't enough for them. You know it isn't, *rakas*. What they need is space."

"What the hell do you call this?"

It was amazing to Tess how utterly in command of her voice Jaana was—a virtuoso soprano of argument. But for the words themselves, they could have been discussing the quality of the marmalade. Jaana crossed from the kitchen to the front door and opened it wide, ostensibly to air out the breakfast smells. Outside there was nothing but trees in front of trees in front of trees. Dawn had come, later than yesterday, earlier than tomorrow.

"It's too much for you. You can't keep it up by yourself." Otso poured his gaze into the well of his coffee cup. No need to actually say: *Because I can't help you.*

Jaana stayed by the open door, her hand on the rough wooden frame. The cottage seemed to expand, full and plump with the morning breeze. "I'm not by myself, *ukko*. She might make a fuss about it, but the girl knows how to use a hammer." She glanced at Tess and quickly switched to English. "What's the matter with you?"

Had her expression been that obvious?

"Nothing," Tess said, pushing herself back from the table and hurrying her plate to the washbasin. Her grandparents' even-toned, incognito argument had all but undone her. Tess was touched, but also so irritated that she felt about as fidgety as her brother. Awful things had happened to her and Axel—she got that. It wasn't fair, but they'd survive. What Tess wasn't sure she could get through, though, was being the awful thing that happened to someone else. Jaana and Otso looked like they'd had a nice thing going. A perfectly manageable little apartment in the city, wheelchair distance from anything they might need. Tess and Axel hadn't asked to be carted off to Finland, but likewise Jaana and Otso certainly hadn't asked to have kids dropped on them out of the dull gray sky. Strange kids on top of that—if Tess was being honest, the fact that they'd never met could just as well have been Sam's fault as theirs. Her grandparents didn't top her list of favorite humans, but she took no pleasure in turning their old, unfamiliar lives upside down.

"Don't go far," Jaana said as Tess passed her,

speed-walking out the open door. "As soon as the light is good, we're going to work on the dock."

It was their last full day at Talvijärvi. Tomorrow they'd catch the train back to Helsinki and begin the process of enrolling in school—a prospect Tess found so unfathomably strange that she saw no point in worrying about it in advance. It was also Halloween. Or at least it would have been, back in Baldwin, but Kari explained that it wasn't a Finnish holiday. He and Kalle knew all about it, though, from the movies. Kalle was even throwing a party for his friends that night. Everybody would dress up in costumes and eat candy and watch slasher films. Tess waited for Kari, all halting and sweat-palmed, to invite her to come. Clearly the boy wanted to, and she'd have said yes. But he never found the guts. Or maybe he wasn't invited, either.

Even with Kari's help, the work on the dock took up the entire day. The first order of business was to look the whole thing over, inspecting bolts for rust, the boards for rot. The slats that Jaana deemed unworthy were pried off their pilings, stripped of nails, and added to the firewood behind the sauna, to be replaced with new ones the color of tanned skin. They scoured baking powder into the wood and rubbed olive oil and vinegar into the stains left by Kalle's idiot friends. But the work wasn't hard enough to keep Tess's mind off Jaana and Otso's fight that morning. Nor did it quiet a buzzing in the back of her mind, something like the bulked-up cousin of déjà vu. Tess was working over a stain at the end of the dock when it hit. She'd been here before. Not just Finland, but *here*.

Tess had long held dear a very particular, very clear memory of splashing in water behind the A-frame. That was impossible, of course. The nearest place to go deeper than your knees was in Mud Lake, where swimming was strictly forbidden. In the summer months, the only time it was warm enough to go for a dip, the shallows thickened into a viscous pudding of duckweed and goose crap. So she always considered it to be a sort of composite memory—splashing around in the Adirondacks and playing in Saara's vegetable garden behind the A-frame. And it would have been a nothing memory, totally insignificant, but for the fact that it was one of only a handful in which her mother made a cameo. Tess could remember a young woman perched on her knees atop a dock. This dock. It wasn't the A-frame; it was the Kivis' summer cottage. Not the Adirondacks, but Talvijärvi.

The thought very nearly made her dizzy.

There was her expired passport, of course, which by now was moldering in some Oswego landfill. But Tess didn't consider those Finnish entry and exit stamps to be proof that she'd ever met the Kivis. She realized, only now, that she'd been choosing to believe that the fight between their families started before she was even born. But she remembered being here, precisely. She remembered her mother on that dock, grinning the way she never did in photographs. If her parents had brought her here, it could only have been to see Jaana and Otso. Had it happened at Talvijärvi, then? Had Tess now arrived at the scene of a family destroying fight? She let her scouring pad drop and turned to face her grandmother.

"Why didn't you tell me that I've been here before?"

"It's all my job, is it? Why didn't you ask?" Jaana was jimmying nails out of a board that looked like it still had a few seasons in it. The wood groaned and popped. "I'm surprised you remember," she said, briefly looking up from her work. "You weren't much more than a toddler."

"You were here, too?"

"Of course I was. And Otso. Your mother, your father. It was here, in Talvijärvi, where the two of them met. Your father had come here to do research for his dissertation." The board came suddenly unstuck, and Jaana fell back on her butt. She'd been pulling too hard. Kari quickly took it from her and retreated to the woodpile behind the sauna. Poor guy—whenever he came over, he got more than he bargained for. "But why would you know any of that?" Jaana said, wiping splinters and grit from her calloused hands. "I don't suppose Sam ever said anything."

"It was all his job, was it?"

"Cute," Jaana said. She retrieved a good board from the stack at the foot of the dock, put some fresh nails into her mouth, and began to hammer it over the gap. Kari should have been back by now. Tess took up her scouring pad again. She could have left things there.

"It isn't my fault that I don't know any of this," she said, working salad dressing into the stain. Soap would have been better, but it was bad for the lake and therefore forbidden. "I know a little, though. I know that you never even called."

"Sam couldn't have been more clear about how he felt," Jaana said. "He didn't want us to have anything to do with you. He stopped us."

"And you let him," Tess said.

She was totally unprepared for how deeply this would cut. The sight of a gouge in Jaana's plated armor was exhilarating, and she regretted it immediately. Still, there was no going back. She kept her attention on the stain, her voice falsely casual. "Blaming my father for everything is just a way for you to let yourself and Otso off the hook."

For a moment she thought that her grandmother might slap her. Jaana leaned forward, as though considering it, but then shifted her weight back onto her haunches and stood. "I don't let anyone off the hook," she said. "Not myself. Not your father. Not even my daughter. Being gone doesn't make either of them guiltless. It just means they aren't around for you to be awful to." Well. That felt enough like a slap. Jaana stooped down to collect her hammer and the spent, useless nails. Out on the pine island the swan let fly a long, quavering call. But it wasn't appropriately poignant or mournful. It sounded like somebody was murdering a clown with a shoehorn.

Jaana disappeared into the cottage without another word. Kari, who'd had the good sense to hide out behind the sauna, slunk back toward the dock. He joined Tess at the end, both of them facing the water.

"I knew your mom and dad weren't in Zanzibar," he said.

Tess didn't know what she expected him to say, but that wasn't it.

"Axel told me a few days ago," he said. "I'm really sorry." He took her hand and held it. It could have seemed creepily opportunistic, but it didn't. It occurred to Tess, suddenly and intensely, that Kari deserved better parents. And a better brother. By every measure, he had more than her—and less.

Tess cried a little then. Kari said nothing. He just held her hand and sat with her. And when she was done, he asked if she wanted to celebrate Halloween.

12

The Castle

Otso had been insistent, back on the day that Tess and Kari brought Axel home from the castle, that the boy join him for a steam. They'd stripped naked together in the little pine sauna, and Otso ladled water over a pile of heated, sizzling stones. It filled the room with steam, dropping a cloak of prickling heat down over their heads. The walls oozed, and the air smoldered in their lungs. "Just breathe," Otso said. He held a whisk of dried birch, which he dipped into a bucket of lake water and then used to strike himself sharply about the shoulders. None of this was even in the running for weirdest thing to happen that day.

Otso's wheelchair sat outside the sauna door, his clothes piled neatly on the seat. Axel's wheelchair was out there as well—though now he finally had a name for the thing. The Hiisi. It had followed them from the castle, beating birds from the bushes, and now it was circling the sauna like a weasel sniffing around a henhouse. It appeared that the Keeper's prediction had held true; the Hiisi was slowly shedding its disguise. The thing had grown bigger than it ever was back home, turning strangely bent and shaggy. The armrests went jointed, jagged—*stretched*. They pulled at the trunks, dragging the Hiisi over log and root as the thing went crawling and rolling, clicking and growling. Axel had been hoping for fantastical, and fantastical had arrived in spades.

Jaana tried to send him straight to bed after the sauna, but Axel resisted. Instead he wandered from window to window, peering out. The Hiisi was still out there, ramming itself into the cottage walls, making framed photographs shake on their nails. But nobody seemed to notice. The thing lingered in the yard for the rest of the afternoon, haunting and hunting. Come nightfall it settled in outside Axel's bedroom, pressing its impossible self up against the glass. Axel watched it from the narrow slab of his mother's bed, never drifting off long enough to dream. But that hardly mattered. His life had all but become one.

It took several days for Axel's strength to

return, and in that time the Hiisi slowly faded into the surrounding woods. But optimist that he was, Axel decided that its sudden appearance could only be a good sign. After all, in Kari's story the Hiisi had been trying to keep poor Väinö away from his wife—away from what Kari had called "the underworld." So if the Hiisi had shown itself at the castle, that must mean that Axel was getting close. And even if the legend of Väinö and Aino were nothing but a fiction, the Hiisi's presence offered a more general hope. Because Axel had come to Talvijärvi to search for his mother's ghost, and when you're looking for a ghost, a *demon* can hardly mean you're on the wrong track—like some kind of paranormal indicator species. Axel's father used to teach a whole unit on indicators, back at the college. Sam could go into maddening detail about the things you could infer from orchids, wild strawberry, or epiphytic lichens—the calling cards of real, ancient woodlands. "Don't worry about missing the forest for the trees," Sam would say. "Because the forest *is* the trees. The forest is the tree. The forest is the branch, and the leaf, and the acorn." When Axel applied this principal to his new magical circumstances, he could only conclude that in a world where the Hiisi existed, his mother could, too.

Axel had plenty of time to mull this over as

he convalesced, stranded in the Kivis' little cottage. The more he thought about it, the more he realized that Talvijärvi also made perfect sense, habitat-wise. This cottage had been in Jaana's family for three generations, and Saara had all but grown up here. What more appropriate place, then, for his mom's bear-shaped ghost to go a'haunting? Sure, Baldwin had been Saara's home too. But she'd lived there for only a few years, and a green card hardly gave her roots. If Saara existed anywhere other than as a pile of bones in the Oakwood Cemetery, she had to exist here, under these old blue spruce trees. Among the rocks and pines of her childhood.

Axel knew that he had no choice but to return to the castle—those ruins were still his best and only lead. He waited as long as he could for his energy to come back, but their impending return to Helsinki forced the issue. He decided to sneak out on their last night at Talvijärvi, the sort of now-or-never moment at the root of most good adventures. And tragedies.

It turned out to be an ideal night for subterfuge—a good chunk of moon swung into the sky, and it gave off such a glow that there was no need for Axel to risk giving himself away with a flashlight. Better yet, Tess had left early for a party at Kari's place and wouldn't be around to catch him sneaking out. Axel waited until after his grandparents' usual bedtime. He dressed quietly, layering sweaters against the dull autumn chill. But as he slipped into the den, he saw that Jaana was still awake, sitting upright on the little sofa. She was crying. Or maybe it would be better described as tearing—her face looked exactly as it always did, only wetter. She hadn't noticed him, so Axel doubled back through the kitchen and slipped out the back door. If Jaana's week of upkeep hadn't included oiling all the hinges, his quest would have ended then and there.

Outside he could hear the breeze in the treetops and faint music coming from the distant party. No creaking wheels, though; no Hiisi. Axel made for the shadows of the birch thicket. His plan was to follow the shoreline past the Hannula house and then cut through the forest toward Erikinlinna. Getting to Kari's was easy enough, thanks to the blazing windows up ahead. Speakers thumped Finnish rap into the forest, and through the windows he could see what appeared to be a Christmas movie playing on the big screen. Or, no—it was definitely a Halloween movie. Santa had a knife, and he was using it.

Axel was just about to cross the gravel drive and slip behind the house when he heard an odd popping sound from the boathouse deck, and something jumped in the brush just behind him. His whole body went stiff. But then somebody on the deck called out: "That's one!" They were all out there, Axel realized. Kalle's friends had lined plastic cider bottles along the railing, and Kalle was taking aim with an air rifle. That jumping sound behind Axel had been a pellet, digging its way into a tree. Axel got down out of the light and the line of fire.

"Schnapps!" a girl on the deck hollered, after Kalle's third miss. It was hard to tell in the gloom, but it looked like her costume was undead Pocahontas. Kalle, who was decked out in a fairly authentic military uniform, obliged her by downing a shot of dark liquid. So it was a drinking game, with weaponry. Splendid.

"How about a turn for jumbo?" Kalle said, his voice sharp and wet after the schnapps. "He's, like, a genius at this." He turned to the far end of the little gathering, where a pair of slightly smaller silhouettes were perched rigidly on deck chairs. This must have been Kari and Tess. Kari seemed reluctant at first, but then a chant of "Jum-BO, Jum-BO" went up among Kalle's friends. He stood, took a few steps forward, and shouldered the air rifle. Axel put his hands over the back of his head, but it was unnecessary. Kari struck down one bottle and the next, until they were all lying label-up in the grass below the deck, urgently bleeding foam. The kids on the deck cheered in a way that didn't seem cheerful, and Kalle offered his brother a victory shot.

"Quit being lame," he said, as Kari tried to hand it back. So Kari drank it. Or at least he pretended to—a lot of it seemed to be pouring down the sides of his face. Axel inchwormed deeper into the woods. Once he was safely consumed by shadow, he stood and made his way around the house. Kari was a nice guy, and he certainly didn't deserve to be humiliated, especially in front of a girl he so obviously had the hots for. But Axel had more important things to worry about tonight.

Now he'd come to the more difficult part. As Axel remembered it, they'd emerged from the spruce wood about a hundred yards down shore of Kari's place. They'd hit the rocky waterline head-on, so his plan was to count out a hundred lunging steps and then turn a sharp right into the forest. This had seemed fairly simple as he'd worked it out in the cottage, but now Axel couldn't count out ten paces before he had to change direction. The lakeshore was totally untended beyond the Hannula property, and the lichen-smeared boulders and dense patches of thorny bramble seemed arranged expressly to block his path. The horizontal corpses of trees bashed flat by summer

actually laughed. Because these were ghosts! This was a haunted wood with swords and battles and shape-shifting local fauna! It was like Axel had been the one to die—died and gone to heaven. Or at least it seemed that way until the Hiisi appeared.

Maybe it had been trailing him the whole time, waiting for the worst possible moment to show itself. The Hiisi nosed out of the trees beside Axel, tattered padding bristling like mange. The magpie didn't like this one bit, and sounded a horrible squawking alarm. "The kid is back!" he screamed. "And Hiisi is with him!"

Whatever these ghosts thought about this demon, it seemed to be enough to unite old foes. Within moments Axel had both sides of this ass-backward battle flying his way with murder in their eyes. The moon peeked out for all of a second, giving him a view of swords and guns, lances and cavalry. Axel turned heel and sprinted. He wondered if, in non-zombie circumstances, dead people could kill or even hurt living ones. The birds were way faster than him, so he figured he'd know soon enough.

The spruces bounced past, and squawking echoed all around. Up ahead Axel saw the house—his disassembled A-frame. But now there was a light in the window, and the front door was open, jagged threads of caution tape dangling loose from the frame. A tall, skinny man stood in the doorway. It could just as well have been Axel's father or Grandpa Paul but for the sound of his voice and the words that he shaped it into.

"Moron!" the Keeper shouted. "Inside!"

Axel made for the open door, feathers brushing his neck and shoulders. Someone pecked him hard on the ear, taking out a little triangle of lobe. Not imaginary—that did *not* feel imaginary. Reaching the door, Axel dove in and rolled over the familiar flooring, crashing into something like a warm shag couch. The Keeper slammed the door shut behind them, bracing his shoulder against it as the birds hurled themselves into the wood.

"Idiot," the Keeper said, fumbling with the dead bolt as he pressed back against the birds. "A whole week I've been waiting, and when you finally show up, you bring these psychopaths with you?"

Funny that he said *I've been waiting* and not *we've been waiting*. Because she was there, too. She was the warm wall of shag that Axel had fallen into. The room was exactly his old living room back home. Except there was no furniture. And where the couch used to be, there was a bear.

13

Boxes from Home

The Halloween party was still going strong when Kari walked Tess out, a little after midnight. He'd put on a brave face all evening, game and passive as his elder brother made him the butt of every joke, but now Kari's demeanor changed. He sat on the bottom step and cleaned his face with the hem of his shirt. He still smelled of the schnapps that Kalle had forced on him—distilled from pine tar. It made Kari's hair stick to his forehead and gave him the unfortunate odor of barbecue sauce. Tess sat down beside him, leaving a very unambiguous chunk of space between them. The last thing she wanted was for her new—and currently her only—friendship to be crushed under the weight of some groping, kissy misunderstanding. To Kari's credit, he didn't make a move, though there was no telling if it was due to wisdom, fear, or the particular funk of the moment.

"You know," Kari said after a long pause. "I don't even think my brother's friends actually *like* him. They're just here for the house." Despite what a jackass his brother had been, Kari seemed to take no pleasure in this thought. It almost sounded like he was sorry for Kalle. Like he thought Kalle deserved better, less-shallow friends.

"Well, it is a pretty nice house," Tess said, half smiling.

Kari snorted. "I prefer yours. I mean the Kivis'."

Neither of them said anything more for a while. The broad gravel drive stretched out at their feet, disappearing into the forest. A small fleet of cars was parked along the drive. Kalle's was at the front—a fat-bottomed pickup truck. It must have been conspicuous as a walrus on the lean Finnish highways.

"How much longer do you have to stay here?" Tess said.

"I don't know. He keeps giving the work crew the day off." Kari glanced at the unfinished wing, beams bright as bone. The work site sprawled, spilling sawdust over the front steps, tarps puckering in the evening breeze. "Maybe a week?"

"Why not call your parents?"

Kari sighed and mumbled something about cell reception and roaming charges, clearly too tired to come up with a more compelling excuse. Or maybe just sick of sticking up for people who seemed not to have earned it.

"Would you like to come back to Helsinki with us?"

"That's nice of you," Kari said. "No. I think I'll stay here. We should—"

There was a weird smacking noise behind them, and they turned to see a shape pressed up against the bright maw of the French doors. It was one of Kalle's friends, writhing and grunting, grinding his hips. "Go for it, Jum-*Bo*!" he stage-whispered. When all they did was stare, he gave up, leaving behind a fuzzy patch where he'd licked the glass. No, whatever Kari might think, Kalle deserved friends no better than this.

"We'll be done soon," Kari went on like nothing had happened. "I can wait." Then, as though these thoughts were somehow connected, he said: "How's Axel?"

"Better," Tess said. "He should be back to normal by tomorrow."

"So he has . . . It's the same as with your grandfather?"

Tess nodded. Though the truth was that she was starting to worry that it could be more than just that. Otso and Axel might have had the same form of dystrophy, but Tess was willing to guess that Otso had never tried speaking to a bird. When she'd confronted Axel about it back at the cottage, he'd pretended not to remember. The kid had straight-up lied to her face. Tess couldn't remember that ever happening before.

Then Kari said something that took her totally by surprise. "You seem like you're a really good sister."

She turned to stare at him. This was embarrassingly, laughably off base. "What are you talking about?"

It obviously wasn't the response that Kari was expecting. "I mean, it must be so hard . . ." He shifted on the step. "Everything you guys . . ." Nope, that wasn't going to work either. Kari knew from her expression that he'd entered a danger zone, and he was searching for a way out. He finally settled for: "I think he's lucky to have you."

Now Tess actually did laugh. After all, she was the sister who'd watched Axel get knocked into the mud at the Battle Re-enactment and still held hands with the douche-bag who did the knocking. She was the sister who was so reluctant to take care of him and so very resentful of her father's expectations on that point that she'd spent the last hour of Sam's life fighting with him. Never mind that lucky *I love you*—it was a fluke, and more than she deserved. Tess was a crap sister, and if Kari weren't so busy trying to flatter his pathetic way to first base, he'd have had the stones to say as much.

"I know Kalle sets the bar pretty low," she said. "But that doesn't mean I'm a good sister."

Kari, bless him, didn't miss a beat. "Don't you talk about my brother," he said. "You don't know anything about Kalle. So shut up about him." They both went silent again, Kari looking a little shocked and terrified by what had just come out of his mouth. He must have thought he'd dashed his chances with her. They were still microscopic, but if anything he'd upped them.

"You're right. Sorry." Tess wanted to apologize before he could, because that would have ruined it. "It's getting late." She stood, brushing sawdust from her pants.

"All right," Kari said. "Cool." His eyes strayed to the hollowed-out new wing, and he kept them there, as though contemplating something pragmatic and work-manly.

Tess just stood there for a moment without moving. "I don't have a phone that works here yet," she said. "Do you have the number for our place in Helsinki?"

"I think so," Kari said.

"Give me a call, then, when you get back."

"Okay," Kari said, all his rejoicing tucked neatly into those two, breathy syllables. "Good night."

Tess set off down the gravel drive without another word, passing Kalle's pickup before cutting around the house, back to the lakeshore. Up ahead the Kivis' cottage windows burned creamily under the lace curtains—no question that Jaana had stayed up to wait for her.

Sam used to wait up for her too. When Tess was younger, he'd been positively delighted by the barefoot, toad-collecting recluse his daughter was turning out to be. Sam had even egged her on, giving Tess the run of the neighborhood and adjacent park by the time she was nine. As long as she passed the winter-jacket test and she didn't have school the next morning, Tess had her father's permission to come and go as she pleased. When she was a kid, that meant hours upon hours in a private little corner of Mud Lake Park. She'd discovered an old stretch of forgotten boardwalk in the hemlock swamp, an oxbow meander that had been bypassed the last time they updated the trail, sitting atop the murk like an anchored raft, secret and hers. From there Tess could spy on turkeys scrambling through the brush, or oblivious joggers from Syracuse on the cleared mulch paths.

Buntings nested overhead during midsummer, and in spring she'd harvest illegal bounties of fiddleheads. The fact that Sam approved of Tess's reasons for staying out after dark—you're looking for a flying squirrel? Well, you'll need a better flashlight than that!—made him overly permissive, even in her estimation. How easy it had been to leverage that accustomed freedom in the service of her own social rehabilitation. She'd set off in her gum boots and overalls, the knapsack slung over her back supposedly filled with binoculars, a Nalgene bottle, and some honey-nut granola, but in actuality stuffed with a complete set of non-moron clothes. Tess dipped into the woods looking like Pippi Longstocking and emerged minutes later as a contemporary human teenager—an unavoidable, essential metamorphosis. One that Axel would go through as well, sooner or later. She hoped.

Tess was nearly at the cottage when she noticed someone standing in the yard, a short ways down from the freestanding sauna. She thought for a moment that it was Jaana, come to pluck her out of the party, but this person was much too small. It was her brother. Axel was fully dressed, his shoes and jeans caked with mud and leaf scraps. As Tess got closer, she saw twigs threading his hair and a big hole torn in his SU sweater.

"Dude. What the hell." Tess turned Axel's shoulders and took his chin in her hand. There was a horizontal branch welt across his cheek, and one of his ears had a small but nasty gash in it. "You've got to be kidding me," she said.

Axel made no response. Tess turned his face to better catch the light from the cottage windows and saw dirt-lined tear streaks running down the perpetual blush of his cheeks. Wherever he'd gone, he'd been crying there. Pretty understandable, all in all.

"Does Jaana know you're not in bed?" Tess asked.

Axel just sort of shrugged. His eyes were big and blank, aimed not at her but at the patch of woods behind her. Keeping her hands on his shoulders, Tess started to lead him back to the cottage door. Sounds from Kalle's party still boomed across the lake. The swan on her island honked back furiously.

"She doesn't give a crap about us," Axel said, addressing not so much his sister as the night itself, the new and puny world. It was a very un-Axel-like thing to say.

"Come on," Tess whispered as they reached the cottage door. "Jaana can be a jerk. But you know she cares about us."

Axel huffed, suddenly put out and fidgety.

"I wasn't talking about Jaana," he said, pulling himself out of his sister's grip. He stepped heavily ahead of her and opened the door, tracking mud into the bright living room. Tess lingered briefly outside before calling after him.

"Who, then?"

But the moment had passed.

Tess could tell that Jaana was livid that Axel had snuck out, but for some reason their grandmother kept it totally buttoned-up. She remained completely silent at breakfast the following morning, glancing at Axel between bites. Tess realized as they ate that her grandmother must have judged Axel to be too fragile to scream at, and for a strange moment she felt almost flattered. Because the old woman never hesitated to come right at Tess, guns blazing. Maybe that meant that Jaana knew she could take it.

They left immediately after breakfast, catching a ride to the station with Kalle. The older boy was clearly hungover, wincing in the sunlight as he helped unload Otso's chair and wheel their luggage up the platform. He was about to make his escape when Jaana collared him, pulling him aside for a little chat. Tess couldn't hear what Jaana was saying, but from the way Kalle was flinching, it looked like she was working some of that anger out of her system. When he finally drove off, Jaana returned to the platform and announced, with no small pleasure, that Kalle was feeling ill. He'd be returning to Helsinki with Kari first thing tomorrow. Tess had already begun to feel a grudging admiration toward her grandmother, and now that feeling seized some major ground. But it didn't advance uncontested—Jaana was exactly the grumpy warrior that Kari needed right now, but she was also the grandma who had chosen to fight not one bit for Tess or Axel.

They arrived in Helsinki to find it gray and overcast, and by the time they piled into the lobby of the Kivis' building, a frigid drizzle was sputtering down. There they bumped into one of Jaana and Otso's neighbors—a man wearing a slicker, a heavy scarf, and a sourpuss face brought on by the bad weather. He greeted the Kivis by name and announced, almost defensively, that he'd been trying to call them all week. He explained that they'd received some packages while they were gone. He hoped they didn't mind, but he'd let the delivery people leave them in the flat. "I tried to call," he said again, as though there were confusion on this point.

"Bad reception at the lake," Jaana said, triumphant. "It's not a problem."

But it turned out that "some" meant *eleven*, and "packages" meant *crates*. Their entire shipment from Baldwin had arrived, well ahead of schedule. The crates filled the living room and kitchen, stacked so densely that there wasn't even space enough to open the door all the way—Jaana and Tess had to slip through the crack and shift some boxes into the bathroom just to get Otso's wheelchair inside. With that done, they gathered in the living room, now a narrow corridor between crates labeled BOOKS and BEDDING and SWORDS(?). Otso's beard fluttered as he huffed and puffed. He'd been right, of course, about the space issue. All four of them fitting into this little flat had been untenable before, but now it was plainly impossible. They could throw out three-quarters of this stuff and still it wouldn't work. But whether or not Jaana was prepared to accept this, Tess wasn't sure.

"Not a word," her grandma said.

No choice but to get started. Axel, who'd been silent as a corpse on the train ride from Talvijärvi, glumly pushed the crate labeled SWORDS(?) into the converted study and began unpacking their dad's blunt armory. Otso set about trying to fold the Fortune book collection into the already sizable Kivi one, layering the titles two deep on the swollen shelves. Jaana and Tess set upon the larger boxes in the kitchen, where her grandmother immediately started a donation pile for redundant mugs, flatware, and linens—sentiment a luxury for people with storage units. When Tess returned to the living room to search for her clothes, she noticed that Otso had gone totally still. He was staring down at Sam's old, leather-bound copy of *Seven Brothers*, in the original Finnish. He set it on the shelf. The next book he pulled out of the crate was a slim little paperback—one of Tove Jansson's illustrated Moomintroll stories, also in Finnish. Tess felt the down on her neck prickling. This had been bound to happen, sooner or later.

"*Rakas . . . ,*" Otso called.

"Can it wait?" came Jaana's voice from the kitchen. When Otso said nothing more, she emerged, one of Sam's frying pans in her hands. "Do you think this would be good for eggs?" she said.

Otso didn't answer. He handed her the Moomin book, glancing sidelong at Tess as he did so. Jaana flipped through the pages and set it on the shelf. She looked into the crate and must have seen that there was a whole set down there—the complete adventures of Moomintroll and his family. Without a word, she and Otso began to go through them. They pulled out an unabridged *Kalevala*. They pulled out Finnish translations of Holdstock, Tolkien, and Lindgren. They pulled out picture dictionaries, grammar readers, and exercise books. Tess and Axel had filled in the blank spaces with careful recitation in number-two pencil—*My mother is from Finland. Finland is in Europe. I live in New York. New York is in America.*

Jaana's calm was worrying. "Do you speak Finnish?" she asked—though her tone, and the fact that she'd said this *in* Finnish, made it not so much a question.

Tess nodded.

Her grandmother was silent for a moment. "Both of you?"

Again Tess nodded.

Jaana's anger, or maybe her embarrassment, made her all but vibrate. "What is wrong with you?" she hissed. "It's a total invasion of our privacy. It's . . . disgusting."

This was, of course, true. But Tess wasn't the type to bring an apology to a knife fight. In this way, she probably took after her grandmother. "It's not my fault if you're ashamed of what we heard. Maybe instead you should be ashamed of what you said." After more than a week of listening to the language, it didn't even feel that strange to be using it.

"And how would you like it if I snuck into your room tonight," Jaana said, taking an almost menacing step forward, "and listened to you and your brother? Or maybe I should have gone to that party with you. You've said nothing about us? Nothing you wouldn't want us to hear?"

"We deserve our confidences as much as you do," Otso said. He sounded severe, and worse, deeply disappointed.

Tess had no answer to this. She let the silence stretch, giving her grandparents a chance to continue. When they didn't, she picked up her box of clothes and retreated to the converted study. Jaana caught her by the wrist as she passed by. "And your accent is *atrocious*," her grandmother said. "You sound like you're speaking Italian." Like Italian was some semiadvanced form of baby jabber.

Jaana discarded Tess's wrist and turned back to the overflowing bookshelf. Tess was a little confused—she'd taken it for granted that this fight, when it came, would be a bloodbath. Certainly she hadn't expected it to end with a little burp of steam and a turning of backs, as it just had. Still, Tess took her time in the shared bedroom, giving her grandparents a chance to cool off. Giving the blood a chance to drain from her cheeks. When she returned to the living room to get another box, she saw that Jaana and Otso were still there, still fussing over the bookshelf. They'd rearranged the spines to give prominent space to

this new Finnish collection, elementary work-
books and all. Otso didn't even try to hide the fact
that his eyes were streaming. He and Jaana looked
so unaccountably proud, so unexpectedly grateful. Tess understood that her father had meant for
this. Whatever had happened between him and
the Kivis, Sam hadn't taught her and Axel Finnish
simply for this little moment of shock. Nor had
he done so to make Jaana and Otso feel lousy for
assuming he wouldn't. He'd taught them Finnish
for the larger moment, in which this smaller one
was set—the kids and their grandparents together
in the first place. He must have planned for this to
happen, must have assumed it would one day. But
what on earth had he been waiting for?

"Dad spoke it too," Tess said.

"Of course he did," Jaana said, turning from
the bookshelf. Her smile was tired, and sad, but
still it was a smile.

The regular work of upkeep had had the effect of
elongating their days at Talvijärvi, but in Helsinki
life sped up again. Now that their grandparents
knew that Tess and Axel had a decent foundation
in Finnish to work with, they moved even faster
to get them enrolled into school. An entrance
exam was scheduled for the following week, and
by Friday Tess and Axel had each been assigned a

tutor to drill their Finnish into better shape. Tess's truce with her grandmother lasted throughout this limbo, and she even gave up on trying to get in touch with Grandpa Paul. Escape didn't just seem unfeasible now. It also seemed like the worse alternative. Besides, Tess hadn't heard a peep out of her grandpa since she'd called him from the marketplace. She wondered if this was calculated on his part—maybe Grandpa Paul was trying to convince her that she'd be better off once she learned not to rely on him for anything. If that was the case, it was working.

Axel's behavior also helped distract them from their smoldering fight. Tess's little brother had gotten over the fatigue that had walloped him in Talvijärvi, but his recovery seemed incomplete. He shuffled along, slack and disinterested, as they toured the halls of what would be his new school. He'd outright laughed when Tess suggested they practice for their placement tests—after all, the only way to exacerbate the already severe social liabilities of the whole new-foreign-orphan thing was to add "dummy held back" to the mix. Grief would have been totally understandable, but this struck Tess as something different—something worse. It was almost as though Axel thought that this imminent new reality didn't apply to him. Like the life taking shape was somehow optional.

But it wasn't until Axel told her about the ghosts in the forest that Tess decided to say something. Honestly, it's not like he gave her much of a choice.

It was Sunday afternoon, and Kari was coming to spend the night. Far from an ideal arrangement, but Kalle needed to make one last trip to Talvijärvi to get the house set for winter, and Jaana had made it clear that taking Kari out of school was no longer an option. Axel made his move about an hour before Kari was set to arrive, yanking Tess into their bedroom, whispering that he had a pressing matter to discuss. She was briefly relieved by the apparent return of her brother's nerdy formality. But everything that came out of his mouth after that straight-up horrified her.

"This is going to sound weird. But the only way I can say it is . . . is just to *say* it. I spoke to Mom. This isn't a joke. I'm not playing. You're going to think it's pretend, but it isn't pretend. I spoke to Mom. To Mom's ghost. She lives at Talvijärvi. Or not, like, *lives*. You know." Axel left it at that for a moment, staring at Tess over the gulf between their beds. "Mom's ghost. That's where she, um, dwells."

As though Tess had somehow missed that crucial bit. "Weird" was a way-insufficient caveat. She was silent for a moment, trying to keep her stare from becoming a glare. "I don't know what I'm supposed to say to that, Axel."

He huffed. "Well, not that. Not anything. Just listen to me, all right?" Axel glanced at the door. "I never expected you to believe me, but you deserve to know. You've seen her, too. She was the bear—the bear that came into our yard on the night Dad died. Remember how we were wondering why no one else saw her? Remember how there was nothing in the papers about it? That's because it wasn't a brown bear. It was *Mom*."

"But another person did see her—her keeper, remember? And also, more importantly, it wasn't Mom. It was a bear. You took a picture of it."

Axel winced, as though this were a wrinkle that he couldn't account for. "That picture," he said. "That's the proof. When I look at that, I see Mom. Not"—he seemed to anticipate that Tess was going to pounce, which she was—"not *metaphorically*, or anything stupid like that. *Mom*. Herself."

"That's not funny, Axel."

"I'm not trying to be," he said. "Also, there wasn't anybody else there. Just the Keeper, and he's not a person. He's something else."

"Okay. Another ghost?" A dumb question, and she felt dumb for asking it.

"Not a ghost, exactly. He's different. What he called himself that night actually fits the best— he's the *Keeper*. But yeah, there are other ghosts. Like heaps of them. He keeps them. He's sort of . . .

I don't know." Axel's stare broke for a moment and drifted, searching. "He's like a shepherd. He helps them when they need help. And do you remember that story Kari told, about the woodsman and his dead wife?"

Tess pursed her lips and gave a little nod. She never should have let them row out to the pine island. Her brother's fantasies didn't need any encouragement.

"The Keeper was in that story!" Axel said. "He was the one who promised to take Väinö into the forest, so he could look for Aino. He's also the one who brought Mom to our house, so she could look for—"

"Hold on a sec." Tess put her hand up in the air. "Just trying to figure out how that works, exactly. Do ghosts fly coach? Or is there like a pet-cargo alternative?" Tess couldn't help the sarcasm, but it was water off a duck's back to Axel. There was no nudging him out of this mania.

"They didn't fly—they don't need to." Axel scooted forward on his bed, just the tips of his sneakers touching the hardwood. "I spoke to them, Tess. I spoke to the Keeper and I spoke to Mom. That's who I was with on the night of the party." Tess remembered Axel standing outside the Kivis' cottage, hair mussed and pants grimy, looking like a shell-shocked urchin. Come to think of it, that was the night he'd fallen into this gloom-funk. "I was with them, but you'll never guess *where* we were." Axel paused, maybe hoping that she'd actually try. But Tess wasn't going to throw so much as a twig on this bonfire.

"We were home," he said. "We were in Baldwin."

Oh. This was, finally, starting to make a little bit of sense. But the fact that it was transparent, fantastical wish fulfillment didn't make what Axel was saying any less distressing. He went on about how he'd stumbled upon the A-frame—as in their actual house, where they used to live, in New York—in the forest behind the Kivis' cottage. That's how their mother's ghost had traveled to America. There was a path running through the spruce trees that could, magically, take you there. A path that stitched the woods of the world together, from the Amazon to Central Park to Talvijärvi. The path was difficult to follow, but if you knew the way, it could take you almost anywhere. The Keeper did know the way, and he'd agreed to bring Saara to Baldwin. "But it wasn't to find us," Axel said, suddenly pulled in and somber. "She was looking for Dad. Mom knew that Dad was going to die, and she wanted to find him—his ghost, I mean. Because this place isn't where he's supposed to wind up." By "this place," Axel was indicating more than just their immediate surroundings. He meant Finland. "Talvijärvi was Mom's home. It's where her heart was. So when she died, she got sent here. But Dad's home is somewhere different, so on the day he died, Mom went out searching for him. But she didn't find him. She still hasn't. And if she can't, they're never going to be able to be together. Mom and Dad will be all alone, stuck in the places they came from. We've got to help them."

That was, apparently, the end of it. Tess took her time. She had a vague sense that a great deal depended on the way she responded to this. Axel had laid his deluded nerd-heart out on the table, and she could either coddle it and hand it back, or she could do what was needed to knock her brother into the land of the fucking big kids. Tess crossed the span of hardwood and joined Axel on his bed. She took his hand in hers, but it didn't have the effortless sincerity of Kari's gesture. She felt like she was onstage for a play, way underprepared.

"I know it's really hard . . ." Sort of a false start.

Axel looked duly skeptical.

"Listen," Tess tried again, "we need to start thinking about this as our life. Dad is gone. Grandpa Paul isn't coming to get us. We aren't going to go back home. This is our home now. The sooner you accept that, the sooner—"

"Were you even listening to me?" Axel pulled his small, sweaty fist out of her grip. "That's not what I'm talking about!"

"It's exactly what you're talking about." Tess had been trying not to get angry with the kid, but maybe anger was in order right about now. This was the exact same crap that their father used to pull. Playing pretend was fine for an afternoon, or a weekend, but it made a lousy lifestyle choice. It was the root cause of the very predicament they found themselves in with the Kivis—Sam had flown them to Battle Re-enactments in Oregon and Maryland, but he'd never flown them here. He'd taught Tess to identify a waxwing by its call but had never let her hear her grandparents' voices over the phone. "You didn't go to our house," she continued, not bothering to blunt the edge of her voice. "And you didn't speak to Mom. Because Mom is dead. Because our house is in New York. And I'm telling you, Axel, next week you're going to be in a new class. You're going to have a chance to make some friends. So you had better quit with this ghost shit before then. I know it isn't fair, but you've gotta grow up a little bit. Actually, more than a little bit."

Axel stood up from the mattress, his expression dead. "I wish I had proof, but I don't," he said. "The Keeper says that the reason you can't see Mom in the picture is because you haven't been on the path. But even if you could see her, I bet you still wouldn't believe me. You'd find a way not to."

"Congratulations!" She felt cruel, but she was getting desperate. "You win that bet. Because there is no proof. Because there are no ghosts. Because *reality*." Tess would have gone on, but Axel had already left the room. She let him escape.

And boy, did he ever. Kalle arrived about a half hour later, parking his pickup in front of the Kivis' condominium to drop Kari off. Tess and Kari had already planned to spend the day in town, which was good, because the last place she wanted to be was stuck in that claustrophobic little flat with her maddeningly weird brother. She and Kari went to the movies to watch Finnish-dubbed superheroes give aliens what for. After that they took one of the trams out to the edge of the blinking city, Kari playing the tour guide. It was already well after dinnertime when Jaana called Kari's phone to say that they'd been gone long enough. They were going to tire Axel out.

"What are you talking about?" Tess said. "Axel isn't with us."

PART THREE
The Path

And he saw the pine-clad mountains,
And the hills with fir trees covered,
But he found no more his homestead,
And the walls he found not standing;
Where the house before was standing,
Rustled now a cherry-thicket,
On the mound were pine trees growing,
Juniper beside the well-spring.

—*KALEVALA*, RUNE XXIX

14

Axel's Escape

Originally, Axel's plan had been to slip away without saying anything to his sister. He'd started packing in the morning, before anybody else was awake, being careful to take only what wouldn't be missed—forgotten tins of sausages and sardines in the back of a cupboard, an old box of rye crackers, two jars of cloudberry preserves. To these he added sweaters and a flashlight, matches and a single fork. Of course, there was also the question of defense; not only from the stalking Hiisi but also the historical grab bag of surly, warlike ghosts. At least in this department Axel was in good shape. Sam's knight-of-the-realm wardrobe included actual steel chain mail, plated with oiled brass. And even though Sam's sword had REPLICA carved into the pommel, it was still exactly what Axel thought a real sword should be: a big-ass metal stick with a pointy end.

He had no doubt that Tess would lose her mind with worry, but he didn't think there was any way to prevent that. After all, his picture of Saara— the only real proof he had—was invisible to her. Without it Tess would never believe the first word of his story, not in a freaking life age of the earth. But Axel began to have second thoughts as his escape drew closer. Maybe he should quit with the assumptions and give his sister the benefit of the doubt. After all, Saara was Tess's mother too. And Sam was her father. That their parents were more than just bones in dirt—and moreover, that they *needed help*—was something Tess deserved to know. Axel decided to give his sister a chance. Maybe she'd surprise him.

Tess so, so didn't surprise him. Axel was on his own. Not that there was anything new about that. He'd been on his own ever since the day his dad died.

Getting his overstuffed backpack downstairs without arousing suspicion was easy enough— Axel volunteered to bring a load of garbage to the chute before the Hannula brothers were due to arrive, and he used that as a chance to stash his backpack behind a potted plant in the lobby.

But the task of sneaking it, and himself, into the back of Kalle's pickup would be considerably more difficult. Everything depended upon how distracted his grandparents were and how long Kalle hung around. But as luck would have it, their reunion was full of commotion. Kalle must have still been smarting from Jaana's talking-to, because he leaped out of the truck and carried his little brother's bag right into the lobby. "Thank you *so much* for taking him," Kalle said, preening before the Kivis, every inch the responsible elder sibling. "I'm *so sorry* for the trouble. Really, I shouldn't be more than a night. Two, at most. Do you have my number? Here. I'll text you."

Idiot. It was no trouble at all for Axel to slip out of the lobby and hoist himself into the truck bed. Kalle had tied a tarp over his gear, and Axel crawled beneath it, lying still. He'd overheard Tess making plans with Kari on the phone and had told Jaana that he meant to tag along with them. It would maybe buy Axel a few hours, and even after his grandparents realized he was missing, there would still be the matter of figuring out where he'd gone. He should have the night, and most of tomorrow, before they worked it out and came roaring up to Talvijärvi. The truck started, and Axel had to restrain himself from hooting. There'd be time to congratulate himself later. In the woods. With his mom.

He still felt dumb for how he'd behaved during their first real meeting. Axel had just been so certain that she'd come for *him*. Because, you know . . . how could she not have? Ever since his father died, his life had been like the depressing first act of a fantasy book. It was ridiculously Rowling or Lewis—hell, even the kids out of *Bedknobs and Broomsticks* were de facto orphans. And when your mom's spirit makes a surprise appearance on the day your dad dies, that kind of invites you to make a certain set of assumptions. Like maybe she's come bearing tidings of comfort—reassurances that things are about to stop sucking and get wonderful. Or even better: She's brought news of some secret, magical heritage, and PS your real, awesome life begins *now*. But when Axel hugged Saara's matted body, the first words out of her mouth weren't even directed at him.

"Get it off me," the bear had said.

The Keeper still had his back braced against the door. A few of the birds were still pecking and hollering outside. "You be nice," he'd said.

"I will not. What is it?" Saara used one of her big, fish-stinking paws to roll Axel away from her. She touched him only gingerly, as though afraid he'd smear.

Then a bar of moonlight came through the window, and for quick moment Axel glimpsed his mother's ponytail, her horn-rimmed glasses, a spray of freckles. He gulped down a breath and held it. This was what Axel had been waiting for his entire life. Everything that came before this moment, the good and the bad—all those autumns at the Annual Battle Re-enactment with his father, all those afternoons getting poked and peered at by a long procession of doctors and specialists— was nothing but a prologue to this exact moment. Axel went to go hug his mother, but the moon had already disappeared and she was suddenly horrible again, all teeth and lips and snout. Tiny eyes.

"We talked about this," the Keeper said. "He's your son."

"This one?" Saara gave a huge, chest-filling sniff, almost enough to change the atmospheric pressure in the room. "Looks weird. Smells weird. Keep it away from me."

The Keeper turned to Axel and smiled lamely. "Sorry. Manners are the second thing to go, after the heartbeat."

Axel had nothing to say to this. He stared at the bear, his mother. His eyes were watering a little bit, but they weren't tears of joy. They were tears of who-knows. Tears of what-the-hell. Really, it shouldn't have been a surprise that his mother didn't recognize him. Their lives had overlapped for all of twenty minutes. But still, hadn't Saara been, like, watching? From up on high, or beyond the veil, or wherever the dead watch the living from? Axel had taken it for granted that his mom would be apprised of current events. He'd been banking on some common ground.

"I think it's probably safe to . . ." The Keeper shifted on the floor, pushed the drapes aside, and peeked out at the yard. A crow collided with the window immediately in front of his face, threading the glass with cracks. "Nope. Perhaps another few minutes."

Saara let out a low, distinctly animal groan. "I'm sick of waiting." Then what could roughly be called an expression passed across her blunt snout. Her small eyes got smaller, and she took a towering step toward Axel. Her wet mouth came much too close. Her teeth were greenish about the middle, black at the roots. "You said this was my son. Sam's son. Maybe it knows where Sam is."

"It doesn't even know where *it* is," the Keeper said.

Saara huffed, blasting a jet of hot air and some flecks of drool across Axel's face. "This was Sam's place," she said, sort of to herself. "I was sure it was his place."

"It could still be," the Keeper said. "Be patient."

"I have been," Saara said. "God, have I been

patient." She took a heavy step toward the front door, floorboards bowing beneath her. "Coming through, old man. I'm going to go check the lake again."

The Keeper glanced once more out the cracked window. "Maybe we should wait until they—"

"Not my problem," Saara said, shoving the Keeper aside with her ox-wide skull and clawing at the handle. When she couldn't open the door by conventional means, she pressed both front paws into it, snapping the frame like soggy cork. And out she went, a big round dent in the night. The Keeper struggled to get the door back on its hinges, and when he couldn't, they retreated to the master bedroom. Axel's bedroom.

"So. Welcome home," the old man said, a little sheepishly.

It was freezing in the bed of Kalle's pickup. Now and again Axel would fold back the corner of the tarp, to track their progress. Residential rooftops took the place of city buildings, which were in turn swapped out for naked oaks and frizzy pines. The road became mostly empty, except for the Hiisi, which had been trailing them since Helsinki.

"The old killjoy is nothing if not single-minded," the Keeper had said. He'd lingered with Axel after Saara left, their voices echoing through the shell of the empty A-frame. The Keeper had explained about the ghosts—how they're all knit to the places where they come from. How even if someone dies halfway across the world, she'll still wind up haunting her true home. That's why Saara was in Talvijärvi and why Sam wasn't. It was also why the castle at Erikinlinna had been stuffed to the gills with long-dead Finns from across the centuries. "The dead come down like snow in the forest," the Keeper had said. "Layer after layer. Everybody in their place."

Despite everything Axel had just been through—setting aside, even, the fact that his earlobe was still throbbing from where one of those undead-soldier birds had pecked at it—he'd found this last bit tough to swallow. Because weren't ghosts supposed to be a special case? Wasn't haunting an activity reserved for melancholy people who had dramatic personal issues to resolve before they could trot off into the great-white-peaceful beyond? But not so, explained the Keeper. The woods *were* the beyond. "Most of the dead are restful," the Keeper said, "and that makes them tough to find. But it doesn't mean they aren't there. The dead are always there."

More interesting than any of this was what the old man had told Axel about the path—a hidden track that ran from one haunted wood to the next. The path was how the Keeper and Saara had traveled to Baldwin in the first place. Axel had accidentally stumbled upon it as he'd searched for the castle and had taken a short walk to America. "That's why the Hiisi is after you," the Keeper said. "Hiisi is *of* the path. It keeps order in the worlds of the dead."

"But it's been following me since summer," Axel said. "Before I ever came to Finland. Months before my father died."

"I wouldn't be surprised if the Hiisi has been trailing you for even longer than that," the Keeper said. "On the first night I met you, I could tell that you already had a foot on the path. That's how you were able to find it so easily. That's why you can see your mother in that picture. I'm not sure if this is because of what happened to Saara when you were born, or because of your . . ." The old man nodded limply, seeming to indicate the entirety of Axel's puniness. "You know. Your *affliction*. Whatever it is that's going to someday kill you." Wow. No tact there. Axel found this strangely pleasing. "But you're not dead yet, and you have no business walking the path. You're disturbing the Hiisi's order—upsetting the balance. The Hiisi feels it keenly that you don't belong. It will do whatever it can to be rid of you."

Axel had almost snorted at this last bit. Not

belonging was the story of his life. "So am I just stuck with it?" he said. "Is the Hiisi going to follow me forever?"

"Heaven forbid!" the Keeper said, placing his mangled left hand on Axel's shoulder, a gesture that was in no way comforting. "If you want the Hiisi to stop, your choices are simple. You can leave the path and go back to, you know, whatever it was you were planning to do with the rest of your life. Or you can just *start belonging*."

"Start belonging?" No one had ever told Axel it was that simple.

The Keeper smiled wide, his awful teeth abuzz. "Fake it, son. The only way to really fit in anywhere is simply to decide that you do. Right now you're upsetting the balance." The Keeper gripped down harder on Axel's shoulder, swaying him forward and back. "But if you can get *both* feet on the path, if you really commit to staying here with your mother and father, then the Hiisi will have no choice but to leave you alone."

"That's it?" Axel said, sort of surprised.

"Oh, I'm sorry." The Keeper scowled down at him. "Did I make that sound easy?"

Now Axel held the tarp over his head and scooted back to the tailgate to get a better view of the Hiisi. It still looked more or less like a wheelchair, but it had lost almost all of its padding, like a bird in molt. The tires were nothing but dented metal rims, toothed with jagged spokes. And the armrests—more like arms now—were twice as long as they should have been, spattered with blood, tufted with sprigs of feather and giblet. There seemed to be a light coming from inside the Hiisi—an electric glow pouring from the gap between the seat and the backrest. It looked kind of like a mouth. The Hiisi matched their speed, cruising at just about sixty miles an hour.

Axel locked his gaze on it and did his best to sort of think in its direction. *Go away,* he thought. *Go away, go away, go away. I am where I'm supposed to be. I am of the path.* When that didn't work, Axel tried saying it aloud. "Leave me alone," he whispered. "I'm going to go find my mother and father, and there's nothing you can do to stop me." The Hiisi rolled on, undeterred. There was a bend in the road, and it turned right after them, going up for a moment on one wheel. Axel decided to stick with what worked. Kalle had brought along a cooler of beer, and he reached back to tip it open and pull out a hefty tallboy can. Then Axel popped above the tailgate, took aim, and threw. The can hit the Hiisi right in the middle of its tatty backrest, flipping the thing. It skidded along the road, hit the embankment, and tumbled into the woods.

"Keep coming," Axel said, "and I'll keep knocking you over."

It was dark by the time they finally left the highway. A big swing gate spanned the gravel drive to the Hannula property, a mile or so away from the lakeshore. The pickup stopped, and Axel felt the shocks stretch as Kalle got out. He could hear the slushy crunch of footsteps across the gravel, followed by the long complaint of metal hinges. As the gate swung noisily open, Axel tossed himself and his gear over the tailgate. He crouched upon the drive, bathed in the red brake lights, while Kalle returned to the pickup. Then, as it pulled away, Axel slipped into the trees.

To have made it this far was already a great sign. The fact that Kalle hadn't received any frantic calls from Helsinki meant that Axel's family still didn't realize he was missing. He'd lie low in the cottage tonight, and as soon as it was light, he'd find the path and follow it back to Baldwin, all the way back to America and his mom. Really, he ought never to have let her leave in the first place. When Saara stalked out of the A-frame, Axel should have gone right with her. But instead he'd just lain there, all weepy and sorry for himself. Mommy hadn't come to rescue him. And also: Mommy was kind of terrifying.

Big deal. She needed help, and so did his dad. Axel wasn't about to give up on either of them.

He traced his way back up the gravel drive, to where it met the dirt branch off for the Kivis' property. He hadn't brought the key for the cottage—slipping it off Jaana's ring would have been a dead giveaway—but Otso kept a spare in the padlocked hillside cellar. Axel wedged the tip of Sam's sword under the latch and leaned his shoulder into the hobbity door. It gave way without objection, and a minute later Axel had recovered the spare key and unlocked the Kivis' darkened summer place. It was just about as cold inside as it had been in the woods, but he'd have to do without a fire tonight. Smoke or lights would have been plainly visible from the Hannula house.

Axel ate his tinned sardines atop one of the rye crisps and then climbed into bed under a steep drift of blankets. He slept deeply, waking up only once to the feel of rough shag on his cheeks. The curled heft of a brown bear, beside him in the bed. But no, it was only a dream. Which, at this point, made it as real as just about anything else.

Axel's first thought when he woke up was that it was unreasonably, unacceptably cold. In the hours since he'd fallen asleep—how many, he couldn't tell, but it was still dark inside the cottage—every bit of heat had drifted away, vented through cracks in the walls, sucked down whole by Talvijärvi. His knees shot up to his chest, and he had to clench his jaw to keep his teeth from chattering. It was then that Axel had his second thought of the day; it wasn't just too cold, but it was also too *noisy*. There was a faint banging, a metallic jostling, coming from the back door. That must have been what woke him up—the sound of something trying to get in.

Axel's hope that it might be Saara lasted only briefly—if his mother's ghost wanted *in*, then *in* is where she would have been, the door flat beneath her paws like a splintery welcome mat. And besides, he was pretty sure he'd be able to smell her, even through the walls. The jostling stopped, and then Axel heard footsteps. They landed with a strange foamy squeak, tapping out a path around the cottage, toward the front door. That ruled out the Hiisi. After a moment of silence, the banging recommenced—first a few noncommittal knocks and then more vague fumbling. The door puckered as whoever was out there pushed on it. Thank goodness Axel had thought to turn the dead bolt before going to sleep.

"No, ma'am," came a muffled voice from outside. "It's still locked." It was Kalle. The fact that Axel had heard only one set of footsteps meant

Kalle must be on the phone—no doubt talking to Jaana, seething in Helsinki. He could only imagine how pissed his grandmother was. There was a long pause as Kalle listened to whatever Jaana had to say. "It really doesn't look like it," he said finally. "But I'll check."

Kalle's steps continued a little farther, followed by the squeal of a glove against glass. That's why it was so dark in the cottage, Axel realized, not to mention so ungodly cold. An early snowfall had blanketed Talvijärvi overnight, crusting the windows. Fuzzy light began to leak into the entryway, that particular blue of predawn, enhanced and reflected by the snow. A moment later the soft glow was sliced open by a yellow flashlight beam. Axel could make out Kalle's dark head pressed up against the window as he searched inside. From that angle, Kalle could see half of the living room and straight into the kitchen. But from the next window he'd have a direct view of Axel, freezing and pathetic. Axel waited until the beam shut off. Then he shimmied silently to the far side of the bed and rolled off the edge, clutching all the blankets to his chest as he did so, stripping the mattress bare. Kalle scraped the snow from the second window and raked the mattress with light. Then he switched his flashlight off.

"It's totally empty," Kalle said—Jaana must

have been holding this whole time. "And it doesn't look like anyone's been here since you left. Are you sure you shouldn't check with . . . No? Of course. I understand." Kalle was quiet for a while, kicking his boots against the back wall, maybe loosing ice from the treads. "That makes sense to me," he said. "I have to go into town. The contractors are having trouble getting out with the snow, so I promised I'd give them a ride. But while I'm out there, I'll ask if anybody has seen him. It could be he slipped——" Another long pause. "Yes, but really, Mrs. Kivi, I'm sure I would have noticed. He must be in the city. Yes. Absolutely. I'll speak to you soon. You gigantic thunder bitch. Why don't you go make yourself a pain in somebody else's ass for a change?"

Jaana must have already hung up, because there was no way Kalle had the guts for that. He tramped off noisily, muttering. Axel waited for the sound to fade before getting up off the floor and peeking through one of the cleared windows. Dawn still seemed a little ways off, but the confluence of moonlight and snowlight gave him a clear view of the unfolding shoreline. A quilt of fresh powder hung heavy over the sauna roof and gathered in aquamarine clumps over the rocks at water's edge. The snow had given flesh to the nude birch trees, and the spruces held massive handfuls of it aloft, as though offering to return it to the sky. The scene was totally beautiful and an absolute freaking disaster. This was no dainty autumn dusting; this was a full-on, upstate-caliber dump. The snow wouldn't just slow Axel down—not to mention potentially freeze his toes off as it trickled into his sneakers—it would also betray him. There was no way to go outside without leaving a set of way-conspicuous tracks. He might as well post signs: *This way to the runaway!*

Axel's breath fogged the inside of the window and crusted to frost. He gathered the blankets tightly around his shoulders, waiting for Kalle to disappear. Before long he could see the faint burn of headlamps through the trees, followed by the rasping protest of a plow on gravel. Kalle should be gone for a few hours, and Axel figured he had time enough for a quick breakfast before setting out. But when he unzipped his backpack, all he found was a mess of glass and petrified orange froth. The two jars of cloudberry preserves that he'd swiped from Jaana and Otso's pantry had frozen overnight and burst. Worse, he'd placed them right next to the open box of rye crisps, which had made a catcher's mitt for the glass shards and frozen berries. Axel had polished off the sardines the night before, so all that remained were a few tins of sausages. The cans looked bloated as a dead fish, frozen as well. The idea of reconstituted meat-sicle was fairly revolting, but Axel was starving. He pried at the pull top of one of the cans and gave the contents a lick.

Okay, maybe he wasn't technically starving.

Still wrapped in his blankets, Axel waddled over to the front door, turning the dead bolt and cracking it open. It was quiet outside, save the ruffle of spruces, the dusty thud of snow clods loosed from their branches by the breeze. Standing there, looking out at the frozen world, Axel very nearly lost his nerve. But this was probably due to the cold and his empty stomach—both things that he could fix, at least in the near term. He slipped on his shoes and headed out to the woodpile, tapping the logs clean of powder against the sauna wall and hauling them back into the cottage. There was an iron lever jutting out of the brickwork above the fireplace, and Axel pulled it wide to open up the flue. A few minutes later he was warming his hands before a perfect little fire. He set the open tin of sausages in the crook between two logs. It very quickly went from looking foul to smelling awesome, the sauce liquefying and bubbling about the rims. Axel set his canteen kitty-corner to the fire as well. Tea or warm mead would have been more fitting, but some hot water would do just fine.

It took Axel a little while to realize that something was wrong. The sausages were partly to blame—he picked them out as they thawed, using a fork to pluck them from the bubbling sauce. Under any other circumstances they would have tasted gross, but on that cold morning they had him nearly grunting with pleasure. But after a while the smell of smoke became too much to ignore. Axel glanced up and saw it thickly pooled about the ceiling. "Oh hell," he said, sort of matter-of-factly. He jimmied the flue lever to make sure it had gone all the way. He closed it and opened it again. The smoke was coming down quickly now, passing the windowsills, like floodwater in reverse. So much for being warm. Axel opened the door again and charged outside, coughing. The powdery snow turned to slush in his hands and sizzled into a sooty mud as he dumped it atop his proud little fire. It took four trips in and out to quench the thing and another twenty minutes of flapping the door open and shut to air out the smoke. It was when Axel was out there, watching the oily curls disappear into the lightening sky, that he realized his mistake. The chimney lid was still on, topped by a neat, triangular dunce cap of snow.

"Stupid," Axel said. "Get on with it."

Axel hoped he wouldn't run into any of the battling ghosts that he'd seen at the castle, but just to be on the safe side, he decided to put on his father's chain mail before setting out. He slipped the jangling thing over his layered sweaters, nearly falling over in the process. The chain mail was absurdly heavy, but Axel though it a reasonable burden to bear, given all the ghost arrows and musket balls that had whizzed by him the last time he was in these haunted woods. Then he left the key in the cottage door and stepped out into the cold.

It was slow going. The snow reached his knees as he passed the freestanding sauna, and his chain mail threatened to tip him over with each lunging step. The Hannula place was quiet up ahead, nothing more than the plowed drive to indicate that anybody had been there since the night of the party. As Axel got closer, he could see that Halloween decorations were still pasted on the windows—cardboard skeletons dancing across the glass. He cut behind the house, slipping between the posts that supported the boathouse deck. Axel had been here just over a week ago, but in that short time the shallows had already frozen over. The far shore was so snowbound that it looked like a bank of cloud, and the only real color to be seen was the orange of the stunted pines on their island. And the light green of the lady's nightdress. Because there was a lady on the island.

She was completely still, standing exactly between the two pines. It was hard to be sure at this distance, but it looked like she was barefoot. She had a lot of hair, half of it piled in a loose bun atop her head, the rest standing at ends in a wiry haze. She was staring at him.

Axel had to take a moment. The sun was burning through the trees at the southeast end of the lake, looking like the beginnings of a forest fire, but the moon was still out. It surrendered the far horizon, pierced by the crowns of spruce trees. And it was the moonlight that must have been revealing the swan—revealing the *ghost*—for who she really was. It was Aino, the lady Kari had told him about. The one whose laminated picture hung in the picnic area outside the ruined castle—Talvijärvi's local legend. Axel realized that in all the commotion back at the A-frame, he'd completely forgotten to ask the Keeper about her. More important, he'd forgotten to ask about Väinö, the grief-sick husband who had set out to find her. The one who froze to death inside the castle. Did that mean that Väinö had failed? Or, worse, did it mean that he'd succeeded? Probably not, Axel decided, because Aino certainly looked like she was alone. In another minute or two the moon would die, and she'd go back to being a swan, roosting on an island of fish bones and her own droppings. Axel suddenly felt very sorry for this lady. It seemed like a bummer of an afterlife.

Aino kept staring as he continued along the shoreline, and just as he was about to turn into the trees, she raised her hand and waved. Not really knowing what else to do, Axel waved back. *Hi there, dead lady*. She went still for a moment, her arm suspended aloft as though held taut by a string. Then her hand started moving again, not side to side, but back and forth. A clumsy, beckoning gesture. The woman took a step forward, lifting a naked foot out of the snow. Her voice glided across the ice, high-pitched and hollow. "Come here," she was saying.

Oh, hell no. Axel's mom was scary enough, and that was his *mom*. He felt sorry for this Aino lady, stuck all alone on that speck of an island, in this frozen nowhere. But her problems were her own, and he certainly wasn't about to take up any side quests. Axel started to back into the trees. Aino took another step toward him, and another, and before Axel realized what was happening, this half-naked lady with cue-ball eyes and electrified hair was flat-out sprinting across the ice. She was waving her skinny arms over her head, shouting: "Come here! Come *here*!" Axel felt like he couldn't move, as though the weight of his chain mail had suddenly quadrupled. He groped at his sides for the handle of Sam's sword, but before he could pull it out, Aino disappeared with a wet, reverberating *crunch*.

The dead woman had fallen neatly through the ice, like a nail hammered home in one strike.

Axel ran into the woods. The snow was shallower in there, under the dense canopy of needles, and he was able to pick up some speed. The chain mail bounced across his shoulders, sounding like a rattling jar of pennies. Up ahead there was a fallen tree, and with some difficulty Axel hoisted his heavy metal self over it, squatting for cover on the opposite side. He stayed there for a few minutes, hacking for breath and sweating under the weight of the mail. He strained his ears for any sign that the madwoman might still be chasing him. All he heard was the breeze and the occasional call of songbirds in the treetops. He peeked back over the log and saw nothing but his own scrambling footprints.

When Axel was finally sure that he was alone, he pressed the tip of his sword into the ground like a walking stick and hoisted himself to his feet. But no sooner had he gotten vertical than something struck him, hard, in the middle of his back. Axel dropped his sword and pitched face-first into the snow. He tried to get up but found he couldn't, the mail a leaden blanket over his back.

"This is you, about to die." Even though he couldn't see him, Axel recognized the Keeper's voice immediately. He heard the grating squeak of gum boots on the snow and felt a sudden closeness beside his ear. The old man's breath stank of tobacco and pine.

"And this is me," the Keeper said, "eating your idiot face."

"You didn't have to hit me," Axel said, still trying to lift himself up. He felt like an overturned turtle. Man, was it embarrassing.

"I suppose I didn't, no," the Keeper said. He watched Axel writhe for another moment before reaching down to help him. Then, once Axel was upright, the old man stripped the chain mail off him and flung it overhand into the woods. "But I could hardly have made my point any better. If the dead want to hurt you, they'll hurt you, metal pajamas or no. Running away is usually going to be your best bet."

"But why would Aino want to hurt me?" Axel said, rubbing his still-sore back with his fist. The Keeper had gotten him square between the shoulder blades with the head of his walking stick.

"Why would I know what she wants?" the old man said. "All I could tell you about Aino is that she's lonely and crazy and mean as hell." The

Keeper's eyebrows arched up slightly. "Tell me . . . how do you know her name, exactly?"

"Our neighbor told us about her," Axel said. "And besides, her story is pasted up in front of the castle." He went to retrieve his father's sword from the snow. "And speaking of that, I need to talk to you about her husband, Väinö."

For a moment it seemed like the Keeper was about to drop his walking stick. Though Axel couldn't tell what was so surprising. "What about him?" the Keeper said.

"For starters, what happened to him? I know that you're that man in the castle. I know that you promised to bring him to Aino and that the Hiisi was trying to stop him. And I know that the spring after he disappeared, they found his body in Erikinlinna."

For a brief but unmistakable moment, a look of relief flooded across the Keeper's broad face. He swung his leg over the fallen tree trunk and sat, knock-kneed as a cartoon cricket. "You know, I offered that coward everything he wanted," the Keeper said. "It isn't my fault that he couldn't cope. Drunks ooze nothing more than doubt and fear, and our dear Hiisi gorged upon this."

"Did the Hiisi kill him?" Axel said.

"Hardly!" The Keeper snorted. "That isn't the Hiisi's style. Remember that the Hiisi keeps order on the path and in the worlds of the dead. It wanted Väinö to *leave*, but killing him would have been as good as a permanent invitation to *stay*. All it did was frighten him." The old man removed his hat, casually dusting the snow off it. There were still flowers in the band, but they were limp and shriveled. "The Hiisi got so very big and terrifying that it scared Väinö off the path entirely. He must have decided to find his dead wife the old-fashioned way. Drinking himself silly and falling asleep in the snow. That'll do it every time. As I said, he was a coward, through and through."

The Keeper put his hat back on, obscuring his rigid lick of red hair. Then he braced his elbows on his knees and rested his chin in the nest of his eight fingers. "This is why you went through all the trouble to sneak up here, I suppose. Burning questions about a pair of country Finns, dead sixty years now? I can't say I see the appeal, but go ahead. Fire away. Would you like to know who attended their funerals?"

Axel hesitated for a moment. It seemed there was something more to this, but what it was he couldn't quite say. Whatever—it couldn't have been as important as Saara. "My mother," Axel said. "Is she still on the path?"

The Keeper extended his arms out, gesturing

at the trees all around them. "I'm afraid so. The hunt is fruitless, but it continues all the same."

"You need to bring me to her," Axel said.

"I do, do I?" The Keeper cocked his head and squinted. "But if I remember correctly, the last time you had a chance to be with Saara, you elected instead to mope. You were so sad that she hadn't come to rescue you from your mundane little orphan drama that you walked right out on her."

"I know that, but—"

"Tut-tut-tut," the Keeper cut him off. "It gives me no pleasure to say this, but your last chance was exactly one chance ago. And anyhow, it's not your decision anymore. They've already come to take you away."

For a moment Axel had zero idea who *they* could have been.

"Jaana," the Keeper said. "Tess too. You running off really upset them. I'm sure they'll want you to speak with someone. There are specialists, you know, to deal with ruined children. It might be good for you—"

"How do you know?" Axel interrupted. He'd begun to get the distinct sense that this was all nothing but a preamble—that the old man just wanted him to twist a bit. It was plain enough to see that the Keeper was, in fact, delighted that Axel had come back.

"Because I have eyes," the Keeper said. "They're just down the path." He pointed with his mangled hand. At first Axel couldn't see anything in the trees, but he did detect a faint sound—a sort of whining grumble. As the sound grew louder, the spruces seemed to thrum with it. Their trunks began to bend. To shimmer and curl, the way the city park had on that day back at the harbor market. And then, quite suddenly, Axel could see the Kivis' summer place. It wasn't that anything had moved—he hadn't, and the cottage sure as hell hadn't. But nevertheless, there it was, not thirty yards away, through a stretch of airy woodland. The sound was coming from a snowmobile idling out front, hopping and gurgling. The cottage door was wide open, and after a moment Tess appeared on the threshold. "He's been here!" she called to Jaana, who was down on her hands and knees in the snow, scrutinizing footprints. They must have already been well on their way when Jaana called Kalle that morning. Axel had hoped to have most of the daylight, but with that snowmobile and his tracks, he probably didn't have twenty minutes.

Then, as though to prove this wasn't simply a hallucination, Tess noticed him. She'd been scanning the trees and her eyes passed over Axel once before actually processing the fact that he was there. "Hey," she said, her voice momentarily flattened by surprise. "Hey!" louder now. Tess raced down the front steps of the cottage and into the woods. But the deeper she went, the more it seemed like she was running *away* from him. The spruce wood folded in upon itself, the trunks rolling over and under one another, obscuring Axel's view of his sister and the Kivis' cottage. Making them far again.

"Not to worry," the Keeper said with grim cheer. "They should be here soon enough. Perhaps they'll make you some cocoa."

Axel had run fresh out of patience with the old man's garbage. "Are you going to show me the way, or do I have to find it myself?"

The Keeper smiled, displaying those horrible rows of urgent teeth. "You should leave that toy behind," he said. "It'll only slow you down." He reached for Sam's sword, meaning to throw it away as he had the chain mail. Axel's body stepped back without his mind telling it to.

"You're not touching it," he said, lifting the point to the Keeper's belly.

"Really, now?" The Keeper cocked his head and took a full step forward. To Axel's horror, the sword sank deep into the old man's stomach, pushing all the way through and tenting the back of his duster where it came out on the other side. It shouldn't have done that—replicas are way too blunt. But it was as though the Keeper were made of soft cheese. "You can't scare a dog with threats of dinner," he said, unsticking himself. "Hang on to it if you want, but it isn't my problem if you can't keep up. I don't wait for stragglers."

And off the Keeper went, deeper into the woods, in search of the path. Axel stood there for a moment, staring down at his father's sword. The dull blade was coated in something dark, but it wasn't blood. It wasn't even a liquid. It was ash— tiny little grains that still smelled vaguely of old fires. The fine ash began to fly from the blade, scattered by the breeze, freckling the surface of the snow.

Axel wasn't a straggler. He could keep up with this.

15

The Blazes

Despite his warnings against falling behind, the Keeper didn't exactly rush. A thin stream of ash poured out of his wound, tracing a dark line across the snow. He hardly seemed to notice. The Keeper puttered, glancing about absently, scanning the roof of blue spruce above their heads. At one point he squatted down to brush away some snow, plucking a little green tendril from the earth below—some kind of vetch or herb. The Keeper brought the frost-wilted thing up to his nose for a sniff and then put it into his mouth, working it over with his tongue. Then he spat it out, mumbling. He reached into his quilt-patched duster and pulled out his long-stemmed pipe, pausing to pack the bowl with tobacco, patting himself down for matches. In the distance, they could hear the gathering hum of the snowmobile.

Axel didn't want to push—he was still spooked by the way the Keeper had impaled himself, by the way he'd seemed almost to enjoy the rush of dull metal into his amazingly soft guts—but this was getting ridiculous. Jaana and Tess would be here any minute. "What are you waiting for?" he said.

"Not waiting," the Keeper said. He got his pipe going, souring the air with a thin veil of smoke. "*Looking*. There should be a blaze nearby, it seems to me." He grabbed at one of the lolling branches above and pulled it down for inspection, loosing a small cascade of snow over Axel's head. The Keeper released the branch after plucking off a few needles, allowing it to spring back into the understory.

"What do you mean a blaze? Like a trail blaze?" Axel shook the snow out of his collar, briefly picturing the color-coordinated paint splashes that marked the paths in Mud Lake Park. Surely the way through the underworld couldn't be marked for tourists.

"In a manner of speaking," the Keeper said.

The soft roar of the snowmobile was growing louder, and Axel heard a voice calling his name. It was Tess. "You mean you don't remember the way?"

"There is no remembering the way," the Keeper said with an exasperated show of thinning patience. He took another branch in hand and shook it clean. "Because the way isn't set. Because the woods of the world are a tangle, and the path is just as . . . tangled." The Keeper squinted—that word, "tangled," seemed to be the best he could do on short notice. "Think of woods as water—as an ocean. With all its tides and currents, surges and waves. There are different oceans, but there's also only one. It's all the same ocean. And it's all the same wood. The path can take us from one part of it to another, but it changes every time the woods do. Which means that the path is different today than it was when you accidentally stumbled onto it last week. It's different at this moment than it was when I first said the word 'moment.'" The Keeper paused to scrutinize this second branch, plucking away another tuft of needles. But for the pitchy undercurrent of menace coursing beneath the old man's voice, Axel could just as well have been listening to his own father. "The map is in the details, and details always change." The Keeper turned on Axel, a disquieting smile peeking out behind his pipe stem. He squatted down and held out his hands, revealing the little stack of needles in each palm.

"Which way home?" he said.

It struck Axel right off that the two piles were not identical. The needles in the Keeper's mangled left hand were a rich, deep green, thick and square-shaped about the middle. It was the same Norway spruce that Axel had been wandering beneath since daybreak. But the needles in the Keeper's right hand were totally different— lighter, flat, and faintly jagged. Canadian hemlock, the trees that clustered in thick hollows back in Baldwin. The trees that towered and pitched over the shore at Mud Lake; the trees his father used to lurk beneath, looking for woodpeckers and owls. God, how perfect was that? Sam had taught him this, and now Axel would use it to find him. He pointed at the hemlock.

The Keeper dropped the needles and brushed his palms clean. He took his pipe from his mouth and smacked his lips, as though savoring the rancid flavor. "Onward, then," he said.

After they found that first blaze, the rest became more obvious. They passed a silvery set of ghost pipes peeking out of the ground like reverse icicles. They rushed under a quaking aspen, what few leaves it still had all spinning in the breeze. Up ahead the snow dispersed and then disappeared. Familiar birds began to flit here and there, cackling in the wavering trees—the birds of home. Blue jays and siskins, purple finches and

American robins. There was a strange darkness up ahead, a deepening smudge of gloom—like night was a place you could walk to. But the Keeper explained that it was nothing to be afraid of. The sun just hadn't risen yet in New York.

They'd gone no more than half a mile, but here they were. Home. Axel and the Keeper emerged from the woods, coming out into a grassy clearing ringed with pine and sugar maple. The moon dominated a cloudless night, and the stars were thick as buckshot on the rims of the sky. It was absolutely silent, Tess and Jaana's calls crushed under an ocean of distance. Axel knew this place—it was one of the meadows at Mud Lake Park, a spot that just some weeks ago had been filled with the striped tents of the Medieval Society. The moonlight was bright enough that Axel could even see where the grass had been worn away under horse hooves. This was the jousting field. Sam had ridden here, in the hours before he died. Pretending to fight, pretending to win.

Axel took a step into the field but was stopped by the Keeper's hand clamping firmly on his shoulder. "Maybe we'd better go around," the old man said, eyes darting across the overgrown heaps of toppled grass. Axel had never heard anything like that in his voice before—it sounded like actual concern. He followed the Keeper's gaze and saw them. Six, seven, more than a dozen corpses were sprawled across the dark. Their hands emerged here and there from the spume of wilting vegetation. Axel could see upturned feet and bent elbows, petrified postures of agony and rest. For an odd moment it seemed like they could be performers from the Battle Re-enactment. Most wore layered leather, fur caps, and outdoorsy beards, like a convention of Davy Crockett impersonators. A few of them were still clutching muskets in their dead fingers. Among these frontier types, there was also a man in a fancy military uniform, his white overcoat stained with dirt and blood. This soldier had been run through with a cavalry sword, and his toppled tricorn hat covered his face. The rest of the dead seemed to have stocky reeds growing out of their chests and necks and stomachs, all fluffy at the tip. The tail ends of arrows.

"It's been a bad year for the dead," a strangely familiar voice said. "A bad few decades, actually."

Axel turned and saw a shape emerging from the shadows, round and pinkish. It was a woman wearing a cotton robe, plaid pajama bottoms, and a tattered set of fuzzy bunny slippers. Her hair was combed and sprayed, swooping down to cover exactly half of her round face. She had what looked like an antique telescope braced across her shoulder, and the copper plating glowed wanly in the moonlight.

It was Mrs. Ridgeland.

"I always think they'll get sick of fighting, but they never do," she said.

The Keeper, for his part, seemed not the least bit surprised to see her. Axel, on the other hand, had to sit down in the grass. Back in Helsinki, when he'd decided once and for all to return to the path and look for his parents, Axel had told himself that he was ready for anything. As it turned out, he was a liar.

"The dead in my woods are no different," the Keeper said, stepping out to join Mrs. Ridgeland in the clearing. He sucked greedily on his pipe and used his walking stick to prod one of the ghostly soldiers, bumping the hat off his face. Axel wished he hadn't. "It's all new grudges on top of old grudges," the Keeper said. "It's exhausting."

"You're still a beginner," Mrs. Ridgeland said. "Give it a century and then tell me how you feel." Now she turned her attention away from the old man and squatted down in the grass beside Axel, using the folded-up legs of her telescope for balance. "It's polite to say hello," she said.

"Hi," Axel croaked.

But Mrs. Ridgeland didn't return his greeting. The half of her face that he could see was twisted into a scowl. "Don't think for even a second that I'm happy to see you here," she said.

"Now, now," the Keeper said, his walking stick still pressed into the dead soldier's chest. "As soon as we find who we're looking for, we'll be out of your neat, neat hair."

"That's what you promised me last time you were here," Mrs. Ridgeland said, grabbing Axel under the arm and pulling him up out of the grass. She was surprisingly strong. "Look how well that turned out for everybody. And now that you've brought the kid, it'll be even worse."

Axel felt like he was lagging behind just a bit. As he scrambled to make sense of what was going on, his mind went back to the day he and Tess had followed the bear tracks out of their garden. He remembered how the bristling prints had stuck to the side of the road, leading straight into Mrs. Ridgeland's yard. Saara must have gone there to ask her about Sam. And suddenly the explanation for what was happening was clear as day.

"You're a keeper, too," Axel said.

"I'm *the* Keeper, thank you very much," Mrs. Ridgeland said, puffing up in her robe just a bit. "When you're in my woods, *I'm* the Keeper. When you're in his woods, he can be." She nodded over at the old man. "But here in Baldwin he's nothing more than an uninvited guest. You both are. I'd appreciate it a great deal if you'd be on your way."

"He never told me there were two of you," Axel said.

The man that Axel knew only as the Keeper snorted loudly, twin plumes of smoke jetting out of his nostrils.

"A lot more than just two of us," Mrs. Ridgeland said. "Every wood on earth has its Keeper."

"Every wood *needs* its Keeper," the old man said. It sounded like a correction. "It's part of the order of things. We're here to remember all the dead among the trees. You could think of us as the designated mourners. It's very glamorous, really." His sarcasm was thick as spit.

"Well, then," Axel said, turning back to Mrs. Ridgeland, "if you're the Keeper here, can't you tell us where my father is?"

Mrs. Ridgeland let out a long, dramatically put-out sigh. "I'll tell you the same thing I told your mother when she was rude enough to visit me at my home some weeks ago. The same thing I've told her many times since then. I haven't seen Sam Fortune. This could mean that he isn't in my woods—that Baldwin isn't his place. Or it could simply mean that I haven't seen him yet." At this Mrs. Ridgeland gave a big, showy shrug. "My telescope is only so big," she went on, "and my woods are brimming with dead. There are new arrivals every hour. Almost all of them were loved by somebody before they died. And none of them are less, or more important, than Sam Fortune."

She went quiet for a moment and stared down at Axel. When Mrs. Ridgeland spoke again her voice was a good deal softer. "You shouldn't mistake me. I'm very sorry about what happened to your father. After all, sorry is what we Keepers *do*. I don't usually get to know anybody well until they settle in my woods, but your father . . . He truly seemed to enjoy being alive. Not many do, or at least not as much as they should." Her gaze drifted now, her voice hardening. "But one thing I can tell you for certain is that wherever Sam Fortune is, it's where he's *supposed to be*. And wherever your mother came from, that's where she's supposed to be. I don't know why you all can't just leave it at that."

To Axel, the answer seemed obvious. "Because where Saara's supposed to be is with Sam. And where I'm supposed to be is with both of them. They're my mom and dad."

"You do understand," Mrs. Ridgeland said, "that your mom and dad are dead."

"Everybody dies," Axel said.

"Dear me." She squinted down at him. "That sounds to you like wisdom?"

Neither of them said anything more. The Keeper took up his walking stick and high stepped over the soldier's corpse, cutting a jaunty angle right through the little moment of gloom that had just settled. "You've seen Saara today, then?"

"Today. Yesterday." Mrs. Ridgeland shook her head. "Much to the dismay of everybody here. She doesn't do well with *no*, that woman." With her free hand Mrs. Ridgeland moved aside the rigid sheet of hair that she'd sprayed into place. Beneath it there was nothing but a few strips of stucco-pale skin, straining against the push of the deep gray ashes that filled her. The ragged rake of a bear's claw had ruined nearly half of Mrs. Ridgeland's face. Axel didn't want to be rude, but he couldn't help it—he stared. His mom had done that.

"The woman's a real terror, to tell you the truth of it," Mrs. Ridgeland said.

"Well, perhaps you could just show us where she is," the Keeper said.

"Oh, I'll point her out," Mrs. Ridgeland said. "But I'm not getting close."

She led the three of them to a mulch trail at the far end of the meadow, which they followed to the main parking lot and the visitors' center. It was so strange—Axel knew no other place on earth as well as Mud Lake Park, but tonight it was almost unrecognizable to him. If the meadow had been the staging ground for a skirmish, there had been an out-and-out massacre in the parking lot. Small fires burned here and there, illuminating corpses scattered like leaves. Many of the dead wore uniforms similar to that of the young soldier in the meadow—white jackets and boots over blue trousers and undercoats, hems and lapels riveted with golden buttons. The moon was still high in the sky, and there wasn't a shred of cloud to offer shade. It looked like it would be a while before these dead would be allowed to flap, trot, and hop their way to shelter. Axel wondered, suddenly, if there were any bears among these moonlit ghosts.

"Why do they all come back as different animals?" he asked.

"They don't *come back*, exactly," the Keeper said, surveying the devastation in the parking lot. "Remember that you're in their world right now. They haven't returned to yours. But to your point—I honestly have no idea. If there's any logic to it, I haven't been able to figure it out. I've seen wealthy men and women arrive in my woods as sparrows and mice. I've seen a little girl, dead before she was half your age, step into the trees as a mother wolf." He seemed to pause and think on this for a moment. "I've often dreamed of how much easier my life would be," the Keeper said, "if your mother had become something with smaller teeth."

Mrs. Ridgeland held up a hand, shushing them. She pointed down to the visitors' center, where a few ghosts had huddled together, and led them to cover behind a small winterberry at the edge of the lot.

"Never a good idea to interrupt the battle," she said.

"What battle?" Axel said. "Who's fighting?"

"Today?" Mrs. Ridgeland made a face as she peered through the branches. "Sometimes it's hard for me to keep track. There have been so many comings and goings in these woods, and enough people put down roots that I'm left with quite the hodgepodge. I've got Algonquin and Onondaga. A handful of backwoods English trappers and rebel veterans who settled here after their war. To say nothing of the newer dead. But these particular ones are . . ." She parted the winterberry and leaned forward just a bit. "They're French."

American history was a weak point for Axel, but he did vaguely recall that the French were among the first Europeans to arrive in this part of the state. And he knew that they and the English, not to mention all the native nations who were here before anybody else, had once fought over this land. It happened hundreds of years ago, but as he stared down at the visitors' center it might as well have been yesterday. It reminded Axel of the inexplicable battle he'd witnessed at Erikinlinna— Vikings getting shot at by twentieth-century infantry. All of them hacking one another to bits, being reset by the moon, and then getting right back to hacking. Now that Axel really thought about it, it was astoundingly stupid.

"Why do they do it?" he asked. "Why do they keep fighting?"

Mrs. Ridgeland blinked at him for a moment, like she didn't understand the question. "They're people," she said simply. "They are fighting about what people fight about."

"But those are *dead* people," Axel said, careful not to sound like he was correcting her.

"All the better for them," Mrs. Ridgeland said. "There are no funerals after the dead go to war." She kept her eyes on Axel as he puzzled this over and seemed all at once to become annoyed. "What are you looking for? You want them to be pure? Washed clean of any pettiness or fear, bright and shiny with love and forgiveness for you? I know that you've spoken to your mother, so you should know better."

Axel hardly had time to feel hurt by this before the Keeper interrupted them with a hiss.

"Speaking of," he said, pointing down at the clutch of overdressed ghosts gathered in front of the visitors' center. One of the men had broken the huddle, and now they could see that Saara was down there as well. Just like the French ghosts, Axel's mother was in her human form in the blue moonlight. She had a thick coil of rope running around her wrists. Her overalls were filthy, and her chin was slick with blood.

"What did they do to her?" Axel said.

"More like what did she do to them," Mrs. Ridgeland said. She still sounded deeply irritated. "Your mother thinks I'm lying about Sam, so she's asking everyone else she can find. When they say they haven't seen him, she asks them again. And again. Believe me, we'd all love her gone."

"Well, neither of us is leaving until we find my father," Axel said.

Mrs. Ridgeland looked from him, to the Keeper, and back again. "Did he tell you about the monster?" she said.

"The Hiisi?" Axel said.

"*You* call it *Hiisi*," Mrs. Ridgeland said, wincing like the word cost her something. She nodded in the direction of the soldiers by the visitors' center. "*They* call it *Lutin*. There are as many words for it in my woods as there are tongues to speak with. But it's all one. Did your happy tour guide tell you that walking on the path would draw out the Hiisi? Did he happen to mention that the farther you go, the more awful it will get?"

"I most certainly have," the Keeper said, unsticking the pipe from his mouth and making like he was offended. "Not that he has to take my word for it—he's seen the monster for himself. In fact, I'd wager that this boy has spent more time with the Hiisi these past months than you have in a hundred years. And he hasn't backed down yet, has he?"

"He's right," Axel said. "I'm not afraid of the Hiisi." Saying the words aloud brought him a little bit closer to believing them.

Mrs. Ridgeland's brows knit together, causing a little puff of ash to fall out of the torn-open side of her face. "Let's set aside, for a moment, the fact that you *should* be. Because this is about more than just you and how brave you are or aren't. I mean, your mother is trouble enough as it is. The Hiisi doesn't like it when the dead stray from their home woods. But you? You're so, so much worse." Mrs. Ridgeland threw up her arms, getting more frustrated the more she spoke. "The Hiisi might forgive a dead wife for wandering, but it will never tolerate a real live boy walking the path. And you shouldn't think for one minute that this whelp of a Keeper can protect you. The Hiisi maintains order among the dead and the Keepers alike. We are as subject to its rules as any ghost."

This last bit the Keeper had, indeed, failed to mention. Axel's surprise must have shown on his face, because Mrs. Ridgeland let out a mean little laugh. "We're nothing but pieces of the order," she said. "One Keeper to every wood. One person to live among the dead—to remember them. Never fewer. And *never more*. Just by being here you're throwing off that balance, and the Hiisi cares only for balance. You must understand that it will ruin whatever stands in its way in order to reach you. Me. Him. Even her." Mrs. Ridgeland nodded down at Saara again, surrounded by French soldiers. "I know that you miss your parents. But you're risking what peace we have by going where you don't belong."

"Then I'll start belonging," Axel said, forcing himself to look Mrs. Ridgeland right in her remaining eye.

The Keeper smiled tightly at this. He seemed about to say something, but at that moment a bright shape stumbled out of the shadowed sugar bush, interrupting them. It was another soldier, his overcoat torn and the tattered uniform beneath darkly striped with blood. But from the way he was moving, it probably wasn't his own blood. When the soldier noticed them all squatting behind the winterberry, he nearly fell back into the sugar bush. He scrambled to unsling his musket, aiming it square at Axel's chest, which seemed pretty unfair, as Axel was the only person out of the four of them who was demonstrably alive. The soldier approached, barking pitchy orders. As he got closer Axel realized how young he was—somewhere between Kari and Kalle in age—and also how utterly terrified he looked. "All right, now," the Keeper said, standing and slowly raising his hands. Axel did so as well—he didn't speak a word of French, but the soldier had made that much plenty clear.

"*Calmez-vous,*" Mrs. Ridgeland said, using her telescope to push herself up.

The young Frenchman seemed to recognize her. Nevertheless, he kept his musket trained on Axel. "*Madame Gardien, pardonnez-moi,*" he said. "*Vous connaissez ces étrangers?*"

Mrs. Ridgeland glanced back at Axel, her expression resigned. "Last chance," she said. "Tell me you'll go home. Back to your sister and your grandparents. I'm sure they miss you terribly." She hardly waited for Axel to finish shaking his head before turning back to the soldier. "*Ils ne sont pas mes amis. Et ils ne sont pas bienvenus ici.*"

Axel didn't know exactly what she'd said, but it sounded stone-cold. The young Frenchman approached them slowly, toeing the grass. In one quick and jerky movement he snatched the sword from Axel's belt. Then he patted down the front of the Keeper's threadbare shirt, the limp pockets of his duster. Finding no weapons, he slapped the still-smoking pipe out of the old man's mouth. "There isn't any need for that," the Keeper said.

"*Tais-toi!*" the soldier said, gesturing with his musket across the parking lot. Again it was pretty clear what he wanted.

"We don't need your help anyway," Axel said, feeling vicious and wild.

"They may not," Mrs. Ridgeland said, "but you most certainly do. And you just turned it down."

"*Dépêchez-vous!*" The Frenchman was shouting now. He pressed the barrel of his musket between the Keeper's shoulder blades and pushed so hard that the old man was forced to take a step. Then the Keeper took another, heading out into the war zone of the parking lot. Axel went with him, his hands still high in the air. They moved carefully around the bodies, some of which were still alive, writhing in the mud of their mingled blood.

The soldier called out as they neared the visitors' center and was answered by a jag of barking French. The officers up ahead left the picnic table and set on them. "*Sont-ils armés?*" one of them asked. He turned the Keeper's duster inside out and confiscated the old man's tobacco with undisguised pleasure.

"Oui, mais seulement avec une épée . . ." The young soldier handed over Sam's sword, earning a few grim chuckles from his superiors. The officers spoke for a while longer, none of which Axel understood. They led him and the Keeper to the picnic table, seating them on either side of Saara. The rope binding her skinny wrists was frayed and ragged, and her fingers were interlocked in a knobby bouquet of bruised knuckles. Her face was mapped in black and blue, and blood still trickled from her lower lip. But that was nothing compared to what she'd apparently done to the soldiers. They had tooth marks on their faces, and a few were missing tufts of hair. One man had both eyes swollen shut.

"I told you not to bring him here," Axel's mother said.

"He insisted," the Keeper said. "Hello to you, too, by the way."

"He shouldn't have come," she said. Then, before Axel could even hope that this was out of concern for his safety, she added: "He isn't any help, anyway."

The battered officers broke off their consultations, and a thickset man with sad blue eyes approached the picnic table. He had a shallow gash across one powdered cheek, though Axel couldn't tell if that had come from the battle or from his conversation with Saara. The thickset man cleared his throat. "We've agreed on some conditions," he said in passable English. "If you three promise to leave immediately, we will grant you safe passage back to the edge of the wood. You can take the path to your home from there."

"No," Saara said. Simple as that.

"But . . . you must." The officer looked a little desperate. "Him especially." He pointed at Axel. This gesture whipped up a brief tempest of nodding agreement from the other surviving Frenchmen.

"Il est une menace!" one grimly proclaimed.

"Il doit être tué. C'est le seul moyen!" another hissed, fingering the decorative guard of his cavalry sword.

"He's too dangerous," the thickset officer said.

"Dangerous?" The Keeper let out a startlingly false laugh. "Are we looking at the same kid?" He reached across Saara to pinch Axel around the biceps, little more than a twig of skin and bone. "A danger to himself, maybe."

The officer waved the Keeper off. "Save your lies for the new dead, serpent." Then he turned back to Axel. "Please understand me. Your mother, we can't kill. And neither can we kill this charlatan." At this the Keeper grinned an unhappy grin.

"If they're truly intent on staying in our woods," the officer continued, "then we can't stop them. They know this. But you . . ." The officer's beautiful blue eyes had become hard and impassive. "It would give us no pleasure to do such a thing. But if that's the only choice we have—if that's the only way we can get the Hiisi to leave us in peace . . . I'm begging you, please don't make it our only choice."

Saara leaned forward, and the fat officer pulled his fingers away from the picnic table, as though afraid she'd bite them. Her eyes seemed not just to twinkle, but to spark. "If it's just the boy you're worried about, you might as well let *me* stay," she said.

Axel hardly had time to tell himself that he shouldn't feel hurt by this—that his mother couldn't help it—because at that moment they were all interrupted by a terrible noise from deep within the shadowed parkland. It sounded something like a wheezy elephant, backfilled with static and reverb, drifting in from beyond a grove of young oaks. A single, trumpeting honk. Then there was silence so sharp and wanting that it made the faded sound seem all the worse. The Frenchmen turned out to the trees and began to whisper, tipping powder down the barrels of their weapons. The young soldier—the one who'd captured Axel and the Keeper back at the edge of the lot—took a few steps out across the asphalt, his musket shouldered.

"Do I have to beg you?" the thickset officer whispered. "Because I will."

Axel was starting to feel a little guilty about this. After all, he had nothing against these people. But he hadn't made the rules, and he'd certainly never asked the Hiisi to start following him. The only choice these Frenchmen were offering him was to give up on finding his father, which wasn't a choice at all. "I'm not leaving," he said. "I'm sorry."

"Me too," the officer said.

The oak grove on the far side of the lot had begun to quake, the few leaves that still clung to their branches snapping off and drifting to the earth below. Then a whole tree snapped—a crack like a thunderclap. The big, broken thing tumbled down and crushed the little winterberry bush that they'd hidden behind with Mrs. Ridgeland. The two trees on either side also went down, their trunks twisting to wet ribbons. Axel could see it now, a proper monster at last. It was still the thing it used to be—still just as horrible as that neat little hospice wheelchair, reeking of the false welcome of antiseptic and artificial pine—but it was also something else. The Hiisi had neither legs nor wheels. Neither a snout nor a seat. It was made of padding and metal, of plastic and rubber, of wire and shadow and light.

The young soldier in the lot had enough time to get off a shot, but he simply didn't. He stood there, a white blip atop the asphalt, utterly awe-struck. The Hiisi shambled brightly over to him and became for a moment nothing but a gaping blaze of light, a mouth without teeth or lips or a face to be set upon. Then the young soldier was gone, swallowed whole. That was enough to knock the officers out of their terrified stupor. The parking lot crackled with the smoky report of muskets, as the ancient Frenchmen scattered and took up firing positions. The thickset one began shoving the prisoners off the picnic table, which he overturned as a barricade. "Look what you've done," he kept saying. "Look what you're doing!"

They didn't stand a chance. The Hiisi crab-walked and shimmied, cheeky and patient as smoke. It grabbed one of the men by his capped head, tossing him up with such incredible force that his body simply peeled away like an apple from its stem, flipping into the night sky. The Hiisi hurled a second officer over the roof of the visitors' center, where he was impaled on the nov-elty Peter Pan weathervane and spun in an absurd, grizzly waltz. A third officer slid past Axel's feet, screaming, held about the ankle by something like a claw and dragged slowly into the glittering nothing of the Hiisi's mouth.

Axel saw that one of the soldiers had dropped his father's sword, and it was lying just a few paces away. He darted out to grab it, meaning to cut the rope binding his mother's wrists. But when Axel turned back, he found that Saara wasn't there anymore. Not knowing what else to do, he dove for cover behind the overturned picnic table, joining the Keeper and the fat officer. It was lucky that he did, because at that very moment a body crashed into the spot where he'd been standing, cratering the fitted flagstones. The body had fallen straight down, as though dropped clean out of the sky. It was the soldier who'd lost his head, Axel realized, completing his return trip to earth.

Where the hell had his mom gone? When Axel peeked around the edge of the picnic table, he could just make out her bobbing ponytail at the far end of the lot, disappearing in the direction of their old A-frame. She must have slipped away while the Hiisi was busy feasting on Frenchmen.

"Nice of her to tell us what the plan was," the Keeper said, pressing himself into the underside of the picnic table. His look of terror was one of the few honest expressions Axel had ever seen the old man wear. "Maybe now would be a good time to, you know, start fitting in," the Keeper said.

"I'm trying," Axel said. Another musket shot burst from the parking lot, followed by a single fading scream. One by one, the Hiisi was finishing them off. "I'm trying, but I don't know how."

"Just believe it," the Keeper said. "You keep telling me this is where you want to be. But it's not me that you've got to convince."

So Axel tried. He held tight to the hilt of his father's sword, drawing what courage he could from it, and stood. He could see the Hiisi over the rim of the overturned picnic table. The impossible thing twisted, gleeful and gurgling. Its blazing mouth hole opened and closed, and it began to slink closer. Then it stopped, seeming to stare back at him. There was a stretch of sudden and deep stillness.

"Stop," Axel said. "Stop," he said again. The Hiisi stayed exactly where it was, sizzling.

"Good boy," the Keeper said, stepping out from behind the picnic table.

"Be quiet," Axel told him. He was repeating the word "stop" over and over again in his head and was worried that if he quit—or took his eyes off the awful thing—then it would leap upon them.

The Hiisi leaned forward and then back. It shuffled from side to side but got no closer. Then it spoke. The voice seemed to emerge out of the wood itself—from every branch and wrinkled leaf, from all the mushrooms and the stones—but there was no question that it belonged to the Hiisi. "Leave," it said simply.

"I will not," Axel said, adding this to the chorus in his mind. *I will not leave—I will not leave—I will not leave.*

"Go home, or I will take you home," the Hiisi said, its voice sprouting once again from the trees.

"This is home," Axel said. "If you take me away from it, I will come back. I will keep coming back."

The Hiisi paused, seeming to consider this. From the corner of his eye Axel could see that the Keeper had been moving all this while, slowly inching around the picnic table and toward the Hiisi. When the old man spoke again, it was to the monster. "You can hear him as well as I can," he said. "He can cut his strings. He can be of the path."

"What is he doing?" whispered the thickset French officer with sad blue eyes. He was standing as well now, gripping the upturned edge of the table.

"I don't know," Axel whispered back.

The Keeper was just a few steps away from the Hiisi. He held his hands up high and threw his head back, leaving his chest and throat exposed.

It was as though the old man were totally unafraid that the Hiisi might do to him what it had done to the Frenchmen. "He can stay," he shouted. "And you can keep your order!"

Axel was totally baffled.

The Hiisi leaned over the Keeper, singeing him with its horrible light. "I don't believe him," said every tree and root and branch in the world. Then, what Axel could describe only as an elbow struck out, whacking the Keeper head over foot like a sack toy. The old man's body flew above the picnic table, crashing through the glass double doors of the Mud Lake visitors' center, knocking stuffed mallards and snow geese from their perches on the walls. Axel didn't watch long enough to see whether or not the Keeper was still moving, because suddenly the picnic table was gone, replaced by a drifting mist of splinters and bolts. The officer was gone, too. Or rather, he was elsewhere—hung like an ornament above Axel's head, held aloft by the Hiisi's sickeningly jointed metal trusses. He was silent as the monster swung him over the cold light of its mouth, seeming to savor the moment before the gulp. Axel would later wish that there were something he could have done for the man. Much later, though. Because at the time, all he could think was *run*.

16

Tracks and Sketches

The sharp smell of smoke hit Tess's nostrils the moment she opened the cottage door, crushing any doubt that her brother had been there. A muddle of Axel-size footprints, outlined in melt-water, were stamped across the kitchen floor. Tess followed the prints into the living room, where she found a splatter of ashy mud oozing out of the fireplace grate and over the hearthstone, staining the tasseled edges of the Kivis' rug. A half-empty tin of ruined sausages jutted from the mess, and when Tess reached down to touch it, she found the rim still warm on her fingertips. But Axel wasn't there. His bed was empty, the comforter lying beside it on the floor.

"He must have just left!" Tess shouted as she

stepped back out onto the freezing front stoop. "He can't be far."

"All the better," Jaana called back to her. She was down by the sauna, tracing deep-set tracks around the woodpile. "The forecast says it's supposed to get even colder in the afternoon."

Tess scanned the tree line, looking to see if her brother's footprints led to the outhouse or the hillside cellar. And that's when she saw him. Or rather, *them*, because Axel wasn't alone. Her little brother was right there, staring at her from a small clearing in the birch trees. Sam's replica sword was clenched tightly in Axel's fist, and he had an intense, almost wild look on his face. But there was also a man, standing beside him, just visible at the edge of the clearing. Even before she processed his features, Tess knew in the pit of her stomach that this was the Keeper. He was dressed exactly as he had been back in Baldwin—the quilted duster, the hat and gum boots. He had the same storkish posture that Tess remembered, the same smile like a mouthful of beetles.

Just the sight of the Keeper was enough to bring back everything about that awful night back home, when Tess had lost her dad forever. Actually, it was worse than that, because now there was plenty of guilt in the stew. It was almost enough to paralyze her, right there, on the frozen stoop of the Kivis' summer cottage. Almost.

"Hey." Tess shook herself out of her own shock and bounded out into the deep snow. "Hey!" she shouted again. But Axel was gone—more than gone, *erased*—by the time she reached the trees. It was almost like he and the Keeper had never been there in the first place. Tess could see far into the winter-stripped forest, but there was nothing out there other than frozen crests and wavelets of untouched snow. The only footprints were her own, extending back to the Kivis' cottage. What the hell was happening?

"You saw him?" Jaana asked, already at Tess's side.

"I think so."

"Think?" Jaana took her by the shoulders, the pressure of her grip almost painful through the down jacket.

"I did. I saw him." *Him*, not *them*, because what could Tess possibly say about the Keeper? Who exactly was it that she'd just seen? The maudlin New York vagabond who'd somehow had a premonition about Sam's death; or the creepy carnie who traveled with a disappearing brown bear; or, strangest of all, the ghost shepherd from Axel's story—chaperone to their pissed-off, undead mom? If it sounded that absurd to Tess, how would it sound to Jaana?

"I think he might be trying to go to the castle," Tess said.

"It isn't far from here," her grandmother said, high-stepping through the powder, back to their idling snowmobile. "If we don't find him first, we can beat him there." She and Tess hopped aboard and rocketed out into the woods.

The first train to Talvijärvi wouldn't have left Helsinki until late that morning, so Jaana had rented a car and driven the two of them up overnight. Otso and Kari remained behind, in case Axel tried to return to the flat, but the farther they drove, the surer Tess became that her brother had run off to the summer place. She and Jaana would have arrived sooner, but for the heavy snowfall that began when they were still a few hours out, the flakes fat and lazy as old moths. By the time they arrived, everything but the highway had become impassable, leaving them with no choice but to head into town. Jaana found a small sporting-goods store, where she all but commandeered this utility snowmobile, leaving her credit card and the words "I'm sorry, but you have to make it happen" with the clerk, who protested in vain that the store was not yet open, nor the sled for rent.

The snowmobile wallowed in the soft powder, but they moved at a good clip, trees zipping by on either side. Jaana crisscrossed the woods behind the cottage, Tess hollering Axel's name from the rear seat. Finding nothing, they decided to follow the track that Jaana had already discovered—a stutter of footprints strung along the frozen lake. The track looped behind the Hannula property and traced the shoreline for a pace before making a sharp turn into the spruce wood. It struck Tess that this was the same route they'd taken out of Erikinlinna. It felt like forever ago, but it hadn't been more than two weeks—that day when Axel's illness had gotten the jump on him and they'd had to carry him back to the cottage.

The ground was more uneven as they sledded into the woods, and the underside of the snowmobile scraped loudly against hidden stones and stumps. Soon they came to a collapsed oak tree, its neat cap of powder gouged from where Axel had scrambled overtop. The dead tree blocked their path, and Jaana began to steer the sled around. It was then that something caught Tess's attention—a sharp glimmer in the morning light. It was roughly the shape of a person—a torso with arms outstretched, just about as tall as a ten-year-old should be. Jaana must have seen it too, because she stopped the snowmobile before Tess had a chance to say anything. They both leaped off, sinking to their shins. But it wasn't Axel. It was chain mail—a shirt of ringed armor, caught up in the crown of a young pine, its weight bending the sapling at the middle. Jaana retrieved the mail and shot Tess a glance.

"Your brother's?" she said.

It wasn't so much a question, but Tess answered all the same. "My father's."

Her grandmother nodded at this, eyeballing the mail for another moment. Together they returned to the snowmobile, where Jaana dropped it into a saddlebag affixed to the seat. They'd hardly gone another ten feet before she cut the motor once again. The snow on the far side of the dead oak was overturned with a mishmash of boot marks and palsied snow angels. It looked like Axel had fallen. Or maybe he'd been pushed, because it was suddenly clear that he was no longer alone. They could see a second set of tracks now, flat-footed craters more than twice the size of Axel's. These tracks seemed to come from nowhere; they simply *appeared*. As though the Keeper had been dropped out of the sky and landed neatly on his feet. Tess still didn't know what to think about the rest of Axel's story, but he sure as hell hadn't been making this part up. He'd tried to tell Tess that he'd seen the Keeper, and what did she do? She'd called her little brother a liar. Worse than a liar—a loser. Tess felt almost light-headed with the shame of it.

"Oh no." Jaana's voice pulled Tess back into the moment. Her grandmother had noticed this second set of tracks as well and had fallen down onto her hands and knees. Jaana's naked fingers pressed into the snow on either side of one of the big, unfamiliar boot prints. "Oh my God." She sounded like she was choking.

"Grandma," Tess said. "There's something I need to tell you."

A few hours later Tess found herself seated on a low wooden stool in the Kivis' freezing cottage, pondering how best to describe the Keeper. A young woman with the Talvijärvi police sat on the stool opposite her, squinting into a sketchpad as though it were the opening of a dark well. This was already their third go-round, and the young artist still couldn't make heads or tails of the baffling face they seemed to be conjuring together. Behind the dry rubbing of the woman's eraser, Tess could hear the crackle of radios and the harsh snap of a camera shutter. The chief of the tiny local police department was a family friend, and Jaana had called him from the road early that morning to say that she thought her grandson might be headed up their way. "No reason to get worked up just yet,

Aarne," Jaana had said. "I had the Hannula boy look in, and he says the cottage is empty. Perhaps you could keep an eye out in town?"

Of course, their discovery of Axel's aborted fire and Tess's mention of the Keeper had changed the flavor of the situation considerably. Even now Chief Aarne was leading a hastily organized search party through the frozen woods. Jaana was out back, digging an icy trench into the yard with her pacing, updating Otso on all that had happened. Tess's grandmother had been so collected on the drive up from Helsinki, so calm and purposeful as they searched the trees beyond the cottage. But now she'd officially lost her shit. Yesterday Tess would have put good money against the prospect of ever seeing the old lady shed a single tear. Today she'd have spent that same massive and imaginary amount just to stop them coming.

"So, would it be—was it perhaps more like this?" The young woman turned her pad around for Tess to investigate. But this one was as bad as the first two; the walleyed, toothy face leering out of the page looked absolutely nothing like the Keeper. It wasn't that the face was too normal, but rather that it was too *real*. Like someone had tried to tease a true-to-life portrait out of a caricature.

"I'm sorry," Tess said. "I don't think I'm explaining it right."

The woman took a moment. She couldn't have been more than twenty-five, and as she scrutinized her pad, the bridge of her nose wrinkled. "Absolutely not. It's not your fault. Why don't we start with a fresh page?" She tore the sketch away, ready to begin again. "We can take our time."

Tess knew, of course, that she believed no such thing. She could almost see the effort that this nice young woman was expending, trying to keep the awful possibilities out of mind. Tess had sat through enough urgently sincere safety-awareness assemblies at school to understand what her mention of the old man would do. A runaway kid was bad enough, but if you throw a strange and unidentified adult into the story, then "this is bad" very quickly graduates to "panic freaking immediately." Tess had understood that telling Jaana about the Keeper would send her—and everybody else—into a frenzy, so she decided to leaven her honesty with more honesty. If she was going to tell the truth, then she might as well tell the complete, moronically fantastical truth. Never mind if no one believed that she'd seen the old man in New York. Never mind if they shrugged off Axel's ghost story, just as she had. Because omitting the supernatural bits wasn't just dishonest, but it also made the story worse. *A stranger had lured her little brother into the forest*—the abridged version was by far more terrifying.

"His face was wider than that," Tess said. "I mean really, *really* like an egg. Almost flat on top."

"All right," the woman said, the arc of her elbow indicating the expansive oval that she was scrawling over the pad. "An egg. Just like an egg."

Tess picked up the discarded portrait off the floor and stared into it. "The teeth here aren't bad," she said. "They were big like this, but also . . . I don't know. Every time you looked at them, they seemed a little different." She went quiet for a moment. How to put that upsetting sight into words? "Like they were swapping places when you blinked."

"That's fine," the young woman said, perhaps deciding to suspend her skepticism. "I'm not sure how to draw that, but I'll try."

They were just about finished by the time Jaana came back inside, looking haggard. Her jacket hung open, and the sweat beading the tips of her close-cropped hair had frozen over, silver on silver. But her eyes were clear, and the dark patch on her fleece collar was the only evidence that she'd been crying. Jaana held a pair of cross-country skis under her arm. Tess knew they didn't belong to her. The Kivis never came to Talvijärvi in the winter, so there was no need for them. "One of your friends took my sled," Jaana said, "so I'm going to need these." She seemed to be addressing the cottage at large. "And the boots that go with them," she said. "Immediately."

"Mrs. Kivi—" the policeman with the camera began. His tone suggested that he was about to say something ridiculous, like that Jaana should rest for a moment. Like that she should wait until they heard back from Aarne's search party.

No need to listen to the tail end of that blather. Jaana cut him off. "Your boots, or I'll just walk," she said.

"I don't think that they'll fit you," the policeman said haltingly.

"Blisters will be the least of my problems, then." Jaana stared at the young man, looking like she'd actually get down and begin untying his laces if he didn't do it himself. So he did.

"I'm going with you," Tess said, getting up from her stool.

"Not until you've finished," her grandmother said. "What you're doing is very important." She already had a foot in one of the policeman's boots.

"We are finished," Tess said.

Jaana shot a glance across the living room, and for a moment the sketch artist writhed in silence. "No, Mrs. Kivi, I don't think we are," the young woman said, peering down into the Keeper's impossible mug. Perhaps she'd been trying to prove a point by drawing the old man exactly as Tess described him, cartoonish hyperbole and all. But in doing so, she'd stumbled blindly into a spot-on rendition.

"Yes, we are," Tess said. "That's what he looks like."

"You ski?" Jaana said.

Tess was from Upstate New York—of course she could ski. She nodded.

Jaana returned her gaze to the sketch artist. "Can she borrow yours?"

"I'm sorry, ma'am . . ." The woman looked at her colleague, exasperated, entreating for his assistance. But the young officer was already good and railroaded, standing there in his woolen socks with pictures of Moomins dancing across them. "We aren't done." The sketch artist seemed to take a breath to gather her courage. "Your grand-daughter is . . . I don't know if she's playing a game, but—"

"Excuse me?" Jaana stopped tightening the boots and took a step toward them. The overlarge things made a menacing thump on the hardwood, untied laces flopping about the sides. The sketch artist gave no answer; she just handed over her pad. Jaana stared down at the grinning portrait. Then she raised her eyes to Tess. "This is what the man you saw looked like?"

"It is," Tess said.

"Then you're done," Jaana said, thrusting the pad back at the sketch artist.

"Mrs. Kivi, I'm only trying to help," she said.

For a moment Tess's grandmother seemed to soften. But before she could make any answer to the young woman, they were interrupted by a clattering from outside. The chief of the Talvijärvi police let himself in and began stamping his boots on the welcome mat to loosen them of snow. Aarne was a big man, with a beard that occupied a wolfish portion of his face. The exposed ridges of his cheeks were bright pink, but it was impossible to tell if this was a condition brought on by the cold, or just the way he was made. "I'm sorry. Nothing yet," Aarne said. "They're doubling around now, in case the boy went back to the lake."

"What do you mean doubling around? You mean they've lost the trail?" Keeping her eyes on Aarne, Jaana knelt down to finish tightening her boots.

"They haven't lost it, but it ends." The police chief waved his hand through the air, indicating some point beyond the cottage walls. "Out past where you found that metal shirt. They—" Aarne coughed and rubbed his hands over his mouth and chin, as if to wipe the word away. "Your grandson must have turned back. But that's a good sign. No ski marks or tread marks. Your boy can't be far."

"Did you check the castle?" Tess asked.

"The tracks don't lead that far, but—" Tess was already getting up out of her stool, and Aarne held his hands out, as though to slow her. "We searched the whole thing anyway. And I left somebody there. If anybody tries to go near the place, my man will see them."

"Good," Jaana said, straightening up and zipping her jacket. "Now, listen, my granddaughter would like to help in the search. Please see that she gets some skis."

Chief Aarne glanced at the bootless feet of his young officer, and Tess guessed that under other circumstances he might have smiled. "Of course," he said. "I have more volunteers on their way to join the search party. I'll ask that they bring a set in her size. Maybe until then, if it would be all right, I could talk to her a little bit?"

Jaana looked at Tess. As frenzied as her grandmother was, Tess had the impression that she would have waited as long as she had to for an answer. "It's all right," Tess said. "I can meet you out there later."

"You probably won't even have to," Jaana said, forcing a strange, under-bitten look of calm. "It can't be long before we find him." Optimism sounded about as natural in her mouth as Japanese. She stepped to the door, pausing for a final moment on the threshold.

"It can't be long at all."

It was a good thing that her brother had left such clear evidence of his escape to Talvijärvi, because had the search for Axel been based on Tess's story alone, then she had no doubt it would have been called off before dark. Nobody said so to her face, but they all plainly believed that she was lying. The people Tess spoke to for the rest of the morning differed only in how they interpreted her motives. A few of them clearly assumed that she was doing it intentionally, either because she had some kind of secret to hide, or because she was simply a profoundly shitty kid. But this was a minority—most seemed to think that she just couldn't help herself. That she was so addled by the trauma of a dead father and a vanished brother that she no longer knew what was true and what wasn't. And as such, these people treated her like some kind of delicate object that might shatter if you moved it too quickly. They listened intently to her story about meeting the Keeper in Baldwin, about Saara's ghost and the physics-defying woodland path, like cheap therapists looking for clues in her dreams. And as kind and gentle as these people were, Tess found that she actually preferred the first group. After all, their nastiness was exactly what she deserved. Because Tess *was* a shitty kid—at least that's how she felt at the moment. Axel had asked for her help. He'd *begged* for it. And Tess had shrugged him off like he was nothing. She'd been shrugging him off for years.

Volunteers arrived as the word spread, sledding in from town and the various lakeside properties. Kalle, shaken with remorse for the role he'd played in Axel's escape, offered up his family home as a base of operations. There Aarne handed out bright neon vests and divided the new arrivals into pairs, assigning them to different search grids in the surrounding woods. The hunt stretched farther and farther afield as the day ripened and burst. By early afternoon a team of sniffer dogs arrived from Savonlinna, and shortly thereafter the forest reverberated with the hectic chop of a rescue helicopter.

Otso and Kari left Helsinki on the evening train and caught a ride to the lake with the police. Jaana and Tess were out in the driveway when the two of them arrived, skis fastened, warming themselves with mugs of tea before heading out to join the search again. Kalle was in the frozen drive as well, handing out thermoses of hot fish soup to returning volunteers. He'd been doing it all evening. As Otso wheeled himself up to the big, bright house, he set his eyes on the young man.

"If I were younger, I would break your goddamn nose," he said. "What's the matter with you?"

"I am so sorry, Mr. Kivi," It was unclear whether Kalle meant this as an apology for his own behavior, or as condolences for what had happened. Maybe both.

"How could you not have noticed that he was in your stupid pickup? How could you not have seen him in the cottage?" There was spit flecking Otso's lip. He looked like he'd just finished up crying, or was about to start.

"I don't know," Kalle said. It was all he said.

Otso's face twisted, his voice cracking awfully. He took a wheezing breath. "Well. I'm upset. Do forgive me."

There was a moment of silence. Jaana broke it by pressing her weight sidelong into her back ski and gliding over the packed snow to her husband. *"Ukko,"* she said, putting her hands on his face, fingers lost in the dense bracken of his beard.

"Rakas." Otso looked up at her and blinked away some tears. He took her fingers from his cheeks and held them in his own shaking hands. Tess suddenly felt a strong compulsion to look away. There was something about this modest

display that was unfathomably, almost terrifyingly intimate. All her grandparents had done was hold hands and trade pet names, not more than four syllables in total. But these were as much real names as pet names, the secret identities that Jaana and Otso would never share with anybody else for the rest of their lives. And beyond.

"You're heading out again?" Otso said, his voice still quavering.

"We're about to." Jaana brought the bundle of their hands up to her lips, exhaling over them. Warming them. "They've given everybody flashlights. And with the snow and the stars, it's bright enough."

"I wish I could come," he said.

"I know you do," Jaana said. Tess knew it too. Her grandfather would have gone right into the woods, plowing his chair through the snow, if only Jaana and the police would allow it.

"And what about you? Are you warm enough?" Otso let go his wife's hands and beckoned Tess over.

"I'm all right," Tess said, approaching with a single push on her outturned ski, as her grandmother had.

"We'll be fine," Jaana said. "She's an excellent skier. You should go inside. Kalle has a good fire going."

"I love you," Otso said. He was still winning

the fight against the tears that so clearly wanted to jump out of his face, but just barely.

"We're going to find him," Tess said.

"Of course you are," Otso said. Before Tess could react, he'd taken hold of her wrist and pulled her close, planting a light, whisker-bristling kiss on her cheek. It was the first time he'd done this. He smelled like an old man, but different from Grandpa Paul, the only other old man she knew. Otso released her wrist and allowed himself to be wheeled to the front door. There Kalle and Kari helped him out of his chair and carried him up the steps and inside.

Jaana and Tess lingered for a moment, light from the Hannula house spilling out over the plowed drive. The stars were bright, and the woods flickered distantly with flashlights from the search parties. Then, without a word, Jaana pushed off with her poles, and together they sailed into the forest.

17

How They Lost Her

A cold snap set in overnight, seeming to freeze everything into place, even the breeze. The previous afternoon had been just warm enough to raise a sweat upon the new snow, melt that had since hardened into a glittering skin of ice. Bluish with reflected starlight, the ice rolled over the forest floor, bunching up around tree trunks like gathered bedding, shattering beneath the gliding press of Tess's and Jaana's skis. Her grandmother took the lead, carving out slick troughs for Tess to follow. The two moved at a good pace, tucking their knees for speed downhill, hardly a stroke wasted between them. Often they would stop to shine their flashlights about the forest, calling out Axel's name. Sometimes the woods would give them an answer: the shrill complaint of a red squirrel, the thumping wing beat of a tawny owl, even the alarmed braying of startled moose. But never Axel calling back. It had been two days since Tess's brother had slipped away from her in Helsinki. Nearly twenty-four hours since Axel had been swallowed up by the forest.

Tess and Jaana skied from the spruce wood to the reedy lakeshore. They slid beneath the star-cast shadow of Erikinlinna, where they encountered two more neon-vested members of the search party. Chief Aarne had set up a constant guard at the tumbledown castle, complete with chemical warmers and winter survival gear, just in case Axel did eventually try to make his way back there. Aarne had done the same thing at the Kivis' cottage and at all the vacant properties along the lake. The men were having an early breakfast when Tess and Jaana passed, taking shelter in the covered picnic area. Coffee steamed in their wooden mugs, and one of them was clutching a little loaf of rye in his bare hands, thawing it out. Right behind them was the display on Talvijärvi's famous ghost, including the laminated picture of Väinö and Aino and their ruined-looking son—the last family that the Keeper had helped to destroy.

"Anything?" Jaana called, hardly slowing on her skis. Given the grim demeanor of the men, she needn't have asked. They shook their heads, and she and Tess pressed on.

From the castle they turned east, swinging up along the far shore. It was more than a ten-mile circuit around the lake, and Tess's legs were gummy with the effort. This was her twelfth hour on these skis, not counting a forty-minute nap back at the Hannula place. Perspiration drenched the insides of her jacket and saturated her scarf, crystalizing wherever it came into contact with the air. In the moments when they stopped to holler Axel's name and shine their lights overhand into the trees, the chill reached almost to her bones. Jaana had said that it was much too early in the season for it to be this cold. The lake shouldn't even have been frozen over yet, but already the ice was thick enough that volunteers had begun to take shortcuts over the shallows. If they stayed really quiet, they could even hear the *trees* freezing. The sap in their veins popped and groaned as it expanded—a conversation that reverberated through the forest.

Tess and Jaana came to a patch of cleared land, stumps dotting the ground like low-set tables, and decided to stop for a breather. Jaana removed her skis and used one to clear the crusted powder from a large stump, giving them a place to sit. It was only after they stopped moving that Tess realized how hard her grandmother was panting—Jaana's face was flushed, almost purple in the dark morning, her mouth a jagged vent of steam. Neither of them had slept more than a couple of hours since Axel had first disappeared, and it was starting to show. Tess sat beside Jaana and caught her breath as well. They were on the north side of the lake, opposite the distant, shimmering windows of the Hannula place. The house hung like a pendant in a chain of lights strung all along the far shores—flashlights from the search parties.

Jaana pulled a thermos of porridge from her knapsack. She poured some into the lid and handed it to Tess with a spoon. They traded bites, marking the slowing pace of their breathing. "I'd like to talk to you about what happened between us and your father," Jaana said. This seemed at first to come from out of the blue. But of all the times in the world for her to bring this up, this struck Tess, somehow, as exactly the right time. "But before I start," Jaana said, "I need to know how much you understand."

"Nothing. Dad didn't talk about it at all."

"I'm not surprised," Jaana said, the spoon stopping on its way to her cold-chapped lips. She and Tess had been operating under a truce since the moment Axel disappeared, but it didn't extend to Sam, dead or not. "That isn't what I meant, though. I meant how much *Finnish* you understand. Because my English isn't good enough for this, and if we're going to talk about your mother and father, then I want to do it right. I need to know that you understand everything I'm saying. And if you don't, I need you to stop me, and I'll try to say it more clearly. All right?"

Jaana handed over the porridge and stared down at her. Tess had the distinct impression that if she didn't agree, her grandmother would have snapped her skis back on then and there, never to mention this again. Tess nodded.

"Your mother could really be a pain in the ass."

Not exactly the way Tess had expected this story to start, but Jaana's expression told her that she didn't mean it to sound biting—her grandmother looked almost amused. "This was partly our fault," she said. "My fault. *Partly*. When Saara was growing up, Otso and I could sometimes be . . . We were maybe a little overprotective. We always knew there was a chance, and not a small one, that someday Saara would get sick. We knew that much and nothing more. The testing back then wasn't what it is today. The doctors didn't know where to look, or even what to look for. But they knew that Otso had it, and that meant that it was fifty-fifty for Saara. Otso's was mild, but Saara's could be severe. You know all this, I'm sure. You must understand it as well as I do."

Jaana stopped here. Tess wasn't eating, so Jaana took the still-steaming porridge back and spooned a little more of it into her mouth. In the distance they could faintly hear Axel's hollered name, fading into the dark. The pine island looked like a rocky hill atop a flat meadow of ice.

"So, yes," Jaana said, "we were strict. And your mother did not react well to this. Saara always, always had to contradict us. She was a lot like you in that way—the moment Saara realized that we didn't want her to do a thing, it became the thing that she most wanted to do in the world." Jaana hardly knew Tess well enough to make an assertion like this, and she would have opened her mouth to say as much, but for the conversational judo that her grandmother had just achieved—arguing would have proven the point. And besides, Jaana didn't seem eager to linger. "Saara was like me, too. She could be an intensely private, secretive girl. I loved my daughter very much, but you must understand, in many ways we were an awful mix. It got worse as she got older. Saara was twenty when the doctors were finally able to make their diagnosis, but Otso and I had known for almost a year by then. We wanted, more than ever, to take care of her. To make sure that she was eating right and getting enough rest. But what Saara wanted, more than ever, was to be rid of us. I would have felt the same thing, in her shoes. And she, in mine." Again Jaana trailed off. She handed the porridge back. "So what I'm saying is this: Yes, your father and I had our differences. But a lot of it started years before we even met him. Sam wasn't the only one to blame for what happened between us."

"Of course he wasn't." Tess couldn't help herself.

"Of course." Jaana gave a tired squint and began to dig through her pockets. She pulled out her cell phone and checked the time—coming up on eight in the morning, but it looked more like midnight. "You know, I'm sure, that he was seven years older than her? And you know, also, that they were seeing each other for less than a month before she went back to New York with him?" This first piece of information was not news to Tess, but the second one absolutely was. She knew that her parents had met when Sam was in Finland to conduct research for his dissertation, but Tess had always assumed that their courtship had been a question of months, if not years. She had no reason to think this, other than the fact that such a thing seemed reasonable. "One day," Jaana continued, "your father is shaking our hands on the back stoop of the cottage, and the next Saara is telling us that she has a ticket to New York. And you know—we took it *well*. We took it better than anybody could have expected. We thought: Why not? Let her spend a summer traveling. Let her give this man a try. Besides, we knew that if we said one word against it, Saara would have traded her ticket in for one that left even sooner. Just to prove that she could!" Jaana threw her hand out, as though casting old frustrations across the ice. "But of course she could. We always knew that Saara could do what she wanted, maybe better than she did."

"It was more than three years before we saw her again." Tess, at first, did not think that she'd heard this correctly. Jaana could tell. "Exactly," she said. "Shortly after Saara left, she wrote to tell us that she was in love and that she had canceled her return flight and didn't know when she'd be back. She told us all of this on a postcard. A *postcard*. It said 'City of Salt,' and it was just the most horrible photograph of a shopping mall, with parking lots going everywhere, forever. Otso and I didn't panic, not yet. Saara was young, so of course she was in love. It's part of the contract, at that age. We decided, for once in our lives, to let Saara do what Saara needed to do. It was, I think, the worst mistake we ever made. The months dissolved away, and we heard from our daughter almost not at all. It was different in those days. An international phone call that lasted anything longer than hello and good-bye could cost a fortune. And letters took their time. But even when Saara did call or write, she said almost nothing. As though Otso and I cared about the weather in Syracuse! As though I were dying to know what she was reading! It was nothing but empty small talk. We became sure that Saara was hiding something from us. And we were right."

Tess knew where this was going. She thought of that expired blue passport with her baby picture in it, the pages empty save a pair of stamps—entry into Finland and then, a full twenty-six days later, reentry to the United States. It struck Tess that there was a strange irony in this. Because for all these years Jaana and Otso had been a secret hiding behind the curtain of her life. But once, Tess had been the exact same thing to them. When Jaana spoke again, her voice was flat, all the hurt in it scarred over. "She never told us she was pregnant. She never even told us they'd gotten *married*. They did it just a few months after she left, so that Saara wouldn't have to worry about her visa. There wasn't a ceremony. They just signed some papers at the courthouse. They didn't even take pictures."

"You would have asked her not to have the baby," Tess said. Even though she was the baby in question in this particular case, she couldn't bring herself to say: *You would have asked her not to have me.*

Jaana straightened up on the tree stump. She took the now-cool porridge back from Tess, upended it into the thermos, and screwed the lid closed. They'd both begun to shiver, but having come this far, there was no stopping. "It's very important here that you not misunderstand me," Jaana said, looking Tess right in the face. "Because Otso and I are happy that you've come to live with us. Not about the circumstances . . . not about anything that's led up to it. But you must know that we love you and Axel very much." She paused, as though actually waiting for an answer. Tess could only nod. "But absolutely," Jaana continued. "We would have asked Saara not to have you. And we wouldn't just have asked. We would have demanded. *I* would have. Pregnancy was so very dangerous in Saara's condition. I would have told my daughter that she was being stupid, and foolish, and risking her life with a man she hardly knew. And all of it would have been true. It's still true now. It's what happened."

That Saara knew her parents would react this way went without saying—that's why she'd stayed quiet about her pregnancy until after Tess was born. Jaana stared grimly down at her own gloved hands. "Do you know what she said to us when they got off the plane? She was walking right toward us like it hadn't been years, holding you out in her arms like she'd been sending us photographs of you the whole time. Like we'd already watched you grow bigger, picture by picture. Saara said: 'Aren't you happy, Mom?' I've never . . ." Jaana's voice got thick and wet, but Tess couldn't tell if it was with sadness or remembered rage. Both seemed appropriate. "We fought all the way home—Tess, you have no idea how we fought. 'I didn't need your permission,' Saara said. As though we thought she *did*! Of course Saara didn't need our permission. I don't know what mistake Otso and I made, as parents, to make her feel like she had to prove the obvious. Gravity exists whether you drop things or not. But Saara, she *always* had to drop them. It wasn't about permission. It was that she didn't tell us. She could have died."

A bit of movement at the edge of the clearing briefly stole their attention. But it was just a rabbit—a big, rangy thing, new white fur still dappled with summer's brown. It hopped a short ways into the open, searching out grass still peeking up among the tree roots. "But you forgave her," Tess said. Again, those scant markings in her expired passport were all the proof she needed. If that fight had been the final one, then Tess's trip to Finland never would have lasted so long. Had things gotten apocalyptic, as she knew they eventually did, then her reentry stamp to the United States would have been dated the very next day.

"How could we not?" Jaana said, still gazing at the rabbit. It didn't seem to have noticed them yet and was hopping ever closer, from stump to stump. Jaana's lips turned up at the corners ever so slightly. "Saara always knew when she had us at a disadvantage. She was back, after all, and as mad as we were, we were also so happy to see her. And she'd brought you, and you were beautiful. Despite everything, it was a wonderful trip. We spent almost all of it right here. Our little cottage on the lake."

"I remember," Tess said.

"Of course you do," Jaana said. Again she fell silent. It felt like the story almost could have ended there. But happy endings aren't endings. They are middles.

"Saara did tell us when she got pregnant with Axel," Jaana said. "As though not keeping it a secret was enough. As though her decision to tell us this time meant that we didn't get to have an opinion about it. She actually tried to keep us from coming. But Saara had as much power to do that as we did to stop her from making her own choices. We flew to New York and rented an apartment in

Baldwin—you know that little building by the diner, overlooking the river? We lived there for almost half a year."

Tess had learned plenty that she hadn't already known in the past few minutes, but this stood out as a shocker among shockers. Jaana and Otso living in New York, even for a short period of time, was somehow even more inconceivable than baby Tess traveling to Talvijärvi. "Paul was already there when we arrived." Jaana said his name like it was a slur in another language. "But not to help. Nothing like that. He'd gotten into some kind of trouble down in Florida, and he was camped out in a tent in Sam's backyard. That drunk was more welcome in their house than we were. Sam said it was because Paul didn't try to meddle in their lives. But there's a reason for that. Paul doesn't love anybody, least of all himself. So why would he bother meddling?"

"That's not really . . ." Tess stopped herself for a moment. She didn't want to approach even the distant cousin of an argument, not today. And besides, since her father's death Paul had done absolutely nothing to earn her loyalty. But that's the thing about family. They don't have to earn it. "That's not fair."

"I don't need to treat Paul with fairness," Jaana said. She went quiet again and seemed to have no inclination to continue. The animal—it was too big to be a rabbit, Tess saw now, and must have been some kind of Finnish hare or jackrabbit— hopped ever nearer. It didn't even flinch when Jaana reached down to refasten her skis. She returned the thermos of porridge to her small knapsack and then propped herself up on her ski poles. Tess could actually hear her grandmother's joints popping. They'd been still for too long and were both nearly freezing. But this was far from an appropriate stopping point.

"And?" Tess said.

"What and?" Jaana said. "You know how the story finishes. Saara died. And all our years of fighting exploded into something else. Sam . . . I have a lot to say about your father. A lot I won't say about him. But whatever else, he loved my daughter. And when Saara died, his love became a furious, snarling thing. Ours did too. I have no desire to remember how ugly—how petty it got. And I could hardly describe it, even if I did. Your father had us removed from the hospital. We tried to have Saara's body shipped home—our home. *Her* home. We spoke to lawyers. We made threats over the telephone. We all burned and burned and burned until there was nothing left."

This was, finally, the end of it. Jaana's face was drawn, as though the telling had cost her something. But she also seemed—not comforted, exactly. But somehow lighter, as though the price had at least bought some small measure of relief. Jaana had probably recited this story to herself, over and over, as much to figure out how things had gone so horribly wrong as to practice for the day when she'd share it with her grandkids. And that task was finished. Or rather, half finished.

"Come on," Jaana said, "stay any longer and you'll stick to that thing."

Tess fastened her skis. She braced her poles against the frozen ground and was just about to hoist herself up into a standing position when the most preposterous thing happened. The hare that had been steadily approaching for some minutes suddenly jumped up into her lap, like some woodland creature out of vintage Disney. "Oh!" Jaana said. Tess was too surprised to manage even that. The animal was heavy as a housecat on her thighs, and it looked up at her with big, glassy, not-so-intelligent eyes. Much of the hare's fur was still brown, but the coloring on its face had already turned white, revealing little scars on its otherwise soft-looking lips. There were also old wounds along its left hindquarter—tight scar tissue, bald as a boiled chicken.

"Is that . . . ?" Jaana trailed off, unable to finish her question. But she didn't have to, because they both knew the answer. It was Bigwig, the family pet they'd left behind in Baldwin. The hare had somehow hopped her way across the world, not only to Finland, but to this exact little corner of Talvijärvi. Tess felt an intense and very sudden swell of mingled guilt and pride. The guilt was familiar—though it had evolved slightly over the last two days. Tess had stopped beating herself up for not believing her brother. After all, who would have, in her shoes? The guilt was simply because she hadn't even really *listened*. But the pride was completely new. Because her little brother had been right, hadn't he? He'd stepped right through the impossible and into the true.

Bigwig shifted around on Tess's lap, trying to get comfortable. She seemed happy and healthy— as well suited to the Finnish winter as any animal condemned to it by birth.

"How could that . . . ?" Jaana was still having trouble making a full sentence.

Tess took hold of Bigwig and stood. She looked down at the snow, where Bigwig's tracks zigzagged across the cleared shoreline and disappeared back into the forest. There was something in there—a dark flicker of movement. Tess's heart caught. She kicked her way over as fast as her skis would take her, sliding past one tree and then another. She was about to call out for her brother when she realized that it definitely wasn't Axel in those trees. It was something else entirely.

"Where are you going?" Jaana said. She sounded strangely far off and muffled. When Tess turned back to answer, she found that she couldn't even see her grandmother anymore. The trees had circled in behind her—trunks and branches in every hue of brown and gray. Some still had leaves, and some did not. Some were heavy with goblet-shaped flowers, while others wore ropy necklaces of hanging roots and vines. It was warm in here, and it stank of blossoms and rotten fruit. When Tess looked down at her skis, she saw that they were slowly sinking into a bubbling patch of coal-black mud. Or, no, it was sand. Fine, white sand.

"I hate you here," a voice said. It seemed to come from all around her. But it was just one voice—the voice of what could only be the monster in Axel's story. The Hiisi. The demon that had chased poor Väinö. Again Tess was hit with that cocktail of guilt and pride. She had no idea that her brother had ever encountered anything so terrifying. But he'd done it. He was still doing it. She caught a glint of movement—a slithering up one of the trunks, leaping from branch to branch.

"I hate you on the path." The Hiisi seemed to be struggling to control itself.

Seeing the Keeper in the woods and holding Bigwig were nothing compared to feeling the Hiisi's voice ripple through her. But she was all in at this point. "Then why did you bring me here?" Tess shouted at the demon. She wasn't really sure where to look, but it hardly mattered—if she fixed her eyes on anything for more than a few seconds, it changed. A cactus came and went, followed by a rosebush and then a palm. Tess was everywhere in the world right now, and everywhere was here. The Hiisi was silent for a moment, so she shouted again.

"Where is my brother?"

"Cottage." The Hiisi coughed the word out over her shoulder, and it bounced about between the dancing trees. "I have chased him off the path, but his threads are straining. If they break, they cannot be mended."

"I don't know what that means." Tess spun around to get a look at the Hiisi, but her skis had become tangled in a mess of succulent creepers, and she fell down hard. Frustration was making her fearless. "I swear to God," Tess said, "if you hurt my brother, I will find a way to hurt you back."

It seemed, for the briefest moment, like the demon was taken aback. "I will not," the Hiisi said, every tree an amplifier for its awful, butchering voice. "You *could* not." When it spoke again, the words came slowly. "Go. To. The. Cottage." As though Tess were a baby, or a pet. "And get your brother."

Before Tess could ask why it would want to help her, the Hiisi seemed to draw itself up close. The wind of its breath passed over her neck, cold as the morning air in Finland. "I hate him on the path. But he will not be frightened off. You're the only way home he has left. Go, now, or you will lose him."

Tess felt something clawing at the back of her jacket, and she twisted around, trying once more to get a look. But it was only her grandmother. It was only Talvijärvi. The trees around her were frozen spruces and nothing more.

"How deep did you go?" Jaana said, helping Tess back up onto her skis. "I lost sight of you for . . ." The blood drained from Jaana's face as soon as she got a good look at Tess's expression. It was as though the impression that the Hiisi had left on Tess, so distinctly strange and terrifying, were contagious.

"Give me your knapsack," Tess said.

Jaana unslung it and handed it over. Tess turned the knapsack around so that it hung across her chest, and then she quickly placed Bigwig inside. As soon as she was in the pack, the hare curled up and went to sleep. Her job was done, apparently.

"We're going to the cottage," Tess said.

Her tone told Jaana all that she needed to know. They weren't quite halfway around the lake, so the quickest route home was the way they'd come. The fact that their skis had already laid down a slick track made the going easier. Tess and Jaana shot across the shattered surface of the snow, catching air on little crests. Her grandmother retrieved her phone from her jacket, and she somehow managed to dial as they went, compensating by leaning into her opposite pole. She called Otso and asked if he could check on the volunteers who were supposed to be staking out the cottage. She called Kalle, who was out searching the western edge of the lake with Kari, and asked if he could do the same. She called Chief Aarne and told him a straight-up lie: "I think we saw Axel. I'm almost sure of it. Please, tell everybody that he might be nearby." The news went out quickly. Shortly after Jaana hung up, they began to hear shouting in the distance, newly electrified with hope. Axel's name, coming from everywhere.

Tess knew that the police had never believed her. They'd released the Keeper's cartoonish likeness to the local TV station yesterday and handed out his picture to the baffled search parties only at Jaana's insistence. But despite that outward support, Tess had no idea what her grandmother actually thought about her story. Jaana had been uncharacteristically evasive on that point, committing only to: "I know you're not lying." Which could have meant: "Yes, you really saw your brother, and we should act accordingly." But also: "Yes, you *think* you saw him. Poor little thing . . ." But in these last few minutes, everything had changed. Jaana may not have been able to see the Hiisi, but Bigwig was undeniable.

Jaana had held the hare in her own hands back in Baldwin.

She'd watched her disappear into the park.

And now Bigwig was here, snug in the hammock of Jaana's knapsack, sleeping beside a thermos of porridge. *'Twas the hare who took the tidings*—the verse sprang up suddenly in Tess's mind. It took her a moment to remember where it came from—*The Kalevala*, that big-ass compendium of Finnish song-poetry and for years her most dreaded study book. It was a random coincidence and also kind of a crappy one. Because the hare in the poem brought a mournful story. Your child is dead. Your child is drowned. Tess shook the poem from her thoughts, skiing faster.

They swung down along the southern shore and could soon see the Hannula house through the spruces up ahead. Just beyond, the Kivis' outside lights were all blazing, a flashlight beam raking the yard. By now Jaana was going at a pace that even Tess couldn't match, the waxed undersides of her skis clattering loudly on the icy gravel of the Hannulas' plowed driveway. A figure in a neon vest appeared up ahead. He was skiing toward them, one gloved hand held high in a frantic wave. It was Kalle.

"Someone's been inside the cottage!" Kalle shouted. Though by the time he was done, he didn't have to shout anymore—Jaana was already at his side.

"Axel? Did they find Axel?"

Kalle shook his head, struggling for breath. "Otso is sure it was him, though. And the police think it hasn't been very long. They've called everybody in to search the woods behind our houses—" As quick as that, Kalle had to shout again, because Jaana was already gone. She sprinted the final distance to the cottage, hardly slowing as she kicked off her skis, flying boots-first through the open door. Tess lagged behind her by only a moment, rushing inside with such speed that she crashed right into Otso's empty wheelchair and sent it rolling back into one of the unadorned walls, knocking rinds of slush from its spokes and stirrups. Otso himself was sitting on the couch in the living room, his trousers soaked to the knees from his trip through the snow, his head in his hands. The entire living room floor was wet with melt. Tess guessed that only moments ago the room had been filled with police and volunteers, but now the only ones left were Otso and Kari. The boy was plopped down on the damp carpet, panting in near agony, still spent from racing back to the cottage with his brother. Jaana ignored him and set upon her husband. She grabbed Otso's hands away from his face and held them. His eyes were pink with frustration.

"They were supposed to *stay* here," he said. "The volunteers weren't supposed to move, in case he came back!"

"They didn't see Axel?"

Otso shook his head. "The searchers posted to Erikinlinna reported a stranger in the woods. Just some crazy old drunk, apparently." Even as he said this, Tess was sure that the crazy old drunk in question could only be the Keeper. "They pulled everyone nearby over to help round him up, but he got away. And in the meantime, they left the cottage empty." Otso was shaking—so mad that it looked like he was about to cry. "Axel was *right here*, and they missed him."

"You're sure it was Axel? You're positive?"

For a moment Otso gave no answer, and Jaana looked as though she might actually shake him. Then he pulled one of his hands out of her grip and cast it in the direction of the coffee table at his knees. There was a piece of unlined paper on it, the top edge jagged from where it had been torn from a pad. It was one of the sketches that Tess had rejected yesterday, the Keeper looking like some toothy moonshiner up for parole.

"The other side," Otso said.

Jaana picked the paper up and turned it over. Tess watched her pupils ping from side to side. "This isn't a bad thing," she said, her voice measured. "It isn't. It means he was close." Otso made no answer. Jaana handed the paper to Tess. Then she returned to the front door to collect her skis. The woods out back were screaming with activity, Aarne and all the other searchers convinced that Axel was still somewhere nearby. But somehow, even before Tess read her brother's note, she knew that he wasn't. Axel was as far away from her as he'd ever been.

The letter on the back of the sketch was written in neat, cautious penmanship. It was maddeningly brief.

Dear ~~Everybody~~,
Dear Tess,
I'm really sorry, but I'm not coming back.
Your brother,
Axel

18

The Long Way

If it weren't for his mother, Axel might not have gotten away from the Hiisi that night back at Mud Lake. The thing chased him through the parking lot, still littered with human-shaped bodies in the moonlight, and out across the big meadows. Axel lost it briefly in the maples edging the road and snuck across to where he thought his old house should have been. But he must have gotten lost in the dark—the A-frame was nowhere to be seen, and the Hiisi was getting closer, gnashing its way through the trees. But for Saara, Axel would have kept right on running. She was hiding in a garbage bin set back from the road and granted him the lean courtesy of a single hoot as he approached. He jumped in beside her, and they held their breath as they waited for the Hiisi to pass them by. The thing took its sweet time, crashing languidly through the forest, jabber-walking this way and that. But these sounds subsided over time. The moon sank, and his mom became a bear again, filling the garbage bin. Axel waited until he was sure she was asleep—ghosts slept, apparently—before leaning against her and closing his eyes.

It was only after sunup the next morning that Axel realized that he hadn't gotten lost at all—the A-frame simply didn't *exist* anymore. The garbage bin that he and Saara had slept in was the same one he'd seen on his first trip back to Baldwin. Axel remembered how Sam's homemade bivouac had been dismantled and how the house itself had been surrounded with orange safety cones and tasseled with caution tape. But that had apparently been just the beginning of Mrs. Ridgeland's plans. In the intervening week, she had weeded every last trace of the Fortunes out of her land. His mother's birch trees were all cut down, the yard leveled, the A-frame stripped to its foundations and then the foundations themselves pried out of the earth like rotten teeth. In the sharp, late-autumn daylight, Axel could see that the garbage bin was filled with the last remains of his life in New York. The curdled chicken wire of Bigwig's hutch and jagged swatches of his father's Birds of the Northeast wallpaper.

Axel climbed out of the garbage bin, walked out across the overturned mud, and sat down roughly in the spot where his living room used to be. Saara leaped out of the bin as well, landing on her wide paws with a snort. She began sniffing about the edges of the property, maybe searching out some lingering whiff of the Hiisi. "What's wrong with you?" she said, glancing back at him. "Why are you crying?"

"It's all gone," was all Axel could say.

Saara took a heavy step toward him, stopping at the edge of the A-frame's fading footprint. "I don't understand," she said. "It was made out of wood, yes? There are other houses, yes? Tons of them, all over the place." It was hard to tell if she was trying to make a point, or if she really didn't understand. Her little bear eyes squinted, making her look simple and mean.

"Lady speaks the truth." This was the Keeper's voice. Axel looked up and saw him standing in what had once been Saara's vegetable garden, sucking forlornly on his recovered pipe. The Keeper looked like he'd had a rough night. Quills and bent feathers jutted from his duster, and a translucent gravel of safety glass had collected along the brim of his hat. When he shifted his weight, a fine shower of ash drifted down from his gaping joints.

"Looks like you made it," Saara said, turning back

to the trees. She didn't seem particularly pleased by this—she was only remarking upon the facts.

"Don't I always, though?" the Keeper said, sounding just as ambivalent about his survival as she did. He took a few creaking steps across the mud, leaning heavily on his gnarly walking stick as he did so. When he reached Axel, he stopped and stared down at him. The old man was either wearing a patronizing sneer, or that was just the new shape of his ruined features. "No thanks to you, I'm afraid," the Keeper said. "Judging by the beastly way the Hiisi treated our French friends, I think it's safe to say that it still thinks that you can be frightened off the path. The Hiisi must reckon you a *coward*. And who knows . . ." The Keeper let out a mean little snort but then had to hug himself about the ribs for a moment, shrinking into a full-body wince. "Maybe it's right," he finally managed.

This stung, but not in the way that the Keeper had meant it to. Axel knew that he wasn't a coward. But he felt sick about what had happened to those soldiers. As far as Axel knew, the dead were indestructible, but still, thoughts of those Frenchmen disappearing into the Hiisi's impossible mouth had kept him up almost all night.

"They're going to come back, right?" he said.

"I don't follow," the Keeper said.

"The soldiers. The next time the moon comes

out, they'll be back." Axel didn't want this to sound like a question. He didn't want there to be any question about it.

"Oh, my dear child," the Keeper said, aping sympathy. "No, they most certainly will not be back." Then, when he saw the color drain from Axel's face, the old man's expression softened. The next time he spoke, he actually did sound sympathetic. "If it makes you feel any better, they're no more dead today than they were yesterday."

That did not make Axel feel better. He felt, rather, like he was sinking into the mud hole left behind by the A-frame. Mrs. Ridgeland had warned Axel last night that he was putting everybody in danger by luring the Hiisi out, but he'd hardly taken her seriously. Because up until that point, the dangers on this little quest had been vivid and exciting, but also mostly toothless. Ghostly soldiers died as men only to spring back to life as birds. Parents died in unacceptable accidents only to be whisked into the woods as ghosts. Here on the path, all losses were supposed to be temporary, all loneliness fleeting.

"So where are they?" Axel said.

"Your guess is as good as mine," the Keeper said. He shrugged, but not unkindly. "I only know that they aren't on the path anymore. Remember—the Hiisi decides who can stay on the path and who can leave it. If the Hiisi were to swallow you, you'd be spat back into that dreary little family just in time to be unpopular at school. But where do the dead go?" The Keeper skewed up his face, as though this were a question he'd never considered before. "That's as much a mystery to me as dying used to be to you." And with that he offered out his left hand, now no more mangled than the rest of him was. Axel took it and pulled himself up. Guilt was settling in his stomach like a bad case of food poisoning, and he felt wobbly on his feet.

Saara took no notice of this conversation. She was peering intently back into the park. "We should be going," Saara said, shifting her weight anxiously from paw to paw. "We're wasting time, just sitting here. I'm going to—"

The Keeper cut her off with a sigh that crackled through the ember in his pipe, expelling a little spiral of sparks out of the bowl. "I'd rather waste time sitting here than waste it walking around that lake one more damn time," he said. "And besides, after last night, any of those Frenchies who made it are going to have zero patience for us."

"I'm not interested in whether they do or they don't," Saara said. She was so eager to get going that her whole body began to rock, and when she spoke again, it seemed mostly to herself. "Maybe the boardwalk? Maybe we should check the boardwalk one more time."

"It won't be any less empty than it was the last time, or the time before that," the Keeper said. "You know, the definition of insanity is doing the same thing over and—"

"The definition of insanity," Saara said, wheeling back around on the Keeper with the broad horror of her head, "is interrupting me."

The two of them went on like that for a while, irritable and bickering, but Axel ignored them. He just stood there, shocked and still in the jagged crater of his old life. And for the first time since he'd encountered the Keeper back in Helsinki, Axel began to seriously consider giving up. He'd come to a point where he could no longer deny that what he was doing had consequences—not just for a handful of eighteenth-century French ghosts, but also for people who were still alive. People who loved him and missed him. The memory of his sister's face, staring at Axel through a bend in the path back at Talvijärvi, straight-up haunted him. And for all the trouble he knew he'd caused, they were no closer to finding Sam than they'd ever been! Instead of clues in his old home, all Axel found was crumbling earth and scraps of garbage. Now it looked more like his Grandpa Paul's disaster of a yard down in the Boils than it did the home where Axel and Tess had grown up. Axel's mind hit a snag on that last thought. It took him a few moments to realize why.

The Boils. It wasn't just where Grandpa Paul lived, but where Sam had grown up. Axel used to suspect that part of the reason their family would visit so often was so that his father could get back out into the creeks and springs he remembered from his childhood. Wow. What an idiot he was.

"Guys," Axel said. Saara had made for the edge of the property, and the Keeper was hobbling after her, still hectoring. "Hey!" he shouted.

"What?" Saara was crossing the road now. She made no indication that she intended to wait for either of them.

"I think I know where my father is," Axel said.

Saara and the Keeper both stopped in their tracks and turned to stare at him. "Well, hell," the old man said. "That's a load off my shoulders."

It was hard to tell how long the three of them walked the path in search of the Boils, but Axel judged it to be at least a full day or two. He hadn't expected it to take that long—after all, the stroll from Talvijärvi to Baldwin was no more than a hundred paces, and a whole *ocean* lay between those places. He thought all he had to do was find the right blaze and follow it to his granddad's home. Simple enough, considering how well Axel knew the Boils; the sulfury reek of the springwater creeks, the feel of fine white dirt between his toes. The stands of bald cypress and sand pine out behind Grandpa Paul's trailer were nearly as familiar to Axel as the black maples and hemlock trees of Mud Lake Park. And on top of that, he had his father's remembered lectures to guide him—Axel knew more about the home ranges of native hardwoods than was reasonable for anybody his age. But in the end these advantages proved to be worth very little. They weren't on the path five minutes before they got good and lost. Axel spotted a runty juniper down the embankment and followed it to a sudden and unfamiliar hillside. The three of them raced up the hill, and when they reached the top, they had a beautiful view of a little village spilling out of the valley below, all made of adobe and thatch. Talk about a wrong turn—this wasn't the Boils, or even America. Apparently, there was a whole lot of world between New York and Florida.

The reason Axel couldn't tell exactly how long they were lost was that time didn't really exist on the path. That's not to say that everything stood still. Clouds still blew from one end of the sky to the other; it rained and it stopped raining; Axel would get hungry and eat, and later on he would be hungry again. Time *passed*. But that passing didn't mean a whole lot without being tied down to a specific place. And Axel had misjudged how disorienting it would be to slip from wood to wood, playing hopscotch across the light and dark sides of the planet. He realized, too late, that it was impossible to keep track of time without a watch or a cell phone. The sun burned high one minute, was gone the next, and set sluggishly moments later, like jet lag in a centrifuge. So they stopped and rested when they needed to rest, and they slept when they could no longer help themselves. Tiny days passed in truncated segments; who could say how many of them?

The fact that it was coming up on winter helped a little—even the slightest trace of snow was a clear sign they were going the wrong way. But it wasn't enough. They came close once, stepping from Vermont to the Everglades, only to turn a corner in the bush and come upon the Mud Lake visitors' center again, the glass double doors still shattered. Another time, after hitting a solidly Florida-like vein of muggy warmth, Axel found himself on the banks of a brown stream choked with sleeping hippos and bald-headed storks. Must have taken a wrong turn at the baobab back there. It would have been awesome if the journey was the point, but it wasn't. Axel's dad was out there, somewhere, and he wasn't about to rest until they found him.

His traveling companions didn't do much to make the time fly, either. You'd think that a major upside to a foot journey with your long-dead mother would be the chance for a little conversation. The chance to get answers to niggling questions, such as: Mom, what's up with the whole secret-grandparents-in-Finland thing? Or: Mom, how to put this . . . ? Having me killed you, didn't it? But Axel had no such luck. For one thing, Saara didn't answer to "Mom," no matter what form she was in. And for another, she was hardly motherly. Saara was a bear, full of hunger and want, usually stinking of whatever it was she'd just scavenged—garbage or beehive or half-rotten deer. The Keeper was no better. He'd been quiet and gloomy since what happened back at Mud Lake, limping along with his eyes on his boots. He only ever perked up when they heard the Hiisi shambling in the distance, which happened more often than Axel would have liked. The monster had been following them since Baldwin, always lingering just out of sight, making its presence known by the terrified birds that it sent hollering into the sky.

It was evening—or at least it was evening in whatever part of the world they'd just stumbled onto—when the Hiisi finally showed itself. The path had led them to an old rockfall of split granite, overlaid with lichen and yellowing scrub. With no way to go around the slope, they decided to climb, scrambling up the stones as the sun set into their faces. It wasn't steep, but it was slow going, the

Keeper prodding each stone with his stick before setting a foot down. They were nearly at the top when they began to hear noises up there—the crumble and tumble of loose rocks. Saara's nostrils flared, her head bobbing as she tried to catch a scent. Axel had been using Sam's sword as a walking stick, but he raised it now, holding it between himself and whatever was on top of the rise. Then it appeared, a silhouette against the setting sun. The Hiisi sashayed lightly from side to side, its bright mouth crackling. Smoke poured off it, trickling down the granite slope like fog out of an open freezer.

"I think we should go back down," Saara said.

Difficult to argue with that wisdom. They turned and began to pick their way down the rockfall, keeping an eye over their shoulders. The Hiisi seemed content to just watch. When they got back down to the base of the hill, they found the woods from which they'd come to be completely transformed. There was ice underfoot, and the air was so cold that it felt solid. Up ahead there was a stone archway and beyond that a stand of bluish spruce. "This is fantastic," the Keeper said, applauding limply, too exhausted to fully commit to his own sarcasm. "This is exactly where we want to be. Absolutely."

Axel glanced back the way they'd come and

saw that the rocky hill was growing steeper. The granite shook itself free of grass and lichen, the slope leaning farther and farther forward until it was standing upright. It took Axel a moment to understand that he was looking at the sheer wall of Erikinlinna. They'd come the fullest of full circles, back to Talvijärvi. He couldn't shake the strange feeling that the Hiisi had herded them here.

"It isn't right," said a voice, in Finnish. It would have made Axel jump out of his skin if he weren't already so keyed up. It sounded like the voice had come from just outside the castle. Axel crept across the snow and peeked around the ruined archway. There were two men out there, seated on a bench at the far end of the covered picnic area. Both were outfitted in survival gear and neon vests. They each held wooden mugs up to their hooded faces, the steam freezing in their mustaches. After a long pause, the one who had spoken continued. "They should at least be honest with the girl."

His companion took his time to answer, sipping loudly on whatever was in his mug. "Perhaps they have been," he said.

"You know they haven't," the first man said. "You saw her face. She hasn't even considered the possibility."

The men were wearing skis, the back halves jutting beneath the bench. Axel glanced out across the much-disturbed snow, where telltale tracks were everywhere. Two grooves, straight as train rails, dotted on either side by the punch holes of ski poles. A lot of people had been through these woods. A lot of people, searching for *him*.

"I suppose," said the second man. In true Finnish fashion, he seemed to want to use as few words as possible. Nevertheless, their gossip was achieved.

"And how's she going to feel if he doesn't turn up? Or, heaven forbid . . ."

The second man nodded to spare his companion from having to complete the thought. "No worse," he said.

"No worse?"

"No worse than if she'd been braced for it." The second man polished off whatever was in his wooden mug. "That's not a thing you can soften. That's as bad as it ever gets." Only then did it dawn on Axel that these two men were talking about his sister—about how she'd feel if no one found him. Or rather, *when*.

The Keeper joined him at the edge of the archway. "Stick around long enough, and maybe we can go to your funeral," he whispered. The men on the bench clammed up and looked at each other, cocking their ears into the air.

"What?" the Keeper said, apparently too

exhausted to care that he'd almost given them away. "I went to mine. More fun than you'd think."

"Is someone there?" the first man called. He must have forgotten that his skis were still wedged under the bench, because when he stood, they got tangled up, sending him tumbling forward. His companion rose to help him.

"Shush," Saara said, approaching as quietly as she could, the snow squealing under her pads.

"Hello?" the first man hollered. He was back on his feet now, held at the elbows by his friend. "Mrs. Kivi, is that you?"

"Lucky guess," the Keeper whispered. "But not the one they're thinking of."

"I said shut up!" Saara wagged her head up at the castle roof. "It's still here."

She was talking about the Hiisi. Axel turned and saw it perched atop the stove-in tower like some kind of magnificently ugly crow, its mouth spilling light down the walls. As though it had ridden the crest of the hill like a wave. The men couldn't seem to see it, but they clearly heard the noises it was making. The Hiisi shifted on its perch, sending chunks of stone tumbling down the tower walls. They landed in the courtyard with a series of big, echoing thuds—clearly the Hiisi was doing this on purpose. The men in the neon vests kicked their way out of the picnic area and began to approach the castle. "Hello?" they called again. Then, more tentatively, one of them said: "Axel? Axel Fortune?"

"Bother," the Keeper whispered, glancing back into the ruins. But he must have known there was no other way out—Axel had been there only twice before, and he even knew it.

The men continued to approach the castle archway. One of them put a hand on a little radio affixed to his shoulder. "We're hearing some movement at Erikinlinna," he said into the mouthpiece. "Stand by, please."

At this the Keeper fell to his knees. He pulled a little bottle of schnapps from one of his pockets and proceeded to empty about half of it all over himself. Then he gathered up a big fistful of snow and poured the rest of the schnapps into that. He looked Axel right in the face. "Don't ever tell me that I didn't sacrifice for you," the Keeper said. Then he stood, pulled the back of his duster up and over his head, and charged out of the courtyard like a madman. Axel could see the Keeper wheel back and throw his boozy snowball, striking one of the two men square in the nose and knocking him back onto his butt.

"Not in *my* house!" the Keeper hollered. "And on *Christmas*?"

Still screaming, the old man scampered insanely

into the forest. The two searchers were so shocked that it took them a second to respond. But when they finally did, they were quick about it. The one with the radio called in to ask for help rounding up a drunk in the woods. Then they skied out into the dark after him, leaving Axel and his mother alone inside the ruins.

The Hiisi watched all of this silently from its perch atop the tower. Then the saplings that filled the courtyard began to twirl, barking with the Hiisi's voice.

"Fools," it said.

The Hiisi leaped down off the tower, crashing through the roof of the covered picnic area. The wooden pillars exploded, and the eaves folded in, catapulting rinds of curdled snow against the castle walls and into the boughs of nearby trees. For a moment they couldn't see the Hiisi, but they could hear it in there, slipping on the snow-strewn floor, smashing into tables, gathering itself back together. A moment later the Hiisi rolled out of the wreckage, clicking and ticking, licking its chops.

"We need to go too," Saara said.

Axel and his mother raced into the woods, careful to go in a different direction from the way the Keeper had gone. They found the frozen lakeshore all dotted with lights from search parties, and twice they had to change course to avoid flashlight beams that came too close. When they finally arrived at the Kivis' cottage, they found it dark against the star-filled sky, obviously empty. There was no place that Axel wanted to go less than that, but the Hiisi gave them little choice. They could hear it sizzle and hiss just a few steps behind. It had eyes only for Axel. It had no eyes at all.

They tumbled into the cottage, Saara's massive body crushing the air from Axel's lungs as she rolled over him. She fumblingly tried to shut the door behind them with her claws, and Axel, still gasping for air, had to help her latch the dead bolt. Saara leaned her bulk against the shuttered door, and they waited. Axel strained his ears, but there was no sound other than the mingled huff of their breathing. And then, from the other side of the cottage, the oiled swish of hinges.

They'd forgotten about the back door. It was, fittingly and horribly, the one with the ramp. The one made to accommodate wheelchairs. Axel turned to see the door swing wide, filled with the Hiisi's nothing guts. It reached a long arm—or something very like an arm, formless and precise as the dark—across the living room. Axel tried to wriggle away, but the Hiisi sensed his movement. It groped frantically, overturning chairs and sending books bouncing against the low ceiling. Saara just stared, utterly useless. Axel's hand fell to his belt and discovered, almost to his own surprise, the hilt of his father's sword. He unsheathed it and struck down as hard as he could. It passed through the Hiisi like it was nothing but air. Still, the monster trumpeted awfully, and as it lurched away, Axel followed it to the back door, slamming it shut. The Hiisi hollered again, thrashing around by the sauna. Then, bit by bit, it quieted down.

They waited. Axel went to check the windows, but all he could see were lights in the distance. A minute passed and then another. Saara began to fret and groan. She tried to get her broad grizzly rear onto the couch and succeeded only in pushing it against the far wall. She stayed like that, half of her butt lifted up onto the couch, mean little ears twitching with agitation.

They kept waiting. Saara glanced about, taking in the sight of her childhood summer cottage like it was a place she'd never been to. Axel looked around too. The cottage appeared to be pretty much as he'd left it. The muddy ash was still frozen in the fireplace, and his stripped bedding lay exactly where he'd dropped it on the floor. There were plenty of people out searching for him, but it was clear that none of them were sleeping here. Axel went to one of the east windows and gazed down shore at the Hannula house. It was like someone had doused the place in gasoline—hot and bright and ugly. He could see silhouettes moving behind the curtains. Even at this distance Axel could tell that one of them was Otso.

"This is where we met," Saara said, apropos of nothing whatsoever.

Axel turned to her. For a moment it seemed as though this might be the beginning and the end of what his mother intended to share. "You and Dad," he said, hoping to prod her. "You and Sam."

Just the utterance of his father's name seemed to have a physical effect on Saara. "Sam," she said. "Sam," like the word was water and she was parched. "He was in Talvijärvi for the summer. He was in the trees, up high in the trees. He didn't have the words." She pressed her tiny eyes closed, her lips curling back over her teeth. It seemed like she, and not Sam, was the one who needed words.

Axel gave her a moment.

"He was collecting samples," Saara said, her eyes still closed. "I had gone out for a walk, and I thought I was alone. Because why would anyone be up there? But when I stopped in some bushes to pee, I heard a noise. It sounded like a person. 'I'm in here!' I called. Sam didn't know what I was saying—he didn't have the words. He yelled back to me, and it made no sense. I spoke English, but I just didn't think . . . Why would someone in the trees be yelling *English* at me? 'I'm in here!' I said. 'Don't come here!' Sam thought that I was in trouble. That I needed help. We were just yelling and yelling and yelling. 'Keep away!' 'Here I come!'" Saara drifted. Her little eyes popped open again.

"I think that you should stay here," she said, as if this thought were somehow connected to the ones that had come before it. It took Axel a moment to understand her meaning. "You should go back to them."

"I don't want to," Axel said. He didn't mean to sound so hesitant and wimpy. So he said it again. "I don't want to stay here."

Saara turned her head sideways, bestial and inquisitive. For the first time since Axel had met her, every bit of Saara's attention seemed to be focused squarely on him. The couch groaned beneath her. "Aren't you homesick?"

"Not for here," Axel said. He turned back to the window so that he wouldn't have to keep looking at her, resting his elbows on the sill. There was a flickering streak in the distance—a pair of flashlights moving quickly on the frozen shore. "Besides, you won't be able to find Sam without me," he said.

"Yes, I will," his mother answered flatly. "I've got forever."

"But I want to find him. I want to find him, too."

"He isn't yours to find." Saara sounded aghast at

the possibility that Axel didn't already know this. "He's mine. And even when we do find him, there's nothing that your father can give you. Not anymore. There's nothing I can give you, either." Axel may have been kidding himself, but he thought he could detect a trace of regret in her voice. "You need to understand this," Saara said. "It doesn't mean I didn't love you when I was alive. It doesn't mean that I wasn't so, so excited to meet you. *When I was alive.* But I'm not anymore."

"But I don't want anything from you," Axel said. He caught himself getting a little frustrated. "And besides, there's nothing for me here. I don't even know who I'm supposed to be here."

"Won't you have to find out, sooner or later?"

"Says who?"

His mother was quiet for a moment, as if she were giving this petulant question more consideration than it deserved. Then she harrumphed, a wet, warm sound. "Says nobody, I guess. Do what you want."

They spoke no more after that. The cottage fell into silence, save the occasional hollering of Axel's name, drifting in from the trees. Had that been Tess's voice, or Jaana's? It was a rotten thing that Axel had done to them—he knew that. They'd be sad. Axel didn't kid himself; they'd be devastated. But they'd get over it.

Eventually Saara got up and began pacing again, eager to get outside and continue the search. Axel was eager, too. He was afraid that if they stayed here much longer, he might lose his nerve. How easy it would have been to just open the door and take the short walk over to the Hannula house. Otso would let him inside, and everybody would scold him, and they'd all weep for joy. Axel decided that there was only one way to keep going. He found a piece of doodled-on paper on the dining room table and a pen in one of Jaana's drawers. It was a short note, but it took surprisingly long to write. When Axel signed the bottom, it was as good as a contract. He was never coming back here.

"Hey!" The Keeper's voice came from just outside. "You two in there?"

Saara was already at the front door. "Is the Hiisi gone?" she called.

"All clear," the Keeper said. "Nobody out here but us saviors."

Saara pawed at the dead bolt, and Axel hurried to unlatch it before she could bust the whole door down. Then he followed her out into the snow. Axel realized, right away, that the Keeper had lied to them. He was standing in the middle of the yard, glowing. He'd lost his hat when he'd run away from the little search party at the castle, and fluorescent light was reflecting off his skull. He wasn't looking at them, Axel realized, but above them. He was staring over their heads, into the mouth of the Hiisi.

It had climbed onto the roof of the cottage. Axel turned just in time to see the thing come down upon him. What a soothing grip it had, cool and clean like washed sheets. The Hiisi took him up, pulling him into the sizzling bright. It was the same thing that it had always been. It was the wheelchair that had followed him to school. It was the numbness in his legs and arms. It was the quiet of an empty house, the loneliness of his father's empty bedroom. The Hiisi was everything that Axel had ever been afraid of. Except, in that moment, it also wasn't. In fact, in those seconds when the Hiisi was about to swallow him, Axel didn't feel any fear at all. Because Axel was of the path now. If the Hiisi pulled him off it today, he would find his way back tomorrow. If Tess and Jaana caught him and brought him to Helsinki, he would walk right back here. Axel could read the blazes now. Every branch was a signpost, every tree a doorway to his new home.

The Hiisi hesitated, Axel still dangling over its shining maw. Then, all of a sudden, it tossed him aside. He landed hard on the ground, the snow burning his palms and bare cheeks. Saara's jaws closed on the hood of his sweater, and she lifted him to his feet.

"So that's it, then?" the Keeper said, his voice high and giddy. He was speaking to the Hiisi.

"The boy seems sure," the Hiisi said, whispering the words through the frozen spruce needles. It sounded vaguely hesitant.

"He is sure. His threads are cut." The old man took one short step toward the monster and then another. "His threads are cut," he said again, all smooth and soothing, like he was trying to calm some wild animal. "He *belongs* now. He isn't upsetting the balance." Another step. "You've got what you need, and the woods do, too." The Keeper was speaking right into the Hiisi's gaping mouth now. With just a twitch, the monster could have ruined him. In the length of a breath, it could have swallowed him whole.

"Get away from it," Axel said. He tried to take a step toward the Keeper, but Saara was still holding his hood in her reeking jaws. She began to back into the trees, and Axel's ankles slid across the ice and powder.

"We have to go," she whispered through her mouthful of cotton. "They'll be here any minute." She was right—Axel could see flashlights approaching from around the Hannula house. He could hear his name hurled out across the frozen lake.

"We can't just leave him there," Axel said.

"We absolutely can," Saara said.

The Keeper had reached out his mangled left hand, as though he meant to try to touch the light inside the Hiisi. "One Keeper for every wood," he said, almost whispering now into the bright abyss. "Just one. You promised."

"What are you doing?" Axel called, still being dragged backward by his mother.

The old man turned back to him, his cheeks shining with black rivulets of ashen tears. "Going home," he said. "Thank you."

And then the Keeper's hand vanished, sizzling away to nothing in the Hiisi. His arm disappeared and then his shoulder. The old man wasn't being eaten—not at all. He was *climbing through*. The Hiisi hacked and coughed, as though trying to spit him back up. But the Keeper seemed as dead set on leaving the path as Axel was on staying there. Finally, the Hiisi gave up.

It swallowed, and the Keeper was gone.

19

The Boy in the Picture

The cold snap lasted four more days, and in that time the search party at Talvijärvi didn't find so much as a footprint from Axel. Expectations had been high at the beginning of the week, when they'd missed him by a hair at the cottage. Chief Aarne requested emergency support from nearby Savonlinna, and by daybreak there was another pair of helicopters in the sky, and the woods were flush with hundreds of men and women in ski outfits and matching vests. They linked arms and walked slowly through the snow, like a chorus line singing a song with only one lyric—only one word. "Axel." His shouted name reverberated for miles, a hot breath of hope cutting through the frozen woods.

Those hopes began to fray as the hours and days wore on without any sign and the temperature stayed murderously cold. One member of the search party discovered bear tracks in the overturned snow, and this animal was added to the whispered fates that were already being passed from volunteer to volunteer. Tess's brother could have been kidnapped. Tess's brother could have frozen to death. Tess's brother could have been mauled and eaten whole. At the end of the third day, Chief Aarne distributed adjustable aluminum poles to the entire search party. Nobody told Tess what they were for, but it wasn't hard to guess—they were to help search for Axel's body, under the snow. Aarne and the police were still being coy about it. They hadn't quit using the word "rescue." Medics remained on standby in a mobile clinic parked in the Hannulas' driveway, volunteers continued to arrive daily from town, and Finnish army helicopters were still doggedly skimming the woods and fields of Talvijärvi. But it was obvious that people were expecting the worst. The patrols went grimly about their work, skiing their assigned lengths of the grid, stabbing their poles into every rise in the snow.

Tess and her grandparents seemed to be the only ones who trusted, without question, that Axel was still alive. But at least for Tess's part, simply trusting that her little brother was alive was very different from trusting that she'd actually *see* him again. Tess still had the note he'd left for her. Axel might have had a penchant for the dramatic, but that made him an exaggerator, not a liar. If he'd committed his good-bye to paper, he must have believed it to be real, and permanent.

Tess still participated in the search, of course. In the mornings she woke up well before dawn and joined Jaana and Kari and the rest of the volunteers. As the cold snap wore on and Axel remained missing, the search grid expanded farther and farther into the unfamiliar woods. But in Tess's heart she knew that her expectations were no different from the rest of the grim-faced volunteers. They weren't going to find Axel, at least not this way. It wasn't until she returned to the Hannula house at night, slick with sweat and numb with cold, that Tess felt the work of recovering her brother really began.

She was determined to read everything she could about the Hiisi and the Keeper and anything else that might be of use. Tess started out by browsing the net on Kalle's computer, but soon learned that what she could find online paled in comparison to what was in Otso's old books. She knew that her grandfather had been a poetry professor back in Helsinki, but it turned out that "poetry" also meant history and mythology and ancient epics all at once. Over the years Otso had brought quite a bit of work up to the cottage, and Tess carted as much of it as she could carry over to the Hannula place. Every night, after a long day out in the woods, she'd settle in with Bigwig on a big, soft couch and continue her search in her grandfather's yellowing books.

There was plenty to be learned about the Hiisi—or rather, about *hiisis*; there was more than just one. Tess had remembered the word to mean a kind of malevolent troll, or demon. It lived deep in the woods and would harass people that strayed inside, sometimes chasing them back to their farms and villages. But as it turned out, that was only one of several possible definitions for the word. *Hiisis* had been playing the part of magical villains only since the Christians arrived in Finland and got their hands on the mythology. Back in pagan times a *hiisi* wasn't always bad; it could even be helpful. And it wasn't even necessarily a *being*—a *hiisi* could also be a *place*. A *hiisi* could be a grove or a clearing out in the wild, a place the early Finns believed to be sacred. A site for the worship of long-dead ancestors.

While this was all interesting, it didn't offer Tess any useable clues about how to get her brother back. She was far more intent on finding information about the Keeper, but there her research was less fruitful. Otso's books had no mention of anything like him . . . or at least not exactly. There was one spirit that tried to lure men into the forest in order to gain its freedom—sort of a corollary for the Hiisi, which tried to chase them out of those same forests. But this spirit was supposed to be a woman, a beautiful one—two things that the Keeper definitely wasn't. And Tess had no better luck searching out more information on the famous ghost of Talvijärvi. All the stories focused on Aino's tragic death and her periodic return to the pine island as a ghost. The fact that her husband had disappeared into the woods only to turn up dead months later certainly gave the tale some extra-morbid flavor, but Tess couldn't find a single version of the story that gave any detail about what he actually *said* before he left. Everybody figured he was simply mad with grief, so there had been no reason to listen to him. And of course Tess had treated her own brother no differently during their last conversation back in Helsinki. But this was a mistake she meant to undo, if she could.

By the time the cold snap finally ended, Tess was running out of things to read and starting to feel as desperate as the dwindling volunteers. Kari suggested that they spend the morning searching the castle once again, and Tess agreed, if only on the chance that she'd missed something useful at that little exhibit on Väinö and Aino. They ate breakfast in silence with Jaana and Otso and left just before sunup.

Outside the weather was the warmest it had been since the day they'd all raced back to Talvijärvi in search of Axel. This would have been a welcome change, but for the rain. A spitting drizzle drifted in from the east with the gathering light, polishing the rounded mounds of snow, melting and freezing all at once. Icicles filled the woods behind the cottage, breaking off under the weight of the rain just as fast as they could form.

It was so slick and treacherous outside that Tess and Kari decided to leave their skis against the back wall of the cottage. They threw ponchos over their winter coats and headed out into the wet mess on foot, stomping hard through the crusting snow to keep from falling over. They were glazed with a film of ice by the time they arrived at Erikinlinna. Aarne was still maintaining a twenty-four-hour watch over the place, and one of his officers stood out in front of the stone archway, hands deep in the pockets of his soggy winter jacket. The officer nodded solemnly as Tess and Kari approached, water tipping off his frozen hood. But he was so afraid of saying the wrong thing to Tess that he said nothing at all, not even "hello."

They passed him by and made for the covered picnic area beyond—though it wasn't so covered anymore. The peaked roof was nearly gone, replaced by an odd jag of upturned beams and shingling. Tess had heard that the roof collapsed under the weight of the snow, but in person it looked a lot worse than that. Rather like a small truck had been dropped on the picnic area and then hauled away. The concrete floor sparkled with ice, and rain poured in through the destroyed roof. Part of the ceiling had pancaked a picnic table, and a stray beam landed right in the middle of the display table housing the historical model of Erikinlinna, leaving the tiny castle just as ruined as the real thing.

Tess picked her way around the debris to the far corner of the picnic area, where the little plaque on Talvijärvi's famous resident spirit was thankfully undamaged. She stared again at the picture of Aino, her blur-faced husband, and their shattered-looking urchin of a son. Some text was stenciled just beneath the photo—Aino's pulpy legend. According to this plaque, the woman had been haunting the pine island for the past sixty years, off and on. Property owners reported seeing her from their decks, and ice fishers said she'd sometimes stick her white face out of the holes they'd drilled. There was even a stretch of summers, back in the 1990s, when the Talvijärvi swimming society had declared the island and all the water around it off-limits—Aino had given some kid such a fright that he'd almost drowned. The plaque also included some text about Väinö, but it was much shorter. LOST IN HIS OWN GRIEF, AINO'S MAD HUSBAND DISAPPEARED.

"It doesn't say here that he died," Tess said, brushing a finger across Väinö's laminated face, obscured by the cloud of its own movement.

Kari looked at her and shifted from boot to boot. He didn't seem to know what she wanted him to say. The truth was that she didn't either. The rain picked up outside, funneling down through the roof and out across the floor.

"You told us Väinö died," Tess said.

Kari nodded. "Froze to death," he said.

"Well, why doesn't it say that here?"

Kari shrugged. "He's not really the main character of that story," he said, as though this explained everything. "Besides, his family was really, really angry. And Talvijärvi is a small town. It could be they didn't want it printed?"

Tess chewed her lip, remembering now that Kari had said that Väinö's family had refused to even attend his funeral. She stayed quiet for a while longer. The rain outside was heavy enough now that it had begun to win its argument with the snow, and the woods were filled with the bubbling sound of water percolating through the slush.

"Do you think any of his family are still alive?" Tess said.

Kari wrinkled his nose. "It was a long time ago," he said.

"Not even him?" She reached out to touch the photo again, this time indicating the child that was huddled between his two doomed parents. He looked about the same age as Axel and nearly as scrawny.

"He'd be really old," Kari said. He squinted at the name printed beneath the child and the date in the corner of the photograph. "It's possible, I guess. We could try looking him up, but—" Kari swiveled as he spoke, turning to follow Tess, who was already making her way out of the picnic area at a fast walk. "But why would you want to?"

"I have a question for him," Tess said, tightening her hood against the weather.

The name of the boy in the picture was Pyry Järvinen, and while the Internet couldn't quite tell them if he was still alive, Tess and Kari did discover that someone by that name owned a house in Talvijärvi. They wrote down the address and caught a ride into town with Kalle, who had just returned from an all-night shift with the search parties out in the woods. Exhausted and bleary as he was, Kari's brother insisted that he wait for them outside of Mr. Järvinen's house, so that he could drive them back when they were finished. "I can nap in the truck," he said, cheerfully pig-headed about it. "Besides, you don't want to walk back to the bus station in this." Kalle gestured out beyond the windshield and the freezing rain that was still pattering down. In the long days since Axel's disappearance, Kalle had more than proven himself worthy of the faith that his younger brother had shown in him. Tess remembered that at one time she'd thought of this blind, defensive trust as a weakness on Kari's part. But it wasn't. Because people—especially family—don't need to deserve your faith before you give it to them. Like Kalle, they could always grow into it.

Tess and Kari hurried up to the house and pressed the doorbell. There was no awning or cover of any kind over the front stoop, and each drop of rain that hit them felt as hard and as cold as a hailstone. They waited. Kari rang the doorbell again, and Tess rapped on the wood.

"Sorry about that," a lady's voice called from inside. "Couldn't hear you over my . . ." The door swung open, revealing a middle-aged woman on the other side of it. She wore a baggy sweater over a pair of pale green scrubs, and her hair was done up in a relaxed bun. One of her ears still had a headphone in it, and the other headphone swung loose across her collar, pumping out faint jazz. Whatever the woman had been about to say, she seemed to see no need to finish it. "Can I help you?" she asked, a little curtly.

"Is this Pyry Järvinen's house?" Tess said.

The woman took a moment before answering. "It is," she said. "Can I help you?"

Had Tess not spoken Finnish, she'd have guessed from the woman's tone that these repeated words meant "go away." She wondered if the woman was the old man's nurse, or maybe his daughter. "Is he at home?" she said. "Can we speak to him?"

"I'm afraid not today, no," the woman said, already beginning to close the door.

"Why not?" Kari said.

"Ask your teacher." The woman frowned at them. "I have half a mind to call her myself. Did you know more than ten students have come by this week alone? I don't care if it's for school— you're all tiring him out."

"We're not in that class," Tess said, slipping her foot into the doorframe.

The woman looked from one of them to the

other. "So this isn't another interview about his mother? The 'famous spirit on the island'?" The nurse—and Tess was sure now that she was indeed a nurse and not a relative—actually used air quotes as she said this. "It's a lousy idea for a class project, if you ask me."

"That's not why we're here, ma'am," Tess said. While this wasn't entirely true, neither was it a full-on lie. After all, she didn't have any questions about Aino. Tess was here to ask about the Keeper—a character who seemed to have been written out of Talvijärvi's quaint little ghost story.

"What do you want with him, then?" the nurse said.

Tess wasn't eager to go the sympathy route, but under the circumstances it seemed like her surest bet. The rain was still coming down, pinging against her skull. "I don't know if you've been watching the news," Tess said, "but my little brother—"

"Oh my." The nurse's eyes widened and her arms went slack. She let go of the doorknob, and the wet breeze blew the door further open. Tess knew that she already had the woman, but she pressed on anyway.

"My little brother went missing right where Mr. Järvinen's father did. I just . . ." Tess let her voice go wobbly and trailed off. She even pretended that she was trying to suppress some tears. But then, before she knew it, she really *was* trying to suppress them. Funny how that could happen.

"I guess I just wanted to talk to him," she said.

"Of course," the nurse said, standing aside to let them both into the tidy little home. "Hurry in. You two are getting *soaked*." She took their dripping ponchos and hung them up in the entryway before leading them deeper into Pyry Järvinen's house.

"Can I fix you two some tea?" the nurse asked, totally contrite.

"No, thank you," Tess said, feeling guilty.

"Well, just let me know if you change your mind." They entered a dark room at the back of the house, where they found an old man slumped in a big wicker chair, bathed in the light of a blaring television set. He didn't seem to notice that he had guests. There was a Moomin cartoon in the DVD player, and the merry voices of the characters were so loud that they caused framed maps and paintings hanging on the walls to vibrate. The nurse picked up a remote that was sitting atop the television and muted it. "Mr. Järvinen," she said, her voice just as loud as the cartoons had been. "Pyry. You have some guests."

Even though the television was muted, Mr.

Järvinen kept his eyes on it for a moment. Then he turned and took them in. He was by far the oldest old man Tess had ever seen—Pyry Järvinen made Jaana and Otso look almost middle-aged. He seemed no bigger than he had in that blurry photograph, as though he hadn't grown an inch since then. He had clear plastic tubes coming out of his nose and running down the sides of his face, and one of his fingertips was hooked up to a little monitoring device. It chirped once, from the corner.

"Hello again," he said. Mr. Järvinen seemed happy enough to see them. "Nice of you to come back."

"You haven't met these two people before," the nurse boomed, her voice endlessly patient and put out all at once. "But this young lady is the one they were talking about on television last night, remember?" Then she lowered her voice and said to Tess: "Mind, he won't."

Mr. Järvinen nodded. His eyes drifted back to the muted cartoons on the screen.

"She's the one whose brother is missing," the nurse said. "That little boy they're searching for up at the lake."

"Terrible thing," Mr. Järvinen said, shaking his head.

"It is," the nurse all but shouted. "It really,

really is." Then she turned back to Tess and Kari. "I suppose I can leave you to it. So you said you just . . . you want to talk to him?"

"Yeah," Tess said, sort of shrugging. "I think it would help." She wished she'd thought to come up with a better lie than that. Goodwill had gotten her and Kari through the door, but it wouldn't last forever.

The nurse eyeballed her for a long while, an equal measure of sympathy and vague suspicion on her face. "Are you sure you don't want anything warm to drink?" she finally said.

"Thank you," Tess said. "Not right now."

"Well. Just holler if you need any help with him." Mr. Järvinen's nurse put her loose headphone back into her ear, but Tess had noticed that she'd switched the music off. "And try not to be too long. I meant it when I said he needs his rest," she said, leaving the three of them in the dark room.

There was a long and tremendously awkward silence. It seemed quieter for the fact that Tess could see the Moomins shouting on the screen but not hear them. Kari wandered past the television, to admire a framed map that had been tacked up to the wall. Tess wondered if it was just so he wouldn't have to look at Mr. Järvinen.

"My mother drew that," the old man said,

his voice warm and foggy. "It's the lake, the way it looked before the mill closed. You can see the mill right . . . *there*." He pointed. "Look," he said. It was only after Kari did look that the old man continued. "You can see the castle, too. And our house—all the houses. Bring it here so I can show you. You can put it in that essay of yours."

"We aren't writing an essay," Tess said. She picked up a stool and placed it as close to his chair as she could. She didn't want to have to yell, lest the nurse overhear her questions.

"Aren't you?" Mr. Järvinen said, glancing from Kari to Tess, confused. But then his confusion ebbed away. "Well . . . I can tell you the same thing I told the others. I haven't seen my mother since I was a little boy. Never bothered looking for her in the first place. Because my poor mother died, and it's no great mystery to me where she is and where she isn't." He winked at them. This was clearly a line he'd used before.

Tess glanced at Kari, and he raised his eyebrows. "I don't have any questions about your mother," she said. "I wanted to ask you about Väinö Järvinen, your father." Considering what an awful dad Väinö had apparently been and the way he chose to exit this world, Tess had expected at least some reaction to the mention of his name. But the younger Mr. Järvinen gave her nothing.

His eyes drifted back to the television, where the Moomin family was putting on a play in a floating theater. Tess got up, shut the television off, and returned to her stool.

"Could one of you please get me the remote?" Mr. Järvinen said.

"In a minute," Tess said. She took him by the hand, hoping to focus his attention, but the old man snatched it right away. So, maybe her mention of Väinö had gotten a reaction, after all. "I guess you don't want to talk about it," she said, "but I have a few questions that I really need to ask you. I think that what happened to your father might be the same thing that's happening to my little brother. I want to know if Väinö ever—"

"Nothing *happened* to my father," Mr. Järvinen said. He no longer sounded quite so foggy, or warm. "He ran away from home. It was a choice he made, not a thing that happened to him."

"All right," Tess said. "I'm sorry. What I want to know is, did he ever say anything to you about somebody named the Keeper?" The old man blinked at her. "Maybe about the man who lived in the castle?" she tried. "The one who promised he could bring your father to Aino."

At this Mr. Järvinen snorted. "Kagg," he said, brushing a wrinkled hand through the air as though to dismiss the word. It had no meaning to Tess, but Kari's attention snapped away from Aino's hand-drawn map.

"You don't . . . You mean Erik Kagg?" he said, looking perplexed.

"You know your history," Mr. Järvinen said, though he didn't sound particularly impressed by this fact. "*Erik Kagg*. It's stupid, I know. I already knew it was stupid when I was a little boy. My God, what a waste my father was."

Tess was getting lost. "Who are you—"

"Kagg was that Swedish count, remember?" Kari said. "We read about him when we took Axel to Erikinlinna. He's the one who built it."

"Erik Kagg, living in his castle." Mr. Järvinen shook his head. "He must have been an old guy by then. Older than me, even." It seemed like he was trying to summon a laugh, but all that came out was a bitter cough. "A waste," he said again, running the back of his hand over his wet lower lip. This had happened well over half a century ago, but the hurt in Mr. Järvinen's eyes still seemed fresh. "You should probably get on back to your class," he said.

"Wait." Tess was having trouble absorbing this information. "Your father said that Erik Kagg was the Keeper?" This seemed, somehow, not quite right to her. She'd spent almost no time with the Keeper, but their conversation back in

Baldwin had given her enough of an impression. The old man had none of the bearing of an ancient Swedish count. Unless perhaps the centuries had softened him?

Mr. Järvinen coughed again, louder this time. He fell into a fit of them, and for a second Tess was worried that his nurse would hear and come running. But the coughs subsided. "I told you that I don't know about any Keeper," Mr. Järvinen said as he emerged from the fit, his eyes watering. "My father just told me that he met the old count in the castle. And that Kagg showed him how to find ghosts in the forest and promised to bring him to my mother." The old man went quiet for a while. He made to wipe his tears away, but they had already sunk back into his eyes. "I used to go out into the woods looking for my father, you know. I did it for years. Just so I could tell him that I hoped he'd never find her. Even dead, my mother was better off without him. We both were."

"Why would you go looking for your father?" Kari said.

"I was young, and I was angry." Mr. Järvinen's head began to list to one side. He stretched his neck, and it popped terribly. "Would one of you, please, just give me the remote? We're missing the best part."

"But he died," Kari said. "Your father froze to death in the castle."

"Bah!" Now Mr. Järvinen did achieve a laugh. "I've no doubt he's dead today, but my father certainly didn't die back then. I'm curious. Which is the version they told you? That my uncles were so angry with him that they forbade us from attending the funeral? Or that I said the body was cursed, and our whole family refused to receive it?"

"I guess . . ." Kari looked suddenly ashamed. "I heard both of those."

"And more, I'd bet. This town hates a story that doesn't have an ending," Mr. Järvinen said, pointing first at Kari and then at Tess, as though he held them personally responsible for that fact. "When spring came, and they found a dead man in Erikinlinna, everybody decided to make that their ending. Never mind that it wasn't Väinö."

"Are you sure that it wasn't your father?" Tess said, leaning forward on her stool. "I mean, it had been months. The body must have been . . ." She didn't really want to finish, and thankfully Mr. Järvinen didn't force her to.

"Oh, it certainly was," he said, sneering darkly. "But my father had a particular feature that made him hard to miss. He was a woodcutter and a drunk—two things that don't mix very well at all. He had a bad accident when I was just a baby and cut his left hand all to pieces. The doctor in town was only able to save three of his fingers. But the body they brought us, rotten though it was, had a full set. Ten fingers. Ten toes. It was probably just some drifter. Or maybe . . ." Mr. Järvinen brightened. He also seemed on the verge of another coughing fit. "Maybe it was Erik Kagg. Mystery solved! Now, would one of you give me that damn remote and rewind my show back to the middle?"

Tess got up off her stool, but then she had to sit back down again. She was shaking. For a moment she could almost feel the Keeper's mangled hand, Väinö's mangled hand, clutching her tight around the stomach. She swallowed a mouthful of spit, worried that she might actually be sick on the poor old man's yellow quilt. Kari noticed immediately.

"Are you all right?" he said.

"Yeah," Tess said. She got up again, and this time she was able to stay standing.

"No," she said.

She walked over to the TV, turned it back on, and reset the DVD. She set the volume even louder than it had been before. Then she took Aino's map of the lake off the wall. The mill, the castle, even the still on the pine island had been labeled in careful calligraphy. Each individual house bore the name of the family that owned it. The woman knew how to draw—Tess could say that much for her.

"I'm going to take this," she said to Mr. Järvinen. "Can I please take this?"

"No, you cannot," the old man said, raising his voice to be heard over the Moomins.

"Okay," Tess said. "I'm going to take it anyway, all right? I'm really sorry, but I need it. I promise I'll give it back."

"No, you . . . What are you—"

Tess opened the fasteners on the back of the frame and pulled Aino's map out. She gently rolled it up.

"Stop that right now!" Mr. Järvinen shouted.

"I'm so sorry," Tess said, her cheeks hot and pink. Then she turned and walked quickly out of the dark little sitting room. Kari rushed to follow her, looking baffled. Väinö's son hollered after them, calling for his nurse. But the cartoons were much too loud, and Tess and Kari had already reached the front door.

20

The Pine Island

It had been only a few hours since Tess and Kari left Mr. Järvinen's house, and already she thought that they might be getting close. They were back at the lake, standing in the same patch of cleared forest where Bigwig had appeared nearly a week ago, poring over Aino's hand-drawn map. Kari was holding his poncho out to shield the map from the rain, but even so the paper was fraying at the edges, coming apart in their fingers. A stray raindrop landed on a corner of the map and passed right through like a wet bullet. Tess felt rotten about it. She promised herself that if she made it through this, she'd find a way to make it up to Mr. Järvinen.

Tess had told Kari everything the moment his

older brother dropped them back off at the lake. Kari hadn't given her a choice—he'd threatened to go right back into town unless Tess explained why they'd stolen from the old man. But it was good—the telling had helped. After all, she was only just starting to put things together for herself. Saying it aloud to Kari was as much a way of explaining it to the both of them. Tess wasn't sure that she had all the details right, but the gist of the story was simple: Väinö Järvinen, the grief-stricken woodsman who had abandoned his son and disappeared into the forest more than sixty years ago, was the Keeper. Väinö was the drifter who had appeared before Tess and Axel back in Baldwin on the night their father died. It was Väinö who had made contact with her brother at Talvijärvi and scooped him out of the world.

"But I thought that what was happening to Axel was the same thing that happened to Väinö," Kari said. "Wasn't he supposed to be a victim of this Keeper guy?"

"He was that, too," Tess said. She had no doubt that a Keeper had once lured Väinö into the woods and shown him the path. And thanks to the younger Mr. Järvinen, Tess had a pretty good idea of who that original Keeper was. But for whatever reason, the job had been passed on to

Väinö. He'd spent decades lost in a wilderness of grief, tricked out of his own life. And now he was the man doing the tricking.

"And the map?" Kari said. "Why do you need it?"

"To find where his cabin used to be," Tess said. She knew that this last leap was the biggest, strangest one of all. To go looking for Väinö at the site of his old home meant that she had to believe that the corpse in the castle belonged to the original Keeper—*Erik-freaking-Kagg*. An ancient Swedish count who by all rights should have been dead for eight hundred years or so. Väinö had taken Kagg's place in the forest, and Kagg had taken Väinö's in the ground. "Erikinlinna was his home," she said. "If Kagg returned there, then maybe Väinö will return to his."

Tess could tell that Kari wanted to believe her but simply didn't. Not even a little bit. But still, here he was, shivering right beside her and holding up his poncho to keep the map dry. A lot had changed since Aino had drawn it. Homesteads dotted the shoreline in her time, but in the many decades since, they'd been replaced by summer cottages, their farms all gone to weed. The mill closed and the forest crept back, advancing on the water. With none of Aino's landmarks left, Tess and Kari had to follow the contours of the shore, orienting themselves by their distance from the island. It lay off to the left, the two old pines bending under the weight of the slush.

"Shouldn't it be here?" Kari said.

"Almost." Tess pointed to a spit of rocky land on the map, curling into the lake like a tail. Then she peered up at the shoreline. They could just make out a few of the rocks in the distance, sticking up out of the ice like dorsal fins. "Past there and over that hill," she said. She rolled the map up carefully and handed it back to Kari, who wrapped it in his poncho. The woods became dense and untended beyond the clearing, so they cut across the shallows. Nearly an inch of rainwater had accumulated on the ice, and it splashed around their boots as they made their way carefully over the slick surface. It was a strange feeling, to be walking through water, atop ice, atop still more water. But it was thick enough—Tess had watched grown men and women from the search parties taking shortcuts across the lake all week long.

They reached the rocks and cut back to the shore. The ground rose up ahead, and Tess saw that what had looked like a hill on Aino's map was actually an outcropping of bald granite wearing a crown of orange-barked pine trees. Kari paused, pressing a gloved hand against one of the trunks for balance.

"Do you smell that?" he said.

Tess did—an oily sweetness hung in the air, rich and pungent against the clean smell of the rain and woods. The odor got stronger as they climbed the rise, and when they reached the top, she could see a few threads of tar-black smoke drifting through the trees. There was something at the far foot of the slope. The snow down there had been trod flat in a rough little circle, all around the husk of a dead pine tree. And within that circle Tess could see a black blotch of smoking ash sitting under a soggy cardboard lean-to. A blue tarp lay crumpled across a bank of overturned snow, partially covering a glinting pile of open cans and empty bottles. It was a campsite.

"Careful!" Kari yelled. But Tess was already sliding down the slope on her butt, going as fast as the ice and snow would let her. The moment she hit level ground again, she was running. According to Aino's map, this was exactly where the Järvinens' cabin should have been.

As Tess got closer she saw that it wasn't a dead tree in the middle of the campsite but rather an upright stack of red bricks. A fireplace and a chimney—the only pieces of Väinö and Aino's home that had survived the endless winters. The campsite around the fireplace looked like it had been only recently abandoned. The embers in the fire pit were still smoking, and an open jar of pickled herring sat atop a stone, slowly filling with rain-water. Beside that was a bottle of syrupy pine schnapps, the cap sitting loose atop the mouth.

"Do you think he heard us coming?" Kari said. He had only just caught up with her and had to lean against a tree, huffing for breath.

"Maybe," Tess said, looking frantically into the woods. The snow out there was ribbed with ski tracks, which meant that the search parties had been back and forth over the past few days. But how the hell had the Keeper escaped notice, right under their noses like this? And how had he slipped away the very moment that Tess found his camp? The Keeper must have departed in a hurry, because he'd left his walking stick leaning against the brickwork of the chimney. His pipe was there, too, sitting neatly atop the crumbling mantel of the naked fireplace. Tess even noticed one of his stupid gum boots jutting out from the other garbage under the tarp, and the sight of it caused her frustration to mount even faster. She didn't know if tears were coming, or a scream, or both. Tess yanked off her gloves and stuck her fingers into the burningly cold snow.

"I think we should go back and tell Aarne," Kari said, still struggling for air. "We wouldn't have to say anything about all the Väinö stuff. This would be enough." He pointed down at the fire and the abandoned meal. "Aarne and the police can search this whole side of the lake."

"This camp has been here for days," Tess said. "They must have seen it and gone right past him." She went over to the chimney and picked up the Keeper's walking stick. It was heavier than she would have thought—solid and old. She picked up his pipe, too, finding the bowl warm to the touch. The tobacco inside was still crackling. The Keeper couldn't have lit it more than a few minutes ago. Would that have been enough time for him to disappear into the forest? Tess turned in a full circle, peering out into the open woodland. Then she set her eyes again on the gum boot. The top half of it disappeared under the tarp. And she realized, all at once, that the boot wasn't empty.

Kari was still talking. "I don't know who this person is," he said, "but if Aarne can find him . . . if the police can talk to him . . ." Kari looked desperate. "It's the best chance we have. We've got to try."

"You're right," Tess said, trying to keep her voice from giving anything away. She set the pipe back down on the fireplace and took a step toward the tarp. "We should go back and get them." She took another step. Slowly, she lifted the Keeper's walking stick into the air, holding it high above her head. Kari seemed like he was about to ask what she was doing, but then his eyes went to the protruding gum boot, and he realized as well. Kari straightened himself up and clenched his hands into fists. Everything went still, even the smoke curling through the air.

Tess aimed for a spot on the tarp about a foot and a half above the boot and brought the walking stick down as hard as she could. The tarp exploded in a scramble of arms and legs, and the Keeper howled in agony. He shot up to his feet in the snow and fell right back down again. The old man's eyes were watering, his face pink with pain. She'd gotten him right in the knee.

"That. Wasn't. Necessary." The Keeper gasped each word through his clenched teeth. He looked different from the way Tess remembered him. The old man had lost his ridiculous hat and traded in his duster for one of the neon vests that had been handed out to all the volunteers—he must have been posing as a member of the search party, which was why no one had thought anything of his camp. But it was more than just his outfit that had changed. The Keeper's entire bearing seemed somehow shrunken, and real. His neck wasn't quite so long, nor his head so broad as it used to be. His clenched teeth looked yellow, and old, and entirely ordinary. The Keeper's attitude, on the other hand, appeared very much the same. His face relaxed as the pain subsided. The corners of his lips pinched up into a smile, propping up his collapsing cheeks. "It's nice to see you, too."

"Where's my brother?" Tess pitched the words at the old man. She held the walking stick high, ready to hit him again.

"I don't know much more than you do," the Keeper said. "He's on the path. On his way to Florida to look for his father. Beyond that, I couldn't say." He braced his hands in the snow and lifted himself up into a standing position.

"Hey!" Kari had been at the edge of the campsite this whole time, frozen in shock. But now he charged up next to Tess, his fists held out awkwardly in front of him. He looked about ready to throw himself on the old man.

"Easy there, humpty." The Keeper held his arms up in a gesture of surrender. He was absolutely drenched—Tess could see that now. His sopping pants stuck to him like skin on a plucked chicken. She also noticed that he was holding a long white feather in his mangled left hand. A swan's feather, mussed and ratty with the rain. "I'm not going to hurt anybody," the Keeper said. "I was only trying to . . ." He took a hobbling step over to the fireplace and cried out in pain. "You really did a number on me. Would either of you mind passing me my pipe before it burns out?"

Tess shot a quick glance at the smoking pipe

sitting atop the fireplace. Then she swung the walking stick like a bat and whacked it off the brickwork. The pipe snapped in two, and the pieces spun off into the woods. The Keeper watched them go. "God," he said, "you're just like your mother."

"Kari," Tess said. "I need you to go back to your house. Get my grandmother, or Aarne, or anyone else you can find."

"No way," Kari said. He was still holding his fists out in front of him. The kid must have never been in a fight—it looked like he was trying to drive an invisible car. "I'm not going to leave you alone with him."

"You have to," Tess said. "They won't know how to get here, otherwise. It'll be fine. I can take care of myself until you get back."

Kari glanced from the Keeper to Tess. "What if he runs away?"

The old man limped over to the campfire and snatched up his little bottle of schnapps before Tess could shatter that as well. He sucked some down like it was medicine. "I'm hardly running anywhere," he said.

"I'll break his leg if he does," Tess said. She really believed she'd do it, too.

"Hear that?" the Keeper said. "I'm in good hands."

Kari looked agonized. He glanced at the far

shore of the lake, his family's summer home just a blip against the trees. "I'll go as fast as I can," he said. "Don't let him get too close to you." And with that he turned and sprinted back through the snow, scrambling up the sloping granite. They both watched him go, and the moment Kari disappeared over the rise, the Keeper's demeanor began to change. His shellacked, self-satisfied grin faded. He suddenly looked rumpled, and old, and tremendously sad.

"I didn't expect to see you here," he said, his voice soft. He seemed unable or unwilling to look her in the face. "But I'm glad to. I mean it. I've been searching for you, you know."

"Not very hard," Tess said.

"I got close a few times," the Keeper said. "That little drawing you had them make didn't have me too worried. As you can see, I'm not my handsome old self. I don't think anyone would look at that picture and then look at me and think: *That's the guy!* But a few people saw me in person the last time I was here. They heard my voice. And every time I tried to get to you, one of them would be out by the house. So I've been hiding out here, making like a concerned neighbor. I've been waiting for them all to give up so I could talk to you. I figured I owed you that much."

"Well, here I am," Tess said. "Talk."

"Yes. Here you are." The Keeper appeared to marvel at this for a moment. "How did you find me, anyway?"

"Your son helped us," Tess said. Just the mention of Pyry seemed to do more to the Keeper than the strike with the walking stick had—for a second she thought he was about to cry. Tess was so furious with the old man that she couldn't help but twist the knife. "I bet you didn't even know that he was still alive."

"Oh, I did," the Keeper said. "If Pyry had come home to my woods, I'd have known. I used to look forward to the day—it would have given me a chance to explain myself to him. But waiting for my son to die wasn't a good enough reason for me to stick around. And I'll see him again eventually." He wrapped his skinny arms around his body, and a shudder ran all the way through him. "You know, I'd forgotten what it felt like to be so cold." He tried to shift his weight onto his bad leg and winced. "And pain," he said. "I didn't remember it could hurt so much." The Keeper took another long pull on his schnapps, and it seemed to lubricate his joints. He tried again to move his knee.

"I owe you an apology," he said. "I know that. I do."

"You owe me a lot more than an apology," Tess said. "You need to take me to my brother."

"I can't do that," the Keeper said.

"Yes, you can," she said. "If you brought him there, you can bring me."

"Not anymore. I couldn't find the path again even if I wanted to. And besides . . ." The old man looked right at her, making eye contact for the first time since Kari left. Tess could see now that he really was crying. "I don't want to. An apology is all you're getting. But it's real. I mean it. If there had been any other way off the path, I would have taken it years ago. But no wood can be without a Keeper. The only way the Hiisi would let me leave was if I could find a new one. Your brother was the best chance I'd had in years."

"So you made him take your place," she said.

"I didn't *make* Axel do anything." Even through his tears, the Keeper looked reproachful at this suggestion. "That's not even possible. The only way to stay on the path is to want it with everything you have. To believe that there's no place else in the world that you can possibly be. That's how I felt after Aino died." He took his eyes off Tess and looked out through the trees, across the shore, at the sodden little island. When he spoke again his voice had gone brittle. "I would have given up everything to see her again—to tell her how sorry I was. I *did* give up everything. Your brother isn't any different. He feels the same way I used to."

"Our dad just died!" Tess hollered at the old man. "Of course Axel feels the same!" She was almost surprised by how loud this all came out. And by the fact that she was crying now too. Because Sam was dead. She loved him so, so much, and he was gone. Now her brother was gone too. This wasn't the way she'd expected her meeting with the Keeper to go—the two of them weeping at each other. "I felt like there was nothing left for me, too. But I don't anymore. That's the point. Feelings can change. People can heal."

"That they can." The Keeper pinched a neon corner of his vest and rubbed it over his face. "Listen," he said. "I'm not going to lie to you. It isn't a good life on the path, as a Keeper. It isn't even a *life*. But your brother will come out when he's good and ready. I promise you."

"You mean he'll have to trick someone into taking his place," Tess said.

All the Keeper could do was shrug. "Kagg did. I did. He will too. There's no shortage of mourners in this awful world. Plenty of them will choose to do much worse to themselves than live in their own grief for a few decades." He took another long pull on his schnapps and stared down at the feather still clutched in his hand. "With any luck he'll figure it out sooner than I did. A lot sooner."

"That's not good enough," Tess said.

"I'm sorry," the Keeper said, "but it is for me. And it's all you're getting." With that the old man turned away from her and began limping toward the lake.

"Stop," she said.

"Stop me," he said, without looking back. The Keeper had called her bluff. He stepped gingerly over the rocky shore and then made his way out across the ice, heading in the direction of the pine island.

Tess caught up with him, the collected rain splashing away from her boots. It had gotten deep enough now that they both appeared to be walking on water. The Keeper still had the worn swan's feather clutched in his hand, and he studied it as he walked. It was very slow going, with that limp.

"You should know that Aino saw what I was doing," he finally said. "She saw and tried to stop it. She was always better than I was."

"It isn't very hard," Tess said.

"That it isn't," the old man said. He tightened his grip, bending the shaft of the feather in half. He dropped it in their wake, and it floated away. Then he took one more swig of his schnapps before pitching the bottle out over the lake as well. It splashed into the water, slid along the ice beneath it, and lay there gulping rain.

Tess began to hear something in the distance—the rising growl of a snowmobile. The Keeper heard it too. He stopped limping and cocked his ear into the rain. Tess scanned the southern shore and saw that it was her grandmother and Kari, come to get her. This was the second time in a week that Jaana had rushed to a grandchild's rescue. God, what they'd put her through. What they were *still* putting her through.

"That kid moves fast," the Keeper said. Then he turned to face Tess again. "It's time for you to go," he said.

"I'm not going anywhere." Tess grabbed at one of the old man's soggy sleeves, but he pulled away. The fabric stretched down over his hand before slipping wetly out of her fingers.

"I'm not kidding," he said, glancing from the shore to the pine island. It seemed like he was gauging the distance. "I'm going to do this whether you're here or not."

For a brief and stupid moment, Tess wondered: *Do what?* But then she realized where they were—roughly the middle of the lake. It was early in the season, and the ice out here was still forming. Still thin. The Keeper shuffled forward a few paces, his eyes locked on the island. The last thing his wife had seen before she died.

"You should do what your brother couldn't

and give it up," he said. "It's our job to love the dead. Not the other way around."

He took a deep breath, as though to give Tess one last chance to back away. Then he bent his good leg and jumped. Even through the sound of the rain, the approaching snowmobile, and the splash of his landing feet on the inundated ice, Tess could hear a horrible, rippling crack. The Keeper jumped again. It was louder this time, and more of a groan, like a voice coming from deep underwater. Tess had very little time to make up her mind. The lakeshore and the island were just about the same distance away, in opposite directions. The only difference was that if she ran back to shore, she'd run alone. And any chance she had of finding her brother would be as good as drowned.

Tess took a lunging step past the Keeper, grabbing him by the wrist as she went by, yanking him toward the pine island. But the old man's arm might as well have been a zipper, because as she pulled, the lake opened up beneath them. She felt the sudden vertigo of loose footing, and then she fell cleanly into a pocket of splashing ice. It felt, at first, like a sharp punch to the head. Like lots of punches. Tess tried to kick to the surface, but her ski boots may as well have been made of cement. Her clothes drank in the lake and dragged her under. The cold down there was so intense it wasn't even cold anymore. It wasn't anything. Tess could just as well have been adrift in space as where she actually was—under the ice, in a lake, in Finland.

21

The Boils

Back in Talvijärvi, neither Axel nor his mother had mourned the Keeper's passing. There wasn't time, and there didn't even seem to be a point. The old man had given himself willingly, even happily, to the Hiisi's glittering jaws. They'd waited a few moments in the birches behind the cottage, to see if he might reappear. But the Keeper was gone. The Hiisi was gone too. The flashlights on the shore drew closer, and Axel began to hear the unmistakable sound of his grandfather calling out his name, followed by the shouts of Tess and Jaana. They couldn't wait any longer. Axel and his mother fled into the forest together, the voices of their family lost under the weight of the congregating trees.

But that was days and days ago—how many Axel couldn't quite count. The search for the Boils brought him and Saara ever deeper into the woods of the world. The forest around them was all at once damp with sunlight and choking on night, bound up tightly in fog and vines and snow. It was exactly as the Keeper had said it would be— an impossible, ever-changing woodland. Axel and his mother passed through the shifting groves, through jungles and swamps and ice-crusted pines. And it wasn't only the forest all around them that was changing. The farther Axel went, the more he could feel it in himself as well.

He first noticed that something was different just a few hours after they left Talvijärvi. Saara had caught a whiff of food, and they stepped off the path and into what appeared to be a little fishing camp. A few men were down at the edge of a mountain stream, casting their lines into the water. They'd left some trout to smoke on an untended grill, and Saara went to work, snapping the fish down whole. Axel took one of the trout in his hands and sniffed it. It had been nicely cleaned and deboned, and the smoked meat was the color of butterscotch. But even though he hadn't eaten in ages, the thought of putting the fish in his mouth made Axel a little nauseous. He wasn't the slightest bit hungry, and wouldn't be again. He remembered that in all the time he'd spent with the Keeper, he'd never seen the old man eat. Apparently, Axel didn't have to anymore either.

But it was more than just his appetite. Axel was transforming in other, stranger ways. These changes revealed themselves slowly, becoming more pronounced with every step. It wasn't until Axel tripped over a log and tumbled into a camel-thorn shrub that he realized how little pain had come to bother him. Axel lifted himself up and picked the barbs from his clothes. He noticed that one of the thorns had passed right through his palm and was sticking out on the other side. He pulled on it, and the thorn slid out without even a drop of blood. He hadn't felt a thing.

Axel had to will himself not to freak out. "You're of the path now," he said aloud. "You're just becoming who you were always meant to be."

He almost believed it.

With time the blazes burned brighter, and Axel began to see traces of the Boils. A patch of wire grass here, a runty juniper there, a sudden stand of hickory trees. Then one morning they arrived at a familiar-looking patch of woods. "Why are you stopping?" Saara said. The air around them had suddenly grown damp and buggy. Her small round ears began to dance to discourage the insects. It made her look a little psychotic.

Axel didn't answer. He looked down at the ground and saw that the shifting mosaic of snow and mud had been replaced by fine white sand. He looked up into the looming trees and then out at the surrounding bramble. After so many wrong turns and near misses, he was a little reluctant to call it. But sand pines don't lie. And neither did Grandpa Paul's trailer, faintly visible through the branches up ahead. Nothing but a ripple in the path, a few short steps, and here they were.

The Boils looked as much like the afterlife as anything Axel had ever seen. A fog rolled in from the scrubby hardpan, reshuffling the sunlight. Spanish moss hung all around like tree-bound kelp, throbbing gray and bright. But if this was the afterlife, it came with mosquitoes and decapitated snakes. It came with cigarette butts and crushed beer cans and crumbling ziggurats of bear scat. It came with rusty lawn furniture and a moldy birdbath shot to bits by years of target practice. It came with Paul.

"This is it," Axel said. "We're here."

Saara neither balked at this, nor showed any great sign of pleasure. She had her eyes on the prize, and the only prize was her husband. She wouldn't celebrate until she found him. "If this is the spot, where is my Sam?" she said.

Axel looked again at Paul's trailer. The screen door hung wide, and a bald lightbulb affixed to the fiberglass lintel flickered and spat. The trailer was ringed with trash, the refuse spreading out into the woods in all directions. Sometimes when they came down for a visit, Sam would spend the first day just picking up garbage.

"He should be close," Axel said. "Have some patience."

"Patience." Saara pressed her soft nose between his shoulder blades and pulled her lips back. "Say 'patience' to me again."

Almost everything that came out of his dead mother's mouth could be construed as a threat, and Axel found that he was getting good at ignoring them. He stepped away from Saara's snout and picked his way through the debris surrounding the trailer. None of the garbage looked fresh. Most of it was weather-beaten, already half reclaimed by the woods. A small fleet of mismatched canoes lay bloated and still, little plants growing out of the mud in their throats. Plastic bags and strips of foil adorned the tops of bushes and the lower branches of trees. It got worse the closer they got to the trailer.

"This is where you wanted to live?" Saara said, stepping gingerly around a pizza box slick with moss.

"It was more Tess than me," Axel said. The

mention of his sister's name briefly filled him with regret.

They were almost at the open door when Axel caught a faint strain of conversation. Somebody inside the trailer was whispering. He stopped to listen. Whoever was in there had a lot on their mind—they were weeping softly, begging, promising that it was all over, that it had meant nothing, that it definitely wasn't *love*. Grandpa Paul didn't say those kinds of things. It was just the television. Axel peeked his head into the trailer and saw the little box set shining on the foot of the unmade bed, the volume lowered to a murmur.

It was even more of a disaster in there than out in the yard. The countertops were stacked with soggy boxes and empty cans, as well as a generous layer of what appeared to be animal droppings. There was a plate on the table, whatever food had been on it long since turned to fuzzy gelatin. Ashtrays overflowed with cigarette butts, and the peeling carpet was polka-dotted with burns. This was rough living, even for Grandpa Paul.

Then, behind the sound of the TV, Axel heard a gentle rustling. It was coming from the bathroom, down the carpeted hall. He leaned farther into the trailer, rapping hard on the doorframe and calling out: "Hello?" The noise in the bathroom stopped, and there was a long silence. Then an armadillo, tasseled with toilet paper and looking like an ugly little Volkswagen done up for a wedding, tore out of the bathroom door, bouncing down the hall in a panic. It wasn't a ghost armadillo. It was a regular armadillo, stinking of Pepto and toothpaste. The thing shot through the trailer door and ran between Axel's legs. It paused for only the briefest moment in front of Saara and then disappeared, squealing into the brightening fog.

"He's not in there," Saara said. Axel couldn't tell if she meant Sam or Paul, but it didn't matter because both were true. It looked like the trailer had been empty for a long time. No wonder Tess hadn't been able to reach Grandpa Paul.

Axel stepped inside to shut off the television and all of the lights. It was probably dumb luck that the electric company hadn't been out to disconnect the power, but they'd certainly be by if the trailer kept draining juice. Then he closed the flapping screen door and returned to the yard. Saara, disinterested in the trailer since the moment she'd established that it was empty, had wandered a few paces off. Her snout was upturned, bobbing as she tried to catch a scent.

"Something's coming," she said, her voice suddenly on edge. The mangy hairs on her neck and shoulders began to stand on end. "Something's here."

"What do you mean, something?" Axel looked over his mother's wooly shoulders and into the sand pines. He saw a flicker of movement in the shadows and then, all at once, the Hiisi appeared. It rolled across Paul's property, bumping and juking over the garbage. It wasn't the same glittering beast that Axel had escaped in Talvijärvi—the Hiisi looked, once again, like nothing but a wheelchair. If it weren't moving on its own, he could even have mistaken it for a real one. Still, it was a terrifying sight. Axel knew what the Hiisi was capable of.

It came to within a few yards of the trailer and stopped. It sat there motionless, watching them. Saara let out a long, pathetic groan and began to back away. Axel pressed himself into the screen door and slowly slid along the trailer wall. Then a breeze cut through the sand pines, and every needle spoke.

"Wait," the Hiisi said.

They did, but it was mostly out of shock.

The Hiisi's wheels rotated, and it rocked forward and back. Then it spun around and returned bouncingly into the sand pines. "Follow," it said. Axel and Saara looked at each other. When they didn't move from the trailer, the Hiisi paused, its back still to them. Axel would have thought it impossible to read the body language of a wheelchair, but somehow he could tell that the thing was getting impatient. *"Quickly,"* the Hiisi said through the voice of the trees. "If you miss this chance, another will not come." And then it disappeared back into the shadows.

Was it offering to bring them to Sam? Saara must have thought so, because she padded off into the trees, after the Hiisi. Axel went with her, and together they followed the monster through the sand pines and into a thick stand of tall reeds. Their passing disturbed a trio of jays, streaks of blue shrieking into the sky. Clouds of bugs clotted the air in here, but they all made way for the Hiisi. The reeds parted as well, bowing down as though to royalty, opening up a clear path for them to follow. Soon Axel could hear a glassy burbling, and they emerged onto the verge of a clear spring pond. This was what gave the Boils its name—warm springs that poured steam into the woods. The Hiisi rolled to the far rim of the pond, its wheels cutting ski-like tracks through the mud.

"Look," the Hiisi said.

Axel saw that signs of his grandfather were rife about the water's edge. A kicked-in cooler sat filled with headless duck decoys, beside an empty plastic handle of cheap bourbon and a car magazine that had been all but veneered into the mud. There were a pair of rotten canvas camp chairs set before the clear water, and standing on the seat of one of the chairs was a great blue heron. Saara's attention snapped toward the bird the moment she saw it. For a second Axel thought she might try to eat the heron, but she didn't. Instead, his mother spoke to it.

"Where is Sam?" she said.

"I wish I could tell you," the heron said, its arrow-shaped face aimed sharply at the water. "He hasn't been by to see me yet." It took Axel a moment to process the fact that the voice coming out of this ragged creature was that of Grandpa Paul. Axel didn't quite realize what this meant at first.

"But he's here?" Saara took a squelching step into the mud ringing the boil.

"Sam's somewhere," the heron said. "He could be here. Should be, I think. But if he is, then he's not letting me know about it." The bird paused for a minute to run his bill through the dirty puff of feathers on his breast. "But I don't suppose I can blame him for keeping his distance." Then the heron turned away from the water and looked Saara in the eye. He appeared to know that this shaggy beast was the dead wife of his dead son. "Who knows," the heron said. "Wouldn't be surprised if he was out looking for *you*. That would be quite the mix-up."

At this Saara fell silent. It wasn't a possibility that she or Axel had even considered. "I'm going to find him," she finally said, sounding more wistful than defeated.

"Of course you will," the heron said. "Or he, you."

"Grandpa?" Axel said. That was, for the moment, all he could say. He fell backward, landing on his butt on the cold mud.

The bird's gaze twirled about for a moment before settling tentatively on Axel. It was as though he couldn't quite see him. "Oh," the heron said. "That's not—no, that isn't right at all. Why are *you* here?"

Axel could have asked his grandfather the same question, but he already knew the answer. Grandpa Paul was dead. Out across the water there was a gnarly old cypress, sodden with moss. Axel remembered it well—a few summers ago Sam and Paul had been able to work together long enough to hang a rope swing from the lower branches. Tess and Axel had spent the whole afternoon casting themselves out over the boil, dropping down into the warm upsurge of water. Axel remembered how the force of the water shooting out of the spring seemed almost strong enough to trampoline him back up into the air. Sam and Paul had watched them from the water's edge, sitting in these very camp chairs, quietly working their way through a cooler of light beer. It had been a great day, maybe the best they'd ever had all together like that. Grandpa Paul must have remembered how sturdy the branch was—how much weight it could hold. Now he was on both sides of the bubbling pond at the same time. He was sitting here in the shape of a heron. And he was floating there, hanging from the rope they'd used for the swing. It looked like it had happened a while ago.

Axel's throat caught, and his hands fell limp into his lap. Grandpa Paul's gaze followed Axel's up the cypress tree, where it snagged on his own hanging body. He seemed puzzled by the sight, as though his old self were nothing but a distant acquaintance—a friend who'd fallen out of touch.

"I was sick," Grandpa Paul said, his yellow eyes brightening as though he'd suddenly remembered. "I had been for a while."

"I know," Axel managed. "Is there anything I could have—"

"No," Grandpa Paul said, his face wheeling back toward Axel. "I was sick, and it was coming for me, sure as time. I'm sorry I couldn't get better." Then he fell silent for a moment. Paul's bird head turned sideways, causing his feathered crest to hang low like rank hair. Just as he had by the sight of his own body, he seemed vaguely baffled to see Axel sitting there on the edge of the boil.

"How did you . . . ?" Grandpa Paul glanced back at Saara. "I didn't think it would be *him*. I've been expecting the other one."

"What other one?" Saara took another step into the mud, her claws sinking deeper. "You mean Sam?"

"No," Paul said, whipping his sharp head about. "The girl. Tess. She's supposed to arrive today."

That got Axel up off his butt. "Why are you expecting Tess?" he said.

Paul's long neck curled, and his wings arched up—it almost looked like he was shrugging. "She's supposed to arrive today," he repeated. "That's why I'm here. I'm waiting for her. I know it's not the best welcome. . . ." His head darted from side to side, mud-streaked beak pointing at the mess around the spring. "But she's been through so much. She's lost everything now. I figured she deserves—"

"What do you mean, *arrive*?" As far as Axel knew, there were only two ways to get here, and one of them involved dying. "Mom, what is he talking about?"

Saara didn't answer him at first. She'd already wandered a few paces off and was staring back into the reeds. Axel could tell that all of her thoughts had now returned to Sam—the only place her thoughts ever went. Finally, she looked back at her son and blinked slowly. "What's that?" Saara said.

God, she was useless. Axel turned his attention to the Hiisi, sitting neat and prim beneath the cypress tree on the opposite bank of the boil. Axel had no doubt now that this was why it had led him here. "Where is my sister?" he said.

The Hiisi didn't answer. It just stared at him through a curtain of steam.

Axel pulled his father's sword out of his belt and said it again. He shouted it. "Where the hell is my sister?"

"What are you doing?" Paul's yellow eyes went wide, senseless with fright. "You're going to make it angry!"

But it was too late. The Hiisi slid wickedly forward, vapor hissing up around its many edges. It bent and unfolded, turning once again into the monster that had chased Axel back in Talvijärvi. The beast that had swallowed the Keeper whole. The Hiisi's mouth arched over the surface of the roiling spring, belching out the light of another day, snow-sheathed trees for teeth. Axel's grandfather let out a terrified squawk and flew up off the camp chair, a ragged silhouette against the fogged-in sky. Axel turned to his mother. She was already backing into the reeds.

"Don't go," he said.

Saara looked back at Axel, the light of the Hiisi shining in her dark eyes and across her broad, wet nose. She seemed, for a moment, to hesitate. But the moment passed. Axel's mother turned and charged into the reeds, their shafts settling back in the wake of her passing. And Axel knew, even as she disappeared, that he could go after her. Wherever his mother was going, he could follow.

He didn't.

Axel was all alone with the Hiisi now. "Where is she?" he asked again.

The monster answered him in a voice of moss and leaves, of branches and rope. "Under"—the Hiisi seemed to take a long breath—*"water."*

"I don't understand," Axel said.

"Your sister," the Hiisi said. "She is underwater. She's coming now. Look."

Axel began to hear a strange sort of crackling from inside the boil. He looked down and saw ice bubbling up out of the spring—big slabs of it, snapping and popping with the heat, spinning as they melted away to nothing before his eyes. And then, after the ice, a man. It was the Keeper, hatless and wearing a neon vest, sprung from the spring like a drowning in reverse. The Keeper splashed about, cussing and bellowing. He found his footing and then crawled toward the shallows, coughing up water. Then, a moment later, something else shot up out of the bubbling pond after him. Axel thought, for a second, that it looked just like his mother. But it was too small. It was too dark. It was a black bear. It was an American bear.

It was Tess.

Axel rushed into the warm water, grabbed his sister by the fur, and pulled her up onto the muddy bank. He looked up at the Hiisi. "Is she dead?" he shouted.

This time the monster didn't hesitate to answer. "Yes," it said.

22

The Bear

Tess could be forgiven for not recalling exactly how it happened—falling into a freezing lake will, of course, disorient a person. Dying is even worse. She remembered being on the ice with the Keeper, the sick feeling that shot right up from her stomach when she felt her footing give way. She remembered the blinding punch of the cold and the drag of her soaking winter clothes. She'd kicked against their weight, but the bright surface up above kept getting farther and farther away. Tess remembered her chest filling up, but not with air. The water was heavy and sharp within her, and slowly she began to go numb. The last thing she felt was a tremendous sense of regret, as painful as the ice water in her lungs. Tess couldn't believe that she'd failed her brother. She couldn't believe that she'd done this to Jaana and Otso. It would destroy them.

But as it turned out, that wasn't the last thing. Something followed the numbness, as Tess drifted down to the bottom of the lake. She felt pins and needles across her body, like the kiss of light rain. Like a soda fizz of bubbles. And suddenly she wasn't cold at all. Tess looked down and saw that the lake didn't seem to have a bottom. It had another surface—a shimmering ripple of light. She splashed right through it and was thrown nearly into the air. Tess felt arms coming around her shoulders, pulling her out of the warm water. They were skinny but very strong. They belonged to her brother.

Axel helped Tess crawl up onto a muddy bank, slapping her back as she hacked and choked. The water came out of her in great bursts, splashing across the mud, spattering her hands. But they weren't quite hands anymore. Tess stared down at her own arms, braced against the bank. It was as though she were wearing a long-sleeved, fuzzy black sweater with matching gloves. In place of fingers she had gray-black claws. Tess tried making a fist, and the claws dug into the mud. Yes, they were definitely hers.

"Tess . . . what did you do?"

Tess looked up from her own perplexing paws and took in the sight of her brother. Axel was filthy. His clothes were caked in dirt and torn at the edges, and there were twigs sticking out of his messy, unwashed hair. His eyes were rimmed with red, and their father's replica knight-of-the-realm sword was hanging limp in his fist. "What did you do?" he said again. Axel looked distraught, but Tess felt nothing other than joy to see him. She jumped up at the kid and they both collapsed into a hug. She had to be careful not to crush him though. Because he was just a little boy, and Tess was a black bear.

"What is happening?" a voice hollered. "Why am I here?" Tess turned from her brother and saw Väinö Järvinen—the Keeper—climbing out of the bubbling water and up the opposite bank. He must have gotten pulled here with Tess, when they both fell through the ice together. Now that he was back on the path, Väinö once again looked every bit the creepy costumed drifter. His body had been stretched to the jaunty dimensions of a marionette, his face pulled broad, his teeth enormous. "Why am I here?" the old man asked. He looked livid, betrayed. "I'm supposed to be done with this!"

The forest all around the spring shivered and whispered an answer back at him. "A Keeper for every wood." Tess had never gotten a good look at it before, but she knew that voice. It was the Hiisi. "That is the order. Your woods cannot go without."

"My wood *has* its damn Keeper." Väinö pulled himself up out of the muck. One of his gum boots got stuck and came off, but he didn't seem to notice. He hobbled up to the Hiisi and stared into the monster's shining mouth. "He's sitting right there." Väinö stabbed a long, crooked finger in Axel's direction.

"He isn't a Keeper," the Hiisi said. "Not yet. If he were, you wouldn't be here."

Väinö put his hands on his head and spun around in a circle, like a child having a tantrum. His face was a stew of disgust and rage. "But the boy cut his threads," he shouted, his voice breaking. "He cut his threads, and you let me go!"

"Not all of them," the Hiisi said. "A thread remains."

Väinö turned back to Tess and Axel, his eyes bulging, desperate. "Her? But she's dead now."

The monster made no answer to this. Axel pulled himself out of Tess's claws and scrambled to his feet. "Does that mean she can still go back?"

"She can," the Hiisi said, its mouth stretching ever wider, as big around as a doorway. A few flecks of spit flew out and landed on the hot mud.

It was only when they melted that Tess realized that they were gobs of snow.

"But only if she goes right now," the Hiisi said.

"Come on." Axel spun around and held his hand out to his sister.

"Where?" Tess said.

"Into the Hiisi," Axel said. "I saw the Keeper do it. It'll take us home."

Only Tess could see what these words were doing to Väinö's expression—her little brother had his back to the old man—but she didn't have time to warn him. Väinö was upon Axel in an instant. He plucked the sword out of Axel's loose grip and shoved him so hard that he fell face-first into the mud. Tess could hear the wind getting knocked out of him, just as she had all those weeks ago, at the Battle Re-enactment.

A growl came tearing out of her, and she lunged at the old man, but Väinö stepped away easily. Tess was unsteady, unaccustomed to having four legs. "Touch my brother again," she said, "and I'll kill you."

"Believe me, kid, I'd like nothing better," Väinö said. And with that he turned the dull blade over in his hand and shoved it into the soft patch behind Tess's shoulder. He had to put all of his weight into it, but the sword broke her skin and went all the way through, skewering Tess to the muddy ground. Axel screamed and threw himself at the old man. Väinö grabbed him by the collar and tossed him nearly overhand into the reeds. Then he braced his remaining gum boot on Tess's ribs and pulled Sam's sword back out. She lay there, twitching, struggling for breath. The pain was worse than drowning.

"I'm finished with apologies," Väinö said, turning back to where he'd thrown Axel. "I've done more than sixty years on the path. I'm not doing another day."

Tess writhed in the mud, turning her pointed face to the reeds. Axel charged out of them, screaming, swinging a heavy stick in his hands. But Väinö whacked the stick away with a light flick of Sam's sword. He turned the blade sideways and whipped it across Axel's face, knocking him down again. Tess's brother lay there for a moment, weeping with fury. When he propped himself up again, she saw that he had a long, purple welt across his cheek. The top edge of it was bleeding.

"You had your chance to leave," Väinö said, squatting down to look Axel in the eye. "You had *every* chance to leave. But this is what you chose, and now you have to live with it. I'm not going to let a dead girl keep me from what I deserve."

These words, "dead girl," seemed to ring in Tess's ears. Because that's what she'd become, wasn't it? Tess had drowned in a frozen lake in Finland. Her body was probably still drifting there, far under the surface of the ice, held down by her ski boots and soaking winter clothes. She wasn't even really here. She hadn't even really been stabbed, had she? Tess concentrated on moving her paws, and as it turned out, they moved just fine. The black bear lifted its head and stirred.

The dead girl got up.

Väinö didn't know what hit him. Tess bit down on the old man's shoulder and pulled him away from Axel so hard that his other gum boot flew off and the sword went spinning out into the water. He squirmed out of his vest and scrambled away from her, surprise and horror splitting his wide face. Väinö tried fighting at first, but Tess was much stronger than him. He made to run, but she was much faster. She had sharp teeth and long claws, and he had hurt her little brother. Terrified, Väinö even tried escaping up a tree. Tess remembered that they always tell you not to climb a tree if a black bear is after you. She taught herself, and Väinö, exactly why that was by climbing right up after him.

If her brother hadn't called her off, Tess wouldn't have stopped until there was nothing left of Väinö Järvinen but some strips of cloth and a pile of ashes. She jumped back down into the mud with Axel. He reached out for her, grabbing tight to a thick tuft of black fur. Then, together, they stepped through the light of the Hiisi.

Axel and Tess found themselves standing in the crescent of naked birches, just beyond the Kivis' summer cottage. The rain had stopped, but it was still streaming down the saturated trees, pouring into the wet snow below. From where they stood Tess could see out over the lake—a flat expanse of white broken only by a little island with two pine trees and the gray-blue hole in the ice. A sled track was faintly visible on the flooded ice, leading to a still rumbling snowmobile, lying improbably on its side by the Kivis' frozen dock. Tess supposed that Jaana must have rescued her. How the old woman had pulled her out of the water, Tess couldn't even begin to guess.

She and Axel left the birches and went down past the hillside cellar. They could hear a commotion coming from inside the sauna, where smoke was whirling out of the tin chimney. Tess wondered who might be in there, but that was silly, because of course she knew. *Tess* was in the sauna. She could feel the warming boards under her back as well as she could the snow crumbling beneath her broad paws. It was a strange sensation, to be in two places at once. To be alive and not quite.

Together they crossed the yard, approaching

the sauna. They hadn't yet reached it when the door slammed open, and out rushed an utterly frantic Kari, his whole face pink and slick with tears. He ran around the sauna, coming up on one leg as he turned sharply at the corner. Kari grabbed a loose armful of wood from the pile stacked beneath the eave and then disappeared back into the little pine building. Tess could hear Jaana's voice in there— calm, crisp, making her wishes known. A moment later Kari raced out of the sauna again and down the shore, probably going to get more help. Tess was glad he hadn't noticed them. She didn't want Kari to see her like this.

They came around behind the sauna, and Tess lifted her enormous body up onto her hind legs so that she could peek into the high-set window at the back. Inside she saw her own blue self, damp and lifeless, all wrapped up in Jaana's heavy down jacket. A good fire had grown to fill the wood-stove. Her grandmother was leaning over her, pushing air into her mouth and compressing her chest so hard that Tess was sure it would leave bruises. Jaana appeared to be whispering some-thing, which Tess heard perfectly, on account of the fact that her grandmother's lips were only inches from her ear.

"You are not to go anywhere," Jaana was say-ing. "You are not to go *anywhere*." Tess could tell, from the thick batter of her grandma's voice, that Jaana would be able to hold it together for exactly as long as she had to.

She fell back down on all fours and stared at her brother behind the sauna. Tess could feel it now. The sharp pressure on her bear's heart and lungs. The need to breathe, because she wasn't breathing.

"What do we do now?" Tess said.

"I think you go inside," Axel answered.

Before Tess could say: "you?" they were distracted by another banging. The back door of the cottage swung open, smashing against the outer wall and shaking on its hinges. Otso flew down the ramp in his wheelchair, blankets upon blankets all stacked over his lap. But he took the turn too hard in the snow, and the chair came crashing down onto its side. Before Tess or Axel could even step toward him, Otso was up again, springing bowlegged for the sauna. Going by the expression on his face, their grandpa was taking this less well than his wife. He just managed to make it through the door before collapsing, pushing Jaana away as she reflexively turned to help him up.

"Just the door," Otso said. "Just the door!"

And with that Jaana shut up the sauna, trapping the mounting heat. Again, Axel and Tess looked at each other in silence. Water trickled from the eaves, away from the tin chimney as it warmed up. It occurred to Tess that there was a question that she'd forgotten to ask. Not that they'd had a chance to do much talking since they'd escaped the Keeper and stepped through the Hiisi.

"Did you find Dad?" she said.

It seemed to take her brother a moment to understand the question. Perhaps he simply hadn't expected it of her. "We didn't," he said.

"I'm sorry," Tess said. "That's a shame." It wasn't condescension, or empty commiseration. It really was a shame that they hadn't found Sam.

"Yeah," Axel said. "It is." Then more brightly: "Mom's still looking."

"That's good," Tess said. She could feel an odd sensation in the tips of her fingers, the tips of her claws. Her chest was about ready to burst.

"Shouldn't you, maybe—" Axel sort of juked his shoulders in the direction of the sauna. "I don't know how long you can . . ."

"Not by myself," Tess said.

He just looked at her, confused.

"I'm not going without you," Tess said. "If you want to stay, I'll stay with you."

Axel sucked his teeth and let out a relieved gulp of laughter. "Don't be stupid," he said. "Obviously I'm coming with you."

But it wasn't stupid. It wasn't obvious, even to

Axel, until his sister had asked and waited for his answer.

"Great," Tess said, beaming a wide, jagged, bear's smile at him.

Together they walked around to the front of the sauna, and Tess used her broad head to push the door open. Axel could see his sister in there, still as clay on the wooden bench, their terrified grandparents arched over her. For a second he was afraid they'd come too late, but then a string of coughs sputtered out of her, fast and hard, emptying Tess's lungs of lake water. The bear lingered for a moment. She looked up at Axel, her rich black fur bleeding color at the tips, her thick muscles turning slowly into air. Jaana and Otso were shouting now. They were holding Tess tight. But it wasn't only her. Axel had come home too. Just a step, just a breath, and here they all were.

They'd arrived just in time for everything.